Water Wizard

John Beresford

For Natalie

CONTENTS

ACKNOWLEDGMENTS

Once again I am indebted to my friend Mik Peach for another fabulous cover (for more of Mik's work, head off to 500px.com/mikpeach), and to Jen from Olde Tinkerer Studio for her simple GIMP tutorial on how to apply a water effect to lettering – a particularly apposite lesson for this story!

Also to a slightly different but still small collection of beta-readers for this work: Natalie & Blythe Beresford, Wendy Gibson – first back in double-quick time with several very perceptive comments – Chris Morrissey (you have him to thank for the explanation of the Berikatanyan Calendar) and last but by no means least Rob Toth, who spent way too much time looking for commas that shouldn't have been there and inserting new ones where they should (as well as many much more valuable comments ☺). As always the book is heaps better for your input and I'm honoured that you took the time to help it along – thank you all!

John Beresford
February, 2020

Also by John Beresford:

The Berikatanyan Chronicles Series

Gatekeeper
Water Wizard
Juggler (coming soon)

Other Work

War of Nutrition
Well of Love
Valentine Wine

i

Map of Berikatanya

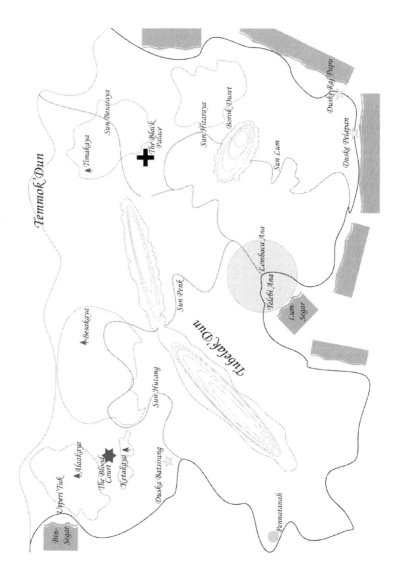

The Story So Far

Book 1 – Gatekeeper

Some years before the story begins, on the earth-like planet Berikatanya, a colourful gathering assembles in the valley between rolling green hills. The hillsides are dotted with observers from two realms but the main throng has assembled in the valley, where four impressive figures stand at the corners of a granite quadrangle. A choir chants—three separate and distinct melodies that join and swell as one—and a lone man takes up a central position on one side of the square. Musicians play, a peal of three bells rings in a hillside tower, and a sparkling mist begins to gather in the valley. Sucked inward it rotates slowly as it accretes, until it disappears into a small, black, star-filled void, dragging three of the four figures, the man and a few of the closer observers with it. The crowd gasps, but the void is gone and nothing remains of those who have been taken except a single yellow ribbon. The bells give one last ear-splitting peal before the tower cracks along its entire height, sending them falling to the rocks below, upon which each one shatters.

Years later the monarchs of the two realms gather again in a memorial ceremony for the lost. The King has attempted to re-forge the shattered bells, hoping the replay will be as close a likeness to the original as possible. But the forging is unsuccessful. One bell is damaged, one cracked, and the third so badly made its tone is painful to hear. The ceremony is a fiasco, and is never repeated.

*

Elaine Chandler is a fire poi artiste in the MeTa (Metropolitan Extended Toronto Area—an urban conurbation that has grown and absorbed 12 million residences stretching from Cambridge along the entire northern coast of Lake Ontario as far as Kingston, and north as far as Orillia including the whole of Lake Simcoe). She has spent four years with a travelling circus company, though she hates large crowds and despises the ringmaster.

Her life before that is a bit hazy. When the cracked brass bell rings, she awakes from a recurrent dream featuring the off-world colony of "Perse." Without understanding how, she knows it holds the answer to the missing part of her memories.

Patrick Glass is a graphic artist. His choice of career is driven by a subconscious desire for control. It's the best match he can find for his needs and abilities but it's not perfect, and he can't hide the fact that he's never settled. He has been passed over for promotion time and again, can't hold down a relationship and, as an orphan, has no family ties either. He decides he must have one last roll of the dice, and he too signs up for Perse.

Terry Spate is a gardener. As far as he can remember it's all he ever wanted to be, and he's been doing it a long time. A lifetime. At least 30 years. Most of his customers think he's a bit slow—mentally and physically. He talks slowly. He moves slowly. He takes his time. But his few friends know he's a warm-hearted man who would do anything for anybody. It's never occurred to them to wonder why such a gentle, unselfish man never found himself a wife, but Terry doesn't stay in one place long enough for anyone to start wondering. He gets on with his job, plants up the gardens of his customers, and moves on. Over the years the gardens he's left behind have become beautiful oases of tranquillity and colour. Some are famous. When visitors ask: "what a wonderful garden. Who designed it? Who planted it?" the owners can only recall a quiet unassuming man who didn't appear to be anything special. And no, they don't know where he is now. They lost touch with him years ago. One day Terry is in the middle of planting an avenue of leylandii at a country mansion. He steps back to line up the next sapling and tramples on a flower in the border of the driveway. His clumsiness in destroying the beauty he tried to create opens a long-forgotten window in his mind. He rests his spade against the trunk of the last tree he planted, takes his jacket, and leaves.

Fifteen-year-old Claire Yamani maintains an outwardly airy mien despite losing her father at the age of eleven in a street crime incident. Since then Claire and her mother have been evicted from one slum dwelling after another in the poorest areas of the MeTa, where sunlight barely grazes the tops of the building and the incessant rain spreads oily puddles on every road and sidewalk. After five years of struggling to find a way out of the grinding and dangerous existence, her mother wins a Lottery place for them on the Valiant. The prospect of a new life in the clean fresh air of Perse fills her with hope and excited expectation.

All convicts are wrongfully imprisoned. Jann Argent is no different. Except for him it's true. He could never remember how he came to be in the room with the dead body, but that didn't stop them convicting him. After eight years on the prison moon Phobos, and three attempts at the Tournament, he wins. Since the authorities cannot allow convicted murderers true freedom, his "prize" is enforced transportation to the new colony world of Perse.

At the spaceport he meets several other characters, each with their own reasons for exile. A young girl and her mother, hoping to start a new life after the death of her father. A gifted graphic artist looking for adventure. A skilled agriculturalist searching for a fresh challenge. And a mysterious, statuesque and quick-tempered woman whose reasons for travelling she keeps to herself.

The Prism ship dominates the spaceport. A massive gleaming tube reflecting the sunlight not from its polished hull but off the low frequency forcefield that surrounds it. Following centuries of tradition the ship is named with hopeful and confident intent: Valiant. Its sister ships Endeavour and Intrepid already left for the new world nine years before. A catastrophic failure of the third launch with enormous loss of life prevented the remaining two ships from departing at the same time. That third ship—

Endurance—was almost totally destroyed causing the colonisation program to be halted until a thorough investigation had been completed. A replacement ship to be named Dauntless has been commissioned and is nearing completion in the adjacent space dock, but the death of so many colonists rocked the popularity of the program. The Valiant has only recently been filled, partially as a result of opening the opportunity to the public through the Lottery. Valiant stands ready to use its graphene prisms to focus gravitational energy and leap away from the solar system at near-light speed, awaiting only its human cargo and their limited possessions.

Even for planet hoppers, Jann Argent travels light. Other colonists have several uniform aluminium flight cases stacked neatly on maglev harnesses. As the only person with a single scruffy backpack, he stands out. Having awoken at a crime scene and spent the intervening years in prison, he has had no opportunity to amass similar crate-loads of belongings.

The travellers watch a public information film about cryosleep, journey times and waking procedures, accompanied by artists' impressions of life on the new world of Perse. There is no way of returning real images from the colony, but even if there was, at the time of Valiant's departure the first two ships have not even completed ten percent of the ninety-seven light year trip.

On Perse, ex-cop Felice Waters investigates strange occurrences, reported as crimes, in the Earther community. People have gone missing, met with freak accidents, been injured or killed. As the Earthers begin to mix more with the indigenous population, reports become more widespread.

With five years of her trip remaining, Claire Yamani wakes due to a cryopod malfunction to discover her mother and the other seven people in her capsule are dead. The ship's systems react to her presence and provide food, water, and entertainment, but with no spare cryopods she's forced to travel alone and keep herself occupied for those five years. The rest of the crew and passengers wake a few days before arrival at Perse. When the ship enters the atmosphere an unusually fierce storm is raging on the planet's surface. Claire watches from a viewport, loving the elemental power, but the hurricane-force winds send the ship crashing into the docking infrastructure and it is forced to ditch in the sea. Many of the travellers, still groggy from the effects of cryosleep, don't make it out before the huge craft sinks. Jann Arden plays a pivotal role in saving many lives, positioning himself in a doorway to help those trapped inside as well as those in the water.

The survivors take stock as they are processed through planetary immigration. They learn that "Perse" was already populated before the Earth ships' arrival. The native people call their planet Berikatanya. Life there is nothing like the public service videos. The newly-arrived Earthers spend a few days "acclimatising" before choosing to join one of the local monarchs—the Black Queen or the Blood King—or electing to remain with the small group of non-aligned Earthers on one of the various projects that are underway.

Claire and Terry take a forest clearance detail. He is naturally drawn to the opportunity to work with the soil and wants to make sure the land is cleared in a sympathetic way. After all spaces at the Black Palace—her preference—are taken, Claire decides to accompany him and spend some time in the fresh air after five years of solitude and recycled life support. In the forest, they work to clear land for the cultivation of crops transported from Earth. The weather is still unpredictable, high winds blowing in a strange synchronicity with Claire's mood. When she's happy and airy the gusts are breezy and gentle. When she's mad or frightened it's more stormy and wild. The native workers are in awe of Claire, believing she is causing the storms. Word of this reaches the Black Queen. She invites Claire to the Palace, where she discovers the previous Air Mage was her father. Claire learns how to control her power and takes up her father's position.

Having read his prison record and seen his heroic rescue efforts, Felice asks Jann to tag along and help her investigate the latest report of an inexplicable event at the Blood King's court. Patrick Glass joins them. Elaine Chandler has already demanded assignment to the Court, seeming to know her own mind better than any of the others. During the journey to Court, Felice explains that the two realms are engaged in a generations-long feud that waxes and wanes between periods of uneasy peace and all-out war. To maintain balance the Elementals divided themselves between the two houses. The Air Mage and Water Wizard align with the Black Queen while the Fire Witch and the Earth Elemental (known colloquially as the Gardener) hook up with the Blood King. Alone of the Elementals left on Berikatanya since the vortex was created in the valley of Lembaca Ana, the Water Wizard has not been seen since for almost a century and is believed dead.

At the time of Valiant's arrival, tensions are escalating again and a few skirmishes have broken out. The travellers are attacked by a raiding party, during which Elaine reveals her powers—she is the Fire Witch. Along with the original Air Mage and the Earth Elemental she fell to Earth through the portal created by an Elemental rite many years before, arriving at different times. As a side-effect of traversing the portal their memories, along with knowledge of their powers and how to use them, was stripped from them. Following their return to Berikatanya, those memories begin to return at a rate inversely proportional to their portal time displacement.

On arrival at Court, Jann is believed to be the Earth Elemental. He is given a position in the Court guard so the King and his cohort the Jester can keep an eye on him while his memory recovers. That process is helped along when Jann, on guard duty in the Court archives, discovers an account of the original portal ceremony. The Fire Witch confronts the King, who attempts to persuade her to rejoin his side. The revelation of her return, and that of the Air Mage, along with the supposition of the Gardener's return, leads the King and the Jester to plot a repeat of the portal ceremony, intending to rid Berikatanya of Elementals and their powers once and for all.

In the meantime, still hoping to exploit those powers to secure victory, the King mobilises forces against the Queen. During the ensuing battle Elaine uses her powers even though they are not fully recovered. Claire, on the opposing side, attempts to counter this but only succeeds in making Elaine's Fire even more powerful. The battle appears to be won by the Blood King when Felice arrives on the battle plain in a flyer, which immediately quenches all Elemental powers. The Blood King is defeated, though no-one really understands why.

After the debacle of the battle, Jann is keen to ingratiate himself with the King. He and Patrick journey to the Valley to recover material the King needs for his new ceremony. There, they meet the Pilgrim, who has lived in the Valley since the first portal incident. He recognises Jann as the Gatekeeper—the one who controlled the vortex and who also fell through in the company of the Elementals. They also discover the Valley is enveloped in an after-effect of the portal: a time-dilation field that slows time down in the area local to the Valley.

Jann and Patrick relay the Pilgrim's message to Elaine. Realising that most of the original participants in the portal ceremony are coming together again, Elaine travels to the coast in an attempt to summon the Water Wizard. Jann and Patrick pay a visit to the Court archivist, who recognises Patrick's favourite doodle as the symbol of the Pattern Juggler—the final piece of the jigsaw, as the Juggler was a key member of the group and the last to be accounted for.

The King and his entourage journey to the Valley,

where he intends to reopen the portal having invited the Queen, with her Air Mage, to attend and play their parts. Lautan arrives in response to his summons, intercepting Elaine on her return from the coast. He carries her warning of the King's intent to Jann and Patrick, and all the players converge on the Valley independently, arriving in the nick of time to stop the ceremony. Thwarted, the King turns instead to the power of his forefathers, which he has resurrected through the ancient blood rituals. He creates clones of the Elementals with the Bloodpower, and begins to open a vortex in the face of their opposition.

In a grisly mirror of the original portal, the final battle plays out in the Valley. Terry, who has belatedly awoken to his power as the Earth Elemental, arrives last, and the Elementals join forces, deploying their powers in combination for the first time to prevent the portal opening and defeat the King and his Blood clones.

Chapter 1

In the upper storey of the Court's westernmost turret, the Blood King lay unconscious. On either side of the ornately carved bed, dense clouds of perfumed smoke belched upwards from gold burners, congealing into a thick blanket above the motionless figure of the monarch. An elderly chambermaid hurried to replenish the incense before scurrying from the room.

Sweat matted the King's once lustrous mane of curled red hair. It wept from his face and brow, staining the crimson satin pillows and rich embroidered linens of the coverlet, and pooling in the hollow at the base of his neck. A tracery of dark blood vessels outlined angry swellings on his head, pulsing under the light from a nearby candle stand. Each of the two dozen wicks added a wispy thread of greasy black smoke to the overburdened atmosphere.

On the other side of the chamber the Jester watched the maid's retreat before crossing to the open window to take a few breaths of the fresh night air. He loosened his mustard-coloured shirt, pulled the frayed tails from the waistband of his bright lemon hose, and mopped his face. Beyond the window the light of the two moons—Pera-Bul and Kedu-Bul—relieved the darkness, casting a ghostly silver pallor on the distant canopy of Ketakaya forest. A quiet knocking disturbed the silence.

'Come.'

The heavy whitewood door opened on well-oiled hinges. A stooped, grey-bearded figure leaned in, appraising the scene with one clear eye, the other staring sightlessly behind its pale cataract.

'Any change?'

The Jester moved back to his seat beside the bed.

'No. He murmurs occasionally, but without sense.'

1

As if in response to these words, the King's shallow breath rattled in his chest.

'Has he taken any food?'

'It's as much as I can do to force a few sips of water into him.'

'Then perhaps lace it with a little honey and milk? He needs something. It's been almost a half-month–'

'Do you think I don't know that, old man? It has in fact been ten days. I have counted every one of them here in this chamber! As I suspected, the Bloodpower served him ill. That dread bane always exacts its own price. He has not moved or uttered any sensible word beyond a cry of pain since our return from the Valley. You are the one with all the scrolls of knowledge. The tomes of learning. If milk and honey is the best you have to offer...'

The old man stepped into the room, an enormous bunch of keys jangling at his waist.

'I am an archivist!' he said, drawing himself erect with an effort, 'not a physician.'

The Jester leaned forward, resting his head in his hands. His voice dropped to a murmur.

'Well then, we may yet have a use for your skills. The King has no heir. Nor did he ever speak of any living family. What do the archives tell us about succession in such a case as this?'

'Succession? Are you so keen to see him dead?'

'Am I not powerless to prevent it? Istania must continue, whether the King survives or no. Who is to rule in his stead? That is the question we must grapple with now, since his malady is beyond us.'

The Keeper's good eye flicked between the Jester and the unresponsive monarch. He tugged at his beard. 'I will see what I can find,' he said, hobbling out of the chamber. The door closed noiselessly behind him.

The Jester fell into a restless doze, perched on a three-legged stool beside the cot. He awoke with a start at the touch of the King's hand on his arm, the flesh cold though

2

the delirium still ravaged him. The dried sweat on his pallid skin had left it with a look of old parchment: worn thin and flaking. The King struggled to pull himself up, a frenzied and feverish expression distorting his face. The Jester reached for a flask of water on the nightstand, but the King gripped his arm more tightly, moistened his lips with his swollen tongue, and fixed him with an intense stare, struggling to speak.

He leaned closer to catch the words.

'Sepuke,' said the monarch, in a voice as cold and quiet as the still night air.

Exhausted, he fell back on the bed, a small moan escaping his mouth. Before the Jester could fathom the meaning of this cryptic message, the King's hand slipped from his arm. His eyes rolled up to reveal angry, bloodshot whites as his final breath gurgled from between his purple lips. Beyond the window, the last light of Kedu-Bul winked out as the moon set. The first drops of the malamajan splashed onto the inner sill, turning it a deeper blood-red under the flickering candlelight.

the palace of the black queen
13th day of run'bakamasa, 966

The imposing blackwood doors stood closed as the Piper ran, breath rasping in his throat, towards the Black Queen's stateroom. The inaugural meeting of the Permajelis was in session, at the third attempt, and he was late! He stopped for a moment in the wide hallway, composing himself. He tugged the collar of his jerkin away from his sweat-dampened neck, smoothed his dyed purple hair, and removed errant strands from his cheeks and forehead. Brushing off the worst of the trail dust from his vibrant amaranthine costume, he rapped on the door and entered the chamber.

Sun demons danced in the foetid air. Even though constructed almost entirely of black stone of one sort or another—slate; jet; granite—the vast heat sink of the stateroom was no match for the fierce Bakamasan day. Incandescent fingers of strong afternoon sun lanced in through the narrow vertical windows, illuminating an ornate blackwood table in the centre of the room. From her seat at its head, the Queen watched him enter, her eyes as dark as the obsidian coronet sitting atop her brushed black hair.

'You're late,' she said, absently stroking the smooth tabletop, the wood so glossy and deep a black that it appeared to shine with a faint blue tinge under the bright sunlight.

On the side nearest the door, five figures sat staring at a spot in the centre of the polished surface. Each in their own way telegraphed an unstated desire to be anywhere else: fixed expressions; a strange kind of stationary fidgeting; white-knuckled steepling of fingers. Apart from the Queen, none of the Permajelis members acknowledged his arrival.

'Apologies, Majesty, I–'

'Don't trouble me with your excuses. I'm sure you have one perfectly prepared. Family troubles, again, is it? Those same unspoken troubles that have kept you away from our Palace on so many occasions recently.'

'Begging your pardon ma'am, but hardly unspoken. My cousin–'

'Ah yes, your cousin,' said the Queen, interrupting him a second time. 'A distant relative whose insurmountable problems are so much more important, more urgent, than any of your duties here. Even the very first Permajelis must wait upon your cousin's unfortunate circumstances, though the peace and prosperity of all Kertonia depend on the decisions we debate here.'

The Piper, who had remained standing in the doorway during the Queen's diatribe, moved to take his seat at the table. The Air Mage, Claire Yamani, shuffled sideways to make room for him. She glanced at him, not daring a smile when the Queen was in this temper. Her fine ash-blonde hair cascaded over the back of her chair, catching a ray of sun and glinting pale gold. The Piper scanned the empty seats on the opposite side of the table.

'I see I am not the only latecomer,' he said. 'It seems unlikely I have missed any decision making today.'

The Queen's intense gaze never left him, but her brow furrowed at his comment.

'Has there been no word from Istania?' the Piper asked, risking a tentative look in the Queen's direction. 'I do hope we will not have to rearrange our inaugural meeting a third time.'

'The King made his agreement to the establishment of a council of peace clear after the Battle of Lembaca Ana,' the Queen said, enunciating each syllable with cold precision. 'We have had no indication from Red House of a change in the royal mind.'

'And yet here we sit, in splendid isolation,' said the Piper, struggling to keep an impish grin from cracking his sombre mask. 'Staring once more at seven empty seats.'

'Enough!' The Queen's rigid, upright posture screamed frustration and impatience, until she slumped back in her chair, releasing a small sigh. 'Oh, what is the point?'

A couple of the attendees ventured a look in her direction.

'Majesty?'

The Piper watched the Air Mage's body language as she spoke. In the days since the battle the Queen had spent a great deal of time in the company of her favourite Elemental.

'I had such high hopes for this Peace Council,' said the Queen. 'Perhaps it was tempting fate to name it Permajelis, or to trust the Blood King would be as good as his word. Easy to agree to anything when being dragged home from defeat on a litter. Why did I think it would be different this time, after all his past behaviour? After his vile blood clones nearly destroyed our entire way of life?'

The Piper leaned forward.

'You have always had the highest of hopes for the future of Kertonia, Majesty,' he said. 'Yes, and Istania too. It is not weakness to seek peace.'

The Queen drew herself up again in her seat. Her hand gripped the arm of her chair, the knuckles showing white against the deep black of the wood. The attendees squirmed, peeping furtively at each other or maintaining their scrutiny of the tabletop.

'Did I mention weakness? No. There is no weakness here. If there is to be no negotiated truce between the two great Houses, or discussion regarding a way forward for... our mutually beneficial assets... then we may as well pursue a policy of enlightened self-interest. I have no doubt that is exactly what the King is doing.'

A murmur of agreement passed along the table. The Piper took to his feet.

'Then we're done here, your Majesty? The Permajelis is dead even before it is born?'

'It is dead,' said the Queen, pushing back her chair. 'Stillborn. And we are done.'

She swept stiff-backed from the room without a backward glance.

puppeteers' meeting hall
22nd day of run'bakamasa, 966

Jeruk Nipis picked at a notch in the surface of the substantial oak table at which he sat, pulling splinters and rolling them between his fingers and thumb. Deaf to the hubbub of conversation around him, and shaded from the torchlight flickering from the wall sconces, his thoughts were occupied by the heavy wooden trapdoor under his left boot or, more properly, what lay beyond it.

In the nine days since the Blood King's death, it had dawned on the King's erstwhile right-hand man that his position was no longer secure. As Court Jester, enjoying the monarch's protection and favour, he had never worried whether his barbed comments and cruel japes were making him enemies. Unrivalled access to the royal ear gave him influence well above his station, which over the years he had exploited to full effect. The old man's death now left him exposed, both to the reality of his lack of power, and to those seeking retribution.

So while the Keeper of the Keys trawled his archives for the letter of the law regarding succession, the Jester's attention had been split between what was necessary for his own protection, and the various options for making his escape at need. These concerns caused him to ruminate on this door. An inconspicuous exit from a room in which he had burned many candles plotting in the company of his compatriots. One he had often noticed without ever considering where it led.

Recently he had with some effort raised the tenacious trapdoor to reveal a steep stone staircase. It descended to a network of dank and clammy passages which he explored for some time. Their haphazard layout and frequent dead-ends tested every nuance of his spatial awareness, honed through years of juggling, acrobatics, and caper-cutting. At length he had come upon a smooth black iron door set into the dark red sandstone bedrock upon which the Court was constructed. A bolt the thickness of his waist held the door fast. Despite its immense girth, and decades of disuse counted only by the sticky webs which criss-crossed the heavy iron bar, it withdrew smoothly and quietly. He expected the door to be rusted shut, but it swung open easily on counterbalanced hinges, allowing him to step onto the shore of a subterranean lake.

Its glassy surface disappeared at the limit of the light from his torch. The sand beneath his feet lay untrammelled; packed into a thin crust by the constant action of the water, rising and falling in harmony with floods and droughts above ground. Under the flickering torchlight it glowed the colour of buwangah wine. The shoreline extended to his left, following the slight curve in the rock wall. While checking whether any other doors opened onto the lake, Jeruk had discovered a small boat tied to a mooring ring. In the unchanging temperature of the cavern, with no living organism to attack its boards, the craft survived in perfect condition. A mast had been stowed along its midline with a pair of sculls on either side.

Satisfied that this made a viable escape route, and the substantial bolt provided sufficient protection from an incursion, he had retraced his steps, kicking dust and stone chippings into the trapdoor's frame until it looked once more unused and unremarkable. His thoughts had turned to emergency provisions for the boat, when a commotion at the other end of the room dragged his attention back to the meeting.

A pair of purple-stockinged legs descended the worn staircase, the colour betraying their owner's identity long before his face appeared.

'About time!'

'Late again Mungo, as usual!'

'Maybe we can finally make a start!'

'No need to have waited on my account,' the Piper replied, taking a seat. He glanced around the table until his gaze came to rest on Jeruk.

'Ah, you *are* here,' he said, raising his eyebrows. 'What are you doing skulking in the shadows over there, and what have I missed?'

Jeruk drew his chair in closer.

'As you may have gathered, you've missed nothing. We've been waiting for you. Quite some time,' he added, nodding at the torches, some of which were already beginning to gutter. 'This evening's agenda begins and ends with you Mungo. What news from the Blacks?'

One of the other attendees slid a mug of beer towards the Piper, who took a long draft. He wiped his mouth on a mauve kerchief before responding.

'Two items of interest. She has the Gardener working

on some kind of earthworks at Lembaca Ana. The details are kept closely guarded but really what else is there to do there but build a seaport? I can't imagine even an Elemental has had time to make much progress as yet, but the Queen is sure to claim any advances Petani may have made as a Kertonian initiative.'

'Preposterous!'

'The land belongs to no one!'

'Typical of the Blacks!'

Jeruk held up his hand for silence. These meetings all too frequently dissolved into outraged name calling.

'Before we become too caught up in the ramifications of a new seaport,' he said, raising his voice to quell the last of the protest, 'you said there were two items.'

'Yes.' The Piper dropped his gaze and shifted in his seat. 'The... ah... lack of response from you, or should I say from the King, to her overtures regarding the Permajelis—'

Mention of the doomed peace council brought a second wave of derision from the assembly. The Jester once again raised his hand.

'Those who cannot maintain order are welcome to leave!' he growled, resting his elbows on the table and steepling his fingers. 'You plot the overthrow of every leader, dream of forming a government, yet time and again you prove incapable of governing even yourselves!'

He waved at the Piper to continue.

'They have now tried to meet three times without success,' the Piper went on. 'Even someone as committed to the talks as the Queen only has a finite supply of patience.'

'And her supplies are exhausted?'

'Indeed they are. She will not call another. You missed a trick there, Jeruk.'

The Piper flushed, his face almost matching his garb.

'A Puppeteer attending the Permajelis would have been well-placed to influence their plans and sow such misinformation as suited your needs.'

'We have you for that Mungo,' Jeruk replied with a sneer. 'Don't we?'

'Not now the Permajelis has been abandoned! You have thrown away that chance. Indeed the Queen has interpreted the lack of interest from Istania as the beginning of another round of hostilities, and instructed her Hodaks to begin mobilising once more.'

Concerned murmurs rolled around the table. A shout of 'Told you so!' went up from the end of the room.

Jeruk stood, glaring at the man. 'Do not believe for one moment this "peace council" was anything other than a diversion on their part! They would have continued with their plans while we sat around chattering about how we could make things better for everyone. The Blacks are only ever interested in making life better for the Blacks! We must look after our own interests, just as they do.'

He retook his seat in silence.

'So we have two beginnings,' Jeruk concluded. 'The start of a tactically advantageous landing point in the Valley, which could open lucrative trade routes with nations as yet unknown, or at least give us an alternative to the overland route from West to East.

'And early indications of renewed hostilities, which if we allow them to continue unchecked will almost certainly cut off our access to that landing point.'

The meeting erupted again as the full implications of his words sunk in.

'Istania has just as much right to the ocean!'

'And just as much need!'

'She needs to be taught a lesson.'

'The threat is clear, even though in its early stages,' said Sebaklan Pwalek, 'but without a leader how are we to proceed?'

'Has the Keeper uncovered any information on succession in the absence of a direct descendant?' asked the Piper.

'He's still working on it.'

'At the rate he works, the seaport will be built and in use before we make a move!' said Pwalek.

'Nevertheless we cannot risk moving forward until we are certain of the Law,' Jeruk said. 'We may be a subversive movement but the people are already restless enough without a monarch. Any overt flouting of authority on our part would be all the excuse the rabble need for outright rebellion. We simply do not have the forces to police the whole of Istania. We are fortunate the Princips are a bunch of feckless inbreds. If they had more political nous we could be contending with a power grab by now. As it is, we are enjoying a period of grace.

'But you are correct,' he continued, rising again to his feet, 'we cannot wait upon the succession. We have to mobilise. If ever anyone is to retake the Blood Throne, they will not thank us for going to war unprepared or ill-advised, but neither would they want us to lose a tactical advantage. We must put brains before brawn. Let us arrange manoeuvres on the hillside at Lembaca Ana. As inconspicuously as possible.'

The Piper snorted. 'A few hundred armed men cavorting about on the grass is not what I'd call inconspicuous. It will inevitably raise concerns.'

'Not as suspicious as a full-scale mobilisation, but in any event with your privileged access to the Queen's ear I expect you can plead our case? Come up with a benign explanation for our presence there?'

The Piper blushed. 'She is already questioning the amount of time I spend away from the Palace.'

'Once this succession business is out of the way and we have deployed troops in the Valley, we shouldn't need to meet as frequently,' Jeruk replied, stroking his chin. 'Our forces will provide valuable intelligence on their progress at the landing, and give us an edge if the Blacks decide to confront us.'

court of the blood king
30th day of run'bakamasa, 966

No fires flamed in the burnished copper bowls of the Blood King's throne room. They sat empty on their red marble columns, not to be lit again until the crowning of a new ruler. A thin shaft of silver from the alpha moon Pera-Bul picked out the white veins of the pedestals, giving them the appearance of an arcane script written by a ghostly hand. The moonlight shone too on the imposing throne, squatting in the semi-darkness like a denizen of the underworld. A sparse dusting of disuse glittered on its surface.

Jeruk Nipis wiped his finger along the stone, leaving a greasy trace in the dust. He regarded the squat structure thoughtfully. Despite long years of service to its owner, he had never occupied it. Even now, with the King twenty days dead, he would not sit there in the seat of power. It called to him like the loudest sirens from Batu'n mythology. It fascinated and mesmerised him; the throne and all it stood for. Though he plotted and schemed for the downfall of both the great houses of Berikatanya, and strove for a time when ordinary people were not in thrall to royalty or Elementals, a small part of him longed to recline on the chill marble, wave the mace of state, and have all around do his bidding.

How they would hate it. And grow to hate him. For the moment, in the minds of the masses, he was still the King's plaything. The Jester. A performer of amusing capers, whisperer of secrets. Tolerated on account of the King's favour. That patronage had plucked him from the filthiest street corners of the most insignificant hamlet in the kingdom. Without it, he could be back there plying his trade as a beggarly street player in less time than it took to tune his celapi. He did not have long. Whispers of resentment and disquiet had already reached him. Istania demanded a leader.

The muted click of the latch heralded the Keeper of the

Keys, who poked his iron-grey head around the door.

'Ah, you are here,' he said, entering. 'Why do you not light a candle at least? Were it not for Pera-Bul's light, I–'

'Have you found it?' Jeruk asked, eyeing the scroll which the Keeper carried tucked under his arm. 'Is that it?'

'This is it, though I know not who filed it. It was in the very last place I looked.'

'What does it say?'

The Keeper approached the throne. 'If you will light a candle as I asked–'

'Not here. Come.'

Jeruk passed behind the Blood Throne. At the back of the throne room a small door stood open, the dim light of a single wick glowing through from the space beyond. He cleared remnants of a simple meal from a table and slid the candlestick into the centre.

'Here.'

The Keeper moved the flame further back. 'This ancient record is the only copy. If–'

'Yes, yes, I understand. Tell me what it says.'

The old man slipped a faded ribbon from the scroll and rolled it out carefully onto the table top. He reached into the pocket of his tabard, retrieving four polished stones which he positioned at the corners of the document before pointing a shaking, wizened finger at the illuminated letter at the beginning of the text.

'The style of this opening paragraph indicates–'

Jeruk grasped the Keeper's hand, pulling the old lore master around to face him. He grimaced at the strength of Jeruk's grip.

'Can you not,' he began through gritted teeth, 'simply tell me what it says?'

The two stood immobile for a moment before Keeper pulled his hand free.

'Yes. Yes of course. My apologies. Sometimes my appreciation of the ancient texts...'

He glanced up nervously. Jeruk stared back, saying

nothing. The Keeper cleared his throat.

'The rules actually appear to be quite simple. Apart from the usual inheritance hierarchy, which,' he added, his gaze flicking from parchment to Jeruk and back, 'clearly does not apply in this case, the only other recognised route to the throne is through combat.'

'Combat?'

'Yes. It's not surprising really when you think of the almost constant warring there has been between the two houses over the centuries. There's no doubt Istania is the more confrontational and has usually maintained the bigger army. It's only to be expected that when there is no natural heir to the throne a successor should be chosen by fighting.'

'Yes, yes, I understand the concept! But combat between whom? Who chooses the combatants?'

'They do. There's an example proclamation in another parchment I found filed beside this one. It gives the prescribed form of letters for the announcement of a tournament and the request for all-comers to declare their interest.'

'All-comers? Anyone can fight for the royal seat?'

'Well... yes. Why not? If there's no heir then Istania needs the strongest leader available. You need not worry, it will be a self-selecting group. There are not so many who will want to rule as you might suppose. We have a strong army, but warriors generally do not aspire to lead. They prefer *being* led. On the other side, those who would seek political power are rarely proficient in the arts of war. They will stand little chance in a combat arena. In these different ways, each group will most likely be dissuaded.'

Jeruk picked up the parchment, ignoring a small moan of distress from the archivist. This could play out well for him after all. A tournament would distract any of his enemies while giving the appearance that something was at last being done to secure the throne—by the very person they had been suspicious of. Any winner would be ignorant of Court protocols and mores, and hence reliant on his assistance.

He traced the faded lines of text. There was no room for delay and yet the period of combat could not be allowed to drag on. He held the parchment out to the Keeper.

'Do the records give an indication of timescales?'

'It is not prescribed,' the man replied. 'The commencement of the contest, and its duration, are both entirely at your discretion, being the most senior of the late King's advisors.'

Jeruk smiled.

'Very well. Bring me the proclamation you mentioned. I will have something prepared.'

foothills of temmok'dun
3rd day of run'bakamasa, 966

It takes me the whole morning to reach the base of the mountain. For most of the journey I can see Claire, waving from the Palace grounds. She disappears from view once I cross the first foothills of Temmok'Dun. It's impossible to tell from the Palace, but these hills stretch for some distance. They become steeper and taller as the mountain approaches, but it's nothing old Perak can't handle.

We have made good time, but Perak is eager for some feed and water, and I should take a bite myself. I've brought provisions for about ten days if I'm careful. I expect I'll find somewhere to hunt or fish before my supplies run out, but right now that remains only a hope so I have to eat sparingly. It's a perfect day for travelling. Not too warm, even though we're in the second half of Bakamasa.

I haven't begun climbing yet but the view from here is already amazing. The black flags and pennants of the Palace—tiny in the distance—and the white tips of the waves in the Eastern bay visible around the curve of the mountain. I can see our whole route. Perak and I followed the river, Sun Besaraya, towards Temmok'Dun. Once we left the lowlands the grass paths gave way to rocks, but it was still firm going and Perak proved sure footed. The river eventually narrowed, squeezing into a foaming torrent beside the path.

The last fifty metres or so were steep. I was forced to dismount and lead Perak by the reins. When we arrived at this deep rock pool we were both ready for a drink! I estimate we're about a third of the way up the mountainside. Its outflow is the origin of the Sun Besaraya, but the exact source of its pristine water isn't visible from here. It's fed from a cataract that plunges down from much higher, filling the air with a fine mist and painting swirling rainbows across the sun-struck cliff face. Now we've quenched our thirsts and I've had chance to scout around a bit, I know I'm going to have to leave Perak behind. He can make his way back on his own but there is no onward path. Not one that a kudo can attempt with any safety, even one as hardy and determined as him. I would never risk taking him somewhere a fall or a misstep could break a leg, or worse, so I always knew there would come a time to say goodbye and push forward on my own. I didn't expect it to be so soon.

He's watching my every move, as if he understands what I'm about to do. It's already almost mid-afternoon; I can't leave it any longer. I'm going to refill my saptak skin, say my farewells, and start that climb.

Chapter 2

The dusk of the Fire season—the end of what the Batu'n call summer - was cooler. Even so, the central basilica of the Blood Court shimmered hazily in the mid-afternoon heat. Jeruk would have been more comfortable had he arranged the gathering during the morning. He ran a finger around the collar of his lemon yellow jerkin, pulling it away from his sweat-sticky neck. Time for further words with the Court seamstress. Leaving his Jester persona behind him was hard enough without this ridiculous costume. The woman had been working on his new wardrobe since the King's death with no sign of progress.

A meagre crowd had assembled to hear his announcement. Most of the courtiers, artisans, and folk from the surrounding hamlets had little interest in Court business, content to catch the details from those who could be bothered to attend. Others would wait to read the notices posted across Istania once he ordered their distribution. He stepped out from the shadow of the Court into the full glare of the sun. At least lemon reflected a lot of the light. He did not envy the bitch Queen, clad in black all year round. Even the Piper's purple robes must be unbearable in this heat.

One of the Court artisans had erected a small podium adjacent to the main entrance. It stood close to the building but offered no protection from the sun. An expectant hush fell as he mounted the platform and held up his proclamation.

'Our beloved King never recovered from the wounds he suffered during his brave battle at Lembaca Ana,' he began, modulating his voice to carry to the back of the throng. 'He journeyed into the care of the Gods on the thirteenth day of Run, leaving no direct heir or living

17

relatives. I instructed the Keeper of the Keys to conduct a detailed search of our ancient Laws of Succession. As a result of his research, and with the agreement of the Princips of Istania, we have concluded that a contest must be held to determine who should be our next monarch.

'This competition will be open to anyone, resident of Istania or no, commoner or high-born, warrior, wizard, or weaver. Candidates must declare themselves before sunset on the last day of Far'Tanamasa. In the event of multiple declarations, contenders will be eliminated by single combat with opponents selected by lot. Competition will commence immediately after the close of nominations, on the first day of Ter'Tanamasa. The archives contain no information regarding restrictions on these contests, so contestants may use whatever skills or weapons they have.'

'When do nominations open?' asked a man standing at the front of the crowd.

'Today,' Jeruk replied. 'You may register—with either myself or the Keeper—at any time during daylight, until they close in sixty days' time.'

'What about you, Jester?' someone shouted from the back. 'Will you be throwing your funny hat into the ring?'

A ripple of laughter spread through the crowd. Jeruk raised his hand to shield his eyes from the sun, trying to make out who had spoken. A tight group of shabbily clothed men at the back of the crowd shuffled nervously, all avoiding his eye.

'I will not,' he replied, eliciting further snorts of mirth. A Tepak of the Blood Guard, who had been standing at attention in the shade of the Court wall, moved forward with a small cohort of Guardsmen. It was enough to silence the throng.

'I will of course continue to act as the new ruler's loyal adviser,' Jeruk continued, 'for as long as they require my services. And I shall be administering the contest to ensure each candidate is treated fairly and equally.'

He paused, ignoring a trickle of sweat running down

his cheek. When it became clear there were no further questions Jeruk nodded to the Tepak.

'Thank you all for your attention,' he said as the Guardsmen moved among the crowd, ushering them out of the courtyard. 'Please pass on the information to your family and friends, and let us hope a strong and capable candidate comes forward soon!'

He left the dusty square, seeking a cool sanctuary inside the Court. Behind him the sound of proclamation pages being nailed to any available vertical surface echoed from the red sandstone walls.

temmok'dun
3rd day of run'bakamasa, 966

My ascent is hard going in places. I'm not used to climbing. Even though I kept myself in shape back on Mars, and Patrick and I did our fair share of travelling, nothing could have prepared me for this. At one point I think my arms are going to be pulled from their sockets! Before long my shoulders are throbbing and my legs shaking. I find a ledge to sit on to take a break and massage my sore fingers. I can still see the pool below, with Perak standing quietly beside it as if he expects me to return. The sun is already about to fall below the top of the mountain. I don't like the idea of spending my first night perched on a tiny outcrop of rock above a five hundred metre drop, so I ignore the cramps beginning to gnaw at my thighs and press on. Parts of the climb are a little easier. I come upon a shear fracture where the mountain has slid sideways and created a plateau. It would be an ideal place to overnight but I convince myself I can see another safe place beyond the next escarpment. Compared to the distance I've already covered, it's a fairly easy haul to that second ledge. Unfortunately that's what it is—a ledge, not a plateau. It's too small to sleep on. Even though the light is failing, I must push on again. I curse myself for not bringing a torch, but I have no means of lighting one, or holding one anyway. I must find somewhere to sleep, and soon, before I lose the light and can't see the handholds.

Eventually I reach a fissure in the rock. The sun has set, the moons have not yet risen, and I can go no farther. I do not have a plateau to sleep on, or even a wide ledge. The crack is barely deep enough to stand in. It could be worse, but I'm about to spend my first night on Temmok'Dun trying to sleep upright, wedged into the rock. I'm not complaining. At least it will keep me dry. The gentle rains of the malamajan won't penetrate, and I'm far enough from the edge not to worry about falling. Small comforts, but I'll take them!

the black palace
10th day of sen'bakamasa, 966

Claire hurried to an early morning Guild meeting. This was her favourite time to be out and about around the Palace, before the heat of late Bakamasa had chance to turn oppressive. Midday especially burned hotter than anything she had experienced during her years in Toronto. That seemed like another life now. It was another life! One in which she had no knowledge of her father's Elemental powers and the status that went with them, and could never have dreamt of taking his place even if she had.

In the time between Albert Yamani's accidental departure from this world and her own arrival, the Air Guild had almost disbanded. Academy classes in the Air powers were still well attended, but the profile of the guild had waned without a strong leader to provide direction and drive. Meetings became rare and incoherent, with no sense of aim or purpose. Even the most advanced of the remaining mages found their powers reduced in the absence of an Elemental, and the guild drifted apart. Inspired by the Fire Guild, which had flourished once more since the return of Elaine Chandler, Claire was determined to achieve similar success in her own domain. She had shared passage with the flame-haired Elemental on the ill-fated Valiant, and seen how quickly she rekindled the embers of her previous life as Fire Witch of Berikatanya. With the Elementals returned, the abilities of established mages and those with nascent powers were re-energised. Claire scouted candidates from across the Kertonian side of Berikatanya, resulting in a near doubling of the intake at the Academy. With the wholehearted support of the other Air mages, and her former tutors at the College, the Air Guild was beginning to show signs of unity for the first time in two generations.

Her mind occupied with thoughts of extending her search for new mages into Istania, Claire rounded a corner and marched straight into the Queen. Her papers scattered to the black slate floor with a loud clatter.

'Oh! I'm so sorry your Majesty!'

The Queen straightened her obsidian circlet and bent to help Claire retrieve her documents.

'No damage done my dear! We are much more resilient than we look.'

'Please, your Majesty, there's no need.' She took a sheaf of papers from the Queen's outstretched hand. 'I can manage.'

The Queen regarded the empty corridor. Her voice dropped to a conspiratorial whisper. 'I've told you, call me Ru'ita. No need for formalities now that we're such close friends. I have few enough of those, and it would be such a refreshing change from all the pomp and pageantry.'

Claire flushed, her pale face colouring to the roots of her ash-blonde hair. Her friendship with the Black Queen had been instrumental in giving her the confidence, and the contacts, to accomplish what she had done with the Air Guild. More, it enriched all other aspects of life at the Palace beyond measure. Even so, she still found it odd to call the monarch by her name.

'Sorry... Ru'ita... I will try to remember.' She took a last bundle of pages from the Queen. 'Thank you.'

'I'm glad I bumped into you actually,' said the Queen, her smile broadening at the unintended pun. 'There is something I must speak with you about.'

'Oh, but I'm already a little late for a Guild–'

The Queen waved aside her discomfort. 'It's not urgent. Really, the Air Guild is a marvel these days, all because of your efforts. I wouldn't dream of standing between you and your work. Come and find me once business is concluded.'

She swept away along the corridor, her long, stiff black dress rustling against the slate floor. Claire took a moment to recover her composure, the morning's agenda temporarily forgotten in the wake of the Queen's enigmatic words. Of all the things Ru'ita might wish to discuss, Claire could think of none requiring a private audience.

She entered the meeting room. Another example of Claire's influence, it had been set aside for Guild use at her request. Its wide windows offered an impressive view over the Palace gardens and the river beyond. At the Queen's instruction it had been furnished with a large blackwood table, similar to the one in the stateroom, but built especially for the purpose by Kertonian artisans. The imposing structure stretched the entire length of the room, its polished surface gleaming in the bright morning light. Two dozen chairs sat around it, each crafted by an individual journeyman. The young craftsmen and women had stamped their personality on the work, including an Air reference on a leg, an arm, or the chair back. Small birds, local insects resembling butterflies, or carved representations of air currents or scudding clouds adorned every piece. Their quirkiness made Claire smile whenever she saw them. In contrast, the seat at the head of the table, created by the master cabinet-maker, was a much more formal affair. Built from rare whitewood, high-backed, with a cushion of deep black velvet embroidered with the sigil of the Air Mage. The chair's wings were carved into an anatomically perfect representation of outstretched ghantu wings, with ornate scrollwork billowing beneath as if lofting the chair away into the atmosphere.

Some chairs remained empty, reserved for students still working their way through the Academy. In the occupied seats, mages engaged in spirited conversation about recent activities and the day's agenda. Claire struggled for a moment to recall the local term for mage. The word came to her as she took her position at the head of the table and a respectful silence fell over the Guild members.

'Good morning suhiri,' she said, setting her paperwork down in front of her.

'Good morning Sakti,' they all replied, using the formal title of the Air Mage. Another small smile passed over Claire's face at the memory of the first time she had been called "Sakti Udara" and her disbelief that the title could possibly apply to her.

'Let us begin. We have a lot of ground to cover today.'

puppeteers' meeting hall
14th day of sen'bakamasa, 966

'Can we have some order, please?' Jeruk Nipis said, raising his voice to be heard above the hubbub. 'Fourteen days have passed since I published the Magisterial Contest proclamation. As yet no candidates have been forthcoming.'

'You've frightened them off!' said one of the few who had found somewhere to sit in the crowded chamber. 'No one wants to have to listen to you whispering in their ear for the rest of their life!'

A handful of others were brave enough to laugh at this quip. Jeruk's sour expression killed the laughter at birth.

'This is not a matter for your amusement! The future of the realm is at stake!'

The bearded man seated at Jeruk's right hand leaned forward.

'Why?' he asked, as the last few embarrassed guffaws died away.

Jeruk had known Sebaklan Pwalek since long before he started attending these meetings. He worked his way up from apprentice blacksmith to become the senior Court Armourer, but although skilled with the crafts of war, he had no stomach for the reality. The interminable years of conflict, largely engineered by the late King, sat ill with his own private philosophies. It was only ever going to be a matter of time before he found his way to the Puppeteers.

'"Why?" Seb?' he replied, 'because with no ruler on the Blood Throne there will be anarchy, or even invasion.'

Pwalek stroked his beard. 'I've always believed doing away with the King was one of our chief aims,' he said, reaching for his second flagon of ale. 'We should look upon him dying without an heir as his parting gift to us.'

'Maybe if the timing was better,' Jeruk admitted. 'If we'd been ready. But we're not in a position to grasp the levers of state at this time. Besides, the general populace would see such a move as opportunistic. We could easily cause more discontent than we solved.'

'But perpetuating the monarchy goes against everything we believe in! Is there not at least a more equitable solution than putting another witless warmonger on the throne?'

Jeruk sat back with an expansive gesture. 'I'm open to suggestions, but bear in mind preparation for the contest has already begun.'

'Without any contestants,' shouted the man seated at the other end of the table, raising a second round of laughter.

'I've been thinking about this for a while,' Pwalek said, turning to address Jeruk directly. 'Assuming the lack of candidates continues, could we not effectively take over— in a non-threatening way—if we set up a kind of government by committee? A Majelis of senior ministers? There are several here who would be happy to serve–'

'Including you?' Jeruk said, smiling.

His friend did not hesitate. 'Certainly including me! I've been here as long as anyone and longer than most. Why not me?'

'No reason. I just wonder if you see this as a slow motion route to the Throne without the inconvenience of a series of bouts at combat.'

Pwalek jumped to his feet, his face reddening beneath his copious brown beard. His chair crashed to the floor behind him.

'What have I done to deserve such an insult? I have no interest in the Throne! I thought you knew me better than that Jeruk!'

Jeruk remained seated, but laid a placating hand on the other's arm. 'Calm down, old friend. I meant no disrespect. The Blood Throne is a powerful prize. Greater men than you have been turned by the thought of it. Our history is littered with stories of plots, counter-plots and backstabbing. You can't blame me for wanting to be certain of your motives.'

Pwalek set his chair on its legs again, sat, and reached once more for his beer. He took a long draught. 'You know my motives better than anyone,' he said, avoiding Jeruk's eye. 'Populate it with a few well-chosen members of our own, including representation from other parts of Istania. It would be a start. We could sell it as an interim measure, pending the arrival of a candidate. Before you know it, the people will have accepted it as fact. How it's always been done. Their memories are short. Even among those few who take notice of such things.'

Jeruk sat quietly for a moment, but his outward calm belied his inner excitement. His old friend had crystallised the nebulous thoughts he had harboured for years. A path forward without fiefdom or favour. It would have to be carefully orchestrated, yes. The idea would be stillborn if even a single candidate materialised.

'We must confirm there are no legal obstacles to such a move,' he said. 'The Keeper must be consulted.'

'I can take care of that,' said Pwalek, rising to his feet more calmly. 'Leave it with me.'

the black palace
15th day of sen'bakamasa, 966

The bright fingers of morning sun had walked the length of the table and passed beyond the windows, leaving the Guildroom with more subdued illumination. The assembled suhiri had dealt with the business of the day—assigning assignments; deciding deadlines; and agreeing the agenda for the next meeting. They filed from the room in small groups. Claire sat back in her winged chair, allowing herself a moment of pride in their accomplishment and progress. Time to find out what the Queen wanted.

The monarch appeared in the doorway.

'My, you do keep good time Claire,' she began, closing the heavy blackwood door behind her. 'We thought you would have concluded your business by now. It seems we were right.'

'I was about to come and find you your Maj– Ru'ita,' Claire said. 'You had something you wished to discuss?'

'Yes. It's a little delicate. You mustn't think we are asking you to spy for us, but... you have been spending a lot of time at Court.'

'Visiting the Keeper of the Keys, yes. He's been helping me with my work.'

'His archives are extensive. Such a shame our ancestors never had the foresight to keep equally careful records. Do your father's books not contain the information you need?'

'No, or at least not much. I'm so pleased to have them, of course,' Claire added quickly. 'They are my only connection with that side of his life. It was hidden from me on Earth. But it seems Father contented himself with conventional uses of his powers. His books record those in great detail. I'm more interested in exploring their boundaries, which are only hinted at.

'So that's why I've had to travel to Istania,' she continued. 'I was bemoaning the lack of Air lore in a conversation with Patrick soon after Jann left.'

Claire's voice faltered at the thought of Jann Argent. More than a month had passed since his kudo carried him out of sight. She had no way of telling how his quest fared.

'Patrick couldn't find any records either. He'd been searching for mention of his own father, but nothing at all exists on the subject of Pattern Juggler lore. When he told me about the scrolls he'd seen in the catacombs the day he visited Jann, and what a nice old man the Keeper was underneath his grumpy exterior, I decided to go and see for myself.'

The Queen laughed. A high tinkling laugh like water rushing along a forest beck. 'Yes, the reputation of his short temper has reached the Palace on more than one occasion.'

'He's been very good to me. Once you know him, he's one of the most helpful, knowledgeable people I've met since I arrived. Present company excepted, of course.'

A faint smile played over the Queen's lips. She walked to the window to stare out over the Palace gardens.

'It's a worry—you spending so much time at Court,' she said. 'It can be a dangerous place, especially for a young woman travelling alone. A young woman whose first loyalty is to the Queen of Kertonia.'

She fixed Claire with a piercing look. 'We are once again moving into troubled times.'

Claire held her gaze for a moment, trying to subdue the conflicting emotions the Queen's fierce demeanour had triggered. 'It would be a brave marauder indeed to risk tangling with the Air Mage of Berikatanya,' she said, struggling to keep an edge of irritation out of her voice.

'And really your Majesty,' she added, risking a return to the formal appellation as a small protest at the Queen's implied criticism, 'what choice do I have? If I want to extend my knowledge and develop Air lore then I must visit the catacombs.

'The old man is protective of his scrolls. He refuses to allow any to be removed from his keeping, but that is the only restriction he's imposed. Provided I take nothing away, and I'm careful with the candles, I have full access to his archives. It takes time to track down the information I need, days even. To travel back and forth repeatedly is exhausting. I'm left with no choice but to stay at Court while I am studying.'

'And what have you learned from all this industrious study?' the Queen asked, turning away once more to gaze out at the gardens.

Claire moved to stand beside the Queen. 'These gardens are a good example. My studies have allowed me to develop uses of Air power to help with both the formal and the kitchen garden. Each now enjoys the protection of semi-permanent air currents to prevent insect attack. I've also invented a method of airborne seed distribution. Planting rates have improved several fold.'

'Most inventive,' said the Queen.

'Thank you Ru'ita. I'm hoping to build on what I've learned for a completely new idea, but I'd rather not say more about it today. I'm not entirely certain it will work.'

'We have no more time today anyway,' said the Queen. She held the door open. 'We trust your studies and investigations won't keep you from today's Eradewan meeting? We are already a little late.'

'No!' Claire said. 'I would never allow anything to keep me from my duties at the Palace.'

'Then let us go,' said the Queen, ushering Claire ahead of her.

temmok'dun
4th day of run'bakamasa, 966

On the second day of my trek the sun rises shining fiercely into my fissure, striking tears from my waking eyes. I enjoy a frugal breakfast looking out from my sanctuary before gathering the mental focus to continue with my climb. As the morning wears on the air turns colder. I guess I'm now at around a thousand metres. The stiff neck and aching limbs of last night have still not worked themselves out. The balmy summer heat of my first stop is a distant memory. It feels more like the tail end of Tanamasa. Later, the wind gets up too, bringing an extra chill to the early afternoon, first pressing me against the rock face and then threatening to tear me from it. It brings faint aromas of trees and grass, a poignant reminder of life totally absent in this barren place. I take a break to put on an extra pair of underclothes and a second shirt, but even so when the day begins to die my shivers soon return. Finally I find a ledge to rest upon, but it offers no shelter. As the heat of my exertions ebbs away I begin to shake so violently I can hardly open my backpack to retrieve my overcoat. I struggle into it and huddle against the mountain. The night is glacial. Even if I had anything to burn, the wind would blow out a fire before it could catch. I take comfort from knowing I am almost at the top. I will surely crest the mountain on the third day.

And I do, soon after daybreak. But on reaching the summit, I feel like the butt of a bad joke. The one where there's always another mountain beyond the one you've just climbed. Not as big as the first—I must have reached two thousand metres by now and this second peak looks like it's a thousand more—but daunting enough when you thought you were over the worst of it. I still have the best part of half a day of light left, so I press on, grateful for small things: I haven't yet seen any snow; and the wind has eased off compared to yesterday.

Now with the light failing once more, I'm in the same

position on the second peak as I had been on the first. I'm praying to all the Elemental Gods that the morning won't see a repeat of the bad joke. I'm wearing every item of clothing I have, and I've eaten three days' food, so my pack is much lighter, but the blisters on my hands and my aching legs can't take another thousand-metre climb.

state room, the black palace
15th day of sen'bakamasa, 966

Claire followed the Black Queen into her state room. Murmurs of conversation died away as the Queen crossed the threshold. Claire was amused to see the Piper already in attendance. Clearly the monarch's obtuse warnings about his habitual lateness had hit home.

'What news from Red House?' she asked, seating herself at the head of the table. 'I expect there have been no further moves to engage us in peaceful debate?'

Harimeladan, the Keeper of the Queen's Purse, leaned forward stroking one side of his forked, pewter-grey beard.

'Red House is ended.'

'What do you mean, Hari?'

'The Blood King died a few days since,' he replied, 'and without an heir.'

A momentary expression of surprise passed over the Queen's face. 'His wounds did not appear to be life-threatening when we spoke after the battle.'

Harimeladan shrugged. 'Bloodpower is not well understood, Majesty, even among those few who wield it. Perhaps his injuries were a side-effect, or they may have been internal. Either way, they were certainly fatal.'

'A long line,' mused the Queen, 'but not an auspicious one. Who will succeed him, do we know?'

'There are reports that a contest is to be held to find a new ruler,' said the Piper.

'We may hope whoever it is will be more inclined to peace than their predecessor.'

'Unlikely, Majesty,' Harimeladan continued, 'since the replacement is being decided through combat. The Jester's proclamation has been posted all over the land, far beyond the borders of Istania.'

'The Jester!' the Queen said, a sneer creasing her face. 'So he is still pulling the strings of state, is he? Whoever takes over the throne may no longer call themselves the Blood King, or Queen, but we would wager they will again come under the baleful influence of that yellow bastard. What is in this "proclamation" of his, do we know?'

The two men continued their double-act, explaining the parameters of a contest in which Claire had no interest. Her attention returned to the Air conundrum she had been working on earlier, until another derisive snort from the Queen dragged it back to the meeting.

'We are surprised the midget doesn't proclaim himself King!' she said. 'He has the head for it.'

'A clever move on his part, Majesty,' the Piper said. 'It is said he is no more liked in Istania than here in Kertonia.'

'Nevertheless the longer that realm exists without a head of state the more lawless it will become,' Harimeladan said. 'Even a war-mongering King is better than no King at all. The old King had a temper but he knew how to keep his subjects in line.'

'We are certain the Istanian people wish for a peaceful existence as much as we do,' the Queen said. 'But wishing for something is a long way from having it. In any case it is moot. Without knowing who will sit on the Blood Throne, or whatever the new ruler decides to call it, further debate is meaningless. Have our scouts and informers keep a close eye on developments.'

'Of course, Majesty,' the Piper nodded. 'And on that note I should say our scouts have reported an increase in Istanian troop movements at Lembaca Ana.'

The Queen squinted at the Piper, gripping the edge of the state room table.

'An increase? We were not aware there had been *any*

deployments by the Reds since the Battle!'

'A recent development, ma'am, and one we have only just become aware of. Almost certainly the work of the Jester and his cronies, since the King was already dead before any forces arrived in the Valley.'

'Damn them!' exclaimed the Queen, 'have they made any move on the harbour works?'

'As far as we know there is as yet nothing worthy of the name "harbour" Majesty. Petani is having great difficulty with his earthworks at the coast.

'Even so, a harbour—should one ever be finished—is a valuable prize. It is hardly surprising the Jester is keeping a watch on our works. There is no suggestion of the troops threatening the workings,' the Piper added. 'At present they are simply observing while making a show of being on manoeuvres. I don't believe we have anything to worry about at this stage.'

'Still, it puts us in a difficult position,' the Queen said. 'We are reluctant to leave our new harbour unguarded, yet any influx of our forces in the Valley will be interpreted as an escalation. In the absence of a King to give them clear and unequivocal leadership, the Istanians must already feel vulnerable.'

'Perhaps,' said Claire, speaking for the first time, 'your Majesty could send hand-picked men to the Valley? In small numbers over several days, so as not to arouse suspicion. They could mingle with the Earth mages and construction workers. If the Reds are camped high on the hillside they won't be able to tell the difference.'

'An excellent suggestion!' the Queen said. 'See to it, Mungo!'

court of the blood king
21st day of sen'bakamasa, 966

Elaine Chandler needed the cool of the morning. Hot words were about to be spoken. Her fiery temper would be that much worse if they had to be exchanged under sweltering heat, but she knew it could not be put off any longer. Not normally one to reflect on Berikatanyan theism, there was a remarkable parallel between the burgeoning heat of the day and the incendiary meeting she was heading for. It sent a shiver down her spine.

The dying days of the season of the Fire God Baka still held surprising warmth. '*Like an old sun that burns hotter as it dies*,' she thought. She had purposely timed her journey to arrive at Court mid-morning, with the air fresh and the travelling easier, but the imposing stone blocks of the keep burned under the early sun. The day already felt warmer than it was.

She hurried inside, eager for the relative cool of the shaded halls and corridors. The Court was no longer her home, but her memories of its complex interior were still accurate. As a girl, she had spent many years here. Later she became one of the two Elementals bound to the Blood King by the principle of Te'Banga. After the King's defeat at the battle of Lembaca Ana she had elected to stay with Claire Yamani and the rest of her companions from the Valiant.

Rounding a corner she caught sight of Claire leaving the refectory in the direction of the catacombs. She called after the Air Mage, her voice echoing along the stone-walled passage, and hurried to catch up.

'If you had mentioned you were visiting Court we could have travelled together!'

The young woman hesitated, her expression and body language betraying her eagerness to continue with whatever mission she was on. Elaine's rare mothering instinct fired up to intervene.

'I'm sorry I don't have time to chat right now,' she added quickly, the girl's tense demeanour dissipating as she spoke, 'but perhaps if we meet later we can share the return journey in each other's company?'

'Yes of course,' Claire replied, 'that would be lovely,

but I really must dash.'

She hurried on without a second glance. Elaine set off again towards the chambers of Kepul Seri, the present leader of the Fire Guild. His doors were closed, but she knocked and entered without waiting. She was not here to stand on ceremony. Seated at his desk, Seri flashed an angry look at the interruption before recognising who disturbed his privacy.

'Bakara,' he said, rising to his feet. 'What brings you to Court unheralded? Is there something I can do for you?'

'Yes,' Elaine replied, closing the door behind her. 'Resign.'

'I have always appreciated the way in which you blaze right to the heart of your business instead of dancing around the edges of it like flames in a fire pit. But resign? What possible reason could I have to resign? Who would take my place?'

'I could quote the greater good. Surely it is obvious the Guild is not working as well as it could be.'

'There is much to do, yes, but much has also been accomplished. None of the other Fire mages have ever suggested they are discontented with my leadership.'

'Why would they? Not one of them is any better placed. You have seen to that. In the country of the blind, the one-eyed man is king. Or perhaps a more appropriate metaphor would be, in a country of total darkness, people will follow a man with a guttering candle.'

The old mage drew himself up haughtily. 'I may not be an Elemental, as you have implied. I cannot deny it. Yet I have stood in your place since the day you fell through the portal and I have grown immensely in the time that has divided us. I am at the peak of my strength. I have years of experience. Years more than you can claim. Let me see, you had only been Fire Witch for what? Six years before you were lost to us? Whereas I have sat at the head of the Guild for sixty.'

'And what have you accomplished in those sixty years?'

the Fire Witch snapped. 'The Guild is much as it was all that time ago. Has it moved forward? No! Has it developed new uses for its powers? No! Forging, drying, and destroying. That's all you are good for.'

'What else is there?' Seri asked, spreading his hands in the air. 'What else has there ever been?'

'You should see the wonders the Queen's new Air Mage has wrought, though she has been out of the Academy less than a season. If that slip of a girl barely off her mother's teat can work such magic with her Guild then there is no reason Fire should fall behind. We are every bit as important to the future of the land as Air, especially now that tensions between the Houses are rising once again. We need to be strong. And more than that we must look to our lore. Sakti Udara is exploring remarkable new ways to use her powers. We should be doing the same. You sit here above centuries of Fire lore but I would wager you are ignorant of the vast majority of it. When was the last time you visited the catacombs?'

Kepul Seri barked a laugh. 'Well there at least is a simple question to answer, Bakara. I have never visited the catacombs.'

'And you find that amusing?'

Elaine flexed her fingers, hinting at their latent power, before forcing herself to relax. This was not about their relative strengths with Fire. Her Elemental abilities far outmatched Seri's. As did her leadership skills. 'The Fire Guild isn't working as it stands,' she repeated, smoothing the last vestiges of tension out of her hands against her tunic. 'The suhiri are split across the land. They have no clear allegiances, no forward path. Perhaps I have stayed silent too long. Allowed the events of early Bakamasa to distract me, and become lulled by the gentle pace of life at the Palace. No more. I appreciate what you have done in my absence, Seri, but you were only ever the caretaker of the Fire Guild. I am the Fire Witch. The seat is mine by right, and it is time for me to reclaim it.'

Kepul Seri had been standing since Elaine entered his chambers. He continued to stare at Elaine for a few moments before collapsing back into his chair like a deflated balloon.

'Well this is as unexpected as it is unwelcome,' he said, staring at the desk in front of him. 'But I cannot deny the truth in your argument. I have never been a scholar. The lore scrolls hold no interest for me. I was content to oversee things as they have always been. It seemed enough. Perhaps that is my age talking.'

Finally, he met her gaze. 'I can raise no objections Bakara. I shall call a special Guild meeting immediately. Will you be here to take over in person?'

'If it can be gathered today. I intend to leave early tomorrow. It's more than a two-day journey to the Palace, as you know, and I must return as soon as possible.'

'Very well. Though we are somewhat dissipated, I believe there are sufficient suhiri at Court to form a quorum. We shall meet this afternoon.'

Elaine let the door fall shut behind her. A flash of purple gown caught her attention as it disappeared from the corridor to her left. She had not seen the face of the man who wore it, but the colour was unmistakable.

Chapter 3

After her unexpected encounter with the Fire Witch, Claire wound her way towards the archives through the twisty little passages of the catacombs. Having exhausted the Air lore in the Keeper's catalogued records, she'd been compelled to search the vast collection of material which even he had never found the time to index—or to read. Her early successes, creating self-sustaining air currents, gave her the idea of using Air power to solve the realm's ongoing problem with communication. In towns and villages, letters were still delivered by runners. Riders covered the more remote regions. But with civil unrest common in both realms of Berikatanya, delivery was uncertain at best. News often went unreported from one season's end to another.

Claire's concept, which she jokingly called "Air mail", used directed currents to carry letters and small packages. Her supposition, that this was no more than a logical extension to her method of distributing agricultural seeds for planting, proved incorrect. The influence of her existing lore only covered short distances. Beyond a kilometre or so, the letters veered off their intended course, or dropped to the ground altogether. There must be a way to operate Air power over greater distances but so far, the necessary insight escaped her.

She found the Keeper's door ajar. A fire burning in his dog grate suggested he had not long left the room, but he was nowhere to be seen. Claire retrieved the last ring of keys from the end of his rack, blowing off the dust and wiping them clean on the cuff of her tunic. The Keeper returned carrying a plate of food in one hand and a flask of wine in the other. He fixed her with an unblinking stare, a gentle smile lifting the corners of his mouth.

37

'Back again young lady? And determined to pursue the most obscure of all our hidden secrets, I see!'

'If you're sure I'm allowed?'

'Goodness me, yes!' the old man said, his smile broadening to a fatherly beam. 'I have few visitors, but of those who do find their way to my humble quarters I would trust you before any. Who knows what wonders you may uncover in today's quest? Visiting the most cobwebbed of my many shelves and crannies whose knowledge has remained lost even to me these long centuries past? I wish you well in your endeavours! For myself, I am content to remain here in the warmth of my fire and refresh my memory of more recent texts.'

So saying, the Keeper placed his modest supper on a small table, settled himself into his favourite armchair, and picked up a scroll of parchment without another look in her direction.

Claire took a lantern from the shelf under the key rack, fitted a fresh candle, and left the old archivist to his studies. The catacombs into which she ventured had lain undisturbed since before the Keeper's time. In this part of the crypt the wall sconces, crumbling to rust, would no longer hold a torch, but they retained enough strength to hang up her light while she found the right key and worked it into the timeworn lock. The dust-clogged tumblers eventually loosened and the hasp fell open. She retrieved the lantern, cleaned its glass, and pulled wide the heavy iron gate, its ancient hinges squealing in protest.

The loud noise in the still air of the crypt sent a shiver through her. It was cold down here, yes, but the reaction was more in anticipation of what she might find. This particular section had remained unexplored even when she had been helping Patrick with his extensive search of the vaults. It had been hard enough to persuade him to revisit the Keeper's domain at all. Even though frustrated at the lack of Juggler lore to be found anywhere at the Palace, he was reluctant to explore elsewhere.

'It's not that I don't want to come,' he had said, after they'd spent an evening discussing potential sources of information. Discussing! Claire smiled. Their discourse had been too one-sided to properly be called a discussion. She had suggested ever more unlikely places where Patrick might look, and he responded by grunting 'tried it', or 'nothing there.'

'How do you know there even is anything written about it?' Claire had asked.

'I don't. Not for certain. It's just a hunch. Well, more than that. I didn't know my father well. Never saw much of him when I was growing up. Nothing at all once I started school. But I remember what sort of person he was. Meticulous. In everything, not only his art. I can't believe he would live here for long as the Pattern Juggler without knowing the lore inside out. If it hadn't already been recorded, he would have committed it to paper. Chapter and verse. That's how he was.'

'If you're so certain, do you have any inkling where he would have kept such precious work?'

'Somewhere safe, that much is obvious. I don't know if the lore would be dangerous in the wrong hands. How many potential Jugglers could there be in the population? Would any of them have malign intent? Who knows? But whether or not it needed to be hidden, he would want to protect it.'

'Sounds like a good reason to look in the catacombs to me,' Claire had replied. 'Anything down there is both safe and secret. Guarded from all but the Keeper. And he's not exactly garrulous when it comes to revealing information others have concealed.'

After pressing the point further, she had convinced Patrick a visit to Court would be worthwhile. He accompanied her on her second trip. The Keeper remembered him, of course. More than remembered; he was deferential to Patrick in a way he had never been to Claire. He gave Patrick the run of the tunnels right away.

But it was no use. He yearned for knowledge of his inheritance, but Patrick didn't possess the temperament to spend time poring over dusty scrolls.

Now, shining her light across the hundreds of racked parchments in this part of the crypt, Claire could almost understand why he had given up after only one visit. Dust clung to every surface, obscuring their titles or any external hint of the contents. She wedged her lantern on a corner shelf to illuminate the largest area. She was made of sterner stuff than the journeyman Juggler! She pulled out the delicate papers one by one and sorted them into piles.

When the flickering of Claire's lamp signalled she was about to lose her light, she was engrossed in an enormous illuminated script written—unusually—on vellum rather than paper. That alone indicated its extreme age. She had never seen another like it. The content of the document proved even more intriguing. Not something she would normally have given a second glance—it didn't concern Air powers or lore—but the opening words caught her attention and wouldn't let her go. Much of the ancient language was impenetrable to her still limited Istanian, but she deciphered enough of the first passage to send shivers down her spine:

"Where a need of second ? arises but no Kayshiru or Banshiru is present, a similar ? ? through the use of Rampiri. These powerful effects can often ? ? care in the order and magnitude of powers combined."

Snatches of the rest of the document referred obliquely to arcane uses of Elemental energies. It seemed to suggest the existence of powers beyond the Four, although they remained unnamed and their descriptions were so esoteric and obscure as to be almost cabalistic.

court of the blood king
22nd day of sen'bakamasa, 966

'Have you had many responses to your invitation?'

Jeruk turned a blank page of parchment face down on his desk before looking up to see who disturbed his concentration. He needed a moment to recognise his unannounced visitor. Kepul Seri, the leader of the Fire Guild, was not someone in whose company he had spent much time.

'Many?' he replied. 'How many would you have expected? Our beloved King is a hard act–'

'I should like to put my own name forward.'

Jeruk exploded into a fit of coughing to hide his amusement, turning back to his desk and reaching for a second blank scroll. It would not do for this suhir to see that the list of candidates was, so far, empty.

'Forgive me. Your offer is as unexpected as your visit. Is the Fire Guild not occupying enough of your time?'

'My services in that sphere are no longer required.'

Jeruk inclined his head in confusion but made no comment.

'Now the famous Fire Witch has returned, she has once more taken up the reins of office.'

'You can hardly be surprised. It is tradition, after all, for the Guilds to be led by their Elementals.'

'Quite so. And I bear no grudge,' Seri added quickly. 'She is far better qualified than I. Not only more powerful, but younger—more energetic. I am content that my leadership in her absence has been sound and the Guild has prospered under my guidance.'

He hesitated.

'I have come to the conclusion that such skills as I have honed during my time with the Guild are exactly those required of a monarch. I–'

'I must ask you once again to forgive me,' Jeruk interrupted, 'but there is more to ruling Istania than administration and delegation! This land has a sustained and not exactly luminous history of unrest, frequently escalating to all-out war with our neighbours. There is no reason to suppose we can avoid similar disputes in future.'

'I am skilled in diplomacy also,' Seri insisted. 'As you may imagine it is no easy task to keep such volatile personalities as the Fire Mages in control.'

'Keeping a lid on a few wizards is a long way from leading the Istanian army into battle.'

'My powers with Fire are prodigious! Even more so now the Witch is returned and our energies are unblocked.'

'But what of battle tactics? Deployment strategies? To say nothing of the kind of charismatic leadership the nation has come to expect from its monarch. Does anyone outside the Guild even know who you are?'

'*I hardly recognised you myself,*' he thought, '*and I've spent my whole life at Court.*'

The ex-Guild leader waved a hand at the blank scroll.

'I wasn't aware I needed your approval for my candidature,' he said, straightening his tunic with a sharp tug. 'Please add my name to the list. At the top,' he added, 'since there are no other names present.'

'Each candidate's details occupy a separate page,' Jeruk said, his gaze unwavering, 'as per the protocol.'

Seri shrugged. 'You will no doubt inform me if and when I must engage in combat with such other candidates as may come forward.'

'Are you expecting your powers to intimidate any potential adversaries? Perhaps dissuade them from joining the contest altogether?'

'I have no such expectations.'

'It's hard to imagine how it could be a fair fight. I've seen Fire used in anger.'

Seri gave Jeruk a cool stare. 'Each will bring their own abilities to the contest,' he said. 'You would not expect a swordsman to fight without his blade. This is no different. There are defences against Fire. My opponent must research them just as I will have to find a way to defeat spear or dagger. Add my name.'

Seri turned on his heel and strode from the room. With a deep sigh, Jeruk reached for a quill.

the granite plain of temmok'dun
6th day of run'bakamasa, 966

The top hundred metres or so of that second peak are easier. Exposure to wind and rain has broken up the rock so there are plenty of hand- and footholds. The incline is more forgiving too. I crest the ridge and utter a cry of relief at the panorama which opens in front of me. A granite plain stretches out for a kilometre or more. I have climbed up between a fork in the rock. The pillars continue on either side for a hundred metres or so before arrowing back down to the plain. I perch on a boulder, trying to make sense of the view. This must have been a high-altitude lake at one time. Where I sit was the outfall. I imagine there was once a spectacular waterfall here. Cascading through a fissure not more than twenty metres wide to fall a thousand metres before exploding into spray atop the first peak. The pool where I left Perak is like a great-great-grandchild of this beast. The inlet must have worn itself another route to the lower levels over time, leaving this basin to empty out. The floor of the plain is dotted with small rainwater pools. All that remain of its former majesty.

But gazing beyond the plain, my heart sinks again. I can see the final escarpment of the mass that is Temmok'Dun rising vertically from the far edge of the basin. I try to stay calm and convince myself a route will reveal itself as I approach, but right now it seems as though I've gone as far as I can. The top of the massive third peak is lost in the clouds—there's no telling how high it goes.

After munching on another bepermak and refilling my waterskin, I set off across the plain. The first bit of level walking I've done the whole trip. If only there had been a way to bring Perak along to make the journey easier!

It's been slow going, being careful not to turn my ankle on a loose boulder, but I'm finally at the rock wall. The perspective from the other side must have been foreshortened. I swear the basin is ten kilometres across.

Or maybe I've been travelling slower than I thought. Either way it's already getting dark. In this fading light I can't see even a single handhold. Hard to describe how dejected I feel right now, but I know it would be stupid to do anything hasty. If I'm going to have to retrace my steps I would have to wait for morning anyway. Might as well hunker down for the night; see if things look better tomorrow. I've been collecting the few bits of scrub I found as I crossed the basin, so for the first time I can get a fire going and enjoy some warmth.

duske raj'pupu
28th day of sen'bakamasa, 966

Sepuke Maliktakta opened his eyes. The thumping noise was outside his head as well as inside. He turned toward the source of the external banging, his cheek burning as it peeled away from the sticky table top. Mingled odours of stale beer and vomit made his stomach roil. He sat upright, catching a half-empty tankard with the sweep of his arm and sending it spinning to the floor. It smashed on the stone flags, its contents foaming in the dusty cracks. A serving girl, her filthy smock gaping to reveal pale breasts the colour of turning milk, moaned and twisted away from him, burying her head against a threadbare settle. She pulled unconsciously at her clothes to cover herself—whether from the cold or immodesty he did not know, or care.

He rose to his feet, the hammering in his head redoubling but still failing to drown out the clamour from outside. A cold morning breeze blew across his face as he cracked open the ale house door. A rider stood there, a hammer held loosely in one hand, a copper nail between his teeth. He was dressed in the deep red uniform of the Blood Watch. Sepuke's sudden appearance caused the man's kudo to shy, its eyes flashing their whites.

'The fuck's all this noise?'

The guardsman raked Sepuke with a glance before driving a last nail into a sheet of parchment pinned to the door. A sneer of disgust lifted one side of his mouth, deepening an old scar that ran the length of his left cheek.

'Royal business. Nothing to concern you.'

Sepuke jerked the door wide and stepped out. Before his ale-sodden brain could form a suitable reply, the man returned to his kudo. He dropped his hammer into a saddle bag, mounted, and set off at a canter towards the other end of the village without a backward glance.

'Sep!'

The familiar voice of Rektan Malikputran rekindled the throbbing of his head while another wave of nausea crashed around his stomach. He staggered into the street and thrust himself shoulder-deep in the kudos' watering trough. The night-cold water sent icy knives through bone and sinew, cutting out the pain. He drank, his headache easing with each gulp.

'Early start, or a late finish?' Rektan asked as Sepuke emerged from the trough in a sun-sparkled shower of droplets.

'Even I don't break my fast by supping ale at the Prancing Kudo,' Sepuke replied, wringing the water from his hair and picking a clump of algae from between his teeth. 'Neither do you, normally.'

'There's trouble brewing,' Rektan said. 'Came to warn you. Etrumus Kepalawan called a meeting last night. He's got everyone riled about your tithe. Says they're not paying any more.'

'Everyone?'

'Near enough. Except those of us you'd expect.'

Rektan proceeded to list the names of their friends and allies. Sepuke knew several were not certain of their allegiance. He let his friend drone on while he switched his attention to the notice the guardsman had posted.

His late majesty King Jadara the First having left no
legitimate heir it is hereby
PROCLAIMED
that the succession to the Blood Throne will be
determined by
COMBAT
to be held over seven days beginning on the
1ST DAY OF TER'TANAMASA
and that all those who consider themselves worthy must
be present for registration at
THE RED COURT
no later than the
30TH DAY OF FAR'TANAMASA.
by order of the High Counsellor of Istania

– Jeruk Nipis

The proclamation was signed in a spidery hand below
the printed name of the "High Counsellor". Not a name
he recognised, but that was no surprise. He had not visited
the Blood Court since he was a boy. Sepuke's bile rose as
he read the parchment again. He ripped it from the door
and waved it in Rektan's face.

'The fuck is this?' he demanded. 'No legitimate heir?'

Rektan scanned the text. 'He never had any kids, did
he?'

'No direct offspring, sure. But he has a cousin.'

'Third cousin,' Rektan said, handing back the scroll.
'And no love lost between you. You despise him, and he
thought you were an arrogant young pup.'

'So? Still family! Still a rightful claim.'

'You serious? You want to sit on the Blood Throne?
Bit of a stretch isn't it?'

'What do you mean?'

Rektan gestured at the deserted main street. 'From lord
of Duske Raj'pupu to Blood King? What makes you think
you can handle that?'

'What makes you think I can't?'

His friend nodded in the direction of the stable block at the other end of the street. A sizable group of men, some of them carrying farm implements, others with lengths of sawn timber, turned the corner and headed toward the Prancing Kudo.

'Let's see how you deal with this lot,' he said, his expression hardening. 'Then you can tell me how good a King you'd be.'

'What were you saying about how many were still on our side?' Sepuke said. Even from this distance he could make out the faces of at least two of his one-time lieutenants.

'Kepalawan can be very persuasive. You could learn from him. Diplomacy is a useful skill for a potential king.'

Sepuke folded the parchment and slipped it into the pocket of his breeches. He loosened his sword in its sheath before turning to face the approaching crowd, rubbing his temples in a vain attempt to silence the persistent pounding in his head.

'You're a little late for the festivities!' he called to Kepalawan at the vanguard of the throng. 'The Kudo will be closed until next delivery.'

'None of us can afford to drink here anyway Maliktakta,' the man replied, his voice hoarse with stress. 'Not while we're still paying your tithe.'

'Is that what this is about, Etrumus? Money?'

'That's part of it. But mostly we don't see why honest hard-working folk should pay for something we're not getting.'

'What is it you're not getting?'

'Protection. This supposed guard against marauders you've been gouging us for the past five years and more.' Kepalawan punctuated every other word with a shake of the short bladed scythe he carried. 'Yes you too Malikputran—and the rest of your men.'

Sepuke's hand strayed close to his sword. 'And who was it defeated the raiders back in '61?' he mused, stroking his three-day-old stubble. 'Was it you, Etrumus? You and your bunch of ingrates with their farm tools? No. It was me. Me and my men. And without us, none of you would have fields to harvest—or even shacks to live in! They'd have been burned to the ground years ago and you with 'em. That's after your women had been raped and your children gutted, of course.'

A few in the crowd pressed forward at his words, the anger plain on their faces, but Kepalawan held them back.

'We're not disputing you saw those raiders off Maliktakta,' he said. 'And we were happy to pay you for the job. But that was five years ago. There's been no sign of them since, and yet still you lord it over us like one of them northern Princips, spending our money on ale and wenches while we're sweating in the fields.'

'Yeah!' shouted a voice from the crowd. 'How'd we know you didn't set them raiders on us in the first place, just so's you could pretend to save our asses?'

A murmur of assent swept over the group. A few raised their rudimentary weapons in a pathetic threat display. Sepuke suppressed a laugh.

'We're not standing for it anymore,' the anonymous voice continued. 'Tell him Etrumus. Tell him what we decided.'

'I think I can work it out for myself,' Sepuke said, holding up his hands. 'You're not paying me any more money and you're going to replace me as Kepta with... who? You, Etrumus?'

Kepalawan shifted his feet, apparently embarrassed his intentions had been so easily read.

'Are you going to run me out of town, too?'

'Yeah!' shouted the voice.

'Well no, hold on,' Kepalawan said, turning to face the townspeople. 'We never said anything about running him out of town.'

Sepuke's hand unconsciously patted his breeches pocket. 'Don't you worry about me, Etrumus. I already made other plans. Save all your worrying for how you're going to lead this rabble. You'll be turning to the drink yourself before long, believe me.'

The apparent ease of their victory took the force out of the group's argument. They broke up into smaller groups, or wandered back to their homes. Kepalawan remained in the middle of the street looking nonplussed.

'Other plans?'

'Yeah. Be careful what you wish for old man. When it's granted you may find it's not worth having.'

'I could say the same about you,' Rektan murmured, hurrying to keep up with Sepuke as he strode off in the direction of the stable block. 'What—you're leaving now?' he added, sitting heavily on a bale of hay to catch his breath.

'Nothing to keep me here,' Sepuke replied, grunting as he heaved his saddle on his kudo's back. He cinched the girth and checked the animal's hooves.

'It's not like you have any friends then. None that mean anything. What about the warm body waiting back at the Kudo?'

'She'll find another cock to satisfy her soon enough.'

'And the friends?'

'Still have each other. Seriously,' Sepuke went on, turning at last to face his comrade, 'you're better off without me. And if I do gain the throne, I'll be in a good position to throw a few royal coins your way. Spruce up the old homestead a bit and give you an easier life.'

'You really think you have a chance? The Blood King's Court will be drowning in political intrigue.' Rektan flashed a wry grin. 'Diplomacy isn't your strong suit. And it's not just people skills you'll need. Don't believe anything anyone says, watch your back, and eat from the edge of the plate.'

'Eh?'

'If someone's going to poison you they'll put it in the middle of the dish. So the royal taster doesn't keel over.'

'I'd never have thought of that.'

'See? You do need me.'

Sepuke clapped Rektan on his shoulder. 'I don't suppose I'll have any trouble with the combat part of it though, eh? Once I've won I'll send a rider for you. You can do all my politicking for me.'

He swung into the saddle.

'You're travelling light,' Rektan said, squinting against the late morning sun.

'I'll drop by home and pick up a few bits. Enough to travel with.'

'What is it, eight days?'

'At an easy pace, yeah. I'm in no rush. Proclamation says I have until the end of next month to register. I guess we were last on their list for posting it, but even so. Plenty of time.'

'Don't forget to write,' Rektan quipped, slapping the kudo's rump as Sepuke urged it into the main street, forcing the few remaining rebels to scatter from his path.

valley of lembaca ana
30th day of sen'bakamasa, 966

Terry Spate sat on an earthy outcrop that had not existed moments before he decided to rest. He rubbed his aching shoulders and gazed out to sea. The choppy waters of the estuary foamed and churned below him as if under the influence of his friend Lautan—the Water Wizard of Berikatanya. No one had seen the old Elemental since their battle with the Blood King and his clones. He had disappeared only a stone's throw from this very spot. The new mountain he helped to create, to defeat those frightful copies of himself and his fellow Elementals, stood as a stark reminder of their victory. Ignoring his protestations that it was the work of the whole group and he did not deserve such a singular honour, it had been named Pun'Akarnya. It translated loosely as "The Pinnacle of His

Career".

While the mountain still glowed in the aftermath of the terrible forces that created it, the Elementals had travelled back to the Black Palace. Terry remained with them for the lengthy celebrations, but the Valley of the Cataclysm called to him on some indefinable, visceral level. He had heard the talk of its value around the Palace, and during his time at the Forest Clearance Project. Of the many battles fought over the centuries for its ownership. The dreams of seafaring exploration that, for want of a usable harbour and the ships to populate it, never came to anything. Terry's expertise lay with land-based earthworks and the cultivation of plants for both food and decoration. Still, he was certain he could make a good fist of a landing point, given the natural shape of the estuary and the abundance of raw materials.

Even in the short time he worked there, his successes at the Forest, with indigenous and Earther plants alike, had reached legendary status. He was happy his efforts resulted in better nutrition and enjoyment for most of the population. Yet still the Valley beckoned. Within a few days of the battle celebrations being concluded he had packed his meagre belongings and set off for the coast. Two of his most trusted colleagues from the Forest, Nembaka and Umtanesh, accompanied him.

Their third workmate Pattana had retired from the team following an injury suffered while working alone in the woods. He had not been happy at the enforced idleness, and missed his compatriots keenly, but Terry had taken time out to craft a small garden for the man, filled with colourful flowers and tasty vegetables from their project. He still visited him occasionally, bringing over additions for his plot whenever they developed a new strain, and filling him in on the latest news from the projects. He was particularly interested in updates about his friend the Air Mage, for whom Pattana had a soft spot, having been the first to recognise her emerging powers.

Pattana's loss hit the team hard, but his replacement Tanaratana had soon proved every bit as resourceful and hard-working as his predecessor. As if responding to the summons of Terry's thought, Tanaratana approached from the direction of the harbour works.

'Petani! This is where you have been hideout!'

'Hiding, Tan.'

Tanaratana's English had improved during his Bakamasa-long association with the Forest Clearance team, but he still needed the occasional pointer. As the native had grown accustomed to the unfamiliar tongue, so Terry had become used to being addressed as the Earth Elemental, Petani. His memories of his origins on Berikatanya were still largely buried in the mental sludge that was the legacy of his passage through the vortex, but his control over his Elemental powers grew surer by the day. He had long since accepted his right to the title. At least, when others used it. He had never been one to embrace change, instead accepting it begrudgingly and at the pace of cooling lava. It would be some time before he no longer thought of himself as Terry Spate.

'What news of our latest attempt at a foundation?'

Tanaratana's face fell, signalling the failure ahead of his words. 'It has fallen for a third time, Petani, sadly. Even after all your efforts and clever use of heaviest stones.'

In the days since his arrival at the Valley, while the Berikatanyan summer waned through Run'Bakamasa and into Sen, Terry's early work had focused on the kind of earthworks most familiar to him. The harbour sections on land were completed swiftly and to his complete satisfaction. He was not concerned with his reputation— such things were for others to worry about. For him the quality of the work was the only thing. He always endeavoured to deliver a project to the very best of his abilities, and enjoyed looking back, taking it all in with the sense of pride and fulfilment that only came from a job well done.

Now here he was at the end of Sen'Bakamasa with Berikatanyan autumn knocking at the door. The days already cooling; the mornings often misted with a chill blanket of early Tanamasa before that season had truly arrived. Soon the different orbits of Pera-Bul and Kedu-Bul—the two moons of Berikatanya—would remember their winter synchronicity, making the seas too stormy and unpredictable to work with. Terry felt an almost overwhelming frustration weighing him down. He rested his chin on both hands and stared in the direction of the harbour.

'To be honest Tan, I'm at a loss how to proceed. Without Lautan to hold back the waters, or some new insight into the materials we have to hand, I doubt we can complete the pontoons before winter.'

'Winter. Our Sanamasa, yes?'

'Sorry, yes. The swells are already too heavy for the stoneworks I have crafted so far. By the time Tanamasa is over they will be too rough to venture near. We would risk being swept out into the bay and drowned.'

Although protected to some extent by the two headlands, the Valley mouth was not an ideal natural harbour. The sea floor close to land shelved gradually into deeper water. In the absence of anything but the most rudimentary dredging tools, the only alternative Terry had thought of was to build out a pair of sturdy pontoons to provide a dock for the deep draught of an ocean-going vessel. Up to now the Kertonian ships existed on paper only, but the craftsmen understood the mechanics of travel upon water from their limited experience boating on lakes and rivers. Without a landing stage of some kind the Valley mouth could not serve as a harbour.

Tanaratana offered a hand to help the older man up off his knoll. 'Let us discuss it further over a hot meal, Petani. Things always look better with a full stomach.'

Tan's suggestion was timely. Terry had not eaten since breakfast. The two men picked their way down the hill towards the camp. Umtanesh and Nembaka already had a good fire burning in the ancient pit outside what had been the refuge of the old man of the Valley. The aged bell maker, known only as The Pilgrim, had not been seen since Patrick Glass rolled back the nebulous time dilation effect as a prelude to the Battle of Lembaca Ana. He perished in the aftermath of the collapse. Having lived for sixty years under its influence most people avoided thinking about what happened to him, especially those who witnessed the near-instantaneous withering of all vegetation as time caught up with the Valley on the seaward side of the curtain.

Nembaka offered a bowl of steaming rebusang. 'Look as though you need this Petani. Tan told you about pontoons, I see it in your face.'

'He did. I am going to have to explain my failure to the Queen at some point.'

He took the bowl, and sat on an unoccupied rock beside the fire, letting its warmth suffuse his chilled body and enjoying the aroma of sweet, herb-infused meat while it cooled a little, the thick rich sauce congealing at the sides.

'I'm amazed we haven't had visit from Istania,' Nembaka mused around a mouthful of stew. 'It not escape their notice that we are working here.'

Terry took his first spoonful. Flavours oozed from the soft meat as he chewed, savouring the exotic mixture of local and Earther vegetables and herbs. No one would ever complain that Nembaka only knew how to cook this one dish when it always tasted so good.

'They have enough to deal with at the Red Court right now,' he said at length. 'Their people are anxious about the lack of leadership, uncertain who will take over once the Jester's jousts are done. The Blood Watch will have their hands full maintaining order. They've no time to spare worrying about what we're attempting here.'

'I hope you are right,' Tanaratana said, wiping the

bottom of his bowl with a large hunk of tepsak. 'We have problems of our own here without having to suffer a visit from those fools.'

'They probably think we the fools, doing what we doing,' Umtanesh replied. 'After today, maybe I agree with them.' He flashed a guilty look in Terry's direction. 'No offence, Petani.'

'None are more aware of our failures than I, young man,' he said, smiling. 'No need to apologise. But I doubt they think us foolish for trying. The great and the good have hung their noses over this place for centuries. We are the first—as far as anyone knows—to make the attempt at realising their plans. I'm sure the Court will turn their attention to us eventually, once those other matters are settled. I must discuss our work with the Queen before then. We have already built something worthy of protection, and yet we have nobody to protect it besides ourselves. Once the new powers at Court discover there is a real possibility for ocean going travel and trade, well, we know how they think. It would not surprise me in the slightest if Istania decides to muscle in on Kertonian progress.'

The thought of a visit from the Istanian military dampened their spirits even after the fine meal. A few moments later the others made their excuses and took to their ahmeks, leaving Terry alone with the dying embers of the fire. The chill of the late summer evening soon overwhelmed the weakening blaze and he sought his own bed, though he expected to find no peace there.

The next morning he awoke to the distant sound of kudo hooves on the Valley's gravel path. He pulled aside the flap of his ahmek. Unusually early autumn mist once again shrouded the morning, carrying noises ahead of their source. As Terry watched, a group of riders emerged from the murk. He counted twelve, all dressed in the crimson livery of the Istanian Blood Watch, their swords clanking against their mailed legs.

puppeteers' meeting room
3rd day of far'tanamasa, 966

The sound of a prolonged fit of coughing drifted up to greet Jeruk on his way down the worn stone staircase.

'Pass him some water, will you? Somebody?' he said as he reached the bottom of the stairs.

Though the man had been a member of their arcane group for several years, Jeruk still could not recall his name. In common with many, he was content to sit at the oak table and complain, without ever stepping forward to actually do anything. Or at least not enough of anything to make him memorable.

'Water be buggered,' replied the man between his coughs. 'Pass me more ale!'

The voice of Olek Grissan made itself heard over the ensuing laughter. A more familiar member of the group, Grissan had joined only a short time after Jeruk himself. 'More than likely the ale you're choking on,' he said.

The other man looked aghast. 'Never!'

He took a mouthful of the amber draught, wiped his mouth and cleared his throat. 'It's all this damned dust down here. And the damp! I don't understand why we still have to meet in the bowels of the Court. The bastard King is dead. Surely the need to keep our meetings secret died with him?'

A murmur of assent passed around the table, Olek nodding along with them. Jeruk walked over to his favoured seat.

'No,' he said, hardly audible over the noise. 'No, it did not. We have our eyes and ears in the Black Palace. Do you believe for one moment the Kertonians do not have similar spies here? I've known most of you for years but even so there are things we do not discuss openly, even down here. In the corridors and assembly rooms of the Court, there are no secrets. No one living knows all the hidden passages and spying alcoves in this ancient place.'

'But–', Olek began.

'Leaving aside the chances of being overheard by informants,' Jeruk continued, ignoring the interruption, 'there are many Istanians who would benefit from learning of our plans, or be tempted to sell their accidentally gleaned confidences. To the Palace directly, or to one of the many seedy intermediaries who flit between here and there like wraiths.

'No, for the time being, we remain here. Few enough know of this place and those that do cannot sneak here without our knowledge. Damp and dusty and uncomfortable it may be. You will have to keep your throats clear as best you can.'

Amid raucous laughter he took the full tankard Pwalek was offering and took a swig, waiting for the mirth to subside. It was evident Olek and a few others were not convinced by his argument but neither were they prepared to press the matter for the nonce. The political game playing, begun before the King's body had cooled to room temperature, meant there were still many hands to be played. No one yet knew how the cards would fall.

His gaze fell on the Piper, for once not late to the gathering. 'What news from Lembaca Ana?' he asked. 'Did the Queen appreciate our neighbourly visit?'

'She has even called an extraordinary meeting of her Eradewan to express her appreciation,' the Piper replied. 'But privately I know she was disturbed by the news. She is not naïve enough to believe the work could proceed without attracting Istanian attention, but even so...'

'She has no plans to send forces of her own?'

'That, I expect, is what the assembly will discuss. We all know she is not afraid of war, even though she would certainly prefer a diplomatic solution.'

'The diplomacy of the sharpened blade,' Olek said.

The Piper regarded him with scarcely concealed distaste. 'One of the few options remaining, since Istania has failed to turn up at any attempts to convene the Permajelis.'

Jeruk's bones ached with the predictability of the conversation. He held up his hands. 'Enough of this! If she has yet to mobilise then there is nothing further we need to consider. I do however have one other item for the agenda. As some of you already know, we have our first candidate for the throne.'

Those in the room who had not heard the rumours sat straighter in their chairs; some of the standing attendees took a step forward.

'Now that our Fire Witch has returned, she has replaced Kepul Seri as leader of the Fire Guild. He is feeling surplus to requirements. He believes he has the skills necessary to sit on the Blood Throne.'

There was a brief pause while the assembly absorbed Jeruk's words, before the room erupted in a cacophony of comments, each louder than its predecessor.

'Ridiculous!'

'A bloody wizard?'

'Who does he think he is?'

'Hardly counts as royalty—he's nothing but a bookkeeper!'

Several of the attendees could not speak past their howls of laughter.

'Gentlemen, please!' Jeruk held up a hand. 'He may not be the ideal candidate but as yet he is the only one.'

'I still say it will be easier for us to retain control if we establish a Majelis to maintain order,' said Pwalek. 'It was hard enough for you to keep a leash on the old King, Jeruk, and you'd known him for years. A new monarch, especially one as puffed up with self-importance and rectitude as Seri, would be near impossible to influence.'

Jeruk rubbed his forehead, considering the point. It was well-made. He knew from their recent conversation that Pwalek spoke from a place of friendship and the common good. They had been friends long before they were comrades-in-arms in the struggle against royal oppression. The man had no hidden motives.

'You're right, of course,' he said at length. 'But we have to jump through the expected hoops. Let us see who else puts themselves forward. Who knows, one of the candidates may prove to be... malleable. There are steps we can take to ensure their victory.'

'But what of my idea?' Pwalek pressed his point. 'Have you had any word from the Keeper as to its legitimacy?'

'Yes. I should have mentioned it earlier,' Jeruk rose to his feet. 'It remains a credible back-stop. The old man has confirmed there are no rules expressly forbidding government by committee. Even better, he has found historical accounts of such an arrangement. After the brief reign of mad King Boris.'

'Does it have to be a back-stop? With only one candidate?'

It was clear Pwalek would not let his idea drop. It would not hurt to be prepared, in the event the plans for a contest should fall through.

'Let's take this away, Seb,' he said. 'We can present some ideas for how a Majelis could be constituted to our next gathering.'

The assembly knew him well enough to recognise the signal that their meeting had ended. They made their way up the ancient steps. When the echoes of the last voice had died away, Pwalek took a seat on the opposite side of the table.

'This tournament is nothing but a diversion. We are wasting time. Organise a governing body, call it what you will, and let's finally be rid of the yoke of monarchy. You want that as much as I do.'

'Of course I do! We've been working for this as long as either of us can remember! But these are dangerous times, Seb. One false step and we'll have open rebellion. There'll be no way back from that. Not for the rest of our lifetimes, which may very well be extremely brief! We must be seen as law-abiding custodians. At least at the beginning.'

'And what of this tournament? If we end up with a winner, then we're back with a monarch sitting on the Blood Throne. One far less susceptible to your influence. We'll have taken several steps back rather than being any further forward.'

Jeruk tapped the side of his long nose. 'What makes you think there will actually be a contest? My declaration? That, my old friend, is what musicians would call an overture. An introduction, only, to the main show. Something to whet the appetite of the audience.'

'Stop talking in riddles. I thought you were trying to drop the Jester persona?'

'The audience are the people of Istania,' Jeruk said, counting out his points on his fingers. 'The overture is the tournament. And the main show is our new Majelis. Our old Keeper is certain to declare it legitimate. Once we have shown there are no suitable candidates, there can be no objection to its establishment.'

'But there is a candidate,' Seb said, 'you just told us.'

'He's an old man. It will come as no surprise to anyone if he doesn't survive the stress of preparing to use his Elemental powers in combat.'

temmok'dun
7th day of run'bakamasa, 966

It feels like I only blinked, but morning is already breaking across the basin. I've woken to the smell of wood ash and the sound of an empty stomach. On this day, the sixth since starting out, I'm given a lesson in serendipity. I'd been right not to be too hasty. The early sunlight strikes the face of the rock, illuminating a huge crack like an inverted bolt of black lightning running down the mountain. The fissure is wide enough for five men to walk side by side. At this time of day the angle of the light penetrates about thirty or forty metres into the gap. There is no end in sight. It dissolves into the gloom. My chest is so tight with excitement I can hardly breathe. Not only is this the only way forward I've found, but it's level!

I make a brief and spartan breakfast and then scout around for more scrub to make a simple torch. The embers of last night's fire are still hot enough to light it. With my torchlight dancing off the nearest wall of the fissure I start in. A few metres from the opening, the going proves nowhere near as easy as it first appeared. Shortly after the gloom point I encounter a rockfall. I can squeeze past the first boulder but the rest of the fall blocks the entire width of the crack. I grip my torch between my teeth and scale the rock pile, waving my head from side to side, trying to shine the flickering light to see a grip, or step. The far side of the mound is too high for the torchlight to reach the floor beyond. I try a controlled slide down the incline. The last few metres are over quicker than I would have liked. I end up on my arse, dust and grit filling my mouth, hair, and eyes. But I am still in one piece! After the major fall there are others, or remnants of the first, but I skirt them easily enough. What I can't avoid is the certainty that the passage is narrowing the farther I go. Pretty soon the light from my rapidly guttering torch is reflecting back off both walls. A few metres more and the cleft closes in front of me with no visible way through. The sides of the fissure are smooth and glassy. Almost igneous. Even if I could see an exit at a higher level, I couldn't reach it.

My torch is almost spent. I retrace my steps to an opening I passed after the main rock pile. It's wide enough to sidle through. For one heart-lurching moment I think I've wedged myself fast between the rock walls. My rising panic gives me the extra energy to push past the narrowest section, and I collapse in a heap in the chamber beyond the cleft. The torch falls to the floor and winks out in the dust. I stand, cursing my luck, but as my eyes adapt I see a faint glimmer of whiteness ahead. Gingerly, with hands on the walls and feet sliding forward in case of chasms, I move toward that light. It's the end of the passage. Outside, a bird calls with an unfamiliar song. There's a nest built on an outcrop close to the exit, two bright blue eggs sitting in the exact centre. Their owner, the bird with the strange call, flies at me in a paternal rage. Covering my head and eyes with my arms I run from the cave. Seeing I mean no harm to its precious offspring, the bird desists, perching on a rock with its head cocked to one side, regarding me with one black eye.

The view from the cliff edge makes me gasp in astonishment and delight. A volcanic bowl stretches out as far as I can see, its floor about five hundred metres below. Above, white clouds amble across a deep azure sky. After the bitter cold of the mountain top, I begin to break sweat. Somehow this hidden wonder is trapping some natural heat. The valley floor is carpeted in green. The treetops reach up almost to my vantage point. The rocks echo with the varied calls of animals that have made this secret paradise their home.

jester's chambers
5th day of far'tanamasa, 966

A gentle knock on the plain whitewood door disturbed Jeruk's dispirited picking at an ancient eight-stringed celapi.

After a frustrating day of meetings—both open, concerned with matters of state, and secretive, concerned with undermining matters of state—he had retired to his chambers to recover his strength and wits. Since the death of the King, he'd had neither occasion nor audience to play. As evening settled around the Court and the blood-red wash of the setting sun gave way to the ghostly silver of the moons, music offered the best way to dispel the day's fatigue.

He had picked up the lustrous old instrument, running his hands across its smooth belly and strong, straight neck.

Even after uncounted years of play, the regimented kaytam frets and opalescent klikeran markers were in perfect order. Kept in its case, regularly cleaned and tuned, this was not a travelling instrument. He took such good care of it partly in honour of the memory of his grandfather, from whom he had inherited the treasured gift. No, not inherited. The old man had passed the celapi on to him long before his death. Long even before Jeruk had settled on a life of entertainment.

'Music is the key of life,' the old man once told him. 'Never believe anyone who tells you different. Elementals wield their powers, but there is magic in music too. It sings the stories, great and small. It asks the fundamental questions and at the same time holds the answers to all of life's problems, if you only know how to listen. Or even better, play. Yes, there is magic in music.'

The thought of musical magic had excited the young Simon Nhej. There was a name lost in time. One which he had left behind in the slums and which nobody at Court would recognise. Simon had asked his grandfather to teach him and the old man agreed with a knowing smile. He did not patronise the boy with words of warning about how hard the eight-string was to master, or how he would be better off starting with six.

Barely a year later, his grandfather's body burning on a community pyre, Simon found himself alone on the streets of the town he had once thought of as home. If it had not been for the celapi and the still-fresh lessons of his closest and only family, he would have starved to death. The season of Sanamasa in the year 941 was the harshest on record. So cold his fingers had been almost too numb to hold the strings against the frets. Yet somehow, he had earned enough coin for food and a hard bed in the cheapest lodging house, and he had survived.

As the night-rains of Berikatanya rattled the windows of his chambers, the tune he struck was as frigid and desolate as the memories of his first lonely winter, twenty-five years before. The rich tapestries and cushions, the overstuffed armchairs and overflowing bowl of fruit, the roaring fire and flagon of rich, red Istanian wine melted away. He was once again perched on the rough wooden slats of his cot in the garret room of the filthiest boarding house in Istania.

A knock came again at the door. He set the celapi down beside his chair.

'Come.'

Kepul Seri entered, his face a conflicted jumble of expressions and emotions.

'I'm so sorry to disturb–'

'You're not disturbing me,' Jeruk said, standing. 'At least, not from anything more than a self-indulgent journey through past melancholy. Set to music,' he added with a wry grin. He pursed his lips, noticing the bead of sweat that ran from under the man's hairline. 'What can I do for you?'

'It has been several days since I approached you about my candidacy–'

'Thirteen, to be precise,' Jeruk interjected. The man certainly knew how to come to the point, although it put the lie to his claim of well honed diplomatic skills.

'Ah, yes. Yes, that's right. So I was wondering if any... er... further candidates had come forward? And if not, what the protocol is for my accession.'

Jeruk turned toward his desk to hide his amusement. 'Slow down, Seri.' He held up the list of candidates, whereupon a single name was written. 'As you can see, there have been no others, but the allotted time for declaration has not yet expired. It is far too early to be talking about accession. I do hope you have not raised any expectations among the Guild that one of their number will be ascending the throne?'

A hint of colour rose in the old mage's waxen cheeks. 'Indeed not!' he said, his eyes wide. 'I am already the subject of enough ridicule from those quarters, without giving them any more ammunition–'

'Have you eaten?' Jeruk asked, interrupting the man again.

'I dined in the refectory earlier.'

'Some fruit then? And a glass of this fine ruby wine to go with it?'

Seri appeared flustered by Jeruk's unexpected display of hospitality.

'Er... yes. Yes, by all means. That would be delightful. If you're sure I'm not keeping you from anything?'

'Nothing more important than ensuring our only candidate for the throne is properly looked after,' Jeruk replied. He selected a dark purple fruit sitting well to the rear of his bowl, removed its stalk and polished it on his sleeve before offering it to the mage. 'Bubayem?' he said. 'A childhood favourite of mine. The flavour is quite unique.'

The Fire mage hesitated.

'I don't believe I've ever seen one.'

'They don't do well this far north. I have them selected and delivered especially.'

The fruit hung briefly in the space between the two men, its dark skin seeming to writhe with reflected candlelight. After a moment, Seri took it from his hand.

'I am always open to new experiences,' he said, sniffing at it as if trying to detect any hint of its "unique" flavour.

'That much is clear, Seri, since you have chosen to subject yourself to the ordeal of our royal contest. You can eat the skin.'

Seri's face puckered as he bit into the soft ripe bubayem. 'A little sour for my taste,' he said, once he had swallowed the first bite.

'Only at first,' Jeruk assured him. 'You will soon find the true flavour coming through, along with the spice that is found closer to the kernel.'

Seri took another tentative bite into the exposed flesh. His cheeks flushed a deeper rosy pink, a pale shadow of the fruit itself. He sucked air over his mouthful and looked around the room, the beginnings of panic clear in his wide-eyed expression.

'My word! Spicy, yes!' He coughed. 'Do you have any water?'

'Only the wine, I'm afraid,' Jeruk replied, handing him a glass.

Seri emptied half the glass in one swallow, and gave himself up to another prolonged fit of coughing. 'Argh! My throat is burning!'

He staggered forward, reaching out to the desk for support.

Jeruk took the glass from the mage deftly, setting it down beside the bowl. 'Please, Seri, sit. The initial burning sensation will soon pass.'

He helped the man to a second armchair close to the open fireplace. 'Can't have you falling down dead now, can I?'

Seri's colour had turned a closer match to the bubayem. He clutched at his throat, his eyes now white with panic.

'Can't... breathe...' he croaked, before being gripped by another more powerful coughing bout.

Jeruk retrieved a small cloth bag from his desk drawer. He carefully dropped the half-eaten fruit into it without touching the exposed flesh. Holding the wine glass by its stem, he threw the contents into the fire where they spit and boiled away in an instant, before dropping the empty goblet into the bag with the fruit. When he turned back to Kepul Seri, the old man was dead.

Chapter 4

It looks like there's a path below the cliff edge but it's too far to jump. I scout around for ages looking for a way to reach it, without any luck. I'm starting to despair when the shifting sunlight casts a shadow on a narrow ledge— probably two or three metres down—hidden from view until now. It's a risk, but my only option. I hang over the edge and try to slide to the outcrop. It can't be more than fifteen centimetres wide. I hit the ledge at speed, almost pitching myself from the rockface, but at the last second I glimpse a small tree rooted in a crack. I make a lunge for it. That little plant saves my life. I take a moment to let my panic subside. I can see the path clearly now, but it's still a fair drop. Something like five metres. I'll have to trust my luck once again. The sharp edges of the rock razor my fingers as I swing over, so I let go sooner than intended, winding myself. After a quick check for broken bones, I take my first proper look at this place.

For a path leading nowhere but this steep escarpment, it is surprisingly well-worn. Evidence of occupation, maybe. From down here the edge of the cliff is out of sight. The rockface looks as if it climbs sheer to the top of the mountainous rim. Anyone approaching from this direction would assume there is no way on. The track winds into the valley, edged by trees and bushes on one side and, for a few hundred metres, rock on the other. It disappears from view around a sharp bend. I can hear running water and the continued calling of birds, much louder now than when I emerged onto the cliff top.

I set off. I can't believe the difference in such a short space of time. It is close to midday and even though I was blue from cold on the mountain, here it's like a summer's day. Around the turn in the path I find the stream.

Flowing rapidly from rain or melt-water, it cuts a channel through the forest. I refill my skin in case I lose the river farther on. From what I've seen so far it's unlikely I'll ever run dry in this place, but I don't want to risk it. After a short walk I pass a thicker grove where the stream disgorges into an enormous lake right in the centre of the crater. I must be in the mouth of an extinct volcano. I strip off and dive in. It's warm! As warm and clear as a bathtub in the distant Black Palace, and full of fish of all colours. Except blue. No barawa fish here. This strange place must have remained isolated from the rest of the country for ages. Once I figure out a way to catch them, I'll have plenty of fresh food as well as water.

I'm still aware there might be others here, so I don't dawdle with my bathing. I'm not worried about my clothes staying wet for long once I'm dressed. At least, not from the lake. More likely to be my own sweat, the climate here is so mild. I have no idea where I'm headed, so I take the first path I come to as I walk the shore. After a short walk, I come upon a simple shelter. Not much more than a few skins stretched between the trees, but it is cleverly put together. My fears of bumping into another crater-dweller are quashed when I find his bones inside.

The sides are open so nothing could sneak up on him unseen, but the hides are angled to give some protection from the prevailing weather. One of them has come adrift and a second is showing signs of age, with small tears where it's fixed to the branches. It will be simple to fix up once I find replacement skins.

My first task, burying this poor guy's remains, is not as grisly as it might have been. His skeleton has been picked clean by the local birds. I'm going to call him Crater Man. I choose a quiet spot away from the paths, and put him deep enough that he won't be disturbed by burrowing creatures.

The karma points I score through my care of his last resting place are cashed in almost immediately. While looking for somewhere to bury him, I discover his store of cleaned hides, along with a small net for fishing. Once again it's fashioned with skill, this time from knotted plant fibres. With Crater Man planted, I turn my attention to repairing the shelter and rebuilding the crude fireplace. A simple ring of large rocks with a spit tied to an A-frame with lengths of the fishnet twine.

With my new home and the fire pit in good order I still have a little daylight left. I grab the net and return to the lake to try catching myself a fresh fish supper. It takes me seconds, only. The fish haven't met enough humans to learn fear. They fall into the net as soon as it's cast. I end up throwing a pile of them back. I couldn't possibly eat everything I caught before it turned bad.

My first night in the valley, I dine like the Blood King himself. Fresh water from the lake, fresh fish from the fire pit. I even picked some dessert from a fruit tree on my way back to camp. It's nothing like a bumerang, but it is sweet and juicy and delicious. It won't take me long to fall asleep tonight, with a full belly, a warm evening, the gentle crackle of my fire, and a few muted calls of unknown animals echoing through the trees.

I wake early the next morning, the sun only recently risen. I hear a snuffling noise before I've opened my eyes. It's a small animal, like a miniature kudo but with a shorter, rounder muzzle, rooting out the last of my fruit for its own breakfast. It's ignored the scraps of fish I left beside the fire so I guess it's herbivorous. It takes fright when I sit up, and runs off. I haven't made a weapon yet, but now I know the crater is home to such creatures I put spear making at the top of my to-do list for today. Man cannot live by fish alone, and if these local ruminants are as tame as the fish I'll have quite the varied diet in my new home.

*

Life in the crater has fallen into a comfortable routine. It wasn't long before I discovered anything I caught tasted better after hanging. I've been fishing or hunting early in the morning, and bathing later. That way my splashing doesn't frighten off the fish. I'm the only natural predator here, so it's no problem gutting my catch or butchering meat and suspending it around my camp on skewers I made from young branches. After lunching on whatever is left from the previous night, I spend the second half of my day exploring. As the days have rolled by I've come to know the crater pretty well, despite its size.

I keep calling it "the crater" but I'd not been here more than a few days before I revised my initial impression. On one of my afternoon walks it dawned on me that it was more likely a caldera. Once I'd fixed the paths and the directions in my mind I wanted to work out exactly how large it is. My initial view of it, from the mountainside, showed it to be roughly oval, so I tried the shorter diameter first. I swerved the morning hunt, setting off after breakfast and walking to the wall below the cliff top where I entered. The round trip took me the best part of a day. Night was falling as my shelter came into view once again. A quick mental calculation gave me a short diameter of fifty to sixty kilometres. My pace wasn't even, so that was my best estimate. The other dimension, the walk to the west wall, could easily take twice as long. No biggie—I already knew the place could support me, and I still had my water skin.

I started out early the next day and arrived at the wall by late afternoon. I'd always planned to camp there, so while I had daylight I scouted the area. The rockface is a lot steeper and taller on that side, but again, no way up. It was a puzzle, knowing that Crater Man had not entered from the same direction as me, but I'd not found another entrance. That conundrum determined my next quest even before I'd finished this one: to walk the perimeter and look for an exit. I spent an uneventful night at the wall and returned to my camp the next day. A second rough calculation gave me the longer distance. More than eighty but less than a hundred kilometres. This place is *big*!

With those two numbers I can estimate how long my new trip will take. At around two hundred and forty-five kilometres, it'll be the best part of five days. Plus a day in total to get to the wall at the start and back to camp at the end. This needs serious prep! I can't rely on hunting for food. No animal will come near while I'm crashing through the undergrowth and there may be no other streams or pools for fishing. I need to pack some food. Cooked meat and fish wrapped in large leaves. A caldera version of a bepermak! I'll need to clean out a stomach and tie it off for a spare water skin, and choose rope for climbing. That will all take a few days to assemble. I've been notching the big tree near my camp for a simple calendar. I set myself a target to have everything ready by the end of my fifteenth day in the caldera, but I missed it. Only by a day though—I set off first thing this morning; day sixteen. My notches tell me it will soon be the last month of Bakamasa. I haven't yet noticed any cooling of the weather. I think it makes sense to begin my perimeter trek where I came into this place. I've traversed the path between there and my camp a couple of times, so I know it's an easy walk. The opposite direction is still an unknown. And when I come back around to that part of the wall, I'll recognise it right away.

*

The perimeter walk took seven full days. I arrived back at the caldera entrance—which I've christened Argent's Gate—on the evening of the seventh day. I camped there last night and made my way home this morning. I found something to wonder at on every one of those days. West of Argent's Gate there's a second, smaller lake. I slept on the shore the day I came to it, intent on a meal of fresh fish, which I've developed quite a taste for. There is another settlement close by. No body this time, thankfully, and a different structure to mine. It took advantage of a natural overhang of the rock. A series of pillars made from small tree trunks formed the front. It had woven bark over the bottom half and rolled skins above, so it could be closed off from the weather. Whoever lived there had gone to a lot of trouble but it was clear the place had been unoccupied for a long time.

The variety of fruit trees in the caldera seems inexhaustible and plentiful: berries, hips, and soft fleshy fruit of all kinds. I also found copious quantities of vine and spent a day collecting and splicing them into a longer, stouter rope.

Around the mid-point of my journey I came to a waterfall. I'd heard it the night before. I figured that if I was halfway through my trek, I must be directly opposite Argent's Gate. This had to be the remains of the river whose original outfall is on our side of Temmok'Dun. The creation of the caldera had diverted it, creating a spectacular cataract here, and forcing it to find another outlet on the other side. I resolved to return to Gatekeeper Falls once I completed my present trip. At that moment I was still eager to discover what other secrets this land had in store.

So my travels gave me a lot to think about, but having arrived home around midday today—the eighth day since leaving—I'm exhausted and blistered all over. I want nothing more than a long swim in the lake and an even longer sleep.

court of the blood king
26th day of far'tanamasa, 966

'Ho there! Who approaches the Court of the Blood King under cover of darkness? State your name and business!'

'My name is Sepuke Maliktakta. I have ridden long and hard to stake my claim to the throne, as proclaimed by the King's High Counsellor.'

'You're a little late sirrah!' called the guard from his perch atop the gate tower. His tone was confrontational, but the flaming torches on the turret walls did not cast enough light to reveal his expression.

'Is this not the twenty-sixth day of Far?' Sepuke replied. 'My journey has been long, but not so much that I have lost count of my days.'

'You have not missed any days, stranger. It is the twenty-sixth, in truth.'

'Then I am in time,' said Sepuke. 'Will you open the gate?'

The guard consulted with his companion, their voices too subdued to carry across the moat. Sepuke dismounted and stretched his aching hamstrings, using his kudo for support.

He had set off from Duske Raj'Pupu with his head still banging from the previous night's ale, and his ears ringing with Rektan's good natured teasing. But what should have been an eight-day ride had turned sour from the moment he left. Though his childhood memories of the road between his village and the Court held true, a series of unfortunate events resulted in the trip taking almost three times longer than expected.

The ancient bridge over the Sun Lum had crumbled into the water—only a few days before his arrival according to the locals—forcing a detour to the next nearest crossing. His kudo Jaraseppu had thrown a shoe. A lengthy search for a blacksmith resulted in an unscheduled stop and a welcome hot meal with him and his wife. The next day Jaraseppu picked up a stone. By the time he noticed, it had become septic. Easy enough to clean out and dress, but the animal could not bear his weight for three days. They were constrained to a walking pace. He encountered raiders close to the Kertonia/Istania border. Giving them a wide berth added another two days. And so it went on. All he wanted now was a hot bath and a reasonably comfortable bed, not to be kept waiting in the cold and dark, with the malamajan almost due.

'Are you going to open the gate, or will I be standing

here all night?'

'Hold your temper, stranger. Someone will be with you directly.'

Sepuke remounted Jaraseppu and set off across the drawbridge at a slow walk. The ancient boards looked as though they had not been lifted since the bridge was built. Tufts of grass and twisted ropes of weed intertwined along its edges, giving way to the inky blackness of the moat beyond. No force had dared assault the imposing keep of the Blood Court in living memory, so the bridge had remained in position astride the deep, sluggish water. The enormous ironwood gate had always been enough of an impediment to unwanted guests. As he approached he heard the sound of gargantuan bolts being drawn. The gate swung open and two guardsmen rode out toward him, dressed in the same livery as those who had posted the notice back home. Blood Watch.

'You are to come with us,' the first intoned as they reined their kudai on either side of Jaraseppu. His mount shied at the closeness of the unfamiliar animals. 'Orders of the Jester.'

'Of course,' Sepuke replied. He betrayed no surprise that the guards were now taking orders from the Jester. Even as a boy he saw what influence the hook-nosed tumbler had with the King. Now his distant relative was dead the stunted man's star would quite likely be in the ascendant. 'Is there a problem?'

'The Jester will explain,' the other guardsman said as they rode beneath the heavy parapet and through the Court gate.

They dismounted together in the barbican. Whisked into the main Court building by the guards before he had chance to ensure Jaraseppu's comfort, Sepuke soon lost his bearings. The wide corridors all looked the same, with identical enormous copper bowls filled with burning embers providing both light and heat. The guards stopped in front of one of the many doors in the passageway.

'Wait inside,' said one, opening the door. 'The Jester will be with you shortly.'

The door closed behind him with a metallic click. He tried the latch. His ears had not been mistaken. They had locked him in! The room appeared at first glance to be comfortable enough, though sparsely furnished. A meager fire burned in a plain grate. A three-horned candlestick standing on a small bureau beside the door provided the only other illumination. Sepuke picked it up and took a turn around the room. A single bed had been made up with fresh linen and a small ceramic bowl of fruit stood on the nightstand next to it, alongside a larger earthenware bowl and a pitcher of water. A towel completed the rudimentary washing facilities. The only other item of furniture, a worn easy chair, stood between the bed and the fireplace.

Sepuke was not a decadent man but he was accustomed to more luxury than this. As he moved to try the chair for size, the lock turned again and the door swung open to admit the Jester. Dressed more sombrely than the bright yellow garb Sepuke remembered so vividly, nevertheless he was instantly recognisable by his crooked nose and short stature. He carried a pen and a sheet of parchment in one hand, while the other gestured in Sepuke's direction.

'Sepuke Maliktakta?'

'Yes sir, very pleased to–'

'You wish to be considered a candidate for the Blood Throne?'

'I do sir.'

'And what makes you think you would be a suitable replacement for King Jadara? Are you skilled in combat? Familiar with diplomacy and politics?'

'Both, to an extent sir. I am come from Duske Raj'Pupu which I have held against raiders for the last six years and where I have maintained law and order for the whole of that time.'

'Leadership of a little known backwater is–' the Jester

began.

'But my personal credentials,' Sepuke continued, ignoring the interruption, 'give me a stronger case than simply that of a competent village leader. The old king was my cousin. I am his last living relative.'

The Jester peered at him closely, stepping forward into the light of the candles. 'I spent almost every waking moment with the King. He never mentioned a cousin.'

'Distant cousin, it is true,' Sepuke admitted. 'I have papers in support of my claim.'

He retrieved three yellowed parchments from his jerkin pocket. 'I enjoyed some time here as a boy,' he added, 'though my relationship with the King was... less than cordial. That may explain why he never spoke of me.'

The Jester took the documents from him, his gaze never leaving Sepuke's face.

'I'm sure I would have remembered a cousin, no matter how distant,' he said, glancing briefly at the scrolls. 'I will have the Keeper of the Keys look over these to confirm their legitimacy. An emergency meeting of the Court leaders will then discuss your case. You must remain here until we are certain of the truth of your claims.'

'Is it customary to whisk away a member of the royal family and claimant to the throne of Istania and confine him to a locked room?' he asked, feeling the colour rising in his cheeks. 'Many years it has been since my last stay here, but no matter what enmities existed between my cousin and myself, his hospitality was never as wanting as this. Is this clandestine farce really necessary?'

A momentary glare of anger crossed the Jester's face, but he hesitated before replying. 'We have had... an incident,' he said at length. 'One of the other candidates was found dead yesterday. I must take all steps to ensure the other claimants come to no harm. *Potential* claimants,' he corrected, with a casual wave of Sepuke's papers. 'You will wait here until my return. A hot meal will be sent up to you. If you attempt to leave I will not be responsible for your safety. The Court is guarded, but the guards cannot be everywhere.'

The small smile that creased his face sent a chill along Sepuke's spine. He turned on his heel and left the room, the lock snicking smoothly into place behind him once again.

black palace
27th day of far'tanamasa, 966

Elaine glanced up and down the long table as she took her seat. The Eradewan appeared to be attended by stand-ins. Apart from herself and Claire, the Elemental Guilds were not well represented. As usual there was no one here from Water. The Water Wizard Lautan had been absent since shortly after the Battle of Lembaca Ana. There had been no word from him in almost a full season. Historically, the Water Guild had been sparsely populated at the best of times, but Earth usually sent a delegate. Terry—or Petani as he now preferred to be called—was still fully engaged at the Landing site. Maybe the small dark-skinned stranger sitting opposite was here in his stead. The Piper had not yet put in an appearance either. The man was almost pathologically late for everything and Elaine had her suspicions as to his reasons. The Queen's counsellors and heads of minor royal houses occupied the other seats.

Her thoughts of the Queen heralded the monarch's arrival. She stalked into the chamber, long black dress billowing out behind her, and took her place at the head of the table. The tall blackwood doors closed silently as she passed through, as if on wheels.

'Come to order please,' she said, her manner businesslike and peremptory. 'We have much to discuss this morning.'

The sight of a slender figure caught Elaine's attention. Dressed all in purple and sweating profusely, he slipped in after the Queen before the doors had fully closed. The Piper.

He hurried to the table. 'Apologies, Majesty, I–'

'Sit down, Mungo,' said the Queen, her expression almost as dark as her bodice. 'For a trained musician, your timekeeping is truly appalling.'

'Apologies,' he repeated. 'I–'

'Spare us your explanations, please. We must make a start.'

The Piper mopped his brow with a mauve kerchief and said nothing more. Elaine could not tell whether his face, its colour rapidly deepening to match his clothing, was empurpled by his exertions or his embarrassment.

'Progress on our Landing project had been good until recently,' the Queen began. 'In the last few days two developments have given us cause for concern.' She nodded in the direction of the dark-skinned man opposite Elaine. 'If you would like to explain the situation, Tanaratana?'

The youth looked daunted by the prospect of addressing a meeting of the great and the good of Kertonia. He cleared his throat and took a sip of water.

'Good morning. My name is Tanaratana. I working with Petani at the Landing site. He is very powerful man, and great teacher...'

The Queen shifted in her seat, fixing Tanaratana with a stare. He glanced at her, but continued without pause.

'...but has still not found answer to the question of how to build stable platform on the water side. On the land side, all is well. In fact, the earthworks were completed before time.'

'Ahead of schedule?' asked the Queen.

'Yes,' replied Tanaratana. 'Some days ahead to tell truth. But then we begin to slip behind. Nothing Petani tried would stand up to forces of the sea. That is where we are now. He still working on the problem.'

'And the second development?' Elaine asked.

'We have visitors in the Valley,' Tanaratana said, taking another mouthful of water. 'Blood Watch.'

Gasps of surprise whispered around the table. The Queen held up her hands for silence.

'This is no more than we anticipated,' she said. 'It was unlikely we could keep our project secret for long.'

Elaine stole another look at the Piper. He had coloured up again. A bead of perspiration ran down his temple.

'The question is,' the Queen continued, 'whether we need to do anything about it. Have the guardsmen given you any trouble, Tanaratana?'

'No majesty,' the man replied. 'So far they just camp on hillside. Not come near our workings.'

'The lack of response to our diplomatic overtures, and their continual non-attendance at the Permajelis gives us enough indication of their intentions I think,' Elaine said. She turned to Tanaratana. 'How many men?'

'Only a small number, Kema'satu. Less than... um... forty men all together, guards and hodaks.'

'Still sufficient to overwhelm the Landing site,' Claire said.

'Exactly what I was thinking,' Elaine added. 'We would be wise to send a force of similar size to protect Petani, Tanaratana, and the others.'

The Queen sighed. 'So we are here again. After all the fine words from the King in the aftermath of Lembaca Ana. All our futile attempts at diplomacy. So much hope, dissolved away before the season is out.'

'Hardly your fault, Majesty,' said the Piper, wiping away the sweat with his kerchief. 'You could have done no more to find a peaceful solution.'

'And yet if we now send a contingent, as our Elementals have counselled, the Reds too will send more men. Soon the hillsides will be thronged with our armies, the turf muddied by the hooves of their kudai. Before long it will once again run red with our blood. Our forces have not yet recovered from their last encounter in that cursed place.'

Elaine felt her palms growing hot. Her topaz bangles sparkled in response to the stirrings of her Fire power. This was not a time for timidity.

'Istania will not hesitate to press any tactical advantage we allow them, your Majesty! It would be a mistake to leave their forces in a position of control in the Valley. In my opinion,' she added as the Queen rounded on her, glaring.

'We will, of course, need *all* our Guilds at full strength should it come to all-out war,' the Queen replied, fixing Elaine with a cold stare.

Elaine's anger swelled. Faint wisps of smoke curled from beneath her hands as they rested on the table. She glanced over at Claire who gave an almost imperceptible shake of her head.

'Majesty,' Elaine replied, 'the Guilds cannot take part in any armed conflict.'

The Queen's eyes widened. 'What do you mean, "cannot take part"?'

'The Te'banga forbids an Elemental from engaging in any conflict which does not have equal representation on each side. In the past, Petani and I were aligned with the Blood King. That is no longer true. He is not here, but he is working for you, ma'am. As am I. As is Claire. And our fourth—Lautan—is Baka knows where. But were he here, he too would take your side, leaving whoever ascends the Blood Throne with no Elemental. Such an imbalance is unthinkable.'

'Do you agree with this, Claire?' the Queen asked, her voice breaking. 'Your ideas for the exchange of flying messages would have given us a considerable advantage over the Reds.'

Claire blushed, her eyes fixed on Elaine, imploring. 'I... well... we would have to debate the exact terms of the Te'banga,' she began, appearing to choose her words carefully, no doubt to avoid further enraging the Queen.

'In any case, Kemasara, the air mail idea is still new. It's unlikely I will have anything usable before the end of Sanamasa.'

Elaine smiled. That was a nice touch, using the Kertonian honorific. The girl was turning into quite the diplomat, and a credit to her Element.

'Tuh!' The Queen's exasperated reaction escalated quickly to anger. 'Do you find this funny, Bakara?'

Before she could explain, the Queen stood, her chair crashing with surprising force onto the polished black marble tiles.

'In any case it is irrelevant for now,' she said, flicking a strand of ebony hair off her face. 'We have days of training before our forces will be battle-ready. We must respond in *some* way to the Red presence in the Valley!'

A houseman hurried to right the Queen's chair as she turned to a silver-haired man seated next to Claire. 'Jurip, see that a contingent of experienced men, matching in number the force Tanaratana has described, is dispatched to the Valley as soon as possible. Tanaratana, they will provide a guard for your return journey.'

The small man inclined his head in thanks.

'Claire, dear, and Bakara too, if she is willing, complete your examination of the detail of your Te'banga with as much haste as you can. We would prefer an answer in the affirmative, but we are sure you will not let that sway you.'

Elaine felt the colour rising again in her cheeks. 'I would be pleased to help, Majesty.'

'Good,' said the Queen, without looking in her direction.

'Might I be of any assistance?' the Piper asked. The first time he had spoken since his earlier attempt to ingratiate himself with the Queen.

'Doubtful,' said the Queen, her eyes darkening once more as she retook her seat. 'Time is of the essence here.'

*

As the meeting broke up, Elaine noticed Claire trying

to attract her attention. Of more urgent concern to her was the Piper, making a hasty exit from the room.

'I'll catch up with you later,' she mouthed, indicating the Piper's rapidly retreating back, and hurried after him. Reaching the door in time to see a purple blur disappear around the nearest corner, she broke into a run.

'You're in an awful hurry for someone who has nothing to do,' she called, intercepting him in front of the deserted refectory.

'Always something to do,' he said, retrieving his kerchief from a pocket and mopping his neck.

'And always in a lather doing it.' Elaine took his arm and steered him into the dining hall. She closed the double doors behind them. 'Especially when late for the Queen's war meeting. Just ridden in from Istania, had you?'

He squirmed under her hold, affecting an exaggerated look of disdain. 'What possible reason could I have for visiting that Baka-forsaken place?'

'I have no idea,' she said, tightening her grip on his arm once more, 'but I saw you there on my last trip. If you came back today that must have been at least your second visit. Busy, busy, busy. Please do not make me rerun the conversation we had at Utperi'Tuk. I have no patience for talking in riddles. Those ears and eyes you spoke of back then, do not reveal their secrets without recompense. What information passes in the other direction, I wonder? I am certain the Queen would be interested to hear my suspicions of how the Reds came to learn so quickly of our activities at Lembaca Ana.'

The Piper reddened, brandishing his sopping kerchief too close to her face. 'You mistake my purpose!' His eyes widened at the sight of a languid curl of flame that caressed Elaine's wrist. He shook off her hand and stepped away. 'You would do the Queen a huge disservice by challenging my loyalty. I am on your side, for Baka's sake.'

'Have a care, sir. That is the second time you have used

my god's name. Elemental gods are not to be mocked by the likes of you.'

'My apologies, Bakara. Your display of power unnerved me. Yes, it is true, I have passed information in the past. But only so much as was necessary to gain the trust of...'

He stopped, dabbing once again at his mouth and neck.

'Of?' She left the question hanging in the air. The Piper's gaze flicked between her eyes and her hands, where she let her Fire power swell until a tongue of flame burned from every finger.

The Piper let out the breath he had been holding, his shoulders sagging under the weight of his discomfort. 'They call themselves the Puppeteers. For obvious reasons.'

'The Jester must be one of them,' Elaine said, quelling her flame. 'Who else?'

'It would serve no purpose to reveal their names. Most are unknown to you. But yes, the Jester—Jeruk Nipis as he is now known—is their leader.'

'And war is their aim?'

'Their short-term aim, yes. And it is exactly what I am trying to stop. I have not lived my whole life serving the Queen without understanding, and even sympathising with, her desire to avoid war and find peaceful solutions to our differences. I told you as much at Utperi'Tuk. But the Puppeteers' aims are more far-reaching. War would only be a means to an end.'

Elaine glanced around the refectory, confirming they were still alone. She stepped closer to the Piper and dropped her voice to a murmur. 'And what end would that be?'

'They believe the common man is ill served by *both* royal houses. They will not rest until they are brought down and a people's republic is established. Whether that means one for the whole land, or one for each of Istania and Kertonia has never been spoken of, but that is what they are working for.'

'Revolution.'

'Rapid evolution, is how they prefer to think of it. But they would not shy away from revolution if it came to that, I'm sure.'

Elaine raised her hands, mentally warding off the idea of a revolt. Her golden bangles flashed in a shaft of late afternoon sunlight that burned in through the refectory windows.

'The one turns all too quickly into the other,' she said. 'Stepping onto that slippery path, even with good intentions, can easily lead to an unforeseen destination.'

The Piper nodded. 'I will do all I can to persuade them to my—to *our*—view,' he said.

Elaine sighed. 'Very well, but there must be no more secrets between us. I cannot afford to waste time worrying which of the Palace intelligence is being passed on to these Puppeteers. And for Baka's sake try to arrange your journeys a little better in future!'

court of the blood king
29th day of far'tanamasa, 966

'Has he eaten?'

Sebaklan Pwalek stepped from the shadows at Jeruk's question. He had ordered this section of the west wing poorly lit. Partly to discourage unwanted visitors and partly to hide his own comings and goings. His most trusted ally guarded Sepuke's chamber. No one was allowed in, or out.

'Yes,' the man replied. 'Just after sunset. He's not happy.'

'Food not to his taste?'

'Don't know about that. I think it's more the imprisonment he hasn't taken to.'

'It's a guest suite, not a prison cell!'

'A guest suite with a locked door is not much different from a prison cell,' Seb observed.

'Since when did you become a philosopher?'

'Three days of sitting in this draughty hallway with nothing but abbaleh for company is not very stimulating. I need something to keep me sharp. There's only so many times I can count the segments of their webs.'

'Did you deal with the guardsmen?'

'On the road to Lembaca Ana as we speak. Poor fools thought it was a promotion to be sent to what they called "the front line." We both know how dangerous a journey that is. Wouldn't surprise me if they never make it as far as the coast. We are the only ones who know there's an angry man shut in a room in the most isolated part of the west wing.'

'How bad is his temper?'

'See for yourself,' Pwalek replied, unlocking the door.

Jeruk stepped inside.

'About time!' Maliktakta said, jumping to his feet. His book fell unheeded to the flagged floor, raising a small plume of dust. 'What is happening? Three days I've been stuck—locked!—in here.'

Jeruk raised a hand. 'Please! Calm yourself! There are procedures—'

'Surely even the worst run Court cannot take three days to examine birth records and family trees? How hard can it be?'

'Yours is not the only case on our record-keeper's desk!' Jeruk snapped. 'It has been many years since the Red Court was without a leader. Historical protocols had to be researched, alternatives considered. You would do well not to be too critical of this interim government,' he continued, clasping a closed fist against his chest. 'Should your claim be verified and you ascend the throne, you would be honour-bound to do better. You may not find it so easy as it appears from the comfort of these guest quarters.'

'Comfort! Ha!'

Maliktakta retook his seat by the fire. Jeruk stepped closer to the flames, the draught by the door making his bones ache.

'My apologies,' Maliktakta said after a lengthy silence. 'It is frustrating to sit here day after day and not know what is going on. I slept late on the first day and woke believing a visit would not be long in coming. When it became clear a third day was to pass without sign of progress I'm afraid I allowed my disappointment to give way to anger. I should not have taken it out on you. My only visitor has been your man, bringing my meals. He would not win any prizes for conversation.'

'You would be surprised. Beneath his gruff exterior lies the mind of a burgeoning philosopher,' Jeruk said with a tentative smile. 'But I am here now, and I did not come to talk of him. Our Keeper has completed his perusal of your documents.'

'And?'

'All seems to be in order.'

'As I knew it would.'

'Which leaves just one final test before you can ascend the Blood Throne.'

'Test? I thought combat was reserved for those who could not show direct lineage?'

'It is. But those who, as you put it, are part of the Blood King's line, are required to demonstrate the extent to which they have inherited the family traits.'

'Traits? What traits? What are you talking about?'

'It is simpler to show you than try to describe it. Come with me.'

He rapped on the door. Pwalek opened it.

'It is time,' said Jeruk, stepping into the corridor. Maliktakta followed, still with a puzzled expression on his face but making no further comment. Pwalek locked the door and fell in behind them.

The hallway into which Jeruk turned was even more poorly lit than the first. He took a torch from the wall and stepped onto a narrow stone staircase, almost invisible in the gloom. Holding the brand aloft, he descended into the cold, clammy darkness. A chill wind blew in through window slits at each turn of the stairs, carrying with it a fine mist of the night-time malamajan.

At the foot of the stairs they passed through a solid iron door into a short corridor, its walls glistening with condensation in the torchlight, before Jeruk turned again onto an even narrower and dustier flight of wooden stairs.

'Hold the rail,' he said. 'This old staircase is stable enough, but if you miss your footing you could take me with you.'

'I suppose I should be grateful you do not pretend concern for my own well-being,' Maliktakta muttered.

The floor at the foot of the second flight of stairs was trodden earth. Jeruk led the way around a large rock pillar, polished smooth by the passage of visitors over the centuries. After a short distance they arrived at the top of a third stone staircase, carved from the wall of a cavernous space whose limits were hidden in the gloom.

'More stairs!' Maliktakta exclaimed. 'Where are you taking me?'

His voice echoed across the empty void—'...king me ...king me'—in a chilling mockery.

'We are almost there.'

A single conflagration burned brightly in a granite pit at the left hand end of the great chamber, illuminating it with writhing, blood-red light. Icy draughts from concealed ventilation channels fanned the blaze into a roaring mass. Orange and red flames caressed the ceiling, leaving greasy soot smears on the stone walls.

In the centre of the cavern a massive wheel of red granite sat above an artificial lake, its oily waters lapping languorously at the rim of the stone before falling back in viscid rivulets that appeared lava-like in the reflected firelight.

'What is this place?' Maliktakta asked, awe and fear giving his voice a tremulous edge. 'It looks like the fiery heart of hell itself.'

'It is the heart, in one way,' Jeruk replied. 'The heart of your family power. The Bloodpower.'

Maliktakta paled, his blood-drained face reflecting several shades of pink under the light of the roaring bonfire.

'Bloodpower? I thought that was just a myth!'

Jeruk smiled. 'It may yet be.'

'The walkway to the Grinding Wheel is over there,' Pwalek said, urging Maliktakta forward.

The path led around the shore of the man-made lake. Maliktakta stared at the glutinous surface of the water as it rolled and swelled, driven by some unknown current. The air was heavy with the smell of wet iron. As they stepped up onto the uneven surface of the Grinding Wheel, the sulphurous stench of the fire overcame the metallic tang. At the centre of the Wheel, the remaining colour leeched from Maliktakta's face.

'Oh, Tana! That's not water, is it?'

Jeruk's smile broadened. 'Of course not. You are not a water wizard. You cannot wield Water power. The power in your bloodline is Bloodpower. It has only one source.' He gestured with a flourish, encompassing the wide lake.

Maliktakta swallowed, small beads of foamy saliva decorating the corners of his mouth.

'Wh-what am I supposed to do with it?'

'I could say that if you have to ask, then nothing you can do with it would make any difference.'

He paused to let the delicious tension build up still further. He had not enjoyed another's discomfort so much for many years. He waited until Maliktakta wiped the sticky white saliva from his lips.

'But I should probably give you the benefit of the doubt, in view of your long years away from Court. You never had chance to be schooled in the dark art. I, however, have witnessed the old King invoke his power. I believe it will be obvious whether or not you have the gift if you follow his example.'

'Which is?'

'Full immersion,' said Jeruk, another devilish smile stretching his lips. 'Full *naked* immersion.'

'You can leave your clothes over there,' Pwalek added, indicating a raised section at the entrance to the Grinding Wheel.

Maliktakta's gaze flicked between the two men.

'And this will prove my claim?'

'The people of Istania have lived long under a ruler with the power,' Jeruk replied. 'They have come to expect it. Especially from one who claims lineage.'

'But if I had simply entered the contest...'

'It's far too late for that,' Jeruk said. 'We have your records. It would be most irregular to attempt to hide your identity from the populace at this stage.'

The younger man's face flushed, whether from anger or embarrassment Jeruk could not tell. He began to unbutton his tunic. Pwalek took the clothes from him one at a time, grinning at Jeruk when Maliktakta turned away from them to remove his underclothes.

'Now, let us see the extent of your endowment,' said Jeruk, bowing low to hide his own smile.

Maliktakta hobbled across the uneven surface to the edge of the Wheel. There were no steps; no obvious entry point to the lake of blood. At last, he sat on the rim and, with a brief shudder, slipped in. His feet touched the bottom when he was still only waist-deep.

'Full immersion,' Jeruk reminded him.

A look of utter horror crossed the man's face. He took a deep breath and submerged himself in the ichor.

Pwalek dropped the bundle of underwear onto the rock. 'The things I do for you,' he muttered, jumping into the pool next to Maliktakta.

He reached beneath the surface and clamped his hands around the other's neck, leaning over him with his full body weight. The blood lake erupted as Maliktakta thrashed his arms and legs in an attempt to dislodge

Pwalek's grip. The Puppeteer was a burly man, at least twice his weight, and had the advantage of surprise, but Maliktakta was a seasoned fighter. Pwalek could not maintain his hold. Maliktakta twisted out from under him, bursting through the surface with a roar.

'Nerka jugu!' he yelled, scrabbling for a hold on Pwalek but unable to see through the gore covering his face. His own vision unhampered, Pwalek landed two swift punches to the other man's head. One skidded harmlessly off his cheek but the second caught his throat square under his jaw and he fell back, coughing, into the lake. Pwalek seized his chance, gulped air, and dived after him. The lake roiled and surged as the two men fought, only an arm or a leg emerging spastically before being dragged under again. It was impossible to tell who was winning, only Pwalek's clothing gave any clue to the owner of the flailing limbs. Moments later, one of the bodies became limp. Jeruk edged away from the rim of the Grinding Wheel as the victor emerged, standing and wiping blood from his eyes.

'Gah!' Pwalek said, flicking rapidly clotting fluid from his fingers and climbing from the lake, his face a tortured grimace of disgust.

Three large bubbles floated to the surface to burst with inaudible pops in the flickering light.

the caldera of temmok'dun
6th day of sen'bakamasa, 966

Soon after that trip around the caldera, I had to admit I was marking time. In many ways this place is idyllic. I know I could be comfortable here. It's like the mythical Shangri-La, catering for my every need other than human companionship. I've long since recovered full health after the ordeal of climbing over the south range of Temmok'Dun. Now, I'm coasting. Nothing I do brings me any closer to my goal. I have explored this place thoroughly, but I haven't yet reached the other side of the mountains. The previous occupant of my shelter has been on my mind a lot recently. Him, and whoever built that other dwelling. What fate befell each of them? And whatever it was, could it be my fate too? Most likely, if I don't make a move.

This train of thought began as a vague feeling of unease, several days ago. It was brought to a sharp focus this morning when I counted the notches on my calendar tree. I have been here almost an entire month! It is past time to make plans. If I'm honest one of the main reasons for my reluctance is the memory of the journey here. I'm in no hurry to freeze my nuts off on the side of a mountain again. Unfortunately, it is the only way forward.

A trip to Gatekeeper Falls is needed to scope the place out. Discover any easy ways to ascend the northern ridge. Once I complete the half-day journey it takes less than no time to work out there are only hard ways. But at least there is a way. Or at least the chance of one. My only chance. To one side of where the river begins its long drop, there's a V-shaped crevice in the rock. It looks close enough to throw my rope up. If I tie a small boulder to the end and wedge it in the V, I can climb up hand-over-hand. I laugh at the thought. Nothing is ever that simple, but it's my only plan.

I return home to make preparations for the journey. The northern ridge is higher than the southern, so it will be colder. I bundle up several layers of clothing. I've never encountered any fur-coated animals in the valley—I guess it's too warm—but I've fashioned extra clothes from the skins of the beasts I've killed. On their own they won't keep much heat in, but in combination I hope they will provide enough protection. I've been drying fish for a few days too. Earlier experiments prove they last at least ten days. I have no idea how long the onward journey will take, but it's all I can do. My last requirement is the anchor rock. It has to be large enough to wedge in the crack, but small enough to throw. I search in the shallows at the lake side and soon find a good one. I am all set.

On the morning of my twenty-eighth day in the caldera I break camp for the last time and return to the Falls. My rope catches in the cleft at the third attempt and I begin the climb. I'm carrying a few extra pounds of food and clothing, so I have to rest about two-thirds of the way up. After a short, strenuous ascent, I stand on a wide ledge looking back over the verdant landscape. My home for almost a month. Beside me the river roars from a wide fissure in the rock, while the northern range of Temmok'Dun stretches above, snow-capped and dark against the midday sun.

Chapter 5

'Come to order, please,' Jeruk Nipis said, standing and raising his voice to be heard above the subdued conversations. The large blackwood table seated eight, but could accommodate twelve at need. At present only five chairs were occupied.

The Keeper of the Keys sat opposite Jeruk, engaged in an animated discussion with Tepak Alempin of the Blood Watch. The old archivist's hands were doing almost as much talking as his mouth. After years spent steeped in the minutiae of Istania's laws and ancient scrolls, he was an obvious choice for the group. Likewise his conversation partner; it was essential to keep the most powerful of the country's fighting forces onside. But beyond that, Alempin had an innate grasp of strategies even away from the battlefield. As the leading Tepak, his political acumen also provided Jeruk with a useful sounding board.

To his right hand sat Sebaklan Pwalek. Secretly representing the Puppeteers, Pwalek was his right hand metaphorically as well as physically. After the events at the Blood Lake seven days earlier, they were partners in crime now too.

'We should drain this,' Pwalek had said to him on emerging from the ichor. 'What purpose does it serve? The Bloodpower must be dead, if the old King's last and closest relative could not summon it in his extremis. There are less grisly ways to dispatch our enemies, and more convenient places in which to dispose of their corpses. Do not ask me to swim in that again.'

A rare and unusual display of assertiveness from his second. Regardless of their years of friendship and their common purpose, he would have to keep an eye on the man.

In the fifth and final seat sat Kilpemigang, Keeper of the Coin. A relatively young man when compared to the rest of the company, taking the position only recently after the sudden and untimely death of the previous incumbent. Kilpemigang was well practised at keeping his own counsel. It went with the job. With luck his inexperience in matters of state would make him much easier to influence than his predecessor.

'I am pleased to declare the inaugural meeting of the Darmajelis open,' Jeruk continued as silence fell around the table. He regarded each of the attendees in turn, assuring himself of their attention, before opening his arms in a gesture of camaraderie. 'After much debate, we have decided this will be our preferred chamber from now on.'

Though the antechamber adjoined the Throne Room, the old King had never used it, opting instead to sit on the throne whenever he held audience. A position from which it was easier to intimidate his visitors. On the rare occasions he bothered himself with paperwork, he had a desk immediately behind the royal seat.

Unlike the King, Jeruk considered this the perfect space. Situated on the north side of the Throne Room, it rarely suffered the direct sun, so it remained cool. The subdued light which found its way through the high windows was ideal for conducting serious business. Once the room had been cleared of its years of detritus he had the Court artisans construct the table according to his own specifications. He was delighted with the result, but even more pleased that it was one at which he was the first to sit. It had no history. No greater man had ever ruled with his elbows resting on its surface or his arse sitting on the chair at its head. Finally, for the only time in his life, he was the first at something.

'Adjoining the seat of power,' he continued, pointing at the door to the Throne Room, 'and yet suitably divorced from it, the physical space matching the political distance we have from the true monarch. And on the subject of the monarch,' he added, 'after our best efforts, no legitimate candidates have come forward to claim the Blood Throne. Strictly speaking nominations do not close until sunset, but as many have observed, the realm is already beginning to suffer from a lack of leadership.'

'The events at Lembaca Ana make that even more obvious,' the Tepak interjected.

'Quite so,' said Jeruk. 'Nothing spooks the populace more than incipient war, especially without a strong commander at the helm. No disrespect intended Alempin.'

The Tepak waved the nicety aside. 'I am a military leader, not a political one,' he said, the suggestion of a frown decorating his brow. 'Men follow me because they are ordered to, not because they choose to.'

'Indeed. Fortunately my old and good friend the Keeper of the Keys, after a lengthy search of the archives, has uncovered no reason why Istania cannot be governed by a council of ministers, and so here we are at last.'

The Keeper got to his feet with some effort. 'Excuse my interruption,' he said, eyeing the Tepak, 'but our position is somewhat more watertight than there simply being no reason *not* to form this Darmajelis. There is evidence, as I have already informed Jeruk, from the early seven hundreds, that Istania had one during the interregnum between mad King Boris and his eventual successor King Jaibarinda. And for those of you unfamiliar with your histories, that was a period of extended peace such as Istania had not known before. Or since, for that matter,' he added, retaking his seat.

Jeruk bowed. 'Well it seems we have something to live up to. As you can see, we are only five at present—'

'There were ten members in that interregnal—' the Keeper said.

'Were there? Yes, well as I was going to say, we may increase our number as and when we decide other representation is needed here. Any further appointments to the Darmajelis will be a decision for the Darmajelis itself. According to the tradition established by the body of records from the time of the first such group, we will henceforth invest ourselves with devolved powers of the monarch. In the absence of a King, this will remain the sole governing entity until such time as another King rises either by acclaim, combat, or any other means.'

'So we are setting no goal to discover a new monarch, nor a time at which this assembly will be dissolved?' asked Alempin.

'As I have said,' Jeruk replied, 'there are no candidates. I do not propose to scour the country enquiring of every mercenary who can wield a rusty blade, or every kudo wrangler I encounter, whether or not they would like to be King. The time for coming forward is over. And clearly it would make no sense to dissolve the Darmajelis after— what? A turn of the sun?—in the absence of a potential monarch. We would only have to convene it again. No, for now you may assume we are the government of Istania for the foreseeable future.'

The Tepak nodded, apparently oblivious to the ridicule implied by Jeruk's response. Perhaps the man was not so politically astute as he had assumed.

'And so, to business,' Jeruk said, taking his seat. 'The first item on the agenda is the deployment of forces at Lembaca Ana.'

pennatanah
1st day of ter'tanamasa, 966

From where she stood, Felice Waters could see clear across the bay. The freshening morning breeze whipped up the waves, sending them to break over the upturned hull of the Valiant, still visible above the surface of the shallow waters. Its polished titanium alloy curves, constantly washed by the foamy spray, sparkled in the early sunlight like a thousand cut gemstones. Felice shivered. The second month of Tanamasa had opened with a vengeance. She pulled her thin jacket closed against the chill wind and walked faster.

She smiled at the simplicity of the local calendar. The Berikatanyan autumn was named for the god of the Earth Element, since brown was the season's principle colour. The worst of the weather was still to come, but she would have been wise to choose warmer clothing before emerging from the comfortable sanctuary of her humble berth.

The last of the senior officers and ship's personnel had abandoned the base soon after Valiant's unfortunate accident, chasing whatever dreams had driven them to the planet in the first place. Their departure left Felice in charge of a small contingent of Earthers for whom a life at Court or Palace held no attraction but who were still to overcome their inertia and decide how to strike out on their own. It had also left her with no shortage of cold weather clothing.

Her route took her past the newly rebuilt mooring mast, its taut steel hawsers singing in the gusting air currents. The wind coaxed a few of the looser lines into a harmonic vibration; clanging rhythmically against the structure. Felice had organised its rebuild, scraping together enough technicians for the task before the main exodus from Pennatanah. After its destructive encounter with the errant Valiant, the engineers decided deeper foundations would be sensible, which made for a lengthy project. The last Prism ship, Dauntless, had reportedly been under construction when Valiant left Earth. Expected to make its departure scant months after the Valiant, its arrival should have been imminent. As yet there had been no sign. Still, Felice stuck to her schedule, checking the communications logs every day.

That was a task for later. Right now she focused on making a start with a new project—something that had been nagging at her almost from the moment she landed on this planet ten years before. Felice wanted to understand Berikatanyan magic. Or more specifically, why some natives of Earth exhibited magical abilities.

Sporadic reports of "Earther magic" had begun from the first days when the crew and passengers of Endeavour had taken their places in Istanian and Kertonian societies. Few, at the start—she believed those initial low numbers were more to do with embarrassment, or fear of these new-found powers—but as time passed the frequency of incidents increased. Every Element was represented, in different strengths. Some significant demonstrations had been recorded, impressive but falling short of an Elemental level of mastery. Since the Earthers had no training in the Elemental arts this was hardly surprising, but even without any skill or knowledge the power manifested. Houses had been burned down or flooded. In her most frequently quoted case, a man ended up with his hand stuck inside a rock after an unexpected burst of Earth power.

On a recent journey to investigate an Earther incident, a chance encounter led Felice to decide the time was right for a more determined investigation into the phenomenon. She met Jo Granger, a scientist from the Intrepid.

'Have you considered a genetic link?' Jo asked as they stoked the fire in a small hut at the far end of her village. It was a balmy day in mid-Utamasa earlier that year, but they had to light a fire to dry out the young girl who experienced a literal outpouring of Water power.

'I've thought about it of course,' Felice replied, 'but I don't have any way of following it up.'

'I can help you there,' Jo said. 'I was an agricultural geneticist back on Earth. Seems a long time ago now! When the colony program was first established the senior science advisers thought it would be sensible to compare Earth crops with any indigenous species we might encounter.'

'So we didn't poison ourselves?'

'Partly, yeah. But we could have done that with

chemical tests. The genetic element was more to determine which of our seeds and plantlets would thrive here. We intended to match the gene sequence of the Earther varieties on record, with whatever we found growing in the same place.

'You have to remember we didn't know what the geological and meteorological landscape would be like. Not in detail. I mean, we knew Berikatanya—or Perse as we called it—is an M-class planet in a temperate zone but beyond that it was all a mystery. We only had space for a set number of samples. We had to do a whole lot better with them than hit and miss. We couldn't afford to plant them wherever we fetched up and hope for the best.'

'So how does all this help with my magic problem?'

'I brought a gene sequencer with me.'

'For plant genes.'

'Well, yes. That's what it was for. But I never used it with plants. In fact it's never been moved since we unloaded the ship. The societies here are so well established we mainly eat what they produce. Except for a few crops whose ideal growing conditions were obvious without resorting to science. But the sequencer will work with any genetic material.'

Felice had stared at her, and Jo had responded with the expression that someone who already understands, reserves for someone they think *should* understand.

'Like blood. Blood from someone who exhibits Elemental powers. I'm not suggesting you walk up to the Fire Witch and ask her for blood!' Jo laughed, a deep throaty chuckle that had made Felice feel a heat in the pit of her stomach that could not be explained by the roaring fire alone. 'But any of the Earthers you've come across will help you build up a genetic profile.'

'Profile?'

'Sure. You're looking for a pattern. A recognisable signature that everyone who can wield this power might have. Once you've spotted any similarities you'll have two things. Proof that there is a genetic link to Elemental power–'

'Which isn't certain.'

'Well no, but at least you'll know, one way or the other. I can help you, if you like. Show you how to work the machine. How to spot patterns in the output.'

'And the second thing?'

'A detector kit. You can recognise the trait in a simple blood sample, once you've run it through the sequencer. Whether the subject has exhibited magic powers yet or not.'

*

Felice unlocked the door of an office unit, indistinguishable from all the other prefab huts at the Pennatanah landing site, most of which she had already searched. There at last stood the sequencer, its amber standby light the only indication it was ready for action. Exactly as Jo had predicted, the device had not moved since being stowed after the unloading and cannibalisation of the Intrepid.

She opened her backpack and retrieved the instruction manual Jo had dug out, along with two glass phials containing DNA samples from the two of them. Obtaining swabs from any of the Earthers who had shown any degree of magical ability would involve a lot of travelling. She wanted to be thoroughly familiar with the analysis process before using real samples. Felice thumbed the sequencer to life and set about preparing her first run.

darmajelis chamber, court of the blood king
14th day of ter'tanamasa, 966

'So you're pretending to be the Darmajelis now?' the Piper said, poking his head around the chamber door.

He had begun the day in high spirits. For once he was certain to be on time for a Puppeteers meeting. He arrived at the subterranean chamber beneath the court crypts to find it empty. Too empty to be explained by his earliness. Belatedly, he remembered Grissan suggesting the group no longer needed to meet in secret. Cursing the Jester for not confirming where the meeting had been moved to, he wasted half the morning scouring the Court for the Puppeteers. He had already checked the Throne Room once, although he doubted the Jester would have the balls to meet there. He was almost on the other side of the main building before it occurred to him its antechambers would be ideal for their needs.

'Come on in Mungo,' the Jester said. 'You haven't missed anything. For once,' he added, to a ripple of amusement around the table.

'Some of us don't need to pretend,' Sebaklan Pwalek said, eyeing the Piper darkly.

Until the moment he took the only vacant seat at the table, he had been unaware who sat on the new governing body. With Pwalek's words, at least one other member was revealed. It was no surprise the Jester's right-hand man had been appointed to watch his back.

'Darmajelis meetings are regular and predictable,' Nipis said, waving the matter away. 'Apart from the two of us, the remaining members are fully occupied. No one else has reason to enter the Throne Room. We won't be disturbed.'

While the blackwood table could seat eight, a Puppeteers meeting was always far better attended. There was hardly room to breathe in the small chamber. Window seats along the north wall, designed for two in comfort, were crammed with four or five. Additional chairs had been borrowed from adjoining rooms, some members leant against pillars or simply squatted on the stone flagged floor. Usually cool on account of its northern aspect, the over-filled room had soon become stifling. The Piper would normally have found it difficult to stay awake in such circumstances, but the parade of Puppeteers business, each new item more irritating than the last, was beginning to wind him up. Reports from their spies at the Black

Palace, the Earther base, and further afield each had to be heard and debated at length. The state of the contest for the Blood Throne was chewed over again, even though there was nothing new to say. The current lack of Elementals at Court, and what should be done about it, rumbled on for far too long given that there was nothing they *could* do about it.

And through every discussion there were those in the group, a majority even, who would search for the conflict in each situation. Eager to exploit their differences in pursuit of hidden agendas, rather than seek more peaceful resolutions. Finally, when the conversation turned inevitably to the forces deployed at Lembaca Ana, he could contain himself no longer.

'Is this the best we can do?' he said, interrupting the Jester in full flow.

'Excuse me?'

'Aren't you sick of it? All we ever talk about is war. How to incite it. How to control it. How to find forces to fight it. How to pay for it. Has it never occurred to you that the cost is measured in more than coin? Don't you ever, even in your most private moment, think peace would be a better option?'

'Now just hold–' Olek Grissan began.

The Jester held up his hand. 'If I may, Grissan.'

He turned to the Piper. 'What's brought this crisis of conscience upon you? It's not much more than a season past when you were an enthusiastic supporter of our cause. Or so I thought. You were supposed to lead the music at Lembaca Ana during the Clone Rout, but if my memory's correct you were late for that too.'

'Yes, and since then you have lost a King,' he said, ignoring the Jester's insult. 'And we, in Kertonia, have tried to broker a peace to prevent further loss of life. An initiative you took great delight in wrecking. I don't suppose we will ever know the King's intentions, but you? You never took a single step in that direction. Your entire focus was on the destruction of the peace process before it even got started. If you could have heard the Queen–'

'Please! Do not extol that Black bitch's virtues here! She does not shrink from war herself, when the mood is upon her.'

'She does not seek it out! It is never her first solution!'

The Jester shook his head.

'You defend her as if your loyalties no longer lie with your brothers here. But this is a diversion only.' He leaned closer. 'War is but a means to an end, as you well know. Our sworn aim is to return both realms to their rightful owners. The people. We have taken a small step here in Istania. We have a ruling body that has dispensed with the monarchy. Something we could only have dreamt of a season or two ago. The next step is clear. The exercises at the coast, if we play them out right, will see the Black Queen fall and give you the chance to set up a similar group across the plain. Another stride towards rule by social collective.'

'But with you in control,' the Piper said, unable to prevent a sneer creasing his face. 'You are no more in favour of a democracy than I am! You are an oligarch, though I'm sure you would deny it with your last breath.'

'I am an agent of change!' The Jester rose to his feet. 'Change that is long overdue. You have been in the company of the Batu'n as long as I. Heard them talk of their society. They do not suffer the yoke of monarchy. They do not bow down before wielders of eldritch powers. Their world is more enlightened, more equal, than we have ever known. They are masters of their own destiny. Do you not want some of that? Don't you dream of seeing it here, as I do?'

'Of course I do! But I don't see the path to it being built on the bones of our people!'

'How else are we supposed to achieve it? Faced with an army of trained men loyal to their monarch, and a few powerful individuals with an overblown sense of their own importance.'

'The Elementals are a force for good!' the Piper said, jumping to his feet and sending his chair crashing onto the flagstones. 'And you will not easily be rid of them.'

'They are mortal just as we are,' the Jester murmured, sharing a look with Pwalek. 'I will not allow this dissent to distract us from our committed path. This band of brothers will not rest until the royal houses and their lickspittle magicians are a distant memory and Berikatanya can be ruled for the good of all!'

Loud cheers rang out around the room, along with cries of 'Well said Jeruk!' and 'Damn right!'

The Jester allowed the noise to die down before turning once more to face him. A chill ran the length of his spine at the menace in the small man's eyes.

'It would be a great disservice to this group, and to the people of both realms, if anyone were to expose our aims and plans at this stage.' He spoke slowly, seeming to weigh each word. 'I know I speak for all of us here when I say the consequences would be severe for anyone so... misguided.'

the black palace
22nd day of ter'tanamasa, 966

Patrick Glass reached his favourite vantage point as the late afternoon sun winked behind the westernmost peak of Temmok'Dun. He climbed onto the flat topped rock that afforded a clear view over Uta Tantaran—the northern plain—now thrown into shadow by the setting sun. The mountain range had been the beginning of Jann Argent's personal quest for answers to his many questions about the power of the Gatekeeper.

It felt like an age since he had seen his friend. Being born on Earth, albeit to a Berikatanyan father, Patrick found the local seasons confusing. He had to count back the days before he could grasp how long Jann had been gone. Almost four months! During their journey to visit the Pilgrim, they had become close. On their return to the Valley it was Jann who had given Patrick the first clue to unlock the powers of the Pattern Juggler, He hoped Jann would find what he was seeking in the far north, and a safe passage back to the haven of the Palace.

Patrick's inability to wield his own power still frustrated him. He took out the Pattern Juggler's amulet from inside his tunic. Rescued from the aftermath of the vortex by the Keeper of the Keys, the old archivist had relinquished it at their first meeting, once he was convinced Patrick was its rightful owner. Now the only connection with his father, the pendant offered no clue to its secrets beyond the familiar pattern of interlocking circles engraved into its face. He traced the design absent-mindedly with one finger.

It felt like a limitless well of energy remained hidden behind an impenetrable barrier. Like the heat of a furnace felt only through its walls, the dense iron obscuring the flame at its heart. Desperate for any insight into the gifts the powers conferred, he had roamed the Palace corridors in search of clues, scrolls, or lore books.

There were none.

Remembering the extent of the archives curated by the Keeper in the crypts of the Blood King's Court, he had allowed Claire to persuade him back to Istania on one occasion. An extensive hunt through the catacombs and discussions with the Keeper himself proved fruitless. Instead he resolved to look inside himself for the answers. On their second trip to the Valley, Jann had shown him how the power could flow from his own natural skill with patterns and graphical images. Armed with that perception, Patrick tore down the temporal anomaly enveloping Lembaca Ana, prior to the Clone Rout. But since then, he had been unable to repeat the feat; incapable of accessing the Juggler's energy in any way.

Ironically, his visit to the Keeper exacerbated his

loneliness. In Jann's absence he had spent more time with the young Air Mage. But Claire was on a quest of her own: researching the lore of Air power. Patrick's description of the Keeper's records had led her to travel with him on his pilgrimage to Court. After her first visit, she spent more time there than at the Palace. He shivered, the feelings of solitude compounding the chill of the evening air. A ghantu bird hooted from a nearby tree, heralding the coming night. He pulled his woollen jerkin tighter around his shoulders and turned up the collar.

'Here you are!'

As if summoned by his thoughts of her, Claire appeared from the gathering gloom.

'I've been looking for you everywhere.'

'Hi,' he said, swivelling round on his rocky perch. 'How's it going?'

'Better than great,' she replied. 'I never did thank you properly for pointing me at the Keeper. The old guy is a fountain of knowledge.'

'You found what you were searching for?'

'I did—and then some. I have so many ideas of how I can use Air power, I hardly know where to begin.'

'That's great Claire.'

While happy for the young woman, the sadness in his voice telegraphed his own frustration.

'No luck your end, then?'

He shrugged. 'There doesn't seem to be *anything* written down. Either that, or it's been hidden away where no one can find it.'

Claire placed a hand on his knee, and hoisted herself onto the rock beside him.

'I'm so sorry,' she said, resting her head on his shoulder. 'Here I am banging on about finding more lore than I know what to do with, and you're stuck with nothing. What are you going to do?'

Patrick did not reply at first. He had no answer to Claire's question; not a single idea how to proceed. The ghantu bird took off with a screech, flying over their heads in the direction of Temmok'Dun. He wanted to fly with it, and leave this enormous problem behind. He let out a lengthy sigh.

'I don't really know. I've been coming out here in the evenings, hoping the quiet of the still night air will give me the head space to remember how I did it the first time.'

'Any luck?'

'No. At least, not yet. I'm not sure I can make it happen on my own. I've tried putting myself back in that place, mentally, where I was when Jann helped me, but even that hasn't produced the goods. Maybe I need a reason to use the power. A task.'

Claire laughed. 'We're fresh out of temporal anomalies.'

'Yeah.' He stared out after the rapidly disappearing ghantu. 'I think that might be a good thing, actually. That was a major problem, for my first outing. Like asking someone to draw the Mona Lisa when they've only just learned to sharpen a pencil. I'm not sure I want to repeat anything on that scale. I might bring down the Palace or something.'

'Wow, really?' Claire's eyes widened. 'Don't think I could ever do anything like that with Air power. Sounds scary.'

Patrick looked at her, his mouth agape. 'You might have something there young lady. This... thing... I can do. It's so powerful, It scares me more than a little. Could be what's blocking me from using it.'

'Which is why you wanted to start small, I'm guessing?'

'True. But what if Juggler power isn't supposed to be used for small things. Or can't be. What then?'

the black palace
22nd day of run'tanamasa, 966

Claire was lost in deep, convoluted thoughts about the vague clues hidden in the ancient lore books littering her desk, when a knock on her door disturbed her concentration. Curiosity quickly overcame her initial irritation. Visitors seldom came to her quarters. Other Air mages preferred to seek her out at Guild meetings, or over a bowl of soup in the refectory, knowing she guarded her private time.

'Come in.'

It took her a moment to recognise the woman who entered. Someone she had not seen since first arriving on planet more than six months before. Felice Waters.

She remembered Felice's kind manner and the practical help she had offered when the survivors of the downed Valiant made it to dry land. All thought of her studies fled her mind.

'Hello stranger! Come in. Have a seat.'

She moved several volumes from an armchair, replacing one carefully in the single space on the shelf above her desk and stacking the rest on the floor. 'What brings you to the Palace? How is life at Pennatanah? I assume you're still there?'

Felice set her backpack down beside the armchair and sat with a deep sigh.

'Pennatanah is still there,' she smiled, 'as am I, yes. You haven't seen it since you arrived. We've reconstructed the mooring stanchion after your unfortunate accident. The Dauntless could be here any day now. Life is quiet. Only a few of us holding the fort now most of you have taken up your new lives.'

'You never wanted to join us here at the Palace?' Claire asked. 'Or over at Court?' she added, not wanting to play favourites.

'I'm not much of a joiner. As I said life at Pennatanah is quiet, and that's how I like it. It's a simple routine. Once the few daily chores are done, my time is my own.'

'So what brings you here now? Can I help with something?'

'I hope so. All this spare time I have leaves me free to

follow up on certain... interests. I was a detective back on Earth as I may have mentioned. New arrivals are still intimidated by ex-cops. It helps the induction process along if I can guarantee I have their attention. The downside is, they tend to call on me to solve any mysteries that crop up.'

'I never knew we had mysteries to solve,' Claire said. 'You mean crime?'

'No. Not really. The natives are pretty good at keeping order.'

Claire smiled at the woman's use of "natives". She had been on the first ship, almost ten years ago, but living at the landing base meant she still thought like an Earther.

'I'm keeping an eye on the tabukki,' the older woman continued. 'You might even say "keeping tabs on them".' She laughed at her own joke. 'You'd think people would take advantage of cryosleep ridding their bodies of all addictions, but no. There's always a few who will go looking for a new high, or even invent one if there's nothing available.'

'So apart from low levels of recreational drug use... what exercises your criminal mind, Detective Waters?'

Felice laughed again. 'Ha! No one has called me that in a long time. I'm trying to get a handle on the manifestation of Elemental powers by colonists. Several Earthers, apparently without any connection to the natives, have shown they can wield the same kind of power as you.'

Claire listened while Felice described the events she had been investigating for several years. Why had these incidents never come to her attention? Surely someone in her Guild must have been aware of the Air related ones at least? None of her Elemental counterparts had ever mentioned such extraordinary and inexplicable events.

'So that's when I began to wonder if there is a genetic link,' Felice concluded.

'Between Earthers and Elemental powers?'

'Between any kind of mage and any ability to use a

power. Which is why,' she continued, reaching for her backpack, 'I have an unusual request.'

She extracted a small glass phial and a cotton swab. 'I'd like a sample of your DNA.'

'But I'm not an Earther,' Claire said. 'At least, not really. Yes, I was born on Earth, but my parents were both Berikatanyan.'

'You're the Air Mage. If anyone has an identifiable genetic trait, it's you. I can use your sample, or more accurately your DNA profile, as a control against which I can compare the others. Assuming you have no objections?'

'No. I mean, it's just a mouth swab, right? You don't need blood?'

'No! Skin cells will do just fine.'

'Are you sampling the others? The Fire Witch is here in the Palace too. Petani is working at the coast right now. He travelled with us on the Valiant, you remember? No one has seen Lautan since the Clone Rout but Patrick is around. Patrick Glass? If there's a genetic link for Elementals then it might be true for the Juggler too. It's a shame Jann is still away. You could have added a Gatekeeper sample to your collection.'

She opened her mouth to let Felice take her swab.

'Every sample helps,' the older woman said. 'Where will I find Elaine?'

'It's almost time for lunch,' Claire said. 'Come with me to the refectory. She's sure to be there soon. But before we go, since you're here, and you obviously enjoy a mystery with a scientific bias, there's something that's been bothering *me* since I first discovered my Elemental heritage.'

'All I know about the Elements is what I've observed,' Felice said. She glanced around Claire's chambers, taking in the piles of lore books and scattered parchments. 'I've not studied them to the depth you clearly have.'

She marked the phial with Claire's name and tucked it

away in her pack.

'This is more about how technology affects Elemental power,' Claire said. 'While I was still aboard Valiant, down here you were experiencing some violent winds. Locals I've spoken to since, and my master Pac Sau'dib at the Elemental academy, have always believed I was the cause. My Air power began to manifest unconsciously as soon as I was close enough to Berikatanya.'

Felice sat quietly for a moment, considering what Claire had said.

'That would certainly fit with what I've seen of Earther adepts,' she said at length. 'Without any guidance or tutoring in the use of their power, the results are often... unpredictable.'

'Yes, I understand that,' Claire said, 'but it's not what I meant. I was on board the Valiant.'

'Why would that make a difference?'

'I don't know. But the first time I tried to use my power in anger was in battle. That very short-lived skirmish at Per Tantaran.'

'I remember,' Felice said. 'I was there. We took a pair of flyers out to quell the fight.'

'Exactly!' Claire said, sitting on the edge of her chair. 'When the flyers appeared, all the Elemental power failed. It was like someone had flicked a switch. If it had been just me I would've assumed it was my fault. The tension of the battle, the distraction of seeing your flyers come over the hills, or whatever. But Elaine was stopped in her tracks too. And she is far better at wielding her power than me, even now.'

'At the base we've known for some time that gravnull fields affect Elemental powers. It's one reason we keep flyer outings to a minimum. The natives don't like them. Most of them think it's bad magic.'

'That's kind of my point. If our Earther technology has that effect on Elemental magic, how come I was whipping up those storms while I was still on the Valiant? I was in a huge bubble of tech! There's no way I should've been using my power, consciously or otherwise.'

Chapter 6

Light flickered dimly through Kyle Muir's eyelids as she fought off the soporific chill of cryosleep. She felt a distant dragging sensation when the robot servos pulled cryogenic fluid syringes from her arms and legs. Had there been a problem? Only moments had passed since she lay down in the pod and heard the quiet hiss of the aerosol anaesthetic sending her to sleep for the journey to Perse. Why were they waking her so soon? The fog of induced coma dissipated. Her pod's polycarbonate hatch lifted to admit the high-pitched whine of the Wormwood "Prism" drive. There was her answer: no problem. They had arrived.

She sat up. The other eight cryopods in her capsule were opening, occupants rubbing their eyes, stretching their limbs, and swinging their legs over the sides of the pods. She glanced into the next pod. Her brother was still asleep.

'Douglas!' she called, jumping out and landing heavily on the stippled steel floor. She nudged his arm.

'Douglas. Wake up. We're here.'

He twitched his arm, shrugging off her touch. 'Get off. Let me sleep. Can't be there yet.'

'I know, it feels like we just left. It's the cryosleep. Come on.'

The first of their fellow passengers had already dressed. Automated lights illuminated the corridor in front of him as he walked from the capsule. Kyle hobbled to her locker, legs buzzing with the worst case of pins and needles she had ever known. She vaguely remembered this after-effect being mentioned in the briefing back at Armstrong spaceport. It would soon pass. She pulled on a T-shirt and a pair of jogging pants before checking on Douglas again. He was still sitting on the edge of his pod.

'Come *on!* We're going to miss everything!'

He rubbed his neck and squinted at her. 'What is there to miss? We won't be landing for days yet.'

'Food!' she replied.

On the wall, beside the legend identifying this as capsule H20, a smartscreen showed the distant orb of Perse. Not yet close enough to have a hint of blue, although...? No, it must be her imagination. Remote telemetry suggested it was drier than Earth, but she still hoped to find an ocean. Having grown up in a small coastal fishing town, she longed to swim in the sea again and feel the waves crash over her face. And Douglas would love to surf—his favourite pastime, since it kept him fit and gave him chance to show off at the same time. Sitting in his pod, her brother yawned. He ignored her, as usual. A wave in the face was exactly what he needed to wake him up and get him moving! Kyle turned on her heel and stalked out of the capsule. Damn him. Let him miss their first meal for almost a hundred years. She was not going to!

The restaurant for their level was located on the other side of the tera-lift. The smell of hot food met her as she entered, causing her stomach to flip over. The cryopods had supplied enough nutrients to sustain life, but her belly was empty. Something she intended to put right immediately. She joined the short queue moments before Douglas jostled her from behind.

'Oi! Watch where you're going!'

'I know where I'm going, thanks. Took a minute until I remembered there'd be food.'

'I told you!'

'OK, not remembered then. Heard with a slight delay on account of that being the last sense to wake up. Allegedly.'

'It would need the mind-numbing effects of a chemically-induced coma to make *you* pass up a chance to eat,' Kyle said. She poked him in his sturdy midriff. 'A hundred years lying on your back hasn't improved your waistline.'

The automated servery dealt rapidly with the small queue. The twins took their meals and found seats close to one of the view ports that lined the opposite wall. They were still too far out to see their destination with the naked eye, but after several decades in a plastic box, Kyle needed the illusion of a vista. For once, Douglas did not object. At least, not about the view.

'This slop is disgusting,' he said, holding up a spoonful and examining it from all angles. 'Smells of dog food.'

'It's not that bad.'

'How long do I have to suffer this? Surely it'll be better down there?' He swallowed the contents of his spoon with an expression of pure disgust. 'Can't be any worse.'

Kyle spun her chair around. Their table sat next to one of the four working areas on this side of the room. Each was equipped with a com terminal. She fired it up and checked the "time to destination" counter.

'Says ten days.'

'Isn't that longer than we were told?'

Kyle shrugged. 'Maybe the improved Prism drive needs a longer deceleration? And we're the last ship, so they wouldn't have bothered to rerecord the briefing.'

'Typical! We're always the last to learn anything. What the fuck am I going to do in this tin can for ten days?'

'Get some exercise? Learn about Perse? You didn't even pick up the info pack before we left.'

'What's the point? Most of it is guess work! No one knows what it's really like down there.'

'Well we'll find out in ten days.'

'Probably be as boring as all hell,' Douglas said. He pushed his plate away. 'I can't eat any more of this. I'll be starving by the time we land. Dunno why I let you talk me into coming.'

'I didn't! You heard what the woman from Colony Assessment said as well as I did. Our aptitude and psych evaluation tests were off the scale. Seemed like too good a chance to pass up to me.'

'I was happy where we were.'

'No you weren't! You haven't been happy since Mum & Dad died. This is a new start for us. Why can't you give it a chance? Some people give up everything for this. Spend their life savings on a ticket if they're rich, or gamble them on the Lottery if they're not. CA scour the planet for candidates with the right skills and abilities. We were handed this new life on a plate!'

'"A new life in the rural idyll of Perse",' Douglas mocked, quoting from the brochure. 'Rural idyll my arse. I had enough of that at home.'

'Well, you wanted a change. I thought we'd agreed we had nothing to lose. There wasn't a single reason to stay.'

'Not for you maybe. I was hoping for my shot at the bright lights. Where am I gonna find that here, eh? Candles and torches'll be the nearest thing to a bright light in the "rural idyll".'

'You'd better make the most of it,' Kyle said, getting to her feet. She had had more than enough of his tantrums for one day. Sometimes he acted as though he were nine, not nineteen. 'Nothing you can do about it now. You're powerless! Muahaahaa!'

valley of lembaca ana
11th day of sen'tanamasa, 966

The irony of working alone was not lost on Petani. He had travelled for a hundred years across millions of kilometres of space, and taken charge of the largest earthworks in Berikatanyan history. Now, he was toiling away in splendid isolation, exactly as he had all those years before on Earth. It was a temporary situation, true, and mostly of his own doing. Discouraged by his failure to solve the conundrum of the harbour, he had granted everyone else the day off. A day of solitary thinking might be enough to dredge an answer from the sludgy depths of his unconscious.

Although alone, he was not lonely. More of a loner than a mixer, he had always been happy to work by himself. Recently, he had come to value the camaraderie of the hard-working Berikatanyans. They made a good team, and had achieved great things at the Forest. The lads insisted this was due to Petani's mastery of Earth power and his legendary ability with growing things. Their awe of his talents meant they could never relax around him enough to become close friends, but their frequent shared meals and banter gave him a warm feeling.

He had failed to live up to his team's high expectations. His day of thinking time was almost done with still no notion how he could craft a harbour within the increasingly choppy waters in the bay. The daylight retreated beyond the imposing mound of Pun'Akarnya. He watched as the reddening orb of the sun dropped behind the new mountain, its last rays glistening and sparking off the glassy surface of the rock. Rock formed in the tremendous heat from Elaine's Fire, which liquefied the deep-rooted material he had compelled to rise from beneath the Valley floor.

Petani continued to stare at the mountain long after the full circle of the sun disappeared. Darkness crept toward him in the shadow of the tower. Something about it spoke to him. If only he could quieten his mind to hear it. There was no hurrying the thought. His slow wits frustrated him—stalagmites formed quicker than his ideas—but there was nothing to be done. It was just the way he was, and he lived with it comfortably enough. Forgoing the creation of a temporary perch with his Earth power, he took a seat atop one of the wooden pillars that supported his land-side harbour structures. The first of the two moons rose from behind him, its bright silver light painting the rocky folds of the mountain in a bas-relief of deep black and lustrous argent. The coming malamajan would have no impact on their creation. Pun'Akarnya would stand for millennia against any kind of weather. Even when the seas had eaten away the coastline and swirled around its feet, the mountain would remain indomitable.

As if rock were being eroded from his glacial mind by those constant rains, a thought finally emerged. The solution to his problem stood right in front of him. His earthworks alone could not defeat the waves, but if he and the Fire Witch worked together, fashioning pontoons with legs of molten rock such as had been created during their epic battle, the harbour would be finished in no time.

*

'There you are!' Umtanesh called as Petani walked out of the gathering gloom and took a seat by the fire. 'We think tides swept you away!'

He grinned broadly. 'I *was* swept away,' he said, accepting a bowl of steaming rebusang from the small Berikatanyan. 'On a tide of inspiration!'

He took a seat between his Forest Clearance companions and the small group of suhiri who had joined them at the Landing to add their Earth skills to his own. Spooning a mouthful of Umtanesh's delicious stew, it took him a moment to notice the cook was staring at him, his mouth hanging open.

'You... you solved the problem?'

Petani sucked air around the hot rebusang. 'I know how to solve it, at least. I can't do it alone. We will need the help of the Fire Witch.'

He outlined his ideas to the group as they ate. The other Earth mages seemed less than enthusiastic.

'You don't like this approach?' he asked Suhir Nyirumi, who sat on the other side of the firepit.

'Apologies, Petani. I mean no disrespect. My thoughts were elsewhere.'

The mages' English, polished during their years spent around Court and Palace, contrasted with that of his

Project companions. Even with the help of his constant tutelage, they remained less fluent. Petani passed his bowl to Umtanesh for a refill. Having not eaten for the whole day, his first helping had already disappeared without any magical aid.

'It must be important to divert your attention from our work here,' he observed. 'Has something happened with our local war heroes? Have they made any moves towards us?'

'No Petani, their encampment remains much as it was. For now, they continue to observe only. No, my concern stems from another event. In your absence today we received a message from the Palace.'

'I saw no rider.'

'The message did not come on kudoback,' Nyirumi said. 'It arrived through the air. It flew here.'

Petani choked on his food.

'It what?'

'Yes, we also were surprised. Part of the message explained that the Air Mage, working with her Guild members, has developed this new use for Air power. Small parchments can be lifted and flown anywhere in the realm.'

'That's wonderful!' He felt a warm glow of pride for the young Elemental, who had become a close friend during their time together at the Forest Clearance Project. Back then her powers were still developing and her heritage as the Air Mage remained as yet undiscovered. 'What an extraordinary idea. But I don't understand,' he went on, 'was there something else in the message that gave you concern?'

'It was not the content of the message, Petani, but rather its provenance. The script itself simply relayed the Queen's desire for news of our progress. But the way it was delivered showed us what can be achieved when Elementals work in harmony with their fellow suhiri. This exciting new use of Air power comes from their Guild work. The Fire Witch is using her Guild also, to train young Fire mages.'

Petani knew where the conversation was leading. He chewed thoughtfully, giving the man chance to speak. In the end it was not Nyirumi who summoned up the courage to voice their concerns, but Suhir Haande, sitting to his left.

'This is not a criticism of you, Petani,' Haande said, squirming in his seat. 'We understand it has taken time to recover your powers. To fit back into the way of things here, after your long sojourn among the people of Earth. But where is our Guild? What are the Earth-wielders doing to match the forward thinking shown by Air and Fire? What exciting new possibilities are there for us?'

'We welcome your solution to the problem of the pontoons,' Nyirumi added. 'It is indeed an inventive idea, and just the kind of thing we were hoping for. With more minds working on problems like these, surely other clever solutions are waiting to be uncovered? We do not want to be seen as the poor relation among the Elemental community.'

'With your leadership,' Haande continued, picking up the thread again, 'an Earth Guild could make great strides.' He held up the parchment message. 'Just as imaginative as this Air Mail idea.'

They fell quiet while he finished his second bowl. There was a visible tension among the two speakers and the few other Earth mages who had been working on the project, but Petani did not feel it. Their concerns washed over him like waves at the coast, and had as little effect as if he had been made of the obdurate stone of Pun'Akarnya. He snapped a twig from the bush beside him and picked a piece of meat out from between his teeth.

'I do not always work well in a team,' he said at length. 'I am well aware of that. You have all surprised me, putting up with me for this long.'

A murmur of embarrassed protest rolled around the

group, which he ignored.

'But I remain Petani. The Earth Elemental. And, if there is to be a Guild, only I can lead it.' He paused again, looking at each of the mages in turn. Some of them fidgeted under his gaze. Nyirumi and Haande weathered his look without flinching. 'So I must put away my personal feelings. You are quite right, all of you. We can achieve more together than we can individually. The very existence of Pun'Akarnya proves it. None of us Elementals could have created it alone, yet there it stands. A testament to what can be done working in concert.'

The tension in the group eased. One of the mages brought round a flagon of ale to toast their new accord.

'When shall we have our first meeting, Petani?' Haande asked.

He glanced around the camp. 'I would say there are enough of us here to make a start right now. I hereby convene the inaugural meeting of the Earther Guild, and swear you all in as members.'

Some of the group laughed politely.

'You will me excuse, Petani,' Umtanesh said, getting to his feet. 'I not part of Guild. We will speak later.'

He began to protest but the young Berikatanyan was adamant he did not want to impose on the private business of the meeting. He ushered his comrades from the fire while the mages toasted Petani's declaration.

'But there are so few of us,' Nyirumi said.

'Indeed. Perhaps that should be our first order of business? I believe you said Elaine—Bakara—has recruited several young Fire mages to her cause? Should we be doing something similar?'

'I know of none,' admitted Nyirumi. 'It has been many years since a new Earth mage arose.'

'Are we restricting membership to our own people?' asked a new voice from his left. A man he did not recognise. 'There are rumours at least one of the Earthers has demonstrated Earth power. Albeit unwittingly,' the man added to general amusement.

'Is this the infamous "hand in rock" story?' Haande asked. 'Do we want such potentially dangerous hampanay in our new Guild?'

'Hampanay!' Petani said. 'It has been many years since I heard anyone called that! I don't think we should hobble our Guild with such prejudices. Earth people have become well integrated here over the years. Unless there are any objections in principle I see no reason why they should not apply for membership. Provided they can demonstrate some ability.

'Where do we find this man, does anyone know?'

the black palace
21st day of sen'tanamasa, 966

Almost a full Berikatanyan month had passed since Claire found Patrick at his evening vigil. He had come out here every night, searching for the elusive mental path that might lead him to a solution—or even a clue—to the puzzle of the Juggler's power. He made no progress, but without an idea of how else to proceed, he continued his nightly ritual. The season of Tanamasa was almost over and the nights would soon be too cold for sitting out. He had not been on the rock long when the sound of voices interrupted his thoughts.

'Ah yes, here he is.'

A Palace guard approached along the narrow gravel path, accompanied by a man Patrick did not recognise.

'Visitor for you, sir,' the guard said. 'Took him to your chambers first off, but I've seen you out here a lot lately so I thought you'd be here.'

'You are Patrick Glass?' the visitor asked, as if unwilling to trust the guard's judgment. Deep lines on the man's face and brow, beneath a thinning crown of mid-grey hair, suggested the stranger had seen maybe sixty summers, but his easy gait and ramrod straight posture were those of a much younger man.

'I am,' Patrick replied. 'And who are you?'

'My name is Penka. I have been looking for you.'

'And so, you have found me. What can I do for you?'

'If you'll excuse me sir, I'll leave you to it. I have to get back to the gate.'

The guard left. The man called Penka approached Patrick more closely, peering at him through the failing evening light.

'Yes, you have his look, though it is many years since I last saw him, and I was only a small child.'

'Whose look?' asked Patrick, beginning to lose patience. He did not appreciate the interruption and was damned if he would suffer riddles too. 'What is this about?'

'The look of your father,' Penka went on. 'You have his distinctive nose. And the same piercing eyes.'

An electric thrill passed through Patrick. Could this be his first clue? The lucky break he had been waiting for?

'You knew my father?'

Penka took a seat on the next rock. 'Not "knew" exactly. My grandfather was his closest friend. They spent much time together. I was a boy, as I have said. Not much more than five years old when your father disappeared.'

'Did you see it?'

'I did not attend the ceremony, no. Not many children did. The Elementals were unsure of its safety. With good reason, as it turned out. But I saw the effect the loss of your father had on my grandfather. He never really recovered.' Penka paused, staring out over the plain. He took a worn kerchief from his pocket and blew his nose into it. 'He died soon after the vortex took your father and the Elementals from us. To lose both of them in such a short time, it was a great blow to our village.'

'You still live in the same village?'

'Yes. My father took his father's place among the elders. When he in his turn passed to Tana a few years ago, I inherited his seat in the chamber.'

Mention of the Earth god made Patrick think of Petani. He had not seen the old Elemental since he had left for the coast. It was a few moments before he realised Penka was still talking.

'...would have come sooner. Word of your deeds did not reach our village for some time.'

'Is it far?'

'Duske Pelapan is quite remote, I suppose. Almost five days' ride from here at a good trot. It sits on the tip of the peninsula immediately south of Borok Duset. We keep to ourselves down there. News travels slowly. When it did arrive it seemed to me there had to be a connection between you and the man who spent many days at our house during my boyhood.'

'How so?'

'Only the Pattern Juggler could have torn down the curtain of time that shrouded the Valley,' Penka replied. 'I never saw your father perform such a deed, but my grandfather told tales of his powers as bedtime stories for all his grandchildren.'

Patrick smiled. 'I would like to hear some of those stories. Earth-bound Elementals had no paranormal powers. If he remembered having them, he never spoke of it. On the few occasions he spoke to me at all,' he added, remembering snatched moments of conversation with a man he hardly knew, during the last of his increasingly rare visits.

'Would you like to see where he lived?'

'His house is still there?'

'It has stood empty since I was five years old,' Penka said, 'but it is still there, yes. None in the village felt comfortable moving into it. I suppose, given the way your father was snatched away from us, many of our people believed he could return just as unexpectedly. No one would ever cross him, however unwittingly.'

Patrick stared at Penka. His expression was unreadable. Could this be a chance to find out more about the man

Patrick himself had not seen since he too was five years old? A strange coincidence.

'Was that fear, or respect?'

'A little of both,' Penka said, smiling for the first time. 'The inhabitants of Duske Pelapan are not the most sophisticated people. They respect power, certainly. And the greater the power, the greater the respect. But your father was well-liked too, in his own right. He was a kind man, and did a lot for the village.'

Not normally one for quick decisions, on this occasion Patrick had already made up his mind. He would visit the village of his ancestors. What else was there to do? Days of sitting out here had come to nothing. This could be what he had waited for.

'I would like to see your village,' he said, climbing from the rock and dusting himself down. 'If you will take me?'

'Gladly. I hoped you would come. Tales of your exploits spread through the village very quickly once word reached us. The other elders are keen to meet you. One or two of them remember your father too.'

'Come, I will arrange quarters for you,' Patrick said, starting for the Palace. 'You must rest first. We can leave tomorrow, or even the day after if you would prefer to extend your visit? I have had a long wait to learn of my heritage. Another day or so will make no difference.'

duske pelapan
30th day of sen'tanamasa, 966

To Patrick's surprise, the village of Duske Pelapan hummed with activity. The two men rode in shortly after midday. He had not expected his family seat to have such a large, active population. Clearly "remote" did not mean "moribund." Several of the villagers waved or called out a greeting as they passed. Whether they knew of Penka's search for the Pattern Juggler, or just assumed any of his travelling companions must be important, he could not tell.

Penka reined his kudo to a halt. 'I'm sure you are keen to visit your father's house, but perhaps we should freshen up first. There is daylight yet, and our journey has been long.'

'A bowl of something would be good, thank you Penka, but let's not leave it too late. I will need time to prepare a bed before dark.'

Penka dismounted, smiling. 'A bed is ready for you here, sir. Though your father's house still stands, you will find it is not a suitable place to spend a night.'

'You are most kind. And please call me Patrick.' He had tried every day to persuade his travelling companion onto first name terms, so far without success.

'As you wish sir. This way.'

With some embarrassment Patrick discovered Penka and his wife had given up their bedroom and were planning to spend the night on two small couches in the living space of their tiny cottage. They waved away Patrick's protestations, and seated him at the head of an ancient table while the slender, smiling woman served bowls of spicy fish soup.

'Thank you, Istri,' Penka said as she retreated to the kitchen. 'Eat, Patrick. The soup is made with the barawa fish that is so popular at the Palace. Here we prefer to cook it until it is much less... blue. We also add local spices to improve the flavour.'

They made short work of the meal. Patrick found the small bowls surprisingly filling and began to think he would prefer to sleep now and visit his family home the next day, but Penka began pulling on his boots as soon as he had tidied away their empty dishes.

'Come, while we still have the light. Your father's house is a short walk from here.'

Penka led the way through the village, the streets quieter now in the late afternoon. A breeze had blown up, bringing with it the sharp tang of the sea. The house, a simple stone-built structure, was visible from the outskirts of the settlement, standing isolated on the cliff top. Even from this distance, Patrick could make out a large hole in the roof. When they were still some way from the building, Penka stopped.

'I will leave you now. This is a private matter. Better that you are alone. Stay as long as you wish. Your bed will be warm on your return.'

He hurried back toward the edge of the village before Patrick could reply. He watched his new friend go before staring down the narrow path at the tiny hut. His father must have lived there alone. It was not large enough for two, let alone a family. Grateful for Penka's diplomacy, he shrugged off his apprehension and covered the final steps to stand in front of the small dwelling. It commanded a spectacular view of the ocean and the rocky coastline. A stone-flagged path led from the door down a steep incline, disappearing over the visible edge of the cliff. Thoughts of where the path might lead were forgotten as he entered the house. Above the door, carved into the keystone of the arch, Patrick saw the complex pattern of interlocking circles so familiar since his boyhood. An involuntary sob rose in his throat. If there had ever been any doubt that this was his father's house, it was banished by that symbol. The mark of the Pattern Juggler. He stepped inside.

*

'The hinges have rusted through,' Patrick said, taking a sip of the clear amber liquor Penka had poured for him on his return. Candle light reflected in the glass giving the drink the appearance of liquid fire.

'No one has set foot inside since your father left,' Penka said. 'Is it very bad?'

'Oh yes. The door falling off was only the first of my surprises. Many of his belongings are laid out in the main living area as if he had only just stepped out—'

'Well of course,' Penka interrupted, 'he was expecting to return.'

'Yes. But now, with the roof having collapsed, everything is covered in rubble, broken shingles, years of dust. And soaked by the rain. It's a miracle I could salvage anything.'

Patrick rested his other hand on an enormous tome bound in tooled leather.

'Where did you find it?' Penka asked, his voice hushed with awe.

duske pelapan
30th day of sen'tanamasa, 966

The first thing I noticed was the smell. More than just damp. There was a spice to it. I recognised it immediately, even though it is one of my most distant childhood memories. Something I hadn't smelt since my fifth birthday. My father's cologne. The inside of his hut is a bombsite —dust and rain damage everywhere; pieces of broken roof strewn all over the living space; birds nesting on the armchairs—and yet that smell still hung in the air. It suffused every cushion, every drape, every rug. And it felt like home. I wandered from living space to bedroom with hardly any idea where to start, or even what I was starting. I rummaged through closets and cupboards, and then as the sun began to slip from view I saw my first clue. Carved into the inner face of the door pillar, a pictogram I recognised. To some it may have looked like a few random scratches, but I knew it was the symbol for a path.

Not just any path. From the position and angle of the carving it could mean only one. The stone-paved track that led to the cliff edge. And its juxtaposition with the Juggler's symbol told me it was the path to what I sought.

I stood in that doorway for far too long, conscious I would soon lose the light and yet enthralled by the view of the ocean. I hadn't seen it since leaving the Valley six months before. Back then the sight had conjured a strange reaction in me. To be honest it wasn't the Valley so much as its proximity to the sea. It spoke to some deep part of me that had remained hidden my whole life. Or I thought it did, at first, but whatever I expected to come from those feelings never materialised. It stayed tantalisingly out of reach in a frustrating emotional mirror of my inability to access my power. As I leant against the doorframe, I knew why. It had been the wrong coast. *This* is the coast I am connected with. Generations of my family—I knew it must surely be more than only my father and grandfather—had lived and died here. It is almost in my genes, that view. The salt tang in the air and the fresh ocean breeze on my face, stinging tears from my eyes to blur my vision until I had to dash them away with the back of my hand. I experienced a bone-deep sense of *belonging* I have never felt anywhere before.

I stepped onto the path, moving slowly so as not to miss the smallest clue. And it was small, when I found it. Tiny. Not on the very last slab—that would have been too obvious. My father was never blatant, with his praise, his criticism, or his hints. The last but one slab had a scratch on its leading edge. Invisible to most, and insignificant to a casual observer who *did* notice it, it was a graphical instruction to descend and keep left. I rubbed away a patch of moss that had encroached over the edge of the slab and discovered the symbol also told exactly how far to drop. Only ten metres or so, which was a relief! I've never been a confident climber and although the path wasn't sheer, it wasn't a walk in the park either.

I was too young to really know my father, but I have a new respect for him having seen how he put together these cryptic clues laying out the route to the secret of his lore. In a way that only one of the family could unravel. I needn't have worried about the climb down. It's not an easy path. Twice it appears almost to end altogether, or at least be too steep to negotiate without ropes and mountaineering gear. But there is a way. There are footholds in the cliff, each with its own clue carved or scratched into the rock, or revealed in a pattern of stones hammered into the earth. Once I began the longest descent—with my heart in my mouth I can tell you—the trail of clues continued on the cliff-face, each at eye level once I had taken a step downward.

I marvelled at my father's inventive genius. There is not one system of patterns that would allow you to decode every clue. Instead, each one in turn, as well as revealing the location of the next, also contains a hint on how to interpret it. My memories of the man himself are faint, but the games he played with me—the ciphers and pictograms and hieroglyphics of his own invention—remain as vivid to me today as when I was a child. It's as if he was preparing me to discover his hiding place, even though the prospect of me ever reaching his old home must have seemed remote indeed.

The last clue revealed the final location of the book. In a place no one would think anything special. Buried under a cairn that didn't even look like a cairn. I would have passed it by if I hadn't been searching for a pattern in the stones. I almost didn't want to take it down. It was an incredible piece of work.

*

Patrick drained the last mouthful from his glass, his fingers tracing the outline of the symbol on the book's cover. He rolled the smoky liquor over his tongue. 'An understanding of geometric shapes and combinations is a family trait. This pattern has followed me around all of my life. So long that I've almost forgotten the first time I saw it. My father drew it for me countless times. It has always been my favourite doodle. It was the symbol that the Keeper of the Keys recognised, and first revealed my heritage. It is carved above the entrance to my father's house and I found it in many other places all over the inside.'

Penka refilled Patrick's glass. 'The book appears to be in surprisingly good condition.'

'It was well protected by the cairn. Another amazing thing—the stones had been fitted together with such precision, inside the small chamber it was completely dry. Remarkable work.'

'Your father was greatly respected in our village, but I would never claim that anyone understood him. It does not surprise me he could hide a complex and important message like that, in plain sight. What are your plans now Patrick? You are welcome to stay here as long as you need.'

'I have a lot of work to do. Not only studying the contents of this—it's a big book! —but I can't impose on your hospitality. It will take a long time to understand all the symbolism in here. I've barely had chance to decipher the first page. No, I must divide my time between the mental challenge and the physical. Study in the evening, and spend the day making good my family home.'

Penka smiled broadly. 'I hoped you would. You will find many villagers are keen to help rebuild the old house. Your father was very popular. I know his son will be made equally welcome. We may be remote, but our artisans are among the best in Kertonia. A few days only, will it take to repair the building.'

'A few days? Surely not. It's a huge task. And your winter is about to set in, is it not?'

'True, this is the last full day of Tanamasa. Tomorrow is the start of Sanamasa, but the worst of the weather is still many days away. We have time. You will see. We have time, and we have the help we need. A month at most.'

'Thank you, Penka. I am overwhelmed. To study my father's lore in my father's house is more than I could have dreamed of. I will sleep better tonight than I have since I first set foot on Berikatanyan soil!'

the black palace
23rd day of far'sanamasa, 966

'I cannot believe he didn't even turn up!' Elaine said, stalking from the Eradewan chamber with Claire Yamani on her heels.

'His lateness is legendary, but he does at least arrive eventually,' Claire agreed. 'Usually,' she added.

The season had turned since Elaine last spoke with the Piper about his duplicity. Recently there had been fewer meetings, but until today he had kept his word. At least as far as his timekeeping was concerned. There was no telling whether he had yet confronted the Puppeteers with the idea of a peaceful solution to their differences, as promised. Over the intervening months Elaine shared with Claire what she knew of the Piper's activities. Right now they were the only two Elementals at the Palace. Lautan had been absent for almost two full seasons. Patrick left for the coast a month ago, before Elaine could bring him into the conversation. With Petani working in the Valley and Jann still Baka-knew-where over the northern mountains, it was up to the two women to help the Queen keep the Eradewan, and the Palace, running smoothly.

'What are you going to do?' Claire asked.

'After I've given him the sharp edge of my tongue, you mean? There are too few of us here for any one of us to shirk his duties like this. But more important, I need to know what the Puppeteers are planning. It must be them driving the military build-up at the Valley. There is no one else but that yellow misfit controlling things at Court. I have told the Queen as much. His "Darmajelis" is nothing but a puppet show in its own right. There'll be another war if we can't do something to stop it, and we are spread too thinly to make a good fist of it from the Black's side. Without intelligence from the Reds we are at even more of a disadvantage.'

They reached the Piper's chambers to find the door standing ajar.

'Mungo?' Elaine called. 'We missed you at Eradewan! What's your excuse this time, you miserable worm?'

She pushed the door open and stepped into the room.

'Hello? Are you here? Speak up man!'

A faint metallic smell tainted the air. The remains of a half-eaten meal sat congealing on a table beside the fireplace, in which dying embers of a fire still glowed. One of the chairs lay on its side, a broken leg beside it. Blood spattered the stone-flagged floor.

'What has happened here?' Claire asked as Elaine moved towards the Piper's bedchamber. The stench of blood became stronger on this side of the room.

'Oh, Baka! No!' she said as the door swung back to reveal the Piper's body lying face up across the bed. The room showed further signs of a struggle. The contents of his night stand had been swept onto the floor, pieces of shattered porcelain ground into the purple bedside rug. Several more sprays of gore decorated the walls. In one, the words

KEB SULPA, KEB MUJAH

had been hastily scribbled. Two pipes, two faces.

The bed sheet, ripped from the mattress, had been used to bind the Piper's hands behind his back. His trademark bifurcated pipe was broken in two. One half had been rammed deep into the dead man's mouth. The other...

Elaine turned away quickly, placing a hand on Claire's shoulder.

'Don't,' she said. 'Stay out. He's dead. Murdered.'

'Oh my God!' Claire said. 'Who? Who would do such a thing?'

'I have no idea,' Elaine replied. 'Someone who questioned the old man's loyalties if you believe that grisly daubing. One thing is certain—we have more than one spy here in the Palace.'

temmok'dun, northern range
18th day of sen'bakamasa, 966

Honestly, if I'd known what was coming, I doubt I would have started. That last day in the caldera had been one of total emotional turmoil. I knew I couldn't stay; I had seen the snow-capped mountains, so I didn't want to go; and it had belatedly occurred to me that with my as-yet-untested "rock and stone" method I could perhaps climb out the way I'd come in after all.

But that smacked of giving up, and I knew I wouldn't have another chance. So there I stood, with the midday sun doing its best to boil my already addled brains, my temporary home behind mc and a climb into the unknown in front of me. Did I say "a" climb? Maybe that's what I thought when I set off, but it soon turned into *several* climbs. There was no easy route over the mountain. Not one visible from the plateau, and not one I found after four attempts. Four false starts, four days wasted, and four portions of supplies eaten. At least my pack is lighter. I've tried to bolster my spirits. I haven't failed four times; I've merely found four routes that don't work. Call me Edison. Unfortunately I'm not a very receptive audience for myself. I'm close to abandoning the endeavour and returning to the warmth and safety of the known. The unknown isn't happening.

Waking with a fresher mind the next day I return to the second route I tried. It was my highest climb. I only abandoned it in hope of an easier route. Now I know there is no easy option, the least hard route is the best I have. Reluctantly I discard my water skin. It's half-empty now anyway and once I'm above the snow line I can melt enough water to live on. If I don't succeed, it will be waiting here for me when I return. Its weight could be the difference between making the climb and not.

I'm notching the walking staff I brought with me in lieu of my calendar tree. On my fifth day since leaving the caldera, the first part of my ascent is soon done. I'm covering familiar ground. When I reach the point where I turned back last time, I stop to consider my options. A narrow ledge angles up to my left with only a few visible handholds widely spaced out. On the right a stairway of wider outcrops set at irregular intervals leads up out of sight around a curve of the cliff. None of the steps is less than a metre high and they will eventually expose me to the strong wind that has blown up. Directly above me, about seventy metres up, another rocky cleft protrudes, asking a question I don't have the answer to. I would have to lean out from the rock to get enough swing on my rope. The angle is bad; each attempt would sap my dwindling reserves of strength. Even if I can secure my rope, I'd have to dangle out over the drop and rope-climb to the lip, with hands already turning blue from the cold. I shiver at that thought. No, that last option is a non-starter. It has to be the staircase.

Five steps further on and I know I've made the right choice, but it's not easy. The wind is horrendous, buffeting and howling around me the whole time. Any exposed skin aches with cold. At the corner, the gale threatens to tear me from the mountain. I cling on, waiting for it to subside. The view from this height is awe inspiring: the caldera nestled among the grey mountains like a fabulous emerald jewel on the finger of a wizened old hag. As I grip the rock, praying to Sana for a break in the moaning maelstrom, I hear a piercing angry cry. A searing pain blazes along my left arm above the wrist. I almost fall. Twisting away from the noise I see a flash of white feathers and hear the shrill squawk again. I cover my eyes. It's some kind of hawk. The beak on it is the size of a man's fist. Its razor edge has laid my arm open almost to the bone. Bright red blood spatters away on the wind as the bird flies in for a third attack. I have no idea what I've done to anger the creature. Perhaps it simply considers me a handy meal? Then I notice the cause of its aggression. Poking from a crack above my head, a few twigs reveal the location of the hawk's nest. Over the whistling of the wind and the screeching of the enraged bird, there's a hint of a thin, reedy peeping noise from inside. I guess this protective mother won't stop until I'm gone. I have two choices: up or down.

Holding my bleeding arm to my chest, I scrabble for a handhold to pull myself around the curve to the next stair. Loosened rock skitters past me, enormous wings beat at me, and the pain from my wound throbs and burns, but somehow I climb. First one stair, then another. Once it sees I'm moving away the hawk abandons its attack. It continues to circle, whether to convince itself I'm no longer a threat, or persuade me not to turn back, I can't be sure.

Three more stairs and I encounter a wide fissure. Grateful for a respite from the wind I crawl inside. My cut is still bleeding profusely. I must bind it. I have nothing but the clothes I'm wearing, but there's no choice. Feel a bit colder or bleed to death? With no ready supply of water I'll pass out from dehydration long before I bleed out. I rip a strip from the bottom of my shirt and tie it around my arm.

With the immediate problem solved, I take a moment for a closer look at my refuge. The vertical crack reaches all the way to the next plateau. Scudding clouds fill the space between the walls. An occasional flurry of snow blows over the edges. This rock chimney offers a much faster route to the top, if I can remember the technique for climbing one. It's tricky with my injured arm out of action. Pressing against the wall makes the pain flare. Fresh blood soaks into my rude bandage. I shall have to make do with my one good arm. The climb is longer and more difficult that way, but after an age I roll out at the top of the crack, exhausted and elated in equal measure.

I scoop a couple of mouthfuls of snow while I recover my breath and take a look around. I've grown used to the "good news, bad news" scenarios this trip throws at me, and this new level is no different. The good news is I've reached the summit of the northern range. As far as I can see there are no new escarpments blocking my path. No more climbing to do. A barren, rocky wasteland stretches away northward, its monotony relieved by small outcrops of darker rock and patchy dustings of snow in places where the howling wind has failed to dislodge it. I can see no end. The walking will be arduous, but more clambering than climbing.

The downside? There is no protection from the weather, or any further predators. The wind cuts across the top of the mountain like a scythe of ice, finding every gap in my home-made clothing and slicing through each. Unless I can find some shelter, a third grisly death will join my list of unappealing choices. Dehydration, fatal blood loss, and now exposure. Standing here thinking about it is not helping, so I start across the bleak and rocky plain with no clear destination in sight. I have no towering mountain to head for; no rock looking any more like a landmark than any other. All I can do is head north, and take shelter in any wind-break I find.

The next few days blend into one. Some nights I'm lucky, finding a depression in the rock that offers respite from the wind. On others I don't fare so well, and spend a fitful night being woken by each cutting gust. Apart from my portable calendar, two things mark the days. My dwindling food supplies, and my increasingly painful arm. It shows no signs of healing. Whether the bird's beak, or its spittle, was laced with a poison, I don't know, but the flesh around the cut is turning purple. The stench each night when I open the bandage makes me retch, but I have no way to clean the wound. I rub snow into it, screaming in agony, to no avail. I have a vague recollection of the healing powers of lichen, and scrape what I can find from the rocks. Is it the right kind? I have no idea. It stings like a bastard when I pack it into the putrid gash, which I hope is a good sign, but the next day I can see no improvement.

Tonight, after tearing another strip of cloth to replace the stinking, pus-soaked rag I've been using until now, I settle down to try and sleep. For once, the wind has eased. It feels warm on the mountain top. There is still no end in sight to the plateau. I have maybe two days' food remaining, but I'm filled with a weird contented feeling. It's already too late to turn back. I am committed. Whatever lies in store is ahead of me, not behind.

In my dreams I am visited by several apparitions. Lautan stands in front of me, water spouting from his hands to quench my incredible thirst. The old Blood King comes by to show me a copy of myself he has made from ichor. A perfect mannequin unaffected by cold, wind, or bird strike. Why am I not fit and healthy like that, he demands? What kind of explorer do I think I am, shivering and cringing on the mountain? He gives me a look of utter contempt, tells me he will never send me on a quest again, and disappears on a fresh wind that has sprung up in the middle of the night. I am still warm, despite that new breeze. I cast around, searching for the source of the heat and suddenly Elaine is here, with fire shooting from her outstretched arms and blazing redly behind her eyes. She seems to be mad at me too, but doesn't speak. And then her fire is in me and I can't breathe. Can't think.

Dawn breaks and I stagger to my feet. The whole plateau spins around me, threatening to throw me from an edge that doesn't exist. I turn away from it and stumble on, not certain which direction I'm taking, not caring. With my throbbing arm held to my chest and my torn shirt flapping in the relentless wind I lurch from one rocky hillock to the next, almost turning my ankle several times. The sound of skittering stones from beneath my flailing feet makes me look down. I can see snow, under the rock, hundreds of metres below me. I shake my head, thinking it to be another illusion, but before I can take a second look there is a thunderous crack. The rock floor of the plateau crumbles underneath me, pitching me to the snow bank I glimpsed only seconds before.

I wake to a blizzard of pain and snow. How long I have lain here, I have no idea. I hardly dare move for fear I will tear some vital part of my insides on a shard of bone and bleed to death, whimpering, in this forsaken place. Tentatively, I stretch my limbs. First one leg, then the other. Apart from the biting cold they seem to be working properly. I sit up, feeling my ribs and my neck, rolling my shoulders. Amazingly, nothing has been broken. The snow provided a soft landing. I look up, thinking there might be more rock to fall, but the top of the valley looks stable for the moment. In front of me the snow bank shelves away, hiding its end from my view. I struggle to my feet, retrieve my staff from where it has arrowed into the powder behind my head, and set off in a whirlwind of white.

I may not have fractured any bones, but my legs have been badly bruised by the fall. I must have turned my ankle too, finally. Soon after starting off it begins competing with my arm for the Pain Championship. I'm limping. Leaning on my staff with my one good arm, I now have only one good leg to go with it. And no food. My pack was torn from me in the fall and ended up who knows where. Most likely buried in the snowdrifts, I have no energy to waste searching for it. I can't tell how long I spent in my delirium on the mountain top, or how much time has passed while I was unconscious. According to my staff this is the tenth day since leaving the caldera, but it could easily be the eleventh or twelfth. The valley I've fetched up in acts like a funnel for the wind. I can hardly stand upright in it. The deep snow whips into impenetrable flurries and eddies that sting my face and eyes until I can't see where I'm going. Can't make out the walls of rock I know must be on either side of me. My good foot catches a large stone and I twist into the fall to avoid landing on my injured arm. Snow blows into my mouth, so fast it has no time to melt before there is more, choking me, making my teeth ache. The pain recedes. The noise of the wind subsides. As

I lay here in the deep drifts of white, the world turns black.

Chapter 7

The village of Duska Batsirang provided exactly the kind of life Piers Tremaine had sought when he first signed up to the colonisation program. One almost totally free of the fears that dogged him back on Earth, which had driven him to move away from his hometown at the earliest opportunity. His nearest university, Sheffield, offered a respected architecture course, but for Piers that was not far enough. Instead he chose Bath. It was the best in the country, so an easy sell to his parents. He never spoke of the real reason for his choice.

Working on the roof of a small dwelling place gave him a fine view of his adopted home. The resemblance between Duska Batsirang and the village where he grew up was striking. Despite running away for most of his life, he had found somewhere that looked so similar to where he had started, he may as well have come full circle.

During those early weeks in his chosen home, he had finally begun to put his fears behind him. To feel free. Almost. In the nine years since Intrepid's arrival, Piers remained the only Earther to move here. Its remoteness made it unattractive to most, but naturally that was one of the things he loved about it. The villagers were wary of him in the beginning, but polite enough. He soon discovered his skill as a stonemason was highly prized. Away from the centres of Istanian civilisation, masons were rare. Before long he came up with a revolutionary design for the traditional stone huts common in many of the local villages. Once the locals saw how the new homes could transform their lives, Piers had trouble keeping up with demand. The work kept him permanently occupied and provided a comfortable standard of living.

'Morning Piers,' said a voice from below.

He slid over to the edge of the roof. Pondok Pemmunak, the prospective owner of the hut he was working on, stood in the dusty roadway, smiling. 'Early start for you, eh? How's it going? Can I move in yet?'

Piers laughed. 'Be another day or so until these tiles are finished. This time of year the inside will take a while to dry before I can fit it out. It'll be next year now, best I can do.'

The man grinned broadly. 'I'm only messing with you. We all know how fast you work. No one faster. It's almost like magic the way they shoot up.'

'It only seems that way Pon. That's why I start early. By the time everyone else is awake it looks like the hut has sprouted overnight.'

Pemmunak walked off towards the main street laughing. The rest of the village was waking now, the street beginning to bustle with early morning activities. The smell of freshly baked tepsak drifted over on a light breeze, reminding Piers that he had not eaten. Similar in many ways to the bread back home, the Berikatanyan version was also unmistakably of this world. It had a blue tinge, for one thing, and the native grain gave it a faint but distinct flavour of mace. Tepsak was a mundane example of the parallels between Piers' new world and his old one. And in the same way that his old world held terrors, the new soon proved to have a terror in store for him too. Something worse. A twist of fate especially cruel because it was so close to his heart. To his reason for living. The villagers still talked of the time he'd become stuck in the stone he worked with. Many of them found it hard to believe it had happened the way it was told. They insisted his hand must simply have slipped into a crevice and jammed. Those who had seen it for themselves knew Piers' fingers sunk into the stone itself like a tepsak-maker kneading his dough.

They saw it, but they could not explain it. And neither could Piers. The woman from the landing site had come to help. She rambled on about Earthers with "powers" while carefully chipping the rock away, striking orange sparks from the stone. Later, Piers went over the events of the day in his mind. He discovered if he concentrated, he could repeat the feat in the privacy of his own hut. He had not slept that night. Being different had tormented his entire life. He had escaped his tormentors to the furthest point man had yet travelled. And here, on this new planet, he had uncovered a new anguish. A new way to be "other." Something stranger and more powerful than anything he had ever conceived. Something he must keep hidden if he was to have any chance of a normal life.

duske pelapan
6th day of run'sanamasa, 966

Patrick sat alone in his father's house. He still could not think of it as *his* house, but it was. After sixty-six days, the place was unrecognisable from the damp, smelly ruin of his first visit. Days full of hard work, good humoured bartering with local tradespeople and artisans, painful but minor injuries, and a great deal of teasing—respectful, but still with a keen edge. These relationships, forged in the cauldron of common purpose, were strong and real. He would always have friends and a home here. A home now secure against the elements: warm, dry, and perhaps, he reflected, just beginning to feel like his.

Penka's initial estimate of the work required had indeed been optimistic. Even so they completed the construction and refurbished the interior before the second month of Sanamasa was half over. For the last month or so the locals had left him alone. Work done, thanks given and meals shared, his new friends returned to their own jobs and lives. Apart from the occasional visit from Penka, Patrick had only his thoughts for company. Naturally, those thoughts turned to the book. His father's lore record lay open in front of him, its intricately tooled cover resting against the polished blackwood of a new table that dominated the centre of the living space. Patrick stared past it, at the unquiet ocean below the house. The winds of winter whipped the waves into whitecaps, surging and breaking on the rocks in a never-ending tale of destruction. Their work was slow, but inexorable. Destructive power had been much on Patrick's mind of late, as the secrets of Juggler lore revealed themselves. The untitled tome was densely populated with symbols, accompanied by very little text. It required great mental effort to decipher the meanings and, once the symbols were understood, to connect them in the correct sequence. He discovered there were many sequences, some more obvious than others, each granting access to one of the Powers of the Patterns. The more he learned, the more terrified he became. A haunted expression never left his face. Through the many days of learning, the dark circles under his eyes grew larger, darker, and more pronounced.

'Are you sure you're alright?' Penka had asked on his most recent visit. 'You're beginning to look quite ill.'

'I'm fine, honestly. Not sleeping much, but apart from that...'

'Are you eating enough? Istri worries. Come for dinner.'

'Thank you, but no. Really, I'm fine. Look.' He opened his well stocked larder. 'You can tell Istri I have provisions enough. I never did eat very much.'

Penka looked unconvinced but did not press the point. He made a dignified, diplomatic withdrawal, for which Patrick was grateful. It was hard enough to grasp the potential of his power without having to explain it to anyone else. Even someone as open and honest as Penka.

The possibilities Patrick had unlocked were not exclusively destructive. In common with much prodigious power, whether gained through status and influence, mastery of a skill, or more fantastical powers such as those of the Juggler, they could be used for good. But a tiny misstep could be massively detrimental. And, what disturbed him the most, the ever-present law of unintended consequence. He may act from the purest of motives and yet deliver something of untold terror.

These were not random thoughts. He had tested some of the simpler patterns in the early days of his learning. The inherent beauty of the pattern, and the unworldly artistry of its result had encouraged him, but the effort drained him. Not only was this lore powerful, it required power. Extreme concentration and focus. After his first experiment he slept for almost a day. Once he had renewed his energies the inspiration of that initial attempt drove him on. Those later tests had frightened him. Each more wide-reaching in its effects and each asking more of its instigator. The dark circles deepened under his eyes as his knowledge and power grew.

And now here he sat, having learned every pattern in the book. In terms of understanding, if not yet of ability, he was his father's equal. Naturally, he had no way of knowing how his predecessor had used the power. Nothing beyond the third-hand accounts of the vortex that had cast him, along with Jann, Elaine, Petani, and Claire's parents, through the void to Earth. Separating them in space and time, and wiping their memories of life on Berikatanya. What his father's exploits may have been before that event, Patrick could not conceive. It was fortunate that traversing the void had such a profound effect on a person's memory. Once on Earth, Juggler powers would have been stripped from him. After his brief taste of them, Patrick could imagine the pain of their loss. A lifetime of learning and power swept away in a moment. Fetching up in an unknown place with no recollection of what had gone before was bad enough. Remembering that you had once been one of the most powerful men on your home world and were now nothing more than normal would be devastating.

What his father had done with the power of the Pattern Juggler was one thing. What Patrick would do with it, quite another. The question occupied his every waking moment. His gut reaction was to walk away. Return the book to its obscure hiding place, take himself back to the Palace, and never think of it again. The only sensible part of that sequence was returning to the Palace. Perhaps he could gain some insight there—from Claire at least and maybe even from the Queen herself—into a forward path. The political situation in Kertonia meant Juggler powers could be called on at any time. May indeed be critical to a positive outcome. He needed to be ready, both in his use of his abilities and in his attitude to them. If he was not comfortable with it, the danger would be multiplied manyfold.

The sound of rain on the roof interrupted his thoughts of preparations for the journey. He opened the door. Outside a gentle drizzle fell, its thin grey curtain blurring the ocean waves in the distance. The sun shone through the mist, casting a hint of a rainbow in the air. It was still mid-morning. It never rained on Berikatanya in the day.

valley of lembaca ana
6th day of run'sanamasa, 966

Petani had to admit the first few meetings of the Earther Guild had gone well. The small group working at the Landing Project had made significant progress. Unfortunately, when his procrastination was thwarted in one regard, it inevitably found another outlet. Since the day of that first meeting he had done nothing to inform the Queen of their current stumbling block. Neither had he made the trip to the Palace—less than a day's ride away at a decent canter—to follow up with Elaine on his idea for the pontoons.

The noonday sun had disappeared behind some unusually heavy cloud as he ambled back to their camp for lunch, stopping for a moment to check the Istanian troop deployment on the opposite hillside. Another contingent had arrived during the morning, pitching their ahmeks alongside the rest of the forces. The encampment, which had been growing since before the beginning of Sanamasa, was by now quite sizeable. They had made no move against him or his men, but there could be no doubt of their intent. The only thing holding them back was his own lack of progress. The Landing remained unusable. There was, as yet, no prize. As he crested a hillock at the midpoint between the Landing site and his base, he spotted a smaller but significant Kertonian force setting up on the embankment opposite the Istanians. The banner of the Black Queen flew over their camp, which was arranged in a defensive formation at the entrance to the Valley. He changed direction, intending to speak with the Queen before eating.

'Petani. Well met,' she called as he approached. Her watch Commander, Pena-gliman Lendan, glowered at him but said nothing.

'Your Majesty,' he replied, with a small bow. 'I would have sent word earlier, but–'

'No matter.' The Queen indicated that he should sit beside them. 'I am kept well enough informed. Of both these troop movements and your lack of progress,' she added, raising an eyebrow.

'Ah yes. Well. It is that I must speak of. Is Bakara here with you?'

'The Fire Witch is needed at the Palace, apparently. And not required here, since—as she has been at pains to point out—no Elemental will take part in any military action unless you all do.'

'A blatant disregard of duty, in my opinion,' Lendan said, not taking his eyes off Petani. 'Nothing short of treason really. No one has seen so much as a glimpse of the Water Wizard since the end of Bakamasa!'

'Why do you ask?' said the Queen, ignoring the Pena-gliman's comments.

'I believe she will be instrumental in my solution to the

problem with the Landing project.'

'So, you have a solution?'

'The idea of one only, as yet. I cannot confirm its viability until Bakara and I have explored the principle.'

'Then you better make haste to the Palace.' She inclined her head towards him with a soft smile. 'Although as it turns out your delay has worked in our favour.'

'Pure luck!' the Pena-gliman said. 'We would have been caught sleeping had the Landing been completed on time. It would already be in the hands of the Reds. Have a care, Petani, lest your own loyalty is called into question.'

Not normally quick to anger, he found this Pena-gliman's negativity intensely depressing. Like an arid patch of ground in which nothing beautiful or nourishing could be grown. He gazed at the darkening sky, allowing his emotions to subside. A large drop of rain hit his cheek. The Queen leapt to her feet.

'What is this?' she said, covering herself with an ebony wrap. 'Rain? In the middle of the day?'

Several more drops followed the first in quick succession. Within moments the shower had become a heavy downpour. The three sought shelter under the Queen's ra-mek. On the other side of the Valley the Istanian forces could be seen scrambling for cover. Nearby, the Queen's troops too were hurrying to their ahmeks and bivouacs.

'The malamajan is an Elemental construct,' Lendan said, swiping a drop of water from his brow. 'Is this Lautan's doing also? If so, he is undoubtedly a traitor! We cannot defend ourselves in this deluge!'

'Neither can our opponents attack,' Petani said, pointing across the Valley. 'Did you not see them taking shelter also? Lautan may be behind this unexpected rain, or he may not, but either way it has the same effect on both sides. It is hardly a weapon of war.'

He stared out from between the embroidered flaps of the ra-mek. Daytime showers were nothing strange to him after his years on Earth, but they had been unheard of on Berikatanya for centuries owing to the ubiquitous charm known as the malamajan. His thoughts turned to the Forest Clearance Project. Much of its planting had been designed with the expected weather patterns in mind. How else, since they were always predictable? A prolonged heavy rainstorm could have immediate and devastating effects there. His friends would soon have a far more pressing need of his help.

duska batsirang
6th day of run'sanamasa, 966

The only illumination inside Piers Tremaine's dwelling place came from the work in front of him. He soon learned that his power would attract attention and had, just as quickly, run out of explanations for the eerie orange light glowing from his windows. It was early afternoon, but day or night the urge to learn more was always with him. Now, his home curtained with old shirts and breeches, he worked undisturbed. No hint of what occurred inside was visible from without.

During the day he should be hard at work on one of his huts, but his latest project remained unfinished. A rare appearance by a travelling stonemason had caused trouble with the prospective owner, Nyaka Baleman. Local people were happy to benefit from Piers' skill. They did not like to think too much about where it came from. Even so, the old incident with Piers' hand had never truly been forgotten. They simply chose to ignore it. It lay like a rock on a riverbed, hidden from view but still disturbing the flow of the water, revealed only during times of drought. Yesterday, the other tradesman had brought the drought. He called Piers' methods unnatural and demanded to know why his client would choose an Earther over a natural-born Istanian. Baleman, intimidated, had thrown Piers off the project. Of course the local artisan had no idea how to finish his work. It would stand half-built until the fuss died away or someone else asked Piers to complete it. His client decided the traveller should build him a new home somewhere else. Piers enjoyed some small, venal satisfaction from knowing it would take twice as long and be half as good as the one he could have had.

While memories of the previous day's confrontation distracted Piers from his task, the rock on which he worked cooled. It set into something bearing no resemblance to his concept. He concentrated anew on the misshapen artefact, reaching inside his mind for the place where his power slept, teasing it into wakefulness once again. The black rock began to glow.

Piers had no lore books to learn from. No mages to teach him. With his limited knowledge of this planet, he was unaware of anyone else with similar power, but he had neither travelled widely nor met with any who had. Locals' conversations often involved Earth, Air, Fire, and Water. No one ever mentioned Stone. His first use of this surprising power had come unbidden, the subject of embarrassing public record and a brief investigation by the Waters woman from Pennatanah. She could offer him no explanation, nor indeed any reassurance beyond the fact that similar things had happened to others from Earth. Piers had been terrified by the incident. His embarrassment, and early adverse reactions from locals, had led him to deny its existence at first, even to himself. Later, he felt a compulsion to discover whether he could make it happen again. Control it, even. Starting slowly at first, he gave in to that urge. Before long it became fascination. His first faltering attempts at fashioning stone objects were as crude as his boyhood sculptures. Little more than molten blobs similar to the shapeless mass sitting in front of him right now. Once his experiments gave him a measure of control, his fascination blossomed into joy. He had found a new means of expression for his lifetime love of stone. It gave him a sense of intense pride and satisfaction. He glanced around the inside of his hut. Nine years of honing his craft had filled it with objects of increasing complexity and beauty. To his eyes, anyway.

The fear never left him though. It rode the joy like a daredevil rider rides an exquisitely beautiful stallion, egging it on to greater feats of danger while the steed's eyes flash white and its mouth foams in terror. Acquired knowledge and skill gave Piers a correspondingly deeper understanding of the mayhem his power might bring. Fine control required immense strength of mind. The slightest slip in concentration could spell disaster. Here in the comfort and safety of his home, an interrupted flow of energy might only result in a malformed rock, slowly cooling on the floor in front of him. In less favourable surroundings, anything could happen.

Piers sighed. His work had solidified once again, after sinking a few millimetres into the stone floor of his hut. Another level of skill would now be required both to shape the stone and to extract it from its basalt shackles. He bent to the task once more. After a few moments, the rock sat proudly atop the floor, held in place by the force of his mind and glowing redly at the point of turning to a malleable lava. Piers struck out again with his thoughts, impelling the rock to the desired shape. Just as it started to reform, the sound of rain on his windows and roof disturbed his concentration. The incandescent stone fell to the floor once again as he moved to the window. He pulled back his rudimentary curtain. A thin but steady rain fell, driving the villagers to seek shelter. In his nine years on Berikatanya, Piers had never seen rain during the day.

forge, the black palace
6th day of run'sanamasa, 966

'Concentrate!' Elaine said, raising her voice over the roar of the furnace. 'This is not a game!'

A group of student fire mages, acolytes seeking

entrance to the Guild, stood in a circle around the furnace at the centre of the Palace forge. Engaged in the final test, Elaine could sense some of them were not giving the matter their full attention.

'And nor is it a joke!' she added, glaring at a pair who grinned at each other. The two flushed in unison and redoubled their efforts. Elaine felt the flow of Fire power increase. The flames glowed a brighter yellow.

One of her first tasks as leader of the Fire Guild had been to commission this new forge. The failure at the old Court forge with something as simple as the casting of a bell had been both an embarrassment and a contributing factor to the collapse of the vortex. As Fire Witch, Elaine took her duties seriously. Such a mistake had to be avoided in future. Now based at the Palace, she supervised the building of a better version, using the latest materials and design. She also moved it outside. Away from the confines of walls and ceiling the furnace could be brought to a more intense heat, allowing new alloys and previously unheard of substances to be developed. It provided a perfect testing ground for the young mages she wanted to attract to the Guild.

Her recruitment program had enjoyed remarkable success. Fire power was latent in many more youngsters than Elaine expected. The best of the first intake now stood around her, focusing their new-found powers on the crucible at the centre of the stone circle that edged the forge.

'That's better,' she said, walking the perimeter slowly, pausing at each student to check their contribution to the whole. 'Feel the power flowing. Free yourself from inhibition and doubt. There are no limits to your ability except those you impose.'

With her encouragement, the furnace grew white-hot, the air above the cauldron rippling and writhing.

'Good. Good! Now concentrate! When your powers reach their peak is the time when control is most difficult, yet most vital. Hold the pattern in your mind, work together. The fire will do your bidding, as long as your focus is true.'

As the final test for Guild admission, Elaine had conceived a complex forging. It depended on all twelve acolytes working in concert. There was no mould. They were not casting metal as had been done for the bell. This was fire forging, something only possible for fire mages, where physical control of the flow of heat was required to shape the artefact to the desired result. Simple configurations could be achieved alone. More complex ones demanded multiple mages operating as a coherent team. This attempt would take the combined efforts of all twelve students, at a level of fine control that only long practice and the highest ability could attain.

A breeze sprang up, blowing Elaine's fiery red hair into her eyes. The cool wind was a welcome emollient to the heat blazing from the forge, but could also be a distraction. Elaine unconsciously replaced the strand of hair and circled the group again, looking for any signs of wandering attention. The acolytes were unfazed. The metal in the crucible began to take on the desired shape under the influence of their united powers. The Fire Witch smiled, permitting herself the beginnings of a swell of pride in her students.

The top of the vessel hissed violently as a large drop of rain fell onto it, followed quickly by two more. The sound broke the concentration of the nearest student, who stepped back and glanced at Elaine for reassurance. She found none. The Fire Witch no longer watched her students. Instead she stared up in disbelief, her mouth open. What was this? Rain, during the day? Her decision to move the forge outdoors was driven by the longstanding certainty of the weather. Another drop landed on her tongue. Within moments a heavy downpour had begun. The flow of Fire power into the forge ceased. Several students ran for cover. Others tried to maintain their concentration and keep up the heat, but were soon drenched. Clouds of steam belched from the quenched furnace. The artefact twisted and buckled as it cooled, while the remaining mages ran to join their colleagues in the nearest building.

'What is *this?*' Elaine cried, frustration and anger boiling over into a bolt of pure incandescent white fire that flew up from her outstretched hands.

The students, huddled together under an awning, gasped as the stone floor of the forge melted to glass beneath the Fire Witch's feet.

pennatanah
8th day of run'sanamasa, 966

Felice Waters had never seen Pennatanah looking so drab. The rain that started in the middle of her ride back from the Palace had not stopped. Through the grey curtain of a gentle but persistent downpour, the small township appeared forlorn and deserted. None of its few inhabitants walked the streets. The noonday sun, imprisoned behind the steel-grey clouds, illuminated the scene with a pale, wet light. Felice dismounted outside the landing station and led her kudo to the shelter of his stable. She rubbed some feeling back into her legs, wincing at the soreness in her thighs.

It had taken her twice as long as usual to make the journey, her sodden breeches chafing against the saddle, rainwater running cold fingers down her neck and back. Roads and paths, which had for centuries only experienced brief overnight rains, turned quickly to mud beneath the watery onslaught. Her kudo had come close to losing his footing several times on the slippery surface. When a sudden deluge had forced Felice to seek refuge in a small copse, she too almost ended up on her arse. Her clothing was soaked and mud-spattered. She wore an overcoat against the cold of the season, but it was not waterproof.

Nothing on Berikatanya was. Generations of locals and three Prism ships full of Earthers had never experienced daytime rain. She needed a shower, a hot meal, and a change of clothes.

Her backpack, filled with phials of DNA samples from her trip, clinked as she set it on her desk. On the other side of the room a red light blinked on her comm panel. It took a moment for Felice to register its import. The message light. There was a message waiting. Dauntless! She hurried over to the terminal. The counter glowed "4". She played the first.

THIS IS PRISM SHIP DAUNTLESS CALLING PERSE LANDING POINT. DAUNTLESS TO PERSE. CREW PREPARING FOR PLANETFALL, WE ARE APPROXIMATELY SEVEN DAYS OUT. PLEASE CONFIRM READINESS FOR ARRIVAL. OVER.

Felice checked the log details. The message had been recorded almost a full day earlier. She cursed her luck. Eleven months of waiting for the final ship to arrive and it called when she was out! She clicked the terminal through to the second recording.

DAUNTLESS CALLING PERSE. DAUNTLESS TO PERSE. PLEASE RESPOND TO EARLIER MESSAGE. CREW PREPARATIONS COMPLETE, WE ARE NOW DECELERATING FOR EXPECTED PLANETFALL AT 16:30 ON 23RD FEBRUARY 2177 UNIVERSAL STANDARD TIME. PLEASE CONFIRM.

She snorted at the arrogance of the phrase Universal Standard Time, remembering a day long past when she would have been comfortable with the term. She opened her date conversion chart, unused since the arrival of the Valiant. Anyone less diligent would have simply counted forward seven days; the Waters' family always preferred to do things by the book. Dauntless would arrive on the 14th day of Run'Sanamasa. Six days from now. Their estimate had been spot on.

The other messages repeated the information from the first, with increasing unease. The captain would expect some delay in reply—local time would be a best guess on board the Prism ship and anyone on planet may be asleep—but when there was no response after twenty-four hours he would be understandably concerned. She fired up the comm link.

'Perse base at Pennatanah calling Dauntless. Perse to Dauntless. Messages received. Sincere apologies for delayed reply, the base was unmanned for a few days. We were not expecting you.'

There was a short pause while Felice listened to the crackle of static before the speaker burst into life.

PERSE! THANK GOD! WE WERE BEGINNING TO WORRY THERE WERE NO SURVIVORS FROM THE OTHER SHIPS! THIS IS CAPTAIN BOGDAN DMITRIEV. YES, SORRY WE'RE LATE. I CAN FILL YOU IN ON THE DETAILS ONCE WE'RE ON THE GROUND. WHO AM I SPEAKING TO?

'Good afternoon Captain Dmitriev. This is Felice Waters, acting... er... commander of the landing base here. You can stop worrying. All the other ships arrived safely. I was on the Intrepid. Been here almost ten years.'

PLEASED TO MAKE YOUR ACQUAINTANCE MS WATERS. THAT'S GREAT NEWS. HOW ARE WE SET FOR A LANDING?

'The mooring mast is in good shape Captain,' she replied. 'Normal landing can proceed as planned. Just like it says in the book.'

The captain laughed, his voice rendered robotic by the comm link.

GOOD TO HEAR. WE DO LIKE OUR BOOK. ANY UNUSUAL WEATHER WE NEED TO BE AWARE OF?

Felice glanced at the rain running down her window and chuckled. Nothing unusual as far as the crew and passengers of the Dauntless were concerned.

'A little rain is all. Probably will have cleared up by the time you get here,' she said. 'You should break out the raincoats though, just in case.'

GOOD ADVICE, PERSE. WILCO. WE'LL BE IN CONTACT
AGAIN ONCE WE BEGIN OUR FINAL APPROACH. DON'T GO
AWOL ON ME AGAIN, YOU HEAR?

Alone in the building, Felice nevertheless coloured up in embarrassment at the captain's words. Years of sticking to her checklist-driven routine and the one time she stepped away from her duties...

'No chance of that Captain! We'll be ready for you, don't you worry.'

OK PERSE. DAUNTLESS SIGNING OFF FOR NOW. OUT.

The comm link carrier died and Felice sat back in her chair. She had told the man they would be ready, but this would be a much simpler induction than any that had gone before. Unless the weather let up there was little chance she could arrange a representative from the Palace. Istania, still in turmoil without a King, would not send anyone, rain or not. It would be down to the few remaining Earthers at Pennatanah to explain the situation to the arrivees as best they could. Her own arrival on Perse and the discovery of its indigent population was a distant memory, but she could still remember the emotions of those first few days. A difficult time which had led to her decision to keep away from Berikatanyan culture as far as possible and stick with the relative certainty of life at the base, where she understood her purpose and had no master to answer to.

Her gaze fell on her backpack, lying discarded on her desk. She sighed. Her pet project would have to be put on hold for a while. She had other priorities now. The first of which, she remembered as she pulled her sodden trousers away from her skin, was a long hot shower.

Chapter 8

forest clearance project
9th day of run'sanamasa, 966

A journey that would normally take a day, two at most, had already cost them five. Petani sat beside a guttering campfire, his head in his hands. Tanaratana fed the reluctant blaze with the few bits of dry wood they had scavenged. Umtanesh emerged from the late evening gloom carrying another small armful.

'Is none to find,' he complained. 'Everywhere soaked.'

The rain, a constant feature of their journey so far, still had not let up. Squally at times, torrential at others, but mainly a fine soaking drizzle. It sought out every loose button or unsecured collar, and wicked its way through to the skin. He remembered with shivering melancholy the industrial-strength waterproofs he had worn on Earth when engaged in large landscaping projects. Those timescales mandated non-stop working in the face of any weather. It made no difference when you were dressed for it. Here, if waterproof clothing had ever existed it had long since passed from memory. The malamajan rendered it unnecessary. It was easier to avoid travel during the brief overnight rains. He shivered again.

'Put another log on, Um,' he said. 'If that fire gets any lower it won't even dry the wood out, let alone burn it!'

A shower of reluctant red sparks spiralled into the night air as Umtanesh's timber landed in the centre of the fire, extinguished almost as soon as they had taken flight by the relentless drizzle.

'How much longer to the Forest?' Tanaratana asked.

Their kudai could hardly achieve a walking pace on the saturated roads and pathways. The risk of slipping in the mud made them skittish. Worse, the animals' hooves often plunged deep into the wet sod. Fighting the ground sapped their strength. Half a day's travelling was as much as they could do before being rested.

'We'll make an early start tomorrow. If we keep to rockier areas, where it's easier for the kudai, I reckon we could be there by the end of the next day.'

'Another two days!' Umtanesh said, a look of utter dismay on his face. 'I never be dry again!'

'Once we reach the edge of the forest we may find some shelter under the trees,' Petani said.

'Or they just slow water down and dump it on us in one go!'

'Anything be better than this,' Tanaratana said, adjusting the spare shirt he had tied around his head and huddling closer to the meagre fire. He stared into the flames. 'Even Nembaka not can cook on this!'

Nembaka, the third Berikatanyan who worked with Petani in the Forest when he first arrived back on the planet, had remained behind at the coast. The only one capable of preparing a decent meal, they agreed it was unfair on the rest of the team to bring him along. Their lack of basic cooking skills and a series of paltry fires made the meals on this trip less than inspiring. Berries and other fruits, supplemented by the limited supply of tepsak they had brought with them. They had a small sack of oatmeal too, but the fire was not hot enough even to make a simple porridge.

'Go to bed on empty stomach again,' Umtanesh said, poking the fire, 'and same tomorrow. Hope Forest crew have wood saved for a decent cooked meal.'

He lay on the damp ground as close as possible to the smoking fire and pulled his sodden coat up around his head. Petani remained where he sat, chewing on the heel of their loaf and dreading what their arrival in the Forest would reveal.

*

His estimate of their remaining journey time proved pessimistic. It was mid-afternoon of the second day when they rode into camp. Their approach revealed few signs of damage. The majority of the Forest Clearance Project work had taken place behind the settlement. The fall of the land hid the clearing, riverbanks, and terraced crop beds from view. They were also obscured by the large ahmeks of the campsite. In Petani's absence a few wooden huts had sprung up, testament to the semi-permanent nature of their successful project. A narrow rivulet of muddy-brown water crossed the forest path in front of them. It flowed swiftly and had already eaten away the edges of the roadway. Petani's kudo snorted. It took some coaxing before the animal could be persuaded to cross the new stream.

At this time of day he expected to find the camp deserted. Working the plantations and extending the forest clearance further north and east was still a full-time job. Project members worked long days. The sound of their kudai whinnying at the abnormally soft earth brought faces to the ahmek flaps and hut doors. The rains had kept the entire squad from their work. David Garcia, still the incumbent camp manager, stepped out into the rain from the nearest building to greet them.

'Hey, Petani! Welcome back! We could sure use your help. Stable your mounts and come inside out of this damned unnatural rain. You'll soon get dry beside our fire.'

Umtanesh cracked a beaming smile.

'Fire!' he said. 'At last!'

duska batsirang
10th day of run'sanamasa, 966

The familiar sound of stonemasons' hammers against rock made Piers Tremaine smile. The rain had not let up since it first rattled his roof four days before, but that apart, all was once again well in his world.

It took almost two days for Baleman to learn that the bullish stonemason, who had lost him the job in the first place, did not have the brains to create new plans. The man even struggled to select a suitable alternative building plot. Baleman ordered him to return to the original site and finish what Piers had started. Another two days passed without progress. The boor had finally admitted he had no idea how to decipher Piers' plans. He sent one of his journeymen to solicit Piers' help.

'Martuk says there'll be no more trouble' said the lad, wiping the rain out of his eyes. 'He's sorry he bad-mouthed you an' he's made it right with the owner. We needs you to come on back and tell us how to finish. What with your strange design and this rain making us slip and slide all over the place, we ain't hardly laid a single stone since we took over.'

Should he tell the boy he could happily finish the build on his own? It was likely the nuance of his argument would be lost. It was not the young apprentice's fault in any case. The blame lay with his employer. In seeking help from Piers the man had effectively lost any argument before it began. There was nothing to be gained from pursuing the matter. And so, on the morning of the fifth day, here he was. Sitting at the top of a wall swinging his hammer, chipping the final few shards from a dressed stone to fit into the top course. Trying not to slip from his perch in the continuing downpour. Even though soaked to the skin, the physical effort kept him warm, and the haft of his hammer felt good in his hand again. Each of the other four with whom he worked—the "head" mason and his three trainees—hammered away at their various tasks, the different rhythms of their blows separating and merging in turn as the work progressed. A masonic symphony in percussion, with the rain providing a surreal accompanying melody as it bounced and dripped off stone and leaf.

There was little in the way of conversation. The local mason Martuk still did not trust Piers. His need outweighed his animosity, but that did not mean he intended to engage in idle chatter. His apprentices were callow youths, not given to debate. It was hard enough for them to understand the simple instructions their master barked out, without expecting them to talk to strangers. When they broke for a midday meal, the others made the short walk to the nearest alehouse, leaving Piers to munch through his plain lunch alone. He sheltered in the small section of the new hut which had been roofed and found a plank on which to sit and watch the rain dripping from the trees behind the hut while he ate. The smell of the wet vegetation and the sounds from the small wood at the edge of the village reminded him of boyhood days spent avoiding the playground bullies who plagued him even outside of school.

He had barely swallowed a single mouthful before a shout from the street outside disturbed his lonely vigil.

'This your doing, Tremaine?'

Piers walked to the front of the building and peered out through the unfinished doorway. A small group of townspeople, some of them previous employers of his, stood in the pouring rain. With a shock, he saw one of them held the sculpture he had worked on last night.

'This unnatural weather? You have a hand in it?'

'What?' he replied, unable to comprehend what the man was saying. 'No, I–'

'Seems a strange coincidence,' the villager continued. 'Never had rain in the day in my lifetime. Then we find this!'

He grabbed the arm of the woman who carried Piers' sculpture and pulled her to the front of the small group. She looked both terrified and defiant in equal measure, but brandished the work in support of the man's words. One of his most recent efforts, he had been experimenting with controlled flow of molten rock, trying to create a waterfall effect. Ironically the piece was his best work so far. With real rain running from it in rivulets it captured the essence of flowing water perfectly.

'No,' the man continued, pointing at the sculpture, anger and fear distorting his face. 'Never had rain. Not before you came. Not before you started making the very stone we stand on look like it's running like a river.'

'This is crazy,' Piers said, stepping out onto the street. He held up his hands in the rain. 'This has nothing to do with me. I work with stone, not water.'

'You make stone *look* like water!' the man replied, his eyes wide with suspicion. 'It's not natural! *You're* not natural. Stop this damn rain right now, you hear?'

The man moved towards Piers, the small crowd at his heels. The woman holding the sculpture held it in front of her as if to ward off Piers' influence.

'I haven't started it,' Piers said. 'How can I stop it?'

'We can destroy this abomination for a start!' the woman yelled, throwing the waterfall sculpture at Piers' head.

He ducked as the stone flew past, hitting the wall of the hut and cracking into three pieces. Some of the crowd looked up, as if they expected the rain to stop immediately, now that the evil talisman had been destroyed. When nothing changed, their anger redoubled. Several voices cried out at once.

'Stop it! Stop the rain!'

'We don't want you here!'

'Damned Earther!'

Piers caught a glimpse of the stonemasons at the back of the crowd. Disturbed by the commotion in the street they had stepped out of the alehouse along with several of the other patrons. A small smile played across Martuk's lips. Piers would get no help from them. He ran back into the building. There was no security in the half-finished structure either. The crowd followed after him, some clambering in through the unglazed windows. He jumped over a sawhorse at the rear and raced for the only safe place he had: his own hut.

Reaching his home with the mob close behind, he slammed the door, dropped the security bar, and pulled his heavy blackwood table over as an extra barricade. Seconds later the villagers hammered on the wood, shouting and screaming for him to come out, stop the rain, leave the village. Several strong kicks rattled the door in its frame, but Piers' security measures held. The shouting continued for some time until he heard a new voice call out.

'Move aside! No door can stand against this!'

Piers braced himself against the far end of his table, sweat running down his face. He had never seen the villagers so angry. They were beyond reason. A chill ran down his spine as an axe struck his door. The wood splintered as the blade was pulled free. When the second stroke fell, its shiny metal edge cut through.

forest clearance project
12th day of run'sanamasa, 966

Not even a full day had passed since Petani's arrival back at the Forest Clearance Project. He was already exhausted. When they had stabled their kudai the day before, little of the day remained. Garcia insisted the three men should rest after their arduous journey. Petani ignored his pleas. He set out immediately to assess the damage and perform what emergency repairs he could in the failing light.

'You worry about the dumwheat,' Umtanesh said.

It was not a question. His friend was well aware of the days of effort Petani had invested in his experimental cereal crop. An inspired cross between Earther wheat and the local grain Berikatanyans used to make tepsak. He expected, or at least hoped, the seed would inherit the best of both worlds. Faster to grow, more resistant to native pests and moulds, and with luck, its own distinctive flavour. The dumwheat plot was the first area they came to. The rains had flattened the stalks to the wet ground. Not a single ear stood. The men set to, trying to recover what little they could of the broken crop.

The damage was much, the effect of their work little,

yet inspired by Petani's leadership the slender Berikatanyans had worked by his side without complaint. It wasn't long before they could hardly see the ground they worked on.

'We must stop now, Petani,' Umtanesh had said, resting a restraining hand on his arm. 'We can do no more tonight.'

'He is right Petani,' Tanaratana agreed. 'So little light, we be doing more damage than we mending.'

Petani did not believe it. His sense of the Earth guided him. They were not making matters worse. But the rain that had dogged their journey constantly, kept up a similar unceasing counterattack to their repairs. They needed an alternative strategy and Petani's tired mind could not conjure one.

He pitched his shovel into the earth in frustration. 'Very well. Let us take some rest and a meal. But we must make an early start tomorrow.'

Even with a belly full of hot kinchu soup mopped up with a delicious crusty tepsak made, ironically, from dumwheat harvested before the rains came, Petani had not slept well. His mind remained awhirl with thoughts of the forest, while his ears were assailed by the constant drumming of rain against the timber roof of the hut.

He was used to hearing rain during the night, of course, but this was different. The measured rainfall of the malamajan fell gently, and for only a short time each night. Designed by ancient Water Wizards to keep lakes, streams, and rivers topped up and provide sufficient moisture for the greenery to thrive, while allowing the populace to move around during the day unencumbered by inclement weather, it never saturated the ground. The first time he sank his hands into Berikatanyan loam he had been amazed at its condition. Dry enough to run freely through his fingers but still holding enough water to support growth. In all his time on the Project he never found an area of drought, or one of bog. The idea of a bog confused his companions.

'What use is wet ground?' Umtanesh asked once Petani described the bog gardens he had created back on Earth. 'Plants not grow properly with damp feet!'

'And if they need more water,' Tanaratana added, 'they grow at side of river, or on shore of lake.'

As a result of this Elemental control, in place for centuries, the landscape had adjusted. There were no complicated sets of run-off channels. If they had ever existed they had long since been overgrown, or filled in through earth movements or the actions of burrowing animals. Running water was found only in streams and rivers, which were adequate to handle the sedate percolations of the nightly rains. Similarly there were no areas of hard pan. No compacted, dried soil. Where there was soil, it was damp and permeable. Where there was not soil, there was rock, or gravel.

But this new, persistent rain was unlike anything he had seen. Unlike anything any living Berikatanyan—be they Kertonian or Istanian—had known. It beat down heavily, eroding the loam to expose bedrock beneath. It coalesced into fast-flowing streamlets that did further damage to the plantations, stripping roots bare of soil and even carrying the plants away.

Tanaratana and Umtanesh had slept as fitfully as Petani, and responded quickly when he could lie abed no longer. They made an early start. The leaden sky held the merest hint of morning when the three men left the warmth of their hut and set off back to the farthest point of the clearing, where they had abandoned their tools the night before. While the planting in this part of the Project was protected on one side by what remained of the forest, on all other sides it was the most exposed of any in the whole clearing. They toiled with renewed vigour, but gradually the exhausting work, the constant rain, and the chill of labouring in sodden clothing took their toll. When Petani finally acknowledged how tired he was, they had been working more than half the day without a break.

'Guys, stop,' he said. He pointed at the edge of the forest. 'Some shelter there. Let's take a breather.'

His workmates would have continued until they dropped if he asked them, but their faces told the story of their fatigue. They crossed the muddy ground, boots sinking ankle-deep and slurping and farting with every step. A strange bird flapped towards them. It struggled to stay aloft in the rain. Beset by peculiar air currents it was blown alternately up and sideways, its flight crabbed and awkward. When it came closer, he could see it was not a bird. It was a piece of parchment.

The sheet fell at his feet, twitched once, and lay still. He bent to pick it up. The ink had become spidery and smudged in the rain but the message was still legible. Signed by the Fire Witch, it read:

RAIN DAMAGE BECOMING SEVERE ACROSS ALL OF KERTONIA. ELEMENTAL CONCLAVE IS CALLED AT PALACE, AFTERNOON OF 14TH RUN. PLEASE ATTEND URGENTLY. ALL OTHER PROJECTS SECONDARY.

He swore under his breath.

'What is it Petani? What does the flying message say?' asked Tanaratana.

He shook droplets of water from the parchment. 'I've been called to the Palace.' He had not recovered his strength after the journey from the Valley. Now here was another demand. The Palace was a day and a half's ride, and the meeting was to take place in two days' time. 'You guys will have to do the best you can here.' He stared through the dripping treeline across the saturated clearing. 'I have to leave right away.'

the black palace & surroundings
13th day of run'sanamasa, 966

'See what I mean?'

Petani stood in the open-air Palace forge, staring at the

stone-flagged floor. The rain had abated to a fine drizzle which beaded on his hair and clothes. The tiny beads caught and reflected the crimson rays of the late evening sun giving him a coat of rubies and a crown of fire. Elaine pointed at a discoloured patch on the surface of the flagstones about four metres in diameter. The rough circle had a glassy sheen that would ordinarily take decades of foot traffic to form.

'I've not seen anything like it,' the Fire Witch continued. 'It's not fragile, like glass. I've had the Palace builders try to smash it up with hammers and chisels. Nothing will scratch it.'

Petani bent to run his fingers over the smooth surface. 'What caused it?' The grain of the original stone had gone. There were no marks or blemishes in the fused area at all.

Elaine's face coloured to the roots of her deep red hair. 'I... lost my temper.' She shrugged. 'These damned rains could not have started at a worse time. Completely ruined the work we were doing.'

He held out a hand. 'Help me up. My knees are not used to spending so much time in the saddle.'

By taking the high path over the foothills of Tubelak'Dun, he had avoided the boggy areas and mudslides that had troubled his kudo Pembumi on the journey from the coast. The mountain roads were steep and littered with shale and pebbles but it was terrain Pembumi was used to. When it slid, it did so in familiar ways. They made better progress than expected. Only in the last few kilometres did they have to negotiate any ground that was affected by the rains. He did what he could with Earth power, finding solid footing where possible, and holding the saturated soil together where there was none, but even this was exhausting work. Both Petani and his kudo arrived at the Palace entirely spent. The animal's legs shook as the old Palace ostler led it away to the stables, muttering under his breath at his poor treatment of the beast. He had been looking forward to a hot bath and a meal. Before he could enjoy either the Fire Witch intercepted him, striding across the basilica. She had offered not even a moment to change out of his mud-spattered breeches.

'There is something I must show you,' she said without a word of greeting, hurrying past the Palace gates toward the outer ward. He followed, having neither the patience nor the energy for an argument.

'Well?' Elaine said, pulling Petani up off his aching knees. 'What do you make of it?'

'I haven't really had time to make anything of it,' he replied, his slow anger rising like lava from the depths of a volcano. 'Like you, I have not seen its like before. My first thought is that it might help with a problem of my own, if we can figure out how it happened and learn how to make it deliberately rather than by accident.'

'A problem of your own?' Elaine let go of his hand. He staggered backward, almost losing his balance on the smooth surface. 'Has it escaped your notice that there are problems everywhere?'

She spread her hands and looked upward.

'This unceasing downpour is affecting the whole country! Whatever problem you have out at the Queen's vanity project is not preventing people from living their lives. It is not killing them!'

Petani's temper erupted. 'No, Witch, it has not escaped my notice. It took me seven full days to journey through it before I could reach the Forest and I laboured there almost another two to repair the damage these rains are causing before I received your summons. Did I take time to rest before answering your call? I did not. I almost killed my kudo getting here by the driest route and I have not slept since the night before last. So no. What small fragment of my awareness remains to me has not yet forgotten the rain or its effects. If you believe we may find a way to help, all well and good, but no matter how much I wish I could aid you in your endeavours, at present I cannot. Not until I have had something to eat and as much of a decent night's sleep as I can muster.'

Elaine's face clouded with sudden concern. She took a step toward him and laid a hand on his arm.

'Forgive me, Petani, I had not realised how hard you have been pressed.'

For once he bridled at the use of his Elemental name. When they had first met they were simply Terry and Elaine. If she thought to get around him now with polite formalities she would be disappointed. But she did not give him chance to react. She turned, slipped her arm through his, and set off in the direction of the refectory.

'Come,' she said. 'Let me fix you that hot meal. I will make sure the stewards have banked up the fire in your quarters and your bed is warmed while we eat. We can talk more about this in the morning.'

Chapter 9

The two Elementals met again for breakfast early the following morning. Still embarrassed by her outburst of the previous day, Elaine called on Petani, eager to ensure he was sufficiently rested and renewed to work on the conundrum of the new material.

'I hope you slept?' she said as they walked arm in arm along the refectory corridor. 'A little?'

'I did, thank you,' Petani replied. 'A full stomach and a comfortable bed made sure of it. And I think the Palace helped too. I have always found this a most peaceful and uplifting place.'

The first rays of the morning sun, poking intermittently between heavy rainclouds, slanted in through the high refectory windows as they entered. It bounced off dust motes and painted vibrant highlights on the drapes and long, polished wooden tables. A hubbub of activity from servers and patrons filled the room, almost drowning the sound of rain on glass. The clicking of cutlery and clanging of pots from the kitchen beyond the servery punctuated the low buzz of conversations. Smells of toasted tepsak, smoked barawa fish, and fried sausage assailed her nostrils. One or two of the Palace regulars greeted her or stopped Petani to enquire on progress at the Landing. The old man was right, there was a friendliness about the Palace and its people. An obvious contrast with the cold and draughty Court of her early days as the Fire Witch.

They assembled their breakfasts and found a seat in a far corner of the dining area, away from the others. In the opposite corner, separated from them by the full width of the hall, a slim, grey-haired man sat facing the wall. With his back to the room, Elaine could not see his face.

'Is that Patrick?' she said.

171

'I think so,' Petani said, turning to look. 'Why? Doesn't look like he wants company.'

'I didn't know he was back. I couldn't get word to him or Lautan. Had no idea where they were.'

She munched on a mouthful of toast, watching Patrick Glass. 'You're right. He's brooding about something. Anyway, I have no time to spend worrying about him. We have more than enough to occupy us with this strange new substance.'

'How do you want to tackle it?' Petani asked. 'Tell me again how you made it. Don't leave anything out.'

'There's not much more to tell.' She recounted the events of the acolytes' test while they finished their meal. They collected rain hats, hastily designed and stitched on the Queen's instructions, from a large wicker basket inside the main door, and walked through the mild but persistent drizzle to the forge. The Palace was woefully ill-equipped to deal with such inclement weather. Normally only guardsmen on night watch ventured out during the rain. Their uniforms were proof enough against the gentle and short-lived malamajan.

A black cloud of ghantu birds sheltering in the nearby trees took off at their approach, screeching with indignation at being disturbed. Beyond the forge, to the west of the Palace, the level of water in the moat had risen more than a metre since the previous evening. In places it had breached the outer bank, submerging small patches of the fields.

'We have to find a way to control this flooding,' Elaine said. 'Surely we can come up with something? Working in concert, as we did at Lembaca Ana.'

'There are only two of us,' Petani reminded her, 'but perhaps Earth and Fire alone will be enough? At the Forest I tried to divert the flow with banks of earth, but the running waters overwhelmed my efforts. The banks collapsed faster than I could build them.'

Elaine continued to stare at the moat. Its waters had

sunk to a new level now the banks were holed; the overflow reduced to a slow trickle.

'I cannot boil the entire moat,' she said. 'Too much water. But see…' She pointed at the overflow. 'Over there? Where the bank is ruptured? I could dissipate a small flow such as that.'

Petani followed her gaze. She gave him time to think, knowing his mind moved at the speed of tectonic plates.

'If I could create small channels in other flood areas,' he said at length, 'Or perhaps drain water into small ponds. You could boil them off?'

'It's worth a try,' Elaine said. 'We can start over there.'

Adjacent to the forge, an intact area of the moat stood above a natural depression where the water could be trapped. The two Elementals made a start, Petani bringing his power to bear to move the Earth and form it into a channel. At first the water flowed too quickly, overrunning the shallow bowl until the old man focused on the outermost edges and raised them enough to capture the outflow. Elaine watched as the pond filled, accessing her power and feeling the Fire build. She released a controlled bolt into the heart of the water. It hit with a suppressed whoosh, blowing a rolling ball of steam and superheated water into the air and destroying the raised wall Petani had created.

'Sorry. I'll control it better next time. If you can build the edge up again I'll have another go.'

Her second attempt was more successful. The water began to boil away. After a few moments the ingress to the pond fell inwards under the power of the running water, sodden clumps of earth splashing into the stream. It began to flow faster than Elaine could handle. With a frustrated sigh she let her Fire die away.

'It is not your fault,' Petani said, rubbing a hand across his face. 'This is exactly what happened in the Forest. The unsupported earth is not resilient enough. There is much strength in running water.'

Elaine noticed where they stood. Rivulets of rainwater ran from the blasted surface of the flagstones. Its glossy sheen seemed to shed the rain like opposing poles of a magnet.

'The answer is here, Petani, as I first suspected. This material can easily withstand the water, if only we could make more of it.'

'But how could we shape it?' Petani asked, his brow furrowed in concentration. Rainwater dripped from the rim of his hat, which was rapidly becoming as saturated as his other clothes.

Elaine shivered. 'One thing at a time, old friend. Let us learn how to make it first, and then worry about shaping it.'

They spent the rest of the morning trying to combine their powers in a way that would form the glassy rock. All their efforts met with no success. Elaine struggled to control her temper as her Fire built and died, built and died, at each attempt. The original sample had been created when she had *lost* her temper, but the line between that unconstrained explosion of power, and a more controlled outburst, eluded her.

Petani was also finding it hard to supply enough raw Earth in the presence of the fierce heat. He dropped to his knees on the stone-flagged floor of the forge.

'It resists my attempts to summon it,' he said with a look of despair. 'It seems to cringe from the heat.'

'I can well understand that, young man,' a familiar voice boomed out from behind them.

The two Elementals turned as one at the words. Lautan appeared, walking from the direction of the river, water running from the hem of his long white cloak.

the black palace
14th day of run'sanamasa, 966

'Lautan!' Elaine cried, rushing over and embracing the

old Elemental in a bone-crushing hug. He was saturated, whether as a result of the incessant rain or his own natural state, she could not tell. Doubtless the Water Wizard had been travelling in his liquid form.

'Bakara,' he said, returning her embrace tentatively before stepping to one side. 'Petani. I hope you both fare well.'

'Well enough,' Petani replied. He glanced upward. 'All things considered.'

'Thank you for coming,' Elaine said. 'I wasn't sure you would hear my summons. We three, and Patrick, are the only ones here so far.'

'I heard it, Bakara, have no fear. When it is you calling, I would hear it were I a world away. As it happens I was making my return anyway. This disturbance in the Water Element greatly concerns me. It flies in the face of all my lore. Had you not called a meeting of the Elementals I would have done so myself.'

'So this is definitely Water then?' Petani asked. 'It's not a natural phenomenon?'

Lautan smiled. 'As far as the rains go, there has been nothing "natural" about them for a very long time. The malamajan, which my esteemed ancestors conjured many centuries ago, has constrained nature to prevent daytime rains for all of those years.'

'Shall we move inside?' Elaine suggested, her desire to continue with their work overtaken by her joy at seeing the old man again. 'I think we're done here for now, yes?'

'Done? Yes,' Petani agreed. 'Done in, too, if we can't find a solution.'

'What were you two doing, standing out in the rain?' Lautan asked as they made their way indoors.

Elaine brought him up to speed as they walked. His raiments dried as soon as they stepped inside, an effect of his magic no doubt. She applied a little heat to their clothes, which steamed gently as they walked, leaving a misty plume in their wake.

'Combinations are difficult to master,' the old Wizard said once she had completed her recap. 'Thus it has ever been. Ancient Water Wizards referred to them as Rampiri, though I have not heard anyone use the term for many years. Consider our respective powers, Bakara. Applying mine atop an expression of yours can vastly strengthen whatever material has been heated, yet too much of either will rend it asunder. The reverse can be even more powerful, and destructive without the proper control. In some cases, a bolt of steam can cause more damage than one of flame.'

The three Elementals passed the Queen's stateroom.

'I suppose we could meet in here,' Elaine said. 'We've been using it for the Eradewan. But I think we'll be more comfortable in my quarters. I'll arrange to have some lunch brought up, if you'll give me a moment.'

She left Petani to escort Lautan to her chambers while she ordered food. When she rejoined them, he had stoked the fire and fetched in extra chairs from one of the adjoining rooms. They were discussing the effects of the rains on the surrounding lands and, of course, the Gardener's pet project in the Forest.

'...so in the end I had to leave them to it and make my way back here,' Petani was saying. 'Is there nothing you can do, with all your powers, to stop this?'

Elaine watched Lautan's reaction. Unlike the others, he was not one to display emotion. She could not remember ever having seen him blush, and despite Water being his Element, he had never shed a tear—at least in her company. The troubled look that crossed his face at Petani's words was more expressive, and more poignant, than either of those reactions. She had always believed him to be the most powerful Elemental. Certainly he was the longest serving Water Wizard in living memory. Now he looked powerless and bereft.

'I cannot, Petani,' he said, his gaze never dropping from the Earth Elemental's eyes, 'though it shames me to admit it. I cannot even explain it, much less stop it. This disturbance is operating at the very heart of Water magic. It is beyond anything I have experienced in all my years, even as a young journeyman of Water lore.'

'The Queen was mightily annoyed when it began to rain in the Valley,' Petani went on, 'but at least it put a stop to any military activity there for the time being. She was convinced you must be the cause of the rain and that if you had started it then you could just as easily stop it.'

Lautan gave a hollow laugh, like the sound of a waterfall plunging into a deep mountain pool.

'She will be further irked then, to learn how ineffective I am in this regard. Nothing I have tried has had the slightest influence. I am at a loss. I believe the best we can do at present is alleviate the worst effects. Perhaps something will come along to shed light on the problem.'

'We must hope so,' Petani said. 'Such ideas as we have had up to now have come to nought. We are at an impasse.'

He continued rambling on about their earlier activities. Elaine could see Lautan was exhausted. His eyelids drooped and the skin of his face began to lose its tone. Soon after the Clone Rout he had told her that after living in water form, it took great effort of will to maintain the integrity of his human frame. She put a hand on Petani's arm and a finger to her lips.

'Why don't you rest for a while, Lautan?' she said. 'Petani and I will find the others and reconvene later once you have had a chance to recover your strength. This afternoon perhaps, or even this evening.'

The old Elemental gave a grateful smile. 'Thank you Bakara. That is most kind. I would welcome an intermission.'

'Very well. Stay here if you will. I shall make sure you are not disturbed.'

'We saw Patrick earlier,' she said as they closed the door on Lautan, who had already fallen asleep where he sat. 'Can you find him? Check his chambers first. I will find Claire. Meet back here at sunset. I'll have a buffet brought up, though the kitchen will not thank me for demanding room service twice in one day!'

elaine's chambers, the black palace
14th day of run'sanamasa, 966

The scene reminded Elaine of the small soirees she used to host in her trailer in those almost forgotten years she spent as a poi artiste. It seemed like a world away now. She suppressed a laugh—it was! A world, a hundred light years, and a lifetime. She was no longer that quick-tempered, wandering, lost woman, but she could still throw a good party.

Except this was not a celebration. The few who gathered in her chambers were not here to dance, or laugh, or make merry. They were some of this world's most powerful advocates and they were here to discuss how to tackle the worst disaster to befall their home in many decades.

The last to arrive, Patrick Glass, sat in one corner avoiding eye contact with anyone. He had filled a plate from the expansive spread Elaine ordered from the kitchens and found a chair as far away from the others as possible. He munched on a leg of dingas, ignoring everyone.

Lautan engaged in muted conversation with Petani. Claire Yamani sat opposite the fireplace in the middle of the room. In this august company she probably deserved to be addressed with her Elemental title as much as anyone, although having been born and brought up on Earth the girl was still a little uncomfortable with the mantle of Sakti Udara. A sparsely filled plate lay untouched on her lap while she gazed into the flames, lost in thought. Elaine knew the Air Mage could debate any subject with any audience and would defend her viewpoint vigorously and defiantly when necessary, but she also had almost limitless patience, as demonstrated by her research into Air lore, which had taken many months. For the moment, she seemed content to wait upon the others before discussions began. Now they were all here, that beginning could be put off no longer.

'I called you together,' Elaine said, pausing to allow Lautan and Petani to conclude their chat, 'to discuss what we can do about the problem we are all painfully aware of. These rains. But before we get into the detail I think it would be worth us each giving the others a brief description of our own personal experiences since last we met, so we're all working and thinking from the same starting point.'

'Experiences?' Claire said, setting down her plate. 'Of the rain, you mean?'

'The rain in particular, yes. But also perhaps a few words on what we've all been doing in the aftermath of our battle at Lembaca Ana.

'Patrick,' she went on, without pausing to give anyone else space to start. 'Would you like to kick off?'

He made a show of finishing his mouthful of dingas. His startled expression when Elaine first spoke his name gave way to one of resignation. He took a small sip of water and cleared his throat.

'Not much to tell, really,' he said, before launching into a short explanation of finding and rebuilding his family seat. When he finished the others waited, expecting more. Patrick stared at the floor. After a few moments he seemed to notice the silence.

'Oh, the rains,' he said, his cheeks reddening. 'They started after I finished my repairs, fortunately.' A small smile played over his lips. 'But they had made the road slippery by the time I set off for the Palace.'

'Indeed,' Petani said, taking the chair beside Claire, who smiled warmly at him. 'When I arrived here my poor kudo Pembumi was carrying almost his own body weight in mud.'

Elaine continued to watch Patrick while Petani spoke. He sat hunched, as if a huge burden pressed on his shoulders. His months at the coast had done nothing to restore his constitution, which had never recovered after his experiences at the Clone Rout. He looked more gaunt now than before he left.

'...kept to the rocky trails for the most part,' Petani was saying. 'Even so those sections of packed earth we had to negotiate, well, some of them had already been swept away altogether. Things will only get worse the longer this goes on.'

He paused to pour a glass of blue buwangah wine. 'As for my work since the last time we were all gathered here, it has been frustrating, to say the least. And for much the same reason—although in the case of the Landing project the water causing the problem sits in Telebi Ana bay rather than falling from the heavens.'

Lautan harrumphed. 'Well, I—'

'If I may,' Elaine interrupted him, 'can we leave Water to the end? It is likely to take up most of the rest of the day, and I'd like Sakti to give us her words first.'

She smiled encouragingly at Claire, who began her own tale.

At mention of the catacombs, a smile creased Patrick's face. 'How is the Keeper?'

'He's keeping well!' Claire grinned. 'When I told him about our meeting, he wanted to pass on his best wishes to everyone. I think we've all met him at one time or another?'

She cast a quizzical look in Lautan's direction.

'What? Oh... hum... yes, indeed Sakti. He and I have known each other for a great many years. Not in a professional capacity, I should add. Water lore is not given to recording on parchment, for, well, obvious reasons.'

In common with many of his fellow Water adepts, Lautan spent a lot of his time in his water form. None of them had ever been motivated to make a physical record of their knowledge.

'With the Keeper's help,' Claire continued, 'and my talented mages in the Air Guild, we've developed several Element-driven innovations, including the one Elaine used to send out the calling notice for this meeting—my Air mail idea.'

Claire smiled. Just the right side of smug, that smile was, Elaine decided. 'It did well to fly through the heaviest of the rains,' she said.

'Mine was still legible when it flew into my hand,' Petani added. 'Though another few moments and it would have been pulp.'

Claire looked flustered. 'Yes, well, at the time we didn't know it would need protection from the rains. We didn't send any trial messages at night.'

'Apart from its effects on your messages, Sakti,' Elaine prompted, 'do you have any other experiences to relate regarding the rains?'

'I was already here at the Palace when we sent the summons,' Claire replied, 'so I haven't experienced the worst of the weather.'

She stood to pour herself a glass of wine and moved closer to the fire. Elaine turned to Lautan.

'I think we have reached the point where we must discuss your experience of this phenomenon, old friend.'

The ancient Elemental seemed to settle deeper into his chair. Sweat stood out on his brow. Elaine half expected him to flow from the seat and soak into the rug. Belatedly, she wished she had not ordered her fire to be banked up so high. It burned now with a fierce yellow glow, flames licking up into the chimney, and gave off a low roar interspersed with sudden cracks whenever a pocket of sap burst from the wood in a jet of incandescence.

Despite her affinity to the flames she began to feel quite faint herself. Baka alone knew how Lautan must feel. She walked over to the door and opened it to let out some of the heat. Framed in the doorway, interrupted in the act of knocking, stood the heavily cloaked and hooded figure of a man. Rainwater dripped from the hem of his cloak, puddling on the floor beneath.

'Looks like quite a party,' he said, flinging back his hood. 'Sorry I'm late.'

Elaine staggered back into her room, her vertigo blossoming into a full-blown swoon. She felt colour rising in her cheeks and for a moment could not catch her breath. Jann Argent stepped through the door.

elaine's chambers, the black palace
14th day of run'sanamasa, 966

Jann entered Elaine's chambers. The heat from the roaring fire hit him like a velvet glove across the face. All conversation had stopped at the sound of his voice from the corridor. They were all here—Patrick, Terry, Claire. Even Lautan! Jann smiled broadly to see the old Elemental again. This already felt like the homecoming he had dreamed of so often since he saw them last.

'Jann!' Elaine said, one hand flying to her throat. 'Welcome back!'

As if a spell had been broken, everyone else stood up and started talking at once.

'You're soaked! Let me fetch a change of clothes for you!'

That was Claire. Ever practical.

'Gatekeeper! Well met indeed! Was your quest successful?'

'Hello young man! Would you like something to eat?'

Before he had chance to respond, Patrick leapt from his seat, strode across the room, and took Jann in a rib-crushing hug that almost stopped his breath.

'Such a long journey without your favourite travelling companion?' he muttered in Jann's ear. 'Don't ever do that to me again.'

Patrick stepped back, raised his voice. 'Good to see you buddy! Welcome home!'

Elaine took charge. She laid a gentle hand on his shoulder. 'For goodness sake let him at least dump this wet cloak and dry off a little!' She released the clasp of his cloak and helped him out of it. He felt warmth from a different direction suffusing his body. The Fire Witch was "drying him off a little" in her own unique way.

'Hello everyone,' he said, the broad smile instigated by the sight of Lautan not leaving his face. 'It's good to be back. Feels like I've been away forever. Yes, Terry, I would love something to eat. Whatever there is, I'll have some, and glad of it. My quest, dear Lautan, is a long and interesting story. But surely there are more pressing issues for a man of your knowledge and experience? What on Earth—or perhaps I should say "what on Berikatanya"– is going on with this damned rain?'

*

Claire returned with an outfit of clean clothes unearthed from his old quarters. Elaine insisted he change in her bedchamber, adjoining the sitting room. Once he had dreamt of visiting that room for a less prosaic purpose, albeit one that also involved disrobing. He never expected to enjoy the privacy of Elaine's bedroom so soon after his return. When he had half undressed, she threw a towel around the door so he could complete the drying process begun by her Elemental magic, flashing him a stomach-churning smile as she closed the door discreetly.

He had lost weight during his travels. His old clothes hung on his frame, but they were comfortable enough and they were *dry!* The first time for eight days he couldn't feel the touch of wet cloth against his skin.

When he emerged, Elaine had ordered the food supplies replenished, the fire restoked, the empty decanters refilled, and the cushions in every chair plumped. Her sitting room looked so warm and welcoming, and populated with dear friends, that Jann felt a sudden pricking behind his eyes. For the most part it had been a lonely five months and he was very glad to be back. Before he had chance to become maudlin, the barrage of questions and comments started up again.

'That's better! Back to your old self!'

'You've lost weight. It looks good on you, actually.'

'Indeed my friend! I should say the outdoor life suits you. You look a picture of rude health.'

'Ready for that bite now? There's a lot more choice than before!'

Elaine let go a loud tut.

'You're all incorrigible. Let him breathe! Sit down Jann. Let Petani bring you something, since he seems intent on getting you fed.'

'Thanks. Anything. It all looks delicious. So, Lautan, I really am interested in your take on this rain. I've never known anything like it. It hasn't let up for the last eight days.'

'Precisely what we were debating when you arrived, Gatekeeper,' the old Elemental replied. 'It is, as I have remarked already several times, unlike any manifestation of Water power I am familiar with.'

'So it is Water power, then?'

'Almost certainly. I feel a disturbance in the energy, though I can neither explain it nor determine its source. The only thing I can say with any certainty is, as we are all aware, it has disrupted the malamajan. Or perhaps corrupted would be a better word, since the power of the original spell is still here.'

'Is there anything we can do?'

'Forgive me, gentlemen,' Elaine interrupted. 'Jann, before you arrived we all shared a few words on what had been happening with us up to the time the rain started. Just so we had a common understanding on which to base our ideas. I think it would be a good idea if you could do the same.'

Jann laughed, almost choking on his first mouthful.

Claire handed him a glass of wine.

'I'm sorry,' he said, once he regained his composure. 'I don't mean to be rude, but what's happened to me since we were last together will take a lot more than a few words.'

'But we're all dying to know,' Claire said, leaning forward in her seat, her eyes bright with reflected firelight. 'What *has* happened to you?'

Jann glanced around the room. Everyone had taken a seat. Everyone had a full plate and a full glass. Everyone was watching him.

'Very well,' he said. 'If you're sure. It's a good thing we have plenty of food and drink. It's going to be a long night.'

Chapter 10

Felice Waters woke to the sound of beeping. The DNA analyser had completed its latest run. Designed for bulk analysis of field samples, Felice had set it to work on a hundred at once; its maximum capacity. Even so, the task proceeded slowly. Compared with a forensic analysis, which typically examined a maximum of twenty markers, it would be more accurate to say it operated at a glacial pace. The problem was, she didn't know what to look for. Or even if the hypothetical genes conferring Elemental powers existed at all. Her only remaining option meant running a complete sequence on each sample and scanning the output for similarities between those who exhibited any ability.

She had returned six days before, armed with swabs from Claire Yamani and the Fire Witch, Elaine Chandler. These gave her control samples for known Elementals against which to compare all the others. Looking for duplicates across the entire genome had been taking forever. She had to focus the search on a subset. The fifteen genes determining eye colour, for example, were not likely candidates for the expression of Elemental powers. If that supposition was wrong then there was not enough of her lifetime left to complete the work!

Halfway through loading a fresh batch of phials into the GenTech 10000 analyser, the comm link crackled into life.

DAUNTLESS CALLING PERSE. DAUNTLESS TO PERSE. COMMENCING ATMOSPHERE INJECTION IN FIFTEEN MINUTES. ESTIMATE PLANETFALL IN FIFTY-TWO MINUTES FROM MY MARK... MARK. PLEASE CONFIRM DOCKING READINESS AND WEATHER CONDITIONS.

Felice thumbed the microphone.

'Pennatanah Landing Base to Prism ship Dauntless. Message received. Docking tower operational and ready. Crew standing by. We have dense, low cloud and heavy rain. Wind around fifteen knots, gusting to forty-five. Temperature five degrees.'

SOUNDS CHARMING PERSE. HARDLY A TROPICAL PARADISE WE'VE COME TO, IS IT?

'Well we are in the middle of winter here, Captain.'

WILL DEPLOY RAIN GEAR FOR CREW. NOT SURE WE HAVE ANYTHING SUITABLE FOR THE PASSENGERS. SEE YOU IN AN HOUR PERSE. DAUNTLESS OUT.

Felice finished loading the analyser. Another hundred profiles would be waiting for her once she and her team had taken care of the ship.

Almost an hour later she stood in the pouring rain with a skeleton landing crew of five, awaiting Dauntless' arrival. In Earth terms it was approaching four-thirty in the afternoon, but the combination of thick cloud and the torrential downpour made the day as black as night. They would not see the Prism ship until it dropped below the cloud, which Felice guessed must be around three thousand metres. While she was calculating the duration of the descent from cloud base to mast, Dauntless punched through the iron-grey murk to the South and was immediately surrounded by a halo of super-ionised water as the gravnull field repelled the rains. The deep blue energy sparked and fluxed, the ship lurching alarmingly and dropping several hundred metres in a few seconds. Felice gasped. Surely there would not be a repeat of the disastrous previous arrival? Out in the bay the silver tip of the Valiant's hull winked in the drenching rain as the waves crashed against the glistening metal, a constant reminder of its catastrophic landing.

As she watched, the hull of the Dauntless turned black against the lowering clouds. Its nose dipped as the ship arrowed towards the ocean, rainwater cascading in torrents from its surface. Seconds later an orange glow suffused the shining alloy. Felice could scarcely believe her eyes. The Captain had engaged the Prism drive! Previously forbidden this close to a planet, she could only suppose the intervening years had offered Earth engineers the opportunity to improve Wormwood's early design. Or maybe whatever problem had beset the gravnull field left Dmitriev with no other option? There was no way to know. She could not contact the ship from out here after the rain fried the only working portable comm link they had. This planet had certainly taken its toll on their vaunted technology. The glinting hull of the submerged Valiant gave mute testimony to that.

'Time to get up there, Cabrera,' Felice shouted against the wind, gusting even stronger now. Since its repair, the landing stanchion needed manual control from a booth located in the middle of the structure. Cary Cabrera had volunteered for the climb and none of the rest of the team had disagreed.

'Take a haz-mat suit,' she added. 'We don't know if that Prism drive is safe, or if they're using it as a last resort.'

'On my way,' the young man replied. He climbed the tower without incident and swung the arm out over the bay.

Dauntless continued to descend at speed. Felice hoped this was a side-effect of the Prism drive, rather than an adverse effect of the weather. The humming and crackling of the pearlescent coral energy field intensified as the ship neared the docking mast, slowing as it angled down through the rain. Water ran from it, splashing into the sea, lost amid the crashing waves. The bright halo of ionisation stood out around the ship a full three metres. Felice felt her hair stand on end despite the rain, but as quickly as the sensation began, it ceased. A thick, jagged, luminescent bolt of lightning leapt from the hull of the Dauntless and struck the mooring mast above Cabrera's booth. The stanchion vaporised in a shower of sparks, but by then the bolt had earthed. The structure held firm, suffering no further damage. Felice's insistence on upping the spec of the build during the repairs had been vindicated. Cabrera reached out to wipe off the spatter of residue from the impromptu brazing which had covered the booth's window, and waved to show he was OK.

Swaying in the gusting wind, the Dauntless inched closer to the arm. Cabrera manoeuvred the docking clamps into position and secured the ship. The deep thrum of the Prism drive abated as the captain reduced power to a hover, ensuring the weight of the ship did not crush the mast. Felice let out the breath she had been holding.

The rest of her landing crew moved steps into place, one of them climbing to the platform to direct the passengers. Moments later the hatch cracked and disembarkation began. Neither wind nor rain gave the new colonists any respite. If anything the foul weather increased in intensity, as if the planet expressed its disapproval at the arrival of yet another batch of aliens. A stream of humanity hurried to leave the ship and find shelter in the arrivals hall. Felice's attention was drawn to a young couple, their black hair flying and whipping in the high wind. The only ones in the group not hurrying, they stood atop the steps engaged in what looked like a heated argument. The taller of the two gesticulated, pointing both at the sky and the ship, and spreading out his arms to take in the whole of the base. The rain had already soaked into their hair and the tops of their short tunics, which provided scant protection from the weather. The wind plucked at the sodden material, threatening to tear it from their backs. The shorter of the two held his coat closed with one hand while grabbing at the other's arm. The taller shrugged off the attempt, stomping down the steps which swayed alarmingly in time with his strides. The rains swept and swirled around the staircase, but as the taller moved away a small tornado of rainwater twisted, catching the shorter one full in the face. Even from this distance, Felice heard the one in front break into a loud peal of laughter.

pennatanah
23rd february 2177

An angry gust of wind flung a swirl of rain into Kyle Muir's face. She staggered backward, almost losing her balance on the swaying gantry. Her damned brother was already halfway down the steps, laughing. What a gentleman! Never even offered her a hand. She held her thin windcheater closer around her neck and started after him, grabbing on to the rail with her free hand. Not a very auspicious start to her new life! And more ammunition for Douglas, who had yet to mention anything he liked about the journey or the planet.

At the bottom of the steps a tall man in a badly worn high-vis jacket directed her to a prefabricated building close to where the ship hovered in the gloom, a faint orange light limning its hull. She could still make out the low frequency hum of the Prism field above the noise of the wind and rain. The buffeting gusts whipped cold salt spray over the sea wall. It tore through her thin leggings, chilling her to the bone. Within moments she was shivering. She caught up with Douglas near the end of the queue to enter the building.

'Do you mind? He's my brother,' she said, bypassing the last of the line to stand beside him.

'Lovely place you've brought me to,' he said.

'Could be worse,' she replied. 'We might have been on that one.'

She pointed into the bay, where the hull of a Prism ship stood out above the inky waters, shining faintly in the dull moonlight.

'Hmph! Even that would probably have been drier than this.'

A taller than average woman with the demeanour of someone in charge stood by the door with arms folded, watching the queue file through. Her stance enhanced the line of her biceps, flexing under a tight black t-shirt as she spoke. Her cropped black hair shone with raindrop jewels, which flew in an arc of glittering silver when she shook an unruly strand off her face.

'We won't begin unloading your belongings until tomorrow,' she was saying, 'but there's hot food in the next room and you can pick up a set of dry clothing and change in the toilets. It's a bit basic. The clothes are piled by size, choose the best fit you can find. You'll soon feel better with a hot meal inside you.'

'It's like a prison planet,' Douglas said, scowling. The lines of his frown had not left his face since they woke. 'Concrete buildings, prison blues to wear, a line-up for your chow. Could things get any worse?'

'Come on, give it a chance. You haven't even seen it in daylight yet.'

The athletically-built woman was still barking out instructions as the queue filed past her.

'You'll find a cotton swab and phial with the clothes. We need you to provide a DNA sample for a survey we're running. Just a simple mouth swab. I'm sure you've all seen it done, but if you're not sure just shout.'

Douglas barked a humourless laugh. 'Perfect! A DNA test too! We'll end up on some database just like real criminals.'

Kyle gave him a shove. 'Stop it. I didn't make you come. It was a joint decision.'

'That would explain it,' he said, 'if I'd had a joint and been high when we decided. I don't have that excuse. You made it sound like an adventure. Now it just looks like a jail sentence.'

'Will you stop going on about prison? Look, dinner is through there.' A double door in the far wall led through to the next block. The aroma of hot food came drifting through. 'You can't say it doesn't smell good.'

He didn't reply, but snatched up a set of cotton

clothing from the nearest pile and disappeared into the men's toilets.

The women's piles gave her the options of slightly too big, or slightly too small. She went large. The bag included a hand towel and the DNA kit the woman had mentioned. She undressed, dried herself, and stashed her wet clothes in the bag along with the damp towel, before swabbing the inside of her cheek. The kit had no instructions, but someone would probably tell her where to hand it in at some point. She slipped the closed phial into the single pocket of the loose trousers and rejoined the crowd of colonists waiting to be served.

Most of the food on offer had a strange blue tinge, but that aside the stew was delicious. Meals on the Dauntless had been rationed, especially in the last few days, and processed until they had no flavour. This was the first time Kyle had enjoyed eating since leaving Earth. When Douglas joined her she was ready for a second bowl.

'You took your time.'

That brought the scowl back. 'Split the first set of these crappy jumpsuits didn't I,' he said. 'Had to go back for a second dib. Embarrassing. Bloody towel's no bigger than a postage stamp.'

The rain battered the roof of the hall. Kyle joined the end of the queue where the last few stragglers, their hair still wet, were waiting for their first bowlful.

'I'm gonna call this bloostoo,' Douglas said when she returned.

'What's this? Humour? Feels better with a full tummy doesn't it? You should have another bowl. We don't know when the next meal will be.'

The black-haired woman had closed the double doors and stood on a small dais at the end of the hall with a group of officials. Or at least, she supposed that's what they were. Right now they looked more like drowned kittens.

'Now that you're all safely disembarked, a quick

welcome to your new home. My name is Felice Waters and I'm in charge of the team here. A few of them are with me this afternoon and you'll meet the rest later this evening. When you've finished your meal,' she said, raising her voice to be heard over the hubbub of conversation, 'please bring your DNA sample to one of us so we can log it in. We'll need your name, and passenger ID, but if you can't remember that just your name will do. We have the Dauntless manifest so we can match you up.'

'No escaping the Gestapo,' Douglas said, scraping the last of the stew from his bowl.

'You going for more?'

'One portion of prison slop will do me for now, thanks. You can have mine. Wait, the head screw is talking again.'

His dogged insistence on finding anything to dislike about Perse before they had even settled in, and his endless prison "jokes" were beginning to wear down Kyle's naturally sunny disposition, but she bit down a retort. She wanted to hear what the Waters woman was saying.

'There are bunk beds in the dormitory blocks and we've put up cot beds wherever we can around the base, but there won't be enough for everyone. Dauntless had a larger passenger complement than the previous ships. The captain will already have shut down the life support systems throughout most of the ship, but in any case you'd get just as wet going back as you did coming off, so better to stay here in the warm and dry. The induction meeting that we normally hold will be a more basic affair than usual–'

'Everything's fucking *basic* here,' Douglas muttered.

'–for reasons that I'll explain at the meeting. We'll get started with that once everyone has eaten and had a chance to claim a bed. Maybe arrange a sleeping rota with friends or family? The sooner you get used to mucking in the better. For now just relax, there's more food if you want it, and get what rest you can. I'll see you again in a little while.'

'Don't you find this at all weird?' Douglas asked, his head swivelling and jerking like a badly controlled puppet as he gazed around the room.

'Of course it's weird! It's another planet for fuck's sake! It was never going to be like Kilclootie! Christ, even Glasgow seems weird when you come from Smallville, Scotland!'

'No. Well, yes, but I mean this.' He waved a hand at the hall. 'They've been here near enough ten years—since the first ship landed—and it still looks like a frontier town. There's something they're not telling us. I didn't expect neon lights and fancy restaurants but after all this time there should be... more. More than this. It's all still prefab and it's *tiny!* Where is everybody?'

'Guess we'll find out in "a little while".'

'And that's another thing. "Induction" meeting that woman said. That's what they call it when you join a new company. A chance for them to start the brainwashing process. Get you to think like they do. Persuade you that all this is normal.'

'Maybe it is. Normal for here, I mean.'

'You have to be fucking joking,' Douglas said, shaking his head. 'If this is all they've achieved in ten years we'll be living the rest of our lives in the dark ages.'

With not much to occupy them, the time passed slowly. She persuaded Douglas into a second bowl of stew, and they both tried a piece of the blue pie served as dessert.

'Why is all the food blue?' Douglas asked, holding up a forkful and examining it from all angles.

'How should I know? Maybe you can ask her,' Kyle replied, waving her empty fork in the direction of Felice Waters, who had returned with a larger team of people and was making her way back to the dais.

She stood behind a low lectern and rapped on it with a nightstick she pulled from her belt. Kyle had not noticed the weapon until then. It gave her an involuntary shiver. Buried memories of wild Saturday nights in their normally quiet coastal town, and the swift justice meted out by the local constabulary bubbled unbidden to the surface of her thoughts.

'Thank you,' Felice called, before waiting for the buzz of conversation to die away. She had quite the megaphone voice when she needed it. 'Rumours circulate quickly, even as early in your new life as this,' she said, looking in turn at each colonist in the front row with the ease of a practised speaker. 'And I'm sure many of you have a whole heap of questions. Let me see if I can predict some of them. Where is everybody? Why is this colony still so undeveloped after all this time? What happened to the Prism ship most of you will have seen in the bay on your way in? But the most important question of all won't have occurred to a single one of you. I guarantee it. That question is: are we alone on this planet? And the answer is no. The people who have arrived here from Earth over the last ten years are not the only people to make their home on the planet you will all come to know as Berikatanya.'

pennatanah
14th day of run'sanamasa, 966

'Yes, you heard me right,' Felice Waters said, raising her voice another notch over the reaction from the hall. 'Perse was our name for this place. The indigenous call it Berikatanya. They are a society mostly medieval in technology, ability, and social development, divided into two realms ruled over—normally—by a monarch. The Black Queen in her Palace in Kertonia, and the Blood King at the Court of Istania. Except that recently the King died, and as far as we know he has yet to be replaced. So one reason for this foreshortened introduction to life on Berikatanya is that neither side has sent a representative. Previous ships were met by one or both of the monarchs, and since many of the colonists came here for the simple life, a majority of them found homes in one realm or the other.'

'We don't have a community of our own then?' called a man from the back of the room. Kyle turned to see who it was, but he was hidden from her sight by those standing around him.

'I'll take questions at the end if you don't mind,' Felice replied, 'but since you've asked, the short answer is yes, there is a small group of people who didn't want to integrate with the natives. They live a frugal life, avoiding contact with the locals as far as possible, including having no trade with them. I can tell you where they are if you're interested, but not how they are faring. My most recent visit was almost a year ago when I introduced them to the only passenger from the Valiant who wanted to join them.

'Anyway, to return to my thread,' Waters continued.

They listened to the rest of her talk, by the end of which Douglas was clearly bored. He had been fidgeting and picking his nose—a sure sign—for some time, cocking his head to listen to the driving rain rattling against the roof. The short version was, they had three options: join the Queen, join the (dead) King, or join the starving Earthers. They would have a day or two to make up their minds, after which they were expected to head off to whichever camp they chose. And it was raining. Well, they knew that. But apparently it was unusual for there to be rain during the day, for a reason Waters had been vague about. The man at the back had asked several more questions. Kyle did eventually catch a glimpse of him. He had a shock of grey hair standing out haphazardly in all directions and a lined face with a small tattoo on his neck which she could not make out at this distance. Kyle wondered what skills he brought. It was unusual for a man of his years to be offered passage. He had wanted to know about the Earthers and also about what use the landing point was put to in the months or years between ships, now that there would *be* no more ships. Waters didn't have an answer to that either.

The buzz of conversation started again once she had finished speaking. A few groups began games of cards or dice. A dozen or so returned to the servery for another helping of dessert. The bad hair man gathered a small group around him. Kyle heard them talking about the possibility of starting a second Earther township.

'What do you want to do?' Kyle asked.

Douglas gave her a sour look.

'You don't want to know.'

'Fine. Well I'm going to find a bed and catch some sleep then. We don't know what tomorrow will bring. Could be a long day. I'd rather be pumped for it than moping about half asleep.'

'Like me you mean?'

'If the cap fits. Any idea where you want to go?'

'Away from here,' he replied, his unhappy expression settling deeper into the lines of his face. 'But I guess that's gonna happen whichever direction we take.'

'I like the sound of the Queen.'

'What do you mean "the sound of her"? You don't know the first thing about her. She's called the Black Queen. The end. Hardly the basis for a decision that will affect the rest of your life.'

'She's a woman,' Kyle said, only half in an attempt to wind her brother up even further. 'Women make better rulers.'

Douglas snorted. She could see he was trying not to smile. He was not as set against this new life as he made out.

'There's still loads they're not telling us,' he said. 'Like why hasn't that dead King been replaced yet? And what are the politics like between these two medieval monarchs? I bet they're fighting each other the whole time. Look at Scotland's history. Clans from neighbouring valleys taking pot shots over the bens at the slightest excuse. Be careful which side you choose.'

Kyle got to her feet. 'I don't think there's any point speculating. We don't know anything, and we won't learn anything until tomorrow. Everyone here is in the same boat. They all seem to be making the most of it.'

The hall echoed with the sound of eating, talking, and the occasional burst of laughter. Small groups of children were busy finding new friends, playing games newly invented for their new lives. Some had already left in the direction of the sleeping rooms.

'Get some sleep. Seriously. You'll feel better.'

Douglas pushed back his chair. 'Nothing else to do,' he said.

They returned their empty bowls to the collection point and handed in their DNA samples. In the bunk room, the rain sounded even louder on the low roof. The large room contained rows of quadruple-tier beds, around a third of them already occupied. Apart from the rain, the loudest sound was gentle snoring.

'I take it all back,' Douglas said. 'It's not a regular prison. It's a prison *camp*. This looks just like Stalag Luft 18.'

darmajelis chamber, court of the blood king
15th day of run'sanamasa, 966

Jeruk Nipis lay awake, the darkness of his chambers relieved only by the dying embers in his hearth and the silvery double fingers of moonlight that painted the end of his bed with cold fire. Sleep did not come easily these days, and not only because of his duties of state. A muted knock at the door disturbed his troubled thoughts.

'Come.'

Sebaklan Pwalek stuck his head into the room. 'Sorry to disturb you.'

'I wasn't asleep.'

'A rider has arrived from the Earther base at

Pennatanah. I think you'll want to hear his message for yourself. I've had him taken to the Darmajelis chamber.'

He closed the door behind him as Jeruk leapt from his bed. He splashed his face with cold water, pulled on a night robe, and made his way along the dark, empty corridors to the stateroom. Inside, Pwalek engaged in quiet conversation with a short, grey-bearded man. Sweat stood out in droplets on the man's forehead. His face glistened in the moonlight streaming in through the high windows, which drummed glassily with the music of the continuing rains. Mud caked the man's cloak. Some had flaked off and fallen to the floor as it dried.

'I rode through the night, sire,' the man said, still a little short of breath. 'Thought you'd want to hear of this before the morrow when choices will be made.'

'Choices?' Jeruk repeated, not understanding the man's intent.

'There's been another vessel from the Earther planet.' Pwalek said. 'It's caught them napping. Waters set up an ad-hoc reception meeting and the passengers will be choosing their sides in the morning.'

'As I was telling your man,' the rider went on, casting a black look in Pwalek's direction, 'I think there's a couple of them Earthers you should be taking an interest in. Might set our cause back if they should decide to go over to the Blacks.'

'Our cause? Do I know you?'

'Brother to Sadra Penganya if it please your eminence,' the man said, 'a long-time attendee of the subterranean meetings and disciple of the Pupp... of, er, those who pull the strings. If you know what I mean.' He tapped the side of his nose in a gesture so unexpected and conspiratorial Jeruk almost laughed aloud.

'Yes,' he said. 'I know what you mean. A couple, you say? How will we know them?'

'A couple, aye. But brother and sister, not husband and wife. They share a look—black hair and pasty white skin, though the girl has more colour than the young man. He looks, well, ill if I tell the truth. Piercing pale blue eyes with dark rings round them as if he's not slept his whole life. Her eyes are blue too, but deeper. Like a rock pool. If you find one, you'll find the other. They're never long out of each other's company.'

'And what is it about them that would interest us?' Jeruk asked.

The man fidgeted under his gaze. A squall of rain hit the windows of the chamber with renewed vigour, rattling like gravel against the glass. The rider nodded in the direction of the windows.

'You'd be best discovering the truth of it for yourself, sire,' he said, 'but I'll say this. It might be more than coincidence that this crazy weather started up at the same time as they appeared.'

Jeruk regarded the man for some time, his thoughts conflicted. He had heard the stories of course—Earthers who could perform simple magical tricks. They had even recruited a couple. Powers or not, most of the feeble-minded "colonists" could be swayed with vague promises of riches and influence. But there had never been any suggestion that any of them were powerful enough to accomplish something like the unending rain they had suffered for the last ten days. To overturn an enchantment that had been in place for centuries would require someone of Elemental-level ability. Unlikely. But if true, then the rider was right. Definitely someone—two someones—who must not fall into the hands of the Black Palace.

'You must ride to Pennatanah,' he said to Pwalek. 'Tonight. Go with him,' he added to the rider, 'so that we can be certain of finding the right couple. There must be no chance of a mistake. Persuade them of their value to the Blood Court. Bring them back with you.'

Pwalek hesitated. 'And what if my powers of persuasion prove no match for the task? Earthers I have encountered have been an argumentative bunch. If these two are so special they won't easily be convinced.'

'Bring them by force if you have to. Take whatever extra men you think you will need to overcome a boy and a girl who are still disorientated by their arrival in a strange new land. But however you accomplish it, do not allow them to take the road to the Palace.'

He looked at the rain, streaming down the chamber windows in thick rivulets, and began to consider how he could turn it to his advantage.

Chapter 11

Jann took the cold plate Claire had prepared for him. The fire had lost none of its strength while he dressed. The room was warm, but not uncomfortable. All eyes remained on him while he settled himself into the last remaining chair. Elaine handed him a glass of wine, her fingers brushing his as he took it from her. He took a sip and perched it next to his plate on a side table. Apart from the roaring blaze in the hearth, silence filled the chamber.

'I set off soon after first light,' he began, 'as Claire knows, because she was there to bid me a cheery farewell.'

The Air Mage coloured at his words, a faint smile lifting the corners of her mouth, but did not interrupt.

'I had no clear idea where I was heading, but I wanted to give myself as much daylight as possible. Chance to find somewhere to spend the first night. It didn't quite turn out as I expected.'

Quickly warming to his tale, Jann recounted the early days of his journey. For the most part, his audience kept quiet. When his account brought him to the edge of the precipice overlooking the caldera, they could contain themselves no longer.

'Incredible!'

'A hidden paradise indeed, Gatekeeper!'

'Did you find anyone else there?'

'Have you been there this whole time?'

'All in good time!' he said, swallowing the only mouthful they had given him time for. 'I haven't even reached the crater floor yet!'

'Was the climb down hard?' Claire asked, refilling his glass.

At the point of losing consciousness in the deep snow on the northern side of the caldera, the fire had burned low in the grate. Jann's plate and glass were empty, and his bladder full.

'Why don't we take a comfort break?' he said. 'Or we can leave the rest until tomorrow? It must be almost midnight and we're not yet halfway into the story.'

'No!'

'Wouldn't hear of it Gatekeeper! I am enthralled with your narrative.'

'I'll fetch some more wood. It's going to be a cold night.'

'And a long one!'

Jann smiled. If they had thought the story enthralling so far, they would shit at the next part.

'Looking back now,' he said, as plates were refilled and the fire stoked, 'it seems obvious that delirium had started to set in before my fall. It wasn't warmer up there; I was developing a fever. Could have been a psychoactive effect of the lichen. Poison from the bird's attack. Or even my own poison, from my putrefying flesh. Whatever it was, I'm convinced it was more than just the cold that made me collapse.'

*

When I woke, I felt cocooned in green. Green light, and green smells. Fractured memories of being fed and tended flashed through my mind. I tried to sit up but I didn't have the strength. It took a few moments for my vision to clear, enough to discover I was lying on a bed of dry leaves and moss. The smell from these was immensely comforting. It explained in part my semi-conscious thought of green aromas. The walls surrounding my cot were fashioned from small branches and woven leaves. Sunlight streamed between the gaps, lighting the interior of the hut. Multiple fingers of gold in which motes of emerald floated and danced. A welcome breeze, gentle and warm, offered some relief from the stifling heat. It stirred the plain woven curtain hanging in the doorway and brought fresh vegetation smells from outside.

'How do you feel? Better?'

A disembodied voice, speaking Istanian but with a strange accent. The face of a young woman swam into view. It took me a moment to focus. Clear, olive skin. Large brown eyes framed by brown hair that swept across her face and tickled my neck as it fell. Full, moist lips curled into a faint smile. She tucked errant strands of hair behind her ear.

'How long...?'

'You have been long asleep. Four days since I found you. Almost five.'

'You found me?'

'Yes. Lucky for you. I was in the mountain. Heading back for home. My kedewada was almost complete. Another day and I would not be there.'

'I don't understand. Kede...wada?'

'It is test. To mark my womanhood, and take my place among the people.'

A coming-of-age ritual. Mountain survival. I would have failed the test. I remembered my arm. Held it out. Its fresh bandage showed no sign of weeping or blood loss.

'Your arm bad infected. The eladok strikes quick and with little ghasteng. Ah, forgive. You would say reason? Excuse? Provocation?'

'Provocation, yes. But you're speaking Istanian.'

'I speak the language of my fathers. Not Istanian. It is Batarian. Your words sound old to my ears. My brother said better to cut off your arm. The poison of the eladok is deadly. If it reaches your brain can send you mad in days only. Already you were rambling. But I say no, I can save. Change bandage every day. Make poultice from luum and luki. Put luum on your bed too, so you enjoy its healing odour.'

'How is it?'

'You will have scar, that for sure. War wound to show grandchildren. You have woman?'

I could feel my colour rising in the warmth of the hut.

'No. I don't have a woman. Or children.'

'So. You will just have to brag about wound to friends. Until woman show up.'

I twisted on the litter to see whether my leg had received similar treatment. It too was bandaged, but also bound with dark brown strands of what looked like bark.

'Your ankle broken. Surprised you could walk at all. Bone had cut through flesh a little. We had to stitch. You cannot stand on it for thirty days, and then only with krupang. Crutch.'

'Here,' she said, reaching behind me to retrieve a length of wood. It had been cleverly cut close to a branch to allow a shoulder to rest in the cleft. Another smaller branch provided a handle. The whole thing was stripped of bark and smoothed for comfort. It glowed greenish-white in the light coming through the walls.

'It is right size for you,' she said, a hint of pride in her voice. 'But not yet.'

'I have to lie here for another month?'

'It is not so bad!' she said, pouting. 'I will bring food, water. Wash you. Change dressing. You just get better.'

'Why are you doing this for me? I don't even know your name.'

'I am called Pennamatalya. I do it because you are my responsibility. I found you. It is the way.'

'Penn...?'

'Pennamatalya.' She laughed, her eyes sparkling in the shafts of sunlight that had shifted and now lit up her face. 'If it fills your mouth too much, can call me Penny.'

'Penny. Thank you. I can't repay this kindness. I–'

'No need for repay. Get well. Then you can meet others.'

'Others? Where are we?'

'You are in my kamesa. Um... village? No, town! Elders very interested in you. They have been visit. I must tell them you are awake.'

Days took on a slow and comfortable pattern. Being

looked after by Penny, resting, napping, eating and engaging her in brief snatches of conversation. She never talked about what else occupied her, but once I'd eaten whatever she brought, or she'd cleaned and dressed my wounds, she didn't stay for long.

As time wore on my frustration and boredom with being confined to the hut made me irritable. Eventually Penny agreed I was well enough to sit outside. She said the sunlight would be good for me. I was just glad to have something new to look at, and to exchange pleasantries with the old women in nearby dwellings. They sat in the sun all day weaving, dyeing, or grinding seeds for bread. One of them offered me a loaf one day. Penny appeared from nowhere and launched into a loud and lengthy argument with the woman, who gave up in the end. Penny refused to explain why she wouldn't let me sample the old woman's bread. Later that afternoon she brought me a loaf of her own, which looked identical to the one I'd been shown earlier but was apparently better for me.

On the third or fourth day after the loaf incident I sat propped against my hut enjoying the warmth, the buzz of conversation, and the last of Penny's breakfast. An old man carrying a large woven basket wandered along the road in my direction. He stopped at every hut, sharing a few words with everyone he met. He seemed to be selling whatever wares he carried, but none of them were buying. As he approached, he smiled in my direction. The deep lines on his weather beaten face creased and folded into new patterns under that smile while his pale rheumy eyes glinted like two shards of opal sitting in a worn leather pouch.

'Greetings, traveller!' he called as he came nearer. 'How goes your recovery?'

'Slowly,' I said, shielding my eyes from the glare, 'but I get a little better each day.'

'Good to hear, traveller, good to hear. They say you almost died.'

I nodded. 'I was lucky. I am being well looked after.'

'Ah yes. Young Pennamatalya is skilled with all manner of healing arts. It is right that you know how lucky you have been.'

Though the old man spoke in vague terms, I felt there was a message wrapped up in his words. I wondered how he knew Penny, but it was a small township. Each of them probably knew what the others were doing.

'What are you selling?' I asked him.

He looked momentarily nonplussed, before shifting his basket from his shoulder.

'These, you mean? Simple herbal pouches. Blends of my own invention. Perhaps one would speed your recuperation?'

He held up a small bag of brown cloth, tied at the neck with a short length of twine. The bag bristled with cut ends of plant stems which poked through the thin material. I had not seen any of the townspeople accept one of his pouches, but he held out the bag, his opaline eyes regarding me unflinchingly.

'I cannot pay you,' I said, not wishing to offend him.

'It is sufficient that I have helped in some small way in your journey.'

I took the bag. 'Thank you.'

'Keep it by your bed,' he said, continuing down the road. 'The fragrance will help you sleep.'

I saw him several times after that day, but he never stopped at my hut again. He would wave and smile, but his route always took him in another direction. Penny continued with her ministrations. I saw her give the pouch a strange look the next day, after I had wedged it into the woven wall behind my bed, but she did not say anything. A few days later she told me I was well enough to start exercising.

'Bones are set,' she said. 'Need to build strength. All this lying around not good. Muscles shrink. Joints get stiff.'

She turned out to be as good at stretching and

strengthening exercises as she had been with herbs and dressings. That first day I was aching all over, and woke in the night with a severe cramp in my injured leg. Penny had a salve for that, too, which she rubbed in thoroughly the following morning. The salve relieved the stiffness in my leg. My other stiffness she pretended not to notice.

After three or four days of static exercising, Penny told me I was strong enough to start using the krupang over greater distances.

'Strength will build quicker if you can walk. Start to carry weight on foot.' She smiled. 'You can explore more of my town. Keep on the flat. And away from the snow!'

'I don't need reminding to stay clear of the mountain!' I joked. Her face took on a deeper colour when I added 'but it would almost be worth it to be looked after by you again.'

Moving around on the krupang was hard at first. My shoulder was not used to the strain. The arm had healed to a thin, livid scar but had not lost any strength. My technique soon improved, and the muscles around my shoulder adapted to their new role. After a few days I could hobble at a decent pace and set out to explore the township properly. That same night my euphoria at my new independence soon crashed and burned.

'Not take it too quick,' Penny said, rubbing more of her salve into my shoulder. 'If trip and fall in early days, can set bone healing back to beginning.'

If I had thought overdoing it was the worst of my troubles, she had further news.

'But,' she went on, 'you not need healing treatments now. Can take care of self.'

She covered her ointment pot and wiped her hands on her skirt. I did not know what to say, or if I should say anything. After more than a month of being looked after every day, taking care of myself felt daunting. I never had discovered what other calls she had on her time. Surely looking after me had been an imposition? One she would gladly be rid of.

'Thank you.' I said. It sounded too insignificant. 'For all your–' I began, but she had already stepped out of the hut and disappeared from view.

elaine's chambers, the black palace
15th day of run'sanamasa, 966

Tanamasa was well into its second month when I began my daily walks around the town. Autumn colours were already painted over much of the mountainside below the snow line and the days were crisp and clear. There was still warmth in the sun, and I dressed simply in the clothes Penny had provided. Most of mine had been cut off my unconscious body so she could clean wounds and apply bandages. The rest disintegrated as soon as she washed them.

I must have misunderstood Penny when she said I could look after myself. She still came by almost every day to bring food and make sure my recovery was progressing. Other townspeople were friendly enough, but circumspect. They would speak if spoken to, and smiled and waved each time they saw me, but they never started a conversation. Occasionally I saw a tell-tale twitch of a door curtain and suspected the occupant had ducked back inside as I passed. None of them walked along with me, or came to visit, apart from Penny. Even the older woman who had offered me bread that one time kept to herself. She never did repeat her offer. I wondered whether I had offended her. More likely Penny's reaction had frightened her off! I saw no other examples of anger or raised voices among the people in all my perambulations. They appeared very content.

Every few days my path crossed with that of the old pouch peddler. We exchanged pleasantries and he always enquired after my health, but he would take the first opportunity to change direction. We never walked together for more than the time it took to move from one hut to the next.

I soon discovered people would answer a direct question. Perhaps their extreme politeness made them uncomfortable with any kind of confrontation, even if only avoiding a response. In this way I learned that they referred to themselves as the Beragan. A word I was not familiar with, but later found out means "civilised people". They use a contraction for themselves too—Bera'n—just as the locals here call Earthers "Batu'n". This was my first clue that the two peoples are, or were, connected. They know about those who live south of the mountains. They call us Binagan or "wild people". I didn't hear a contraction for that. Maybe they don't speak about us often enough. A few referred to us as Keti Caraga. The warring tribes. I guess given the stormy relationship between Court and Palace over the centuries, they pretty much know what they're talking about! When she brought my evening meal that night, I asked Penny about it.

'You should speak with the Elders,' she said. 'They ask after you all the time, more since you start walking.'

'Ask after me?'

'Yes. They want to know everything. Who you are. Where you from. What made you cross the mountain. No one ever did that before. Some of our young ones—the bravest—have tried in the past. During their kedewada. None returned. I think our Elders are... surprised. By your strength.'

'I almost died.'

'Yes, but you not die. All our people did, or why have they not returned? What makes you so special? Is what they want to know.'

'I don't know what to tell them. If you hadn't found me, I would be dead too. Just like the others. But what about us "wild people"? You still haven't told me how you know about us. If no one from here has ever made it over the mountain...?'

'Speak with the Elders. Is not for me to tell.'

She would say no more. I tried to raise the subject again several times over the next few days, but she pretended she had not heard me, or spoke of something else.

The Elders might have asked frequently about my progress, but they did nothing to approach me about a meeting. I did not even know who they were. By now I'd walked the length and breadth of the township. No one revealed themselves as an Elder, or pointed one out to me. I tried engaging anyone I met on the question of "wild" people but, like Penny, they would not talk about it. All of the Bera'n were adept at steering the conversation to more mundane matters. The closest I ever came to the tiniest fragment of knowledge was from the pouch seller, one sunny afternoon. He seemed more than usually chatty. Perhaps the warmth of the day—one of the last we would see before winter set in—had made him less guarded, or maybe he had seen me about so often he had become used to our exchanges.

'It is an ancient story,' he said, when I brought the conversation round to the warring tribes. 'I knew you must be one of them as soon as you came. No one has passed the mountains since they were raised up.'

His unusual turn of phrase gave me pause, but I shrugged it off mentally. Obviously he didn't mean raising the mountains had been a deliberate undertaking. The limitations of language, or the differences in their dialect from my own experience, had made it sound like a conscious act, but he would have meant raised by geological action. Or volcanic, given my ideas of how the caldera had formed.

'No one speaks of it now,' he went on. 'Ancient history. And troubled times. We doubted they could ever become truly civilised, and so it has proved.'

I tried to press him on the matter but as always he skipped to a different topic, refusing to be drawn further.

'I have heard the Elders wish to speak with me,' I said, determined to press on in the face of his reticence. He was not the only one who could change the subject. 'Yet I have never met one. I wonder—do you know the Elders? Could you introduce me?'

The old man smiled. 'The Elders move in their own circles,' he said. 'When they are ready to speak with you, you will be told, have no fear. But I will say this,' he went on. 'They do not countenance wild behaviour in any form. They will only meet with civilised people. Perhaps they await some evidence from you, in either direction.'

Without another word, he was gone. A quick turn into a side-street and he disappeared in the late afternoon shadows. I continued walking, less reliant on my krupang by then, but carrying it with me for help over rough ground, or if I stood still for long periods. I thought about what the herb seller had said. Wondered how I could prove my lack of wildness, or my level of civilisation, which I believed to be at least as high as the simple people living in the town. All I had done since I arrived was accept Penny's diligent care, and pass the time of day with anyone else I encountered. It wasn't much, but none of it could be called "wildness". I had not raged at my wounds, complained of pain even when at its worst, or ever lost my temper. What could I do to raise my chances of being seen by the Elders?

As always, I put this point to my only sounding board—Penny—that evening. We sat on cushions outside my hut in the gathering dusk. The air was still warm. A few children played in the street even though it was getting late. Their parents called them in one by one as we talked, sharing a glass of fruit juice from the pitcher she had brought over.

'Be yourself,' she said. 'That is all I can say. Elders are wise. If you are false, they will know. If you try to impress, they will know. Just be. I know you are not wild. They will come to know too. Trust.'

And so the days passed. I had long since given up scoring notches on bits of wood to mark their passage. I still had my staff, and as time wore on I took to walking with it in preference to the krupang. A psychological boost, perhaps. I felt less like a cripple. But during the days I had spent in and out of delirium, and later when confined to the hut, I'd had no way of marking the days on its shaft. I didn't know how many I'd missed, so the whole thing became pointless. As the season turned and the early days of Sanamasa brought the chill of winter to the air, I became less concerned with how long I had been away. Instead I focused my attention on the question of how much longer I could stay. I was doing nothing to earn my keep, yet these were poor people, with little to spare. But if I did not stay, where would I go? Retracing my steps would likely get me killed, and in any case there was no way back over the southern range. But what of further north? What would I find there? And how would I travel? I had seen no sign of kudai or other beast of burden during my stay. Everyone travelled on foot. I did not relish the prospect of leaving my comfortable berth and the pleasant evenings spent in Penny's company in exchange for a hard life on the road to who knew where.

Sometime during what I judged to be the latter half of Far'Sanamasa, I visited the outskirts of the town, where the lowland forests of the mountain range approach close to the outermost dwellings. I liked to walk there. The breeze often brought the smells of the forest on the air, and the calls of animals dwelling in the shade of the trees would echo through the woods, reminding me of my time in the caldera. Those houses were filled with children, whose company I had come to enjoy. They were less guarded than their parents and would treat me as just another one of their community. It doesn't sound much, but when you have been an outsider, any chance to join in is welcome, even if only with a child's game.

I could hear one such game in progress while I walked

that day. As I drew nearer the shouts and screams of excitement turned unmistakably to ones of terror. I quickened my pace until the group of children came into view. I could see one—a young girl—had become separated from her playmates. The other youngsters cowered behind a low wall. Between the wall and the lone girl, a kuclar stood, its teeth bared. Strings of thick saliva dripped from its jaws and a low growl came from deep in its throat. Its eyes flicked in my direction as I rounded the corner before fixing back on the girl. It took a step forward. The girl screamed again.

It was unusual for a shy animal like the kuclar to venture into town, but we were already well into winter. Food would be scarce. Hunger had driven the beast to overcome its fear of human contact. There was only one thing to do. I ran to position myself in front of the girl, ignoring the pain that stabbed from my ankle.

'Go to your friends! Run!' I shouted as she stepped behind me. I threatened the predator with my staff.

'Yahh!' I yelled. 'Get back to the forest!'

The cat hesitated, its gaze darting between my staff and the running girl. She was vulnerable for a moment only, having emerged from my protection but not yet reached the wall. The animal took its chance, leaping at the child. I moved to intercept its path, shouting, closing my eyes against the expectation of its teeth on my arm. The wood of my staff felt hot in my grasp and a strange feeling of calm suffused me. I don't remember opening my eyes and yet the scene was suddenly there before me. The air in front of the kuclar rippled as if it were rising from a sun-warmed rock, and then the beast was gone. Another child screamed and I fell to my knees on the cold ground, shaking with delayed shock.

The children, many of them still shouting and crying, ran off to find their parents. My trembling gradually passed. I levered myself upright with my staff and made my way back to the hut. That evening Penny came by as usual with a small tureen of stew, enough for two, and a pitcher of fruit juice. For the first time since leaving the Palace I would have preferred wine! We ate in silence; unusual for us. I did not feel like talking, but her lack of conversation surprised me.

When we had finished eating, she poured our juice and handed mine over, staring into my eyes with a strange expression.

'The Elders want to meet with you tomorrow morning,' she said.

elaine's chambers, the black palace
15th day of run'sanamasa, 966

The following day was overcast, the iron-grey sky matching my mood. I admit I felt anxious about meeting the Elders. During my months of convalescence I had not uncovered a single fact about them, had never met one, but had observed many times the awe they inspired in the townspeople. Almost reverence. I had no idea what they actually did, how many of them there were, or anything else about them. I was about to find out, and the prospect filled me with a strange mix of fear and excitement. I walked through the streets toward the hut Penny had directed me to, remembering what I had been through, and who I was. Why should the Gatekeeper be afraid? I survived the portal, imprisonment, the Tournament, the Blood Clones, and the mountain no one had crossed before. I was strong, and I was resourceful.

But more than that, I had been on a quest to discover my position in this world. A world I had been wrenched from and cast back to, but which I still didn't really understand. Perhaps these Elders could offer me some insight, or perhaps not. And if not, I resolved at that moment to continue my quest further North until I found whatever answers were to be had.

I arrived at the door. From the outside, the hut

appeared no different from any other I had seen in all my wanderings. A little larger, perhaps, but it did not sit in the centre of a town square, or in any other way betray any significance. I did not want to barge in unannounced, so I rapped on the smooth-worn wood of the door frame and waited.

'Enter, Gatekeeper,' came a voice from inside.

Whatever I had been expecting, it was not that. Composing myself, I lifted the curtain aside and stepped through the doorway.

Inside the hut a few candles and a small dog grate filled with embers provided scant illumination. Even compared to the dark skies outside, the interior was gloomy. I stood by the entrance for a few moments to allow my eyes to adjust. Unlike my own dwelling, this had only a single room, almost unfurnished. On the smooth dirt floor, eleven villagers sat in a circle. A twelfth occupied a single chair. A simple three-legged affair made of wood, with a high back covered in the patterned skin of an animal I had never seen.

'Come, take a seat among the Elders,' said the old man in the chair. It was the herb-seller.

This day, hardly begun, was already full of surprises. He indicated a space in the circle. I sat, ignoring a twinge from my ankle as I tried to cross my legs. I rested my staff across my lap. Questions burned through my mind, uppermost among them how the old man knew I was the Gatekeeper. Unsure of the protocol at this gathering, I held my tongue and waited for one of the others to speak. Apart from the single chair there was no indication of a group hierarchy.

'Your recovery is complete?' the herb-seller asked.

I supposed this was for the benefit of the other Elders. I had seen their leader almost every day since first setting foot outside my hut and he always enquired after my health.

'Thank you, yes,' I said. 'Penny... er... Pennamatalya has

been very attentive. I owe her my life, in more ways than one.'

The old man smiled. 'My daughter is skilled in many things,' he said. 'You have enjoyed her company, I understand, even after your wounds had healed.'

I felt my face growing hot. 'We have become... good friends.'

'You have shared her bread.'

Even then the significance of the bread escaped me. It came to me later with a flush of embarrassment. At the time, I took the old man's statement at face value.

'Yes. She has been very kind. I don't really know anyone else in the community. I don't even know what this place is called.'

He smiled again, his eyes twinkling in the firelight. 'This is the town of Tenfir Abarad. It means "cradle of civilisation" in the ancient tongue. We do not keep written records. Our history is passed down through the Elders. I am Penjal Mpah. The others in this assembly can introduce themselves to you later.'

'Thank you for all you have done,' I said, 'and for inviting me to this meeting. My name is Jann Argent.'

'And you are the Gatekeeper.'

'Yes. How did you know that?'

'We had long suspected. Even though the true extent of your ability remains hidden from you, many of us are sensitive to the presence of power in others. And now, of course, we have the evidence of your recent demonstration.'

'What do you mean?'

'Your encounter with the kuclar yesterday. You showed considerable courage. Your intervention certainly saved the life of one of our children, possibly more. That alone would have been sufficient to prove you are a civilised man, which is something that has been troubling us since your arrival. How can someone from the southern lands be truly civilised? And yet, here you are. But beyond your bravery in protecting our kin, the way you dispatched the animal revealed that our suspicions were correct.'

'I still don't understand. The animal disappeared. I assumed it had run off.'

'It ran, that is true. But it was running toward you. You opened a gate right in front of it, and it passed who knows where.'

His words stunned me. My first reaction was disbelief. I had been alone. I could not have summoned a gate without help. And yet, I remembered the strange appearance of the air around the kuclar before it pounced.

'A gate? No! How is that possible? I can only do that in the presence of the four Elements.'

The Elder sat on Penjal Mpah's right held up her hand. 'That may have been how you have done it in the past Jann Argent,' she said. 'But it is not a requirement, except for the very largest portals. Do you have experience of such a portal?'

'Yes,' I admitted, struggling to maintain my composure. 'My memory of it is still unclear, but its effects were considerable.'

The woman nodded. 'Such gates, or portals, can be very dangerous. But smaller gates can be opened by drawing on the power of two Elements only. And once you are adept, you will be able to open a simple gate using nothing but the power of your mind. In those places where they are close to the surface.'

'Dipeka Kekusaman is one of those most sensitive to power,' Penjal Mpah said. 'It was she who first brought your ability to our attention.'

'Forgive me,' I said, 'I do not mean to doubt you, but two Elements? I didn't even have those to call on.'

Dipeka Kekusaman smiled, gesturing at my lap. 'You had your staff.'

'Yes.' I rested my hand on the smooth wood. 'But what use is that?'

A murmur passed around the circle. The man on my

left spoke. Possibly the oldest person in the room. His face was even more deeply lined than the herb-seller's. His beard touched the floor in front of him. 'After all this time, they have still not uncovered second tier powers, Penjal. Until yesterday, Jann Argent had only worked with Earth, Air, Fire, and Water.'

I turned to him, still feeling totally confused. 'Yes, those are the four Elements. I have met the Elementals who wield them. I am privileged to call them friends. I know nothing of second tier powers, whatever they are.'

'You are holding one in your hand, Gatekeeper,' the man said. 'Wood. It combines the natures of Air and Water. Draws part of its manifestation from them both. But it also confers its own strengths to those who can wield it.'

I gripped the staff more tightly, remembering how it felt hot before the kuclar leapt toward me. I had assumed it was heat from my own hand, the rush of fear through me. Could it have been the wood itself?

'But... how? I am not an Elemental. I didn't even know about the power of Wood until a moment ago.'

'Your own ability will draw power from wherever it can, Gatekeeper,' Dipeka Kekusaman said. 'An Element, or any combination. Including Wood and Stone.'

'Stone?'

'Stone is the other second tier Element,' Mpah said. 'It combines Earth and Fire in the same way that Wood combines Air and Water.'

'The Elementals I know have never mentioned these,' I said. 'We have no one who can use such powers.'

'This story is all connected, Jann Argent,' he said. 'Perhaps a brief history of this land will help you understand. Berjengo?

Berjengo was the man on my left who had spoken earlier. To my surprise he stood and walked to the chair, which Mpah vacated for him, coming over to sit beside me.

'In the beginning,' he began, 'All people were civilised. But many centuries ago, twins were born to one of our most powerful mages. These two became bitter rivals as soon as they were old enough to fight. At first they argued over playthings. When they were old enough to learn, they quarrelled with their teachers, but each would always take the opposing view to the other.

'We have argumentative children, naturally,' Berjengo said with a smile, 'but we expect them to grow out of it at an early age and adopt the civilised ways of their parents. Everyone tried to set these two a good example, to chastise them in positive ways, to look for the good in anything they did. But all was in vain. The brother and sister fought all day, and all night. When they were old enough to take partners, each would pick fault with the partner of the other. Soon even the in-laws were resentful, and so the fighting escalated.

'Naturally, being so riven from each other intellectually, morally, and socially, they formed friendships with different people. It seemed to the Elders of the time that the siblings spurred their companions to adopt their rash and uncivilised ways. Fights broke out in the streets. The only ale house in the town barred them both. Our people lived in fear of encountering their marauding gangs and being caught up in the violence. Eventually, the Elders had no choice. The brother and sister, along with their partners and all of their close friends, were banished. The only time such a measure has had to be taken in all our long history.

'Having packed their belongings, the two groups left Tenfir Abarad, travelling in different directions. They established separate settlements: one in the East, and one in the West. For a time, peace reigned. The town was restored to order, and we heard nothing from either camp. But our serenity was not to last. Less than a year after leaving, fighting broke out between the two new townships. Skirmishes, at first. Raids in either direction. It was not long before they armed themselves. The fighting became more extreme. More bloody, and more frequent. Travellers to and from our own town were set upon on the road, robbed and beaten. Then one was killed. Parents came to the Elders in fear for their children's lives. And indeed for their own.

'The Elders debated the problem for many days. They consulted with our mages, counsellors, the parents of the twins. Several solutions were suggested and discarded. Having had no success with banishment, a more drastic and permanent answer was required to restore order to the north.'

'It was at this time,' Kekusaman said, 'forgive my interruption Berjengo, that our most adept mages experimented with a portal. Similar in size and strength, I suspect, to the one you have experience of. But while we learned how to create such a terrible device, we had no one with the knowledge to control it. Our strict moral code would never allow us to dispatch a group of people into the void with no concept of their destination, no matter how heinous their crimes. We had to abandon the vortex and seek another solution.'

She nodded at Berjengo. 'Please continue my friend. I thought it worthy of mention, since the Gatekeeper has encountered one.'

'So scouts were dispatched to investigate the lands to the south, as far as the coast,' Berjengo went on, picking up the thread of his story. 'Our ancestors had explored that far in the distant past, but there is a reason we call this place "the cradle of civilisation". We have everything we need here, and had discovered nothing in the south to encourage us to move. And yet the land between here and the coast was found to be fertile, with good water supplies, plentiful natural resources of wood and stone for building. The Elders were convinced it would be a suitable location for the warring tribes, as they had become known, to settle. Some thought it far enough away to prevent further trouble. Others still believed a more permanent solution was required. The Elders consulted with the most adept Stone mage of the time. They conceived a plan to raise a mountain range between us. This was so audacious it was met with considerable scepticism from many of the Elders. Nevertheless the Stone mage was certain that with enough help he could raise an impassable spine of rock across the entire breadth of the peninsula. The warring tribes would be shut in the South for all time.

'Clearly, we could not allow any Stone mages to join them. Though limited in number and ability compared to the original mountain builders, still it would risk undoing all our good work. Even a narrow gorge or canyon would be sufficient to free the tribes to trouble us anew. And if we must prevent Stone mages, then Wood too had to be restricted in order to maintain balance. In the end one mage from each discipline agreed to travel South. During the debate it became obvious that some Stone power may be needed at that side of the new mountain. We had to ensure it did not encroach too far into the southern lands. We also thought to craft the rock face so it appeared impassable, thus discouraging any attempt to return. The other part of their mission was to suppress the expression of latent Stone and Wood powers. They took with them artefacts to help with this, and agreed to keep the effect of these items secret even from their own descendants.'

I was puzzled by this. I had seen no evidence of Elemental exploitation during my entire time in Tenfir Abarad. I did not want to interrupt Berjengo but my curiosity got the better of me.

'Do you not make use of the Elements now, then? I have not seen any overt usage in my time here.'

The old herb-seller turned to me. I had at first thought he was the chief Elder, but once he relinquished his seat the whole set-up was revealed as a more egalitarian power-sharing co-operative.

'The deliberations of the Elders in those times had to take into account many things,' Mpah said. 'One aspect concerned the forward path for our society. They could not escape the thought that something of our way of life had brought about the troubles. Hubris, or over-reliance on magical means. You must remember, Gatekeeper, the people we banished were our kin. Children, friends. The Elders had to make every effort to ensure they could thrive in their new society. We were in a stronger position. So they elected to send our Elementals and their mages with the outcasts. Earth, Air, Fire, and Water all travelled south, along with the clandestine agents of Stone and Wood. But forgive me—I am encroaching on Berjengo's expertise. Please continue my friend.'

The bearded Elder took up the story once more.

'Indeed. As Penjal has said, the minor Elements formed such an integral part of our lives it was decided the warring tribes had greater need of access to those powers. On the other side of the coin, the presence of Elementals would help to keep peace between them. We have long been aware of the hereditary nature of Elemental power, so the minor Elements aligned themselves in antagonistic pairs to minimise the chances of Wood and Stone powers arising again naturally. Water and Fire joined one camp, while Air and Earth took positions in the other. By this time the sibling rivals had adopted colours and banners of their own, but I cannot recall exactly which took the Black and which the Red.'

For some reason it surprised me that the colours had survived.

'Those colours are now ingrained in their two societies,' I said, 'but over centuries the Elements have realigned into their natural pairings. I guess the reason for the original loyalties was lost in time, although they maintain their insistence on balance. So until recently the Blood Court was served by Fire and Earth, and the Black Palace by Air and Water.'

'Black Palace!' Mpah cried. 'How grand it sounds! It seems their arrogance has not diminished over the years! I suppose they are still at each others' throats?'

'My journey began a few days after the most recent battle,' I said, 'but to be fair, the Black Queen does try to seek peaceful solutions. War is never her first choice.'

'A descendant of the sister, most likely,' Berjengo said. 'The brother was always the more violent of the two. But I should finish the tale of the mountain. It was quite a subterfuge. Something that sat ill on the shoulders of the Elders. But they recognised the necessity, if peace were to return to the north. And indeed if the warring tribes were ever to have a chance of cohabiting without the constant threat of death. We sent delegations to each camp with news of the fertile lands to the south. Warmer climate, abundant fresh water, livestock, and building materials. We sold to them the idea of life there, and they bought it. Land divisions were discussed and agreed, for the most part. Our tales do tell of an area they disputed. Some coastline at the midpoint between the two states. Once the map was settled and preparations made, the tribes set off across our lands. The ceding of our Elementals proved to be the final sweetener. It convinced them we were telling the truth and working in their best interests.

'The prospect of life in the absence of eldritch powers was daunting, but we believed our reasoning was sound. Before they left, we asked the Elementals to establish some long-lasting enchantments to help us over the hump.'

A light went on in my head. 'Is that where the malamajan originated?'

Berjengo smiled. 'Yes, indeed, Gatekeeper. That was one of the major changes of those times. And the power of the charm survives to this day! Is it still the case in the south?'

'It is. That, and the obscuration of Wood and Stone powers, seem to be the major successes of your ancestors' plan. I am only sorry I don't have better news about fighting. The warring tribes are still warring.'

'Yet you said the Elements were aligned "until recently" Gatekeeper. What changed?' Mpah asked.

'During the most recent battle, all the Elementals joined forces to defeat the Blood King. Er... the Red side as you know it. He had summoned a power that had not been used for many years. One which horrified all who saw it. The Elementals realised that only by working together could they defeat it. Afterward, with their new-found camaraderie they decided in future never to divide their loyalties.

'I have no more recent news to impart than that,' I told them. 'When I left, an uneasy peace had settled over the southern lands, though their main causes of dispute remain unresolved.'

The meeting dissolved into a more general discussion on the issues we had raised. Power, both magical and political, and its various manifestations. I wanted to learn more about Wood and Stone, but on a more personal note I brought the subject back to my own use of Gatekeeper powers.

'It is the reason I started out on this quest in the first place,' I said. 'To discover what the power is, exactly. What it can do and how I can use it. What did you mean when you said some gates are closer to the surface?'

As the only person present with a deep understanding of the power, Dipeka Kekusaman answered the question. 'Gates exist everywhere, Gatekeeper. The more practised you become, the easier you will find it to discover them. But their openings are at different levels. I do not fully understand it, but the deeper, and larger the gate, the more power it requires. Both to open it in the first place and to keep it open. The portal you experienced in your past could only be opened with all four Elements working in concert, and in a particular way. On the other hand, the gate you opened yesterday required only Wood. Some even smaller gates will eventually be accessible with nothing but the power of your mind, as I have said.'

I knew then that I would have to spend more time with Kekusaman. The Bera'n had already told me they kept no written records. Only her verbal accounts of how to use the power, how to find gates, and anything else were available to me, but I also knew I had to leave. To bring back all the knowledge of Wood and Stone. I remembered the tale Felice Waters told me on the road to the Blood King's Court soon after the Valiant arrived. Of the young man with his hand stuck in a rock. Could he be a Stone Mage? Or maybe he had opened a tiny gate—only the size of his hand—and closed it again before he could move out of its way?

I thanked the Elders for their openness and frank discussion, and explained why I needed to leave.

'I do not know how I will make the return journey,' I said. 'It almost killed me on the way here, and there are at least two insurmountable obstacles in the other direction.'

Dipeka Kekusaman smiled. 'There are no insurmountable obstacles for you, Jann Argent,' she said. 'You will see.'

*

The room had developed a chill during Jann's narrative; the fire burning to nothing but embers. As he concluded his story, a houseman who had been waiting patiently beside the wall moved to rearrange what remained of their spread and collect the dirty plates. Patrick raked the ashes and threw another log onto the fire.

He turned to Jann. 'And did you?' he asked.

pennatanah
15th day of run'sanamasa, 966

Kyle Muir had fallen asleep to the sound of rain drumming on the roof. She woke to the same sound. It was as if she'd not been asleep at all. Surprised to discover Douglas's cot already empty, she found him at breakfast.

'Early start for you,' she said, carrying a small plate of

food to sit opposite him. Last night's meal still sat heavily in her stomach, but without knowing what the day would bring she decided to eat at least something.

'Yeah,' he said around a mouthful of what looked like sausage but tasted like chicken. 'Couldn't wait to get started with all the excitement.'

'A good night's sleep hasn't improved your mood then, you grumpy sod?'

'If I'd had a good night's sleep, it might have. Damn rain kept me up half the night.'

As he spoke, a fresh squall hit the roof of the hall, resounding around the other passengers while they ate.

'Maybe it'll ease up a bit later,' Kyle offered.

'It better. Wherever I decide to go, I don't want to be travelling on whatever medieval transport they have lined up for us, in the pissing rain.'

'Wherever *we* decide to go.'

'I guess. Do we have to stick together though? What if we don't like the same place?'

The thought of being separated from her brother sent a chill down Kyle's spine. He was probably only trying to wind her up, but even so it was not an attractive prospect.

'Let's see what's on offer before we go assuming we'll want different things. Knowing you, you won't be happy with any of the options!'

'And you'd be happy with any of them, I suppose?'

'I can find something to like about most places,' she agreed. 'Nothing wrong with that.'

While they were talking, Kyle noticed Felice Waters in conversation with a stocky, leather-clad man. He fixed Waters with a stern expression and pulled at a long brown beard while she spoke. Both his beard and hair were heavily streaked with grey. Waters had pointed them out to the man and he was now making his way across the hall toward them.

'Look out,' she said to her brother, 'someone's after you.'

Douglas turned too quickly in the direction of her gaze, knocking his almost-empty plate to the floor. He had a guilty conscience, even here.

'Who's he?' Douglas asked.

'How should I know? I guess we're about to find out.'

The man picked up a chair from the next table and sat beside them.

'Good morning,' he said, in heavily accented English. 'You are Douglas and Kyle Muir?'

'Who's asking?' Douglas said.

Kyle punched his arm. Always with the suspicion!

'My name is Sebaklan Pwalek,' he said, 'advisor to the present leader of the Darmajelis of the Blood Court.'

'Sorry, I wasn't really paying attention yesterday. Is that the King, or the Queen?'

Kyle swiped him across the shoulder. 'It's the King's side, only there isn't a King anymore.'

'Your sister is correct,' Pwalek said. 'We have no King at present, but one will soon be found. In the meantime we have convened the Darmajelis to govern Istania, and I am one of its members. We would like to invite you to join us at Court. We believe we each have something to offer the other.'

'Oh?' said Douglas, retrieving a piece of the chicken-sausage that had fallen from his plate onto the table, and biting down on it. 'And what is it you're offering us?'

'The... er... president offers much,' the man said. He was sweating profusely, despite the chill in the hall. Damp circles shadowed his armpits and he gave off an odour of wet animal hair. 'In the absence of a King, we intend to seize the opportunity to create a more equal society where everyone has a voice. Where each is as powerful as the other.'

He stumbled over the word "powerful". Why? Compared to other natives they'd met, his English was very good. His heightened colour compounded Kyle's certainty there was more to it. She did not trust him.

'Why would this Court be a better choice for us than the Palace?' she asked. After Felice's brief talk, she had visions of life in a Palace, led by a Queen. It seemed far more attractive than whatever this man was offering. Even the name of the place put her off. Blood Court! Ugh!

'The Court is nearer, for one thing,' he said. 'These rains are not normal, but there is no sign they will stop. In this weather it is more than a four day ride to the Palace. You could be at Court in less than half the time. But also we offer you a suite of rooms. We have lake and forest nearby for exploration. Many craftsmen to help if you wish to learn new trade. Perhaps even a seat in government, if politics or administration are of interest?'

Douglas picked up his plate, which had survived its plunge to the stone floor, and affected a detailed examination of his fingernails while the stranger outlined his offer.

'I'm struggling to see what we've done to earn this idyllic life you describe,' he said. 'We are not skilled in any craft, including politics. We don't own anything of value. We've only just arrived. What we have is not much more than what we stand up in. Why us?'

Kyle watched the newcomer licking his lips and fidgeting in his seat as Douglas spoke.

'You are both young,' he replied, 'and strong. Earthers have a frontier spirit which will serve you well at Court. Enthusiasm and energy are far better rewarded there than at the Palace. Theirs is a more... backward society. Still locked in the feudal ways of old. The death of our King has ushered in a new era of enterprise. I know you will have a more rewarding life with us.'

On the other side of the hall a small group of similarly clad men waited. One of them signalled to this one.

'I can see you need time to consider,' he said, pushing back his chair. 'I will remain here until midday, talk to others in your group, see if some of them can be persuaded to join us. Spaces are limited. I will come and find you later if any remain. Unless, of course, you find me.'

With that, he left them to join the others.

'"Spaces are limited",' Kyle said, mimicking the man's voice. 'That's used-car salesman talk if ever I heard it. "Last one on the lot, don't miss your chance. I've had a couple of people checking this baby out already today." What a crock. I don't like him.'

'You want to be a fairy princess in a big castle,' Douglas said, 'and have tea with the Queen. If they even have tea here.'

'We don't actually know anything about either of them,' Kyle said. 'I heard some of the others talking about extending the colony here. Rebuilding the place.'

'Too much work! I don't want to be humping prefab sections for months on end in the pissing rain.'

'You'll have to do something to earn your keep. That man—Polak or whatever his name was –'

'Pwalek.'

'Right. He made it sound as if we'd be treated like visiting dignitaries. It won't be like that at all. And why was he so interested in us?'

'We're just the first people he came to.'

'No. There's more to it than that. I saw him. Talking to Waters. He was looking for us.'

'Don't be stupid! How could he be? No one knows us here!'

'I know what I saw. It's weird.'

'You're just looking for any excuse to go to the Palace. At least five days trekking through the pouring rain. I bet there's nothing to choose between them really. They're all as backward as the most primitive tribe on Earth. If I have to pick one I'd sooner go with the closer option. At least we'll be dry and settled while anyone heading for the Palace will still be soaked and travelling.'

'I don't know. I don't like it.'

'Well you do what you want,' Douglas said, getting to

his feet. 'I'm going to Court. If I can find that Pwalek guy before his spaces run out.'

They each glanced around the hall. Pwalek and the group of men had disappeared.

'Can't have gone far,' he said. 'See you later.'

Kyle sat alone at the table. Something about Pwalek did not sit right in her mind, but she had to agree the shorter journey was more attractive. Douglas' wind-up about life as a princess was closer to the truth than she would have admitted, but she knew this was no fairytale. As always, the prospect of being alone in a strange place, compared to being with her brother in an equally strange place, was enough to tip the balance. She followed him out of the hall.

Chapter 12

Alone on the coast with no recollection of how she had come there, she watched torrents of rain lash the rolling waves. Fierce lightning flashes seared the night sky to stab at the restless sea, while icy winds whipped the swell to foaming peaks. She would not have recognised the location but for the fact she stood on a sturdy wooden jetty that stretched out into a large bay. It was Lembaca Ana, and it seemed the Gardener had completed his works without telling anyone. Perhaps he intended the surprise to be a gift?

The Queen shivered in the freezing air. She had no cloak, and no entourage to provide one. What was she doing here, in such frightful solitude? A shout echoed across the valley from behind her.

'Ru'iiiiita!'

It was Claire! Riding in the vanguard of all the Elementals, their kudai slipping and snorting as they strove to pick a safe path down the hillside.

A loud maniacal laugh from somewhere out in the bay drowned the Air Mage's cry. The Queen peered through the rain. Seen dimly at first but coming quickly into focus, the bearded face of a young man emerged from behind a thundercloud, his piercing icy-blue eyes staring right into her soul. He laughed a second time, his eyes glinting with menace, as the rains redoubled their intensity, drenching the Queen to the skin. She shivered again with cold, and with fear.

The Elementals would save her! But no! As she watched, the unremitting downpour undermined the already slippery path. A kudo at the back of the group lost its footing and skidded into the one in front, setting off a catastrophic chain reaction of sliding and falling that knocked the group over like a set of ninepins. With shouts of mounting terror, they tumbled to the edge of the cliff and out into the raging waters below, their voices stilled into deathly silence as they slipped beneath the boiling sea.

Seconds later a lightning bolt blazed from the sky to hit the jetty beside the Queen. More intense than any other, she was momentarily blinded by the cold white light. When her eyes recovered she saw the wood of the jetty had absorbed the charge and now glowed an alien blue, sparking and coruscating along its entire length. She felt no effect from the bolt, and yet the eerie after-light seemed to offer comfort from the storm. She bent to examine it more closely but lost her balance on the slick surface. The malevolent laughter of the face in the clouds echoing in her ears, she fell headlong toward the dark water.

The Queen awoke with a start. The sheet beneath her saturated with sweat, her chambers chilled from the continuing rain, there was nevertheless a source of heat in the bed with her. She took her hands out from under the covers. Around her wrists the inky black circles of her obsidian bangles, which she had worn for as long as she could remember, were hot to the touch.

the black palace
15th day of run'sanamasa, 966

The morning after Jann Argent's return, Claire was still trying to get her head around his story. The revelations about the ancient history of the two Berikatanyan states were surprising enough. The knowledge that there were other Elemental powers beyond those familiar to her, and the other Guild leaders, was mind-blowing.

Their gathering had finally broken up shortly before dawn. Lautan and Petani retired once Jann completed his account. The rest of them stayed behind to discuss its implications.

'I keep coming back to this old tale of the man with his

hand in a rock,' Patrick had said. 'It seems more than likely he has some ability as a stone mage. Do we know where he lives?'

'Felice only spoke in general terms,' Jann replied, 'but I'm sure she said he settled away from Court or Palace. A more rural village, somewhere to the South.'

'We must find him,' Elaine said, 'and quickly. Before word of Wood and Stone reaches the Istanians. They will doubtless have heard the tales too. They'll want to exploit this man's powers, such as they are, for their own ends.'

'What about the new arrivals?' Claire said. 'No one from the Palace has visited Pennatanah yet, but Istania will certainly send someone. If any of them have latent powers, like I did, we should be there to explain things to them.'

'We have no time to lose,' Elaine said, pressing her point. 'We must travel tomorrow. We can journey together until we're through the Forest.'

'And then what?' Patrick asked. 'We need to decide who will go where.'

'The best knowledge we have of Stone power is only second-hand, from Jann. He should seek out this man. I will go with him.'

'In that case, I'll travel on to Pennatanah,' Claire had said. 'I know how strange and unsettling it feels to have unconscious control over the elements. I have the best chance of spotting anyone in similar straits.'

'I know that feeling too,' Patrick added. 'I'll come with you.'

'What of Lautan and Petani?' Elaine asked. 'One of them should tag along with each group. Claire, you and Petani have worked together. Why don't you take him with you? Lautan can come with us.'

And so it had been decided. They each tried to rest, knowing the journey would be long and arduous. Even so Claire had arrived at the refectory long before lunch service started, unable to settle with the enormity of their task weighing on her mind. The daunting prospect had affected the others too: she did not have to eat alone for long.

Conversation over the breakfast table was muted. Restricted to shared jokes about lack of sleep and the now inevitable rain, which lashed the windows of the large hall with continued vigour. Everyone avoided mention of travel, or their chances of success. The servery provided fresh and dried provisions for the journey to the Forest Clearance Project. They intended to rest there and replenish the supplies. The weather and the deteriorating roads would slow their progress. They had planned for a four-day ride instead of the usual two.

The kudai made their feelings known while being saddled. Dragged from a warm, dry stable into the cold steady drizzle of a grim, grey Sanamasa day, they snickered and bucked while the travellers cinched girths and fastened traces. The Queen appeared during their preparations. She too looked tired. She bore a small pile of clothes.

'Take great care on this journey,' she said to the group. 'Kertonia cannot afford to lose any of you, especially in these strange times. Our scouts report some sections of the roadways have collapsed but all are passable at least as far as the foot of Tubelak'Dun. Beyond that, they have not ventured.'

'Thank you, your Majesty,' Elaine said. 'We are grateful for the knowledge.'

'We have had the court seamstresses prepare these,' the Queen added, handing the garments to the Fire Witch. 'They are not entirely proof against the rain, but they will shed some of it. They are designed to dry out again quickly. There is no warmth in the fabric, but perhaps some protection against the wind.'

Elaine distributed the Queen's gift to each member of the troupe, starting with Jann. Claire unfolded what proved to be a large cloak, similar to a poncho. It slipped over her head and covered her as far as the knees. One size fits all. The design included a hood, tightened with a simple drawstring. The weave was treated with something that gave it a sheen. Rain ran off it easily when it hung down, or beaded on a horizontal surface.

'These are most welcome, ma'am,' Claire said.

'It is our pleasure, my dear. A small token, only.'

The Queen hurried back indoors. Elaine and Claire combined their powers to protect her from the worst of the storm as she walked. She threw a grateful smile over her shoulder at the Elementals before crossing the threshold.

Claire caught Jann staring after the Queen, a strange, intense look on his face.

'What?' she said.

'Hmm?'

'What's with the thousand-yard stare? Did our Queen grow horns?'

'Come on,' Patrick shouted before Jann could reply. He was already mounted. 'The sooner we start the sooner we can make our first camp.'

So saying, he led the way through the Palace gates and on to the gravel path leading to the moat. Lautan remarked on the height of its waters as they crossed, the hooves of their kudai echoing beneath the bridge. They rode alongside the outer bank for some distance before heading north toward the nearest river crossing, which the scouts had claimed was still passable. Claire thought Lautan looked uncomfortable and dejected in the rain. Normally the presence of water buoyed his spirits, but she guessed this unnatural downpour had the opposite effect. He had already admitted to being powerless to stop it, which was reason enough to be depressed.

The gravel under their kudai's hooves provided a good soakaway for the rain. They reached the river crossing without incident. The stone-built bridge had indeed weathered the storm so far, but there were signs the fast-flowing river had eroded its foundations. As the afternoon wore on and the rain showed no signs of slowing, their new cloaks lost their water shedding ability. They hung heavily against their legs and the kudai's flanks.

'We will be losing the light soon,' Jann said, 'especially with this heavy cloud cover. Tubelak'Dun is only a short distance further. I suggest we press on to the foothills and try to find shelter there for the night.'

A murmur of assent passed around the group, each huddled under a sodden cloak, each hoping they would find a decent campsite to provide some respite from the weather. The rain pitched and swelled, but never slowed to less than a heavy drizzle, occasionally throwing a squall into the faces of the riders, making the kudai snort and buck. Their plodding pace was only partly due to the uncertainty of the footing. The poor animals were just as miserable as their riders.

The diluted orb of the sun, which had never broken through the cloud during the day, began to fade toward the Western mountains by the time the travellers crossed into the lowest of the foothills. Their path to the Forest skirted the northern tip of the range, rising to less than a hundred metres above the plain. This area was lightly wooded. They stopped at the first copse that afforded any shelter, dismounted, and fed their kudai before beginning a search for enough dry kindling to make a fire. The damp wood spit and crackled as the flames took hold with some assistance from Elaine's power. Claire spread their cloaks in nearby branches to dry while Jann and Patrick prepared a meal. She conjured an air current, but with the wind already laden with moisture it didn't help much.

'Can't you do *anything* about this damned rain, Lautan?' Jann asked, brushing a flying ember from his sleeve.

'Alas, Gatekeeper,' the old wizard replied, squeezing water from his beard and wiping his hands on his cloak, 'as I have said, I am at a loss to understand what is causing this. And since I cannot comprehend it, I know not how to stop it.'

Claire felt a lump rise in her throat as Lautan took a

seat and rested his head in his hands. Even the sweet aroma of herbs and meat from the stew pot, now beginning to bubble over the fire, did nothing to lift the Elemental's mood. While their simple meal sang its cooking song, she took the chance to ask a question that had bothered her since leaving the previous night's meeting.

'You obviously found a way back over the mountain,' she said to Jann. 'How did you do it?'

Firelight played over his face as he sat staring at the pot, giving it an occasional stir.

'Dipeka Kekusaman was quite right. Once I started looking for gates—once I knew what to look for –there were several I could use without much effort. My staff helped me to find even more. There was one close to Tenfir Abarad. It led back to the caldera, so I regained my camp in a single step. I stayed there overnight. More from nostalgia I guess than any need to recuperate. Translating through a gate doesn't take much energy, for me at least. Next day I scouted around and located a second gate on the lake shore. It took me right through the mountain. I emerged beside the pool where I'd left Perak. I have no idea whether it was simply coincidence—finding a gate that linked two shores. The old boy was still waiting for me. Maybe he had some instinct compelling him to wait, I don't know. There's plenty of grass and scrub there for him to eat, and a pond full of fresh water, so it's more likely he had no reason to leave. Once I'd found him it made sense to ride back. I didn't bother looking for any other gates.'

Jann divided the stew into bowls, the others coming to his call. Claire paused with her sunyok halfway to her mouth.

'If there are gates all over, and they're so easy to find, why aren't we "gating" our way to the Forest?'

Jann laughed, covering his mouth with the back of his hand. 'When I'm travelling alone, all I need is a gate large enough for me.' He waved his hand around the campsite. 'Look at all this. Opening a portal large enough for all of us, our provisions, and the animals to pass through would need some serious Elemental power.'

'So?' Claire said. 'Look around yourself! We're all here. There's no shortage of power on this trip! There must be more to it than that.'

Jann's face reddened under the light from the flames. Claire did not let her gaze fall, or break the silence.

'It's complicated,' he said at length. 'It's not like opening a door. Once a door is open, it stays open until someone closes it. And you can see through to the other side. Patrick and I met an old man on our first visit to Lembaca Ana. I never knew his name. We called him the Pilgrim. He told me the Gatekeeper can see in both directions at once, standing on a threshold. That I would always know the start and end point. But he was wrong. With some gates it's like that, but not always. The other side is often indistinct. Foggy, sometimes, or gloomy. Sometimes it shifts.'

'In what way? You mean the view of the other side moves around?'

'Not like swivelling a telescope. More like a flipbook. You're not always sure which view is the truth. Sometimes it's not clear where the gate will lead. Small gates, those close to the surface, they're simple. Deeper gates are more unpredictable. Harder to find, harder to be certain where they go. And then, of course, they need to be held open. I have to maintain the power during the transition.'

'What if you didn't?'

Jann blanched. 'I don't know. I know where the gates begin. I might know where they end. I'm not exactly sure where they go in between. But I wouldn't like to be in one when it closed. That kuclar, in the village...'

'When you saved the girl?'

'Yes. I didn't have time to check where it went. I didn't even know I was creating a gate really, not at the time. I just reacted. Opened it as the cat pounced. Closed it as soon as it had entered. The animal could be anywhere. Or nowhere,' he added, staring into the fire.

'It was easier when I was travelling back. It didn't matter to me where the gate went. I got lucky. They were shallow gates and I could see where they were going. But I could as easily have ended up further north. So what? I figured I'd find another and try again. I wasn't running to a timetable, I only had myself to worry about. I was practising. Still am. There are so many variables. So all things considered, I thought it was probably best to do this journey the traditional way. Even with the rain. Safer. Gates are tricky.'

Silence fell again between them. Jann continued to stare at the flickering flames. Who knew what demons her questions had conjured in his mind? She shivered, in spite of the heat from the fire. She knew from her own experience that high magic did not always go to plan. At least Air power was not capable of throwing a person into an abyss of nothingness.

road between pennatanah and court
15th day of run'sanamasa, 966

Kyle Muir could not remember a time when she had felt more miserable. Except maybe the day she'd had to abandon her few friends when the family moved to the United States after her father's promotion. He'd called it a new start, but it always seemed like the end of something to her. Nothing like that glorious sunny day, a hundred years ago, when they boarded the Dauntless. At the beginning of their trip to a new world, Kyle believed she was on the verge of a marvellous adventure. Now, on yet another journey to a new domicile, her odyssey had turned into a cold, sodden, shivering nightmare. The sea crashed against the coastline to her left. What looked like a mountain range stood guard to her right. The views would have been spectacular if they were not rendered grey and featureless by the incessant rain. The locals, even the earlier colonists from Earth, were strangely unprepared for wet weather. The cloak she had been given had long since become saturated. It clung to her like a frigid lover, caressing her thighs with clammy hands and sending new shivers through her already trembling body.

The weather was bad enough, but on top of that she had to put up with her brother's foul temper, which worsened with every gust of wind. As if attracted by her thought, Douglas reined his kudo to a halt, turning in his saddle to make himself heard.

'Does this fucking rain ever stop?' he shouted.

Before she could answer, another drenching blast caught her from the seaward side, threatening to unseat her. The kudo snickered in disgust at the renewed strength of the downpour. To her dismay she realised her brother was laughing.

'I guess it does have its entertaining side,' he said once he recovered his breath. 'Although watching you get wetter doesn't make me feel any drier.'

A peculiar air current swept the rain into eddies around Douglas' mount. For a moment the rain appeared not to touch him at all. She shook her head, cold wet strands of hair slapping her face and sticking where they touched. When she looked again, he seemed every bit as saturated as she was. Silver ribbons of dripwater ran from the hem of his cloak. His close-cropped hair stuck to his skull, giving him the look of an animated corpse.

'You *aren't* any drier,' she retorted. 'If anything, you've always been wetter than me.'

'Keep telling yourself that dear sister,' he said, facing forward in his saddle and spurring his kudo on against the grey curtain of rain. 'The only thing dry about you right now is your sense of humour.'

Their pace was impeded by the dray wagons travelling alongside them. They bore the Muirs' few belongings, along with those of the others from Dauntless who elected to join them at Court. Something else Douglas had complained about when they were preparing to leave the landing site.

'I thought we were special,' he had said to Pwalek earlier. 'You said a place had been reserved for us.'

'And so it has, young master Muir, but these others seek a life at Court also. Who am I to deny them? Each must find his own path. I repeat: you will find yours considerably different from these others.'

'Considerably *better*, I think you said. Chambers reserved for us, you said.'

A blood vessel stood out on the man's temple, pulsating in time with his heartbeat. A fast beat: a sure sign of heightened emotion. She understood that reaction to her brother all too well.

'Leave it Douglas. I'm sure Pwalek is as good as his word.'

'Thank you my lady. If we can only complete the journey, you will see the truth of it.'

Douglas reined back again, interrupting her remembering. 'Can't these damned carts go any faster? I can feel my skin starting to wrinkle. If I don't get out of these clothes soon I'll catch fucking pneumonia.'

'If we didn't have the wagons,' she replied, 'there would be no dry clothes for you to change into.'

Her logic, though undeniable, served only to worsen her brother's mood. He never had liked being wrong about anything. He rode off again and did not return until Pwalek halted the convoy close to a wooded area through which the road passed. Since leaving the gravelled roadway behind, their progress had been even slower. The dirt road, now little more than a streak of mud across the landscape after days of constant rain, sucked at the kudai's hooves. The uncertain surface threatened to throw their legs from underneath them at any moment.

'This is the last shelter until we reach the Sun Hutang,'

Pwalek said. 'There is little sign of the rain stopping, so I suggest we camp here and get some rest. The river was swollen when I came through last night and will likely be even higher by now. We will need all our wits and strength to make a safe crossing. Better to do it tomorrow than try now, when the animals are tired from the day's trek.'

He dismounted and led his kudo onto the grassy verge. Kyle followed his example. The animal nuzzled her hand in gratitude before cropping at the wet grass. Pwalek barked instructions to the other colonists. Fetch wood, move the wagons under cover, build a fire. They all looked as miserable as Kyle felt. Cold, wet, and sore from a day in the saddle which none of them were used to. At least she was spared that. One of her childhood joys had been to join Douglas riding along the coastal paths, picnicking on the cliff tops and watching the white horses in the bay, or her brother surfing. They were both skilled riders, but he could keep his surfboard. Kyle had never understood the appeal.

'You can get changed behind that scrub,' said Pwalek indicating a denser clump of bushes to her left. 'Take it in turns if you're shy.' He let out a hollow laugh that gave Kyle another shiver.

The clothes in her chest were uniformly damp, even when she dug down to the bottom. Nothing in this place was weatherproof! Douglas helped another man, possibly called Adrian, to light a fire, but the wood they had found was too wet to catch. Could there possibly be anything left to annoy him today? She watched his face redden and his grimace deepen and still the fire would not start. The rain rattled noisily in the branches of the trees, a large drop finding its way through and falling onto the back of her neck.

'Ugh!' she said, spinning sideways to protect the outfit she had retrieved from getting any wetter. She had hoped at least to eat, and snatch a little sleep before being soaked to the skin once more.

After changing, she did feel a little warmer. Pwalek had finally found enough dry kindling to persuade the fire to light, although Douglas made it smoke by dumping the wetter wood onto it. The acrid plumes caught in her throat and eyes, making her cough.

'Anyone would think you'd never made a camp fire before,' she said.

Douglas flashed an angry look in her direction but did not respond.

'The dry wood burns too quickly and there is too little of it,' Pwalek said. Kyle did not know why he needed to defend her brother's ineptitude. 'I'm afraid our choices were a smoky fire or a very brief one.'

'Why is nothing on this planet waterproof?' she asked him, voicing her earlier thought. 'With this much rain surely you have suitable cloaks or at least tents to provide some shelter?'

'Tents?' the Istanian said. 'This is not a word I know.'

Kyle explained.

'Yes,' he said, 'ahmek. We have them, but for battle camps or long time projects only, with more people. They are large and heavy, not easily carried on the backs of kudai. Not suitable for small groups of travellers. Our people rarely travel at night.'

'What's night got to do with it?' Douglas said. His tone made Kyle's teeth itch, but she did not risk asking him to dial it down. 'Surely you travel in the day. When it's raining?'

Pwalek gave him a strange look. 'It does not rain during the day.'

Douglas barked a disdainful laugh, his arms raised in a sweeping, all-encompassing gesture. 'What's this then?'

'It is unusual,' Pwalek replied. 'Unheard of, I would say. The malamajan has kept the rain to a short period of the night for centuries past. Only in the last few days has this daylight rain been happening.'

'Malamajan?' Kyle said. 'What is that, some kind of

climate control? Even we don't have that technology. I can't believe you have it here.'

'I do not know "climate control". The malamajan is a manifestation of Water power.'

'What the hell is Water power?' Douglas asked, throwing another thin branch onto the fire, which was burning more fiercely now and with less smoke. He fixed Pwalek with a strange look, his eyes catching the firelight and appearing also to smoulder.

'Water is one of the four Elements,' Pwalek said. 'They are all around us here. Our mages can control them. Some of them only a little. But the four Elementals can command them.'

'You're going to tell me the others are Earth, Air, and Fire, aren't you?' Douglas asked, his face twisted into a sneer.

Pwalek's eyes widened. 'Batu'n do not usually know of this. How is it you have the knowledge?'

'I read the comics,' Douglas laughed. 'You can't be serious? We could have used a fire mage earlier to get this bloody thing started. What's a Batoon?'

'You are. Batu'n is what we call people from your world.'

'If you lot are so good at controlling things, why doesn't your Water dude, whoever he is, stop this damned rain?'

'Elementals do as they will,' Pwalek replied with a shrug, 'their reasons are a mystery to me. The Water Wizard has a great many years' experience, but he has not been seen in these parts since the great battle.'

'Just bloody marvellous,' Douglas said.

Pwalek poked at the fire with the last dry stick. 'We need more wood," he said, getting to his feet. 'This will not last the night.'

Douglas hoisted himself onto a low tree branch. 'Told you it would be shit here,' he said. 'Even their bloody magicians are no good!'

He had chosen to sit in the same tree that dumped a large raindrop on Kyle earlier. As she watched, another fell from the uppermost branches, missing her brother by millimetres and splashing onto the branch beside him. The annoying prick had the luck of the devil, and Old Nick's temper too.

'We could have stayed at Pennatanah and avoided all this,' she said, resting a hand on the trunk of Douglas' tree but keeping an eye out for further raindrops. 'I overheard some of the others talking about starting a proper "Earther" colony, separate from Court or Palace. We would have stayed dry.'

'We wouldn't have been special there,' Douglas replied. 'We will be special at Court.'

'You don't even know what he meant by that,' she said. 'His English isn't that good. It could mean anything. Or nothing.'

'No. He wanted us. I have no idea why, but he sought us out. Life at Court is going to be good.'

He smiled, probably the first time Kyle had seen him look happy the whole day.

'Much better than if we had stayed with the Batoon.'

She gave his knee a slap.

'Batu'n!' she said. 'Don't try and pretend you're already one of the natives. They've had ten years of dealing with us. You won't fool anyone. Except yourself,' she added, watching another raindrop fall from the canopy. It too missed her brother. *Luck of the devil.*

The next day began even greyer, even wetter. The rains, which had not let up overnight, started the morning with renewed vigour. They slanted in under the trees, soaking those few colonists who had slept nearer the roadway. Pwalek announced they had no time to scout for more dry timber, so after a desultory cold breakfast they packed up and hit the road. Within moments of starting out, Kyle was drenched to the skin once again.

forest clearance project
16th day of run'sanamasa, 966

The Elementals crossed into Besakaya Forest soon after midday on the third day of their journey. Progress had been painfully slow since they reached the central mountain range of Tubelak'Dun. The continuing downpours had saturated much of the ground, with new areas of flooding around every turn. Claire watched with a feeling of helplessness as Lautan fought to control the floodwaters to maintain a clear path for them. They had made another early stop the day before, reaching the Sun Hutang and finding it impassable. They camped close to the riverbank, intending to seek out another crossing with the advantage of new daylight and a full night's rest.

The roar of the river had soon lulled Claire to sleep. For once her dreams were not filled with terror. Nightmares had troubled her long before leaving the Palace. Friends being washed away in raging flood waters, drowning in the moat, or waking to find her bed floating in a lake of stinking, foetid swamp water. Yet camped only metres away from the fast-flowing river, her sleep was undisturbed.

That morning they followed the course of the river for several kilometres and eventually had to admit they were unlikely to find a crossing. Lautan declared he would create one, and without further ado stepped into the torrent with his arms raised. For the first time, Claire heard him use an incantation. Normally the ancient Elemental wielded his power easily, accessing his core in a way familiar to Claire with her own power, but without words or gesticulation. That he spoke at all, and moved his hands in arcane ways, meant redirecting the flow of the river took all his concentration and strength. Under the influence of his magic the current bent around him, leaving a small area of riverbed in his wake.

Their kudai baulked at stepping into this space, but seeing Lautan's intent, the riders pressed them to the water's edge. Still they shied away from the raging torrent. Claire saw Patrick wave his left hand. For a moment his gesture left a trail of dark smoke in the rain, but before she could focus it was gone. She felt the tension in Pembwana's body disappear. Her mount, together with all the others, walked into the maelstrom as if it were just another woodland path. The Water Wizard continued his slow march across the river, the rest of the group keeping as close behind him as they could without distracting him.

On reaching the opposite bank, Lautan collapsed to the ground, his face pale with exhaustion. The river crashed into the space he had created as the last of them stepped ashore, sending a gout of spray that soaked Claire and Patrick anew. She dismounted and rushed to Lautan's side.

'Is there anything I can do?' she said, taking his hand.

The old man gave her a weak smile, his rheumy eyes looking at each of the party in turn, seeking something. At last, Elaine moved into view.

'Perhaps a little of your sustenance, Bakara,' he said, wheezing. 'For once I feel the need to be warm and dry.'

'Of course, old friend,' the Fire Witch replied, closing her eyes in concentration and sending gentle waves of heat in his direction.

They had remained on the riverbank while Lautan recovered his strength, and then set out once more for the Forest. Claire fell in beside Patrick as they rode.

'What did you do?' she asked quietly.

'Hmm?'

'I saw you. Before we crossed. You did something to the kudai. Something to take away their fear.'

Patrick frowned. 'I'd rather not talk about it.'

'It's Juggler power, isn't it? It's what you learned at your father's house.'

They rode in silence for some time before he answered.

'Yes. But it scares me. I haven't used it since I returned, and I won't. Only in extremis. It is a dangerous lore. I can't tell you. I can't even think about it without breaking into a sweat. But there was no other way. The kudai were terrified, and Lautan could not have held the waters back for long. Please don't say anything to the others.'

'But–' Claire began, before the tormented look on Patrick's face silenced her. In all her time at the Palace, and in the company of the Keeper of the Keys, she had never heard anyone speak of the Pattern Juggler's powers. Now her friend had learned something about them, it seemed the knowledge gave a hint why the subject was shrouded in mystery. She spurred Pembwana forward, leaving Patrick to his thoughts.

She caught up with the Fire Witch, who had taken a position at the head of their line and was trying to dry out the roadway with blasts of Fire. The effort took its toll on her too, Claire could see. The entire width of the path was a boggy quagmire with no easy or safe route to guarantee a good purchase for their animals' hooves. Elaine concentrated her power on a narrow section of road in an attempt to create such a path. Progress was slow, and it was clear her strength would be exhausted long before they made the Forest.

'Can I help?' she asked. 'Maybe hot air would dry the mud faster?'

Elaine swept her face with the back of a hand. 'Air is harder to heat than mud,' she said, out of breath. 'But by all means summon your power. It can do no harm.'

Claire bent her will to the task, but it was soon apparent that drafts of moisture-laden air had almost no effect on the sodden roadway. Lautan joined them, looking a little recovered.

'There is a run-off ahead,' he said. 'It is that which is muddying our path. I believe I can redirect it into this gulley.'

He gestured at the ditch which ran along the side of the roadway.

'Perhaps you can boil it off Bakara, before it overflows once more?'

The plan worked, after a fashion, but both Elementals were close to exhaustion. By the time the Forest came into view they could do no more.

'We must stop here, under the trees,' Elaine said, her face drained of blood and resembling a grey mummer's mask. 'I can ride no longer without sleep.'

Petani rode up beside them, his face creased into a scowl. 'You're stopping here? I had hoped we would press on to the Project. It is not far now. I must find out how the crops are faring, and the team. I have seen the conditions thus far. I have a feeling they will be in need of my help and I cannot delay.'

Elaine offered the old man a weak smile. 'For you, Petani, I will suffer in the saddle a little longer, though it will be a wonder if I stay in my seat.'

So they resumed their journey. The path beneath the trees, protected from the worst of the rain, was in better condition. Progress improved. Only in one place had a river breached the trail. Lautan deflected its course while they crossed, their kudai's hooves crunching on exposed gravel but otherwise unaffected. They emerged from the darkened Forest into the Project clearing as night fell. Several of the Project members, busy lighting torches around the camp, hurried over to greet them. At the sight of the Earth Elemental, the nearest let out a cry of delight.

'Petani! You have come! At our greatest need! We have prayed to Tana for your return, before all is lost!'

Petani almost dropped from his saddle. He gripped the young man's shoulders. 'Lost? The Project is lost? Come, show me.'

He strode off into the clearing, the younger man at his heels. Two of the others followed, repeating what the first had said almost word for word.

'Go after him, Claire,' Jann said. 'Find out what can be done tonight, if anything. I will see to the others and the kudai.'

'I will come with you,' Patrick said, swinging a leg over

his mount and sliding gracefully to the muddy ground. He pulled his hood tighter around his face and followed Claire.

As they neared the main area of planting, the worked soil, now turned to deep mud by the continuing rain, sucked at Claire's boots. Every footstep was a slipping, sliding invitation to fall. From ahead in the gloom, Petani's anguished cry echoed across the clearing.

Claire crested a small rise with Patrick at her side. Even in the failing light, the extent of the devastation was clear. Parts of the plantation had been washed away wholesale. Others were beaten flat by the pounding of the rain. To Claire's left, on the far side of the Project, trees at the edge of the remaining Forest had had their roots undermined. They lay collapsed across the crops in a jumbled heap, branches pointing skyward as if in accusation of the rains. Their exposed roots, washed clean of soil, gleamed white in the deepening gloom like skeletons picked at by carrion crows. One had fallen right across the middle of the garden, crushing blooms beneath its colossal trunk.

She rushed to Petani's side. Tears streamed down his face, mingling with raindrops.

'It is even worse than I dared think,' he said, swallowing a sob. 'I cannot leave it like this. They need my help. All that work. Ruined.'

His knees sagged. If Claire had not been there to support him he would have collapsed into the mud. Patrick grabbed his other arm.

'Come away old friend,' he said. 'We can do nothing tonight. Get some rest. Take a hot meal. We will come back at first light and take a better look.'

'Meal?' Petani cried. 'I cannot eat! I can hardly even think!'

'You must eat,' Patrick insisted. 'You can do no good here without your strength and your wits about you. Come, let's get you out of this damned rain.'

They led the old man back to the campsite. The

Berikatanyans chattered incessantly, and so quickly that Claire could not follow what they were saying, beyond the obvious expressions of relief that Petani had returned and their certainty that he could make everything better.

In the team hut the rest of their group sat with the Project members beside a small fire pit, their cloaks and boots strewn around it to dry. Elaine massaged Jann's shoulders while each of the others took tentative sips from large, steaming mugs of soup, the rich comforting smell of the broth a welcome alternative to damp earth and wet clothing. Jann passed over a mug which Petani took reluctantly. After tasting the soup he finished it as fast as he could drink without burning his mouth. He handed the empty mug back to Jann.

'Thank you. I think I could try a little more.'

Once the soup was finished Patrick added a few more logs to the fire. The Project leader David Garcia poured wine for those who wanted it and bumerang juice infused with forest herbs for the others.

'I'm sorry you had to come back to this,' he said once everyone had been served. 'We did our best...'

The old Elemental laid a hand on the man's shoulder. 'No one could have stopped it,' he said. 'Even I am at a loss to know what to do. But whatever can be done, I will stay to do it.'

'We have business elsewhere, Petani,' Elaine said, taking some soup for herself. 'If we do not find a way to stop these rains, anything you do here will be in vain.'

The old Gardener took a sip of wine, staring into the fire. Claire watched his conflicting emotions play across his face in the flickering firelight. They had been close companions back in the early days of this Project, but she knew she could not help him now. Even if he could be persuaded to leave, his heart would remain here, distracting him from other purposes.

'Nevertheless, I will stay,' he said, draining his glass. 'You must do what you think is right, as must I. The

Forest needs my help before I can offer it elsewhere. And now,' he said, rising to his feet with a grunt, 'I must get some rest. There is an awful lot of work to do tomorrow.'

'Umtanesh has prepared your old ahmek,' Garcia said. 'It is still pitched in your favourite spot.'

'Thank you,' Petani said as he left the hut.

The others drifted away one by one until at last only Claire, Patrick, and Jann remained sitting in the reddening light of the dying fire. Outside the hut the rain continued to fall, but had lessened to a stiff drizzle that made a constant scraping sound against the wooden roof.

'More wine?' Jann asked.

'No, thank you,' Claire replied. 'We still have a way to travel tomorrow. I can't ride with a wine-sodden head.'

'How long do you think he will stay here?' Patrick asked. 'And what does he think he can do?'

Claire shrugged. 'He will stay as long as he believes he should. This place is close to his heart. He poured a lot of himself into that garden.'

'I remember his tale, back at the Armstrong spaceport while we were waiting to board,' Jann said. 'About the crushed flower at the posh house he was working on. That was just one flower, and it was enough to bring him here. Half his entire garden is destroyed now. What's that going to do to him?'

'It's not his own doing, though,' Claire replied. 'I remember that story too. He trod on that flower. It was the carelessness that hit him so hard. This is different. It's not his fault. But if he doesn't do everything he can to put it right, that *will* be his fault. He can't turn his back on it.'

'It's just a garden though,' Patrick said.

'I can't explain it,' Claire said. 'You'd have to work with him as long as I did to understand what it means. But in any case it's not just the garden is it? The whole of the rest of the Project is trashed. It's pretty obvious the team can't fix it on their own, and he wouldn't leave them to it. It's not in his nature.'

'Even when there's a more pressing need?' Jann said. 'We didn't come this far to mend a few broken flower beds.'

'That's a bit harsh. There are five of us and only one of him. I guess he thinks we can carry on without him, but Garcia and the rest of them here can't.'

The conversation went around the subject again several times. Frustrated by the others' inability to see Petani's point of view, Claire left them to it.

The next day dawned grey and cold, with the overnight drizzle seemingly set in for the day. They said brief farewells before Petani left for the clearing, and saddled up their kudai under the shelter of the treeline. Nembaka had packed some meat and fruit into vine leaves for the journey. They set off, heading for the south-western edge of the Forest. They saw several more fallen trees whose roots had been undermined, but none had fallen across the path. Around noon they emerged from the Forest into the full force of the rain once again, which by that time had become stronger.

'Let's not hang around in this,' Elaine said. She pointed south. 'Your path to Pennatanah leads in that direction Claire. We are taking the other road to the coast. Be careful! With any luck we will see you back at the Palace in a few days.'

Claire turned Pembwana south, with Patrick falling in beside her.

'Take care yourselves!' she called over her shoulder.

pennatanah
16th day of run'sanamasa, 966

Closing the lab door behind her gave Felice Waters a feeling of blessed relief. From the rain, certainly, but she had almost grown accustomed to that. Right now, the colonists were giving her a worse headache. In the past, delegations from Court and Palace had pitched newly arrived passengers with embroidered tales of how life could be for them if they only chose it. Blacks and Reds, as they called each other, were always keen to make an impression and attract the best of the crop. Istanians and Kertonians both valued the skills Earthers brought with them, but had also quickly recognised the benefits of the frontier spirit that had led most of them to board a Prism ship in the first place. They wanted to exploit it quickly, before it evaporated.

This time, apart from the unexpected appearance of the intense and slightly scary Sebaklan Pwalek yesterday, there had been no word from either camp. If anyone had asked, Felice would have said it more likely for a delegation to come from the Palace. They were in better shape, politically, with the Istanians still coming to terms with how they should govern their realm in the wake of the Blood King's death. Felice and her team did their best, of course, but they were not salespeople. Having themselves chosen to remain at Pennatanah they could hardly extol the virtues of life in the Black Palace or the Blood Court. They had neither the inclination nor the experience to paint a verbal picture for the new colonists. Left to their own imaginations, most of them were taking longer than usual to make up their minds. With the exception of the Muir twins' party, which left yesterday in the company of Pwalek and his men, all of the remaining passengers from the Dauntless were still here. Felice already longed for the base to return to its normal status as a quiet backwater.

For today, though, she had done all she could for the colonists. Her attention returned to her pet project: DNA monitoring. Her pile of samples, swelled by several hundred new arrivals, sat in a plastic tub on her desk. They needed to be catalogued before being run through the analyser and the results entered in her simple database.

Felice picked up two samples that had slipped from the tub. Labelled "Douglas Muir" and "Kyle Muir", they had been opened. Not only opened: analysed. Two sheets of paper sat in the output hopper. An odd coincidence that these were the ones Pwalek asked about, and two of the few already to have left Pennatanah. A cursory glance at the results revealed nothing out of the ordinary, but since the arrival of Dauntless had interrupted her project she didn't have much of a benchmark to compare them with. She shrugged, dropped the Muirs' results and samples back into the tub, and set to work to finish processing the earlier ones.

It was tedious work. The analyser could deal with a hundred samples at once, but for multiple runs the constant unloading, cleaning, reloading, and restarting was mindlessly repetitive. Right now she was more interested in processing her control group: the three Elementals' specimens, along with Jann Argent and Patrick Glass. Once their results had spooled from the printer, she kicked off another run including a sample taken from a "talented" Earther, and sat down at her desk to compare the early results. It did not take long. The Elementals' graphs shared a very distinct sequence of spikes, unlike anything Felice had seen before. She was not a molecular biologist, but during her time in the New York police force she had seen plenty of DNA results. None of them looked like this.

Patrick Glass was another matter. He differed from the Elementals, but also had a unique pattern of his own. Felice ran a hand through her hair and massaged the back of her neck. Sitting hunched in the same position had left her with a nagging ache. Looking at these results nagged at her too. They were trying to tell her something, but she could not work out what. More data was required. The analyser spat out its latest sheet. Felice turned to load the next batch of samples.

Chapter 13

Jann could hardly believe the change in less than a day. When they entered the Forest, the road had been hard going but still passable with care. Overnight the canopy of trees shielded them from the worst of the rain. This morning their only path had become a slippery quagmire. The kudai shied and snorted at each slip, or refused to walk forward at all. The riders were forced to dismount and lead the spooked animals through the mud. Their progress slowed from snail's pace to glacial.

Soon after they separated from Claire and Patrick, the river burst its banks. The flood tore out the roadway from in front of them and threatened to pitch Lautan into the foaming waters. Elaine caught his arm at the last instant.

'Thank Baka we were leading the kudai,' she yelled over the roar of the river. 'Had we been mounted you would have been lost for certain, old friend.'

'Indeed Bakara, we must thank the Gods for small mercies.'

Lautan watched the river for a few moments, unmoving.

'Are you alright, Lautan?' Jann asked. 'Take a moment. That was a close call.'

'It is not my fall that concerns me Gatekeeper,' the Water Wizard replied. 'This is the Sun Hutang. The same waterway we encountered before the Forest. It snakes down to the coast from here. I had thought it swollen yesterday. Now, as you can plainly see, it is in full flood. I doubt it will be possible to cross.'

The truth of Lautan's words was obvious. Even where the banks had not been breached the water was only millimetres from overflowing. It sped by, roiling and splashing, carrying broken tree branches and the occasional drowned animal which had fallen from an upstream bank. As they stood watching, a section of roof, no doubt torn from a submerged hut, swept by. It crashed against the opposite side, splintering into shards with a hollow rending sound.

'Must we cross?' Jann asked.

Lautan wiped a gout of river water from his face. 'Unless we are to travel four times further than we intended. The Sun Hutang meanders in a double loop from the Forest. We are close to the midpoint here. Our path lies straight ahead, with Duska Batsirang on the other side. If we remain on this bank we could most likely cross closer to the coast. But then we may as well have journeyed with Sakti Udara. Our route would intersect with theirs. Such a diversion would add many days to our journey.'

Cries from the opposite bank interrupted their deliberations. A small group of villagers waved frantically.

'Help us!'

'Please, come quickly!'

'Grandmother is drowning!'

Through the grey curtain of rain, the rooftops of a few small huts were visible. The village, standing in the path of the floodwaters, had been overwhelmed.

'We must help them Lautan!' Jann said. 'Can you not make a crossing as we did before we entered the Forest?'

Lautan looked concerned. 'The river flows much stronger here, Gatekeeper. I do not believe I can staunch it.'

The old Elemental looked across the waters at the panicking villagers.

'Nevertheless, I must make the attempt. Bakara! Do what you can to assist me!'

He strode to the water's edge. With his wrinkled hands held aloft he bellowed an incantation and stepped into the maelstrom. The fast flowing water swirled and spattered over his legs. Jann felt certain he would lose his footing on the riverbed, but within seconds a small space appeared in the current. The river parted to allow Lautan to walk. With a fierce, fixed expression of concentration he pressed on, his voice cracking with the effort of shouting his enchantment. Elaine rushed to join him. She held her arms out in front of her, in contrast to Lautan's open gesture. Bolts of flame, hotter than anything Jann had ever seen her produce, shot from her hands. The sight of her true power, immensely greater than he had conceived, contrasted with the gentle affection she had shown him since his return. She was magnificent. The words of Fire power, guttural and harsh, joined Lautan's as Elaine conjured every ounce of her strength and focus into the tight beam of conflagration. Where it touched the water, jets of steam exploded, blowing fountains of water up and over the Elementals to fall harmlessly beyond them.

Left behind on the bank, Jann grabbed the reins of their three kudai. He stepped into the wake of his friends, before the river had chance to reclaim its course. Without Patrick's influence the animals were skittish. Perhaps remembering their earlier crossing, they allowed Jann to lead them into the maelstrom. The whites of their eyes flashed at each new bolt of power from the Fire Witch. Jann caught a glimpse of the villagers on the opposite bank, their expressions of terror soon hidden behind a cloud of steam. He searched his mind for any hint of a gate, but there was none. The embrowned river water washed round his knees. The smallest diminution of force from either Lautan or Elaine would be disastrous for all of them.

Moments later, they made the far bank. Lautan collapsed, coughing and retching with the effort. Elaine stood doubled up with one hand resting on a large rock, gasping for breath. The three villagers surrounded Jann. They were all young women, barely in their teens. Tears streamed down their faces, mingling with the rain. Their long hair, moulded to their heads, looked like a trio of blond helmets.

'Please help us,' the tallest said. 'Our huts were washed away and our animals drowned. And now grandmother is trapped by the flood.'

'Go!' Elaine gasped. 'Help them. We will follow once we catch our breath. Go!'

The women hurried away in the direction of the huts. Their village had been built on the plain beside the river to benefit from the rich deposits of nutrient-filled mud carried downstream during the annual Utamasan thaw. The torrent had overwhelmed it; floodwater covering the land as far as Jann could see. The brown sea covering the ground was several metres deep and had washed away houses, crops, animals, and people alike.

'There!' cried the girl, pointing.

On the roof of a wooden hut, floating on the dun-coloured water, an old woman perched. She held one arm round a rickety chimney and waved with the other. Her voice could hardly be heard over the drumming of the rain and the roaring of the river. Farther down the bank the remaining villagers stood by the water's edge, calling to the woman to hold on. The hut drifted slowly away from them, driven by the currents and eddies. Jann cast around for some way to reach the old woman. There were no ropes or branches to hand, nor anything large enough to use as a raft.

Lautan and Elaine joined him. The old Elemental sized up the situation in an instant. Dropping his pack to the ground, he dived into the water, the outline of his body dissolving as he entered the new lake without a splash. Only a stream of cleaner water through the brown gave any hint of his passage. A small fountain erupted in front of the floating hut, resolving itself quickly into the upper torso of the Water Wizard.

Jann could not hear their conversation, but Lautan beckoned the woman over to his side of the roof. After a moment's persuasion, the girls' grandmother slid off into his outstretched arms. He bore her back across the water, reminding Jann of a mythological rendition of Neptune he had once seen in an old book of fairy tales back on the prison moon of Phobos.

When he reached the bank, Lautan handed their grandmother to the waiting girls.

'Thank you, thank you!' they said, favouring him with awed looks.

The terrified woman quivered from shock, incapable of speech, but bowed to Lautan once she was certain of being on dry land. The Water Wizard stepped out of the lake, his bottom half taking shape as he did so.

'I am happy to have been of service,' he said, his voice still retaining a bubbly quality. 'If only I could have done more.'

The villagers made no attempt to approach, and the girls hurried their grandmother off to safety and a set of drier clothes.

'That was well done, Lautan,' he said.

'Thank you Gatekeeper. A small enough accomplishment compared with my failures so far with these infernal rains.'

'You got us across the river,' Elaine said. 'That was no mean feat.'

'And something I could not have achieved alone, Bakara,' the old man said, 'so thanks are also due to you.'

'Now there's no longer anyone in imminent danger of death,' Jann said, 'where do we go from here?'

road to duska batsirang
16th day of run'sanamasa, 966

Jann's question gave Elaine a moment's pause. She was not familiar with this part of the country. Their immediate problem—the enormous lake of muddy river water that lay before them—cut off the direct route to Duska Batsirang.

She turned to the older Elemental. 'Lautan? You know

this river well. Clearly we cannot go forward. Which path should we take?'

'I have been thinking on this, Bakara. I believe, although it may appear to fly in the face of logic, we would be better advised to retrace our steps. Travel upstream a short way from here. Our choices are limited since we must follow the river to circumnavigate this flood. Were we to take the downstream route it is likely we would encounter further flooding, perhaps even worse than this. We may in any case be forced to backtrack, losing precious time.'

Elaine looked downriver as Lautan pointed. Low cloud and persistent heavy rain obscured much of the view to the southwest, but she could see that the land sloped away to the coast. The Water Wizard was right. More flooding seemed inevitable.

'Whereas upstream,' Lautan continued, 'the land is higher, the river calmer. We need travel only a short distance before we arrive at a point, somewhat closer to the Red Court than our present location, where we can turn south again for the coast.'

'Sounds good to me,' Jann said, 'let's go.'

Elaine bit down a retort at Jann's intervention. She enjoyed her reputation for being quick in thought and deed, but she was never impetuous. She was glad of Jann's return, but the man could take an irritating turn without the slightest excuse! Lautan's counsel had been sound, but she would have preferred the decision to move to be hers.

The kudai were still uncertain of their footing, so the troupe set off at a walking pace. They led the frightened animals beside the foaming waters of the Sun Hutang for some way. Eventually they came to a path that allowed them to leave the river behind. Elaine's cloak, long since saturated by both rain and river water, hung on her like a cold shroud, dripping on her already wet legs as she walked. She considered drying herself with her powers, but the effort would have to be constant to have any effect against the equally persistent rains. After the experience of two river crossings when the need for her abilities had been urgent, she endured the discomfort and kept her power quiescent.

'Is it much farther to this turning point?' she asked Lautan. It would not offer them any respite from the downpour, but at least they could put further distance between them and the river. Once the torrent was out of sight their kudai may relax enough to allow them to ride.

'Not long now,' he replied, pointing. 'Up ahead, beside the large ponektu tree is where the path forks.'

The ancient ponektu stood as a botanical signpost beside the path on the opposite side from the river. Three large branches grew in coincidental alignment with the three directions which met at the crossing. Back the way they had come; onward to the Court; and left to the coast and Duska Batsirang. The roar of the river became more distinct as they approached the tree. Elaine held tightly to Jaranyla's reins when the animal began to shy from the noise.

'Softly, softly Jara,' she crooned to the beast. 'We will soon be away from the river. Calm yourself.'

Jaranyla regarded her with a white-eyed stare, but ceased pulling on her traces.

Lautan reached the tree ahead of the others and let the reins of his kudo drop. The animal stood shivering where it stopped, too frightened even to nip at any of the lush grass that carpeted the verge beneath.

'We're not stopping here, are we?' Elaine said. 'These leafless branches provide little shelter from the infernal rains. I would rather press on.'

'Indeed, Bakara, I am in agreement,' Lautan said. 'I was merely waiting for you to catch up.'

The old man's eyes twinkled and a slight smile creased his face. In spite of her black mood, Elaine too smiled. There was little enough joy to be found on this cold, wet trek to the coast, but the Wizard's gentle humour lifted her spirits a little.

Without warning, the noise of the river increased to a thunderous roar. Her kudo reared, snatching the reins from Elaine's hands before turning and galloping away from the river.

'Jaranyla!' she called. 'Stop!'

Before she could start down the path after the terrified animal, the riverbank exploded. Time telescoped for Elaine, an enormous wall of water and debris falling toward her as if in slow motion. Free of corporeal limits, her mind raced to seek an escape, but her body refused to move. She had no time to react, or even to duck. Elaine's thoughts, running as fast as her kudo, had already accepted the grim reality unfolding before her eyes when the air in front of her rippled and split with a soundless rending. With her heightened perception she watched the world separate from itself, revealing with impossible slowness a limitless black chasm like the terrible maw of a nightmarish beast, swallowing anything and everything before it. The approaching cascade disappeared, falling beyond the shimmering curtain and leaving only a boot's depth to splash around her legs and feet. A tremor passed through her.

'Baka be praised,' she breathed. 'What happened?'

Lautan turned to her, his face white. 'Some blockage further upstream must have burst under the pressure of water. The sudden flood breached the riverbank.'

'But where did it go?'

'The Gatekeeper. He saved us.'

'Jann!' Elaine said, turning to thank him. 'Jann?'

Lautan placed a hand on her arm. Tears welled in his rheumy eyes.

The Wizard's reaction did not register for a moment. Elaine continued to scour the riverbank and the paths in every direction for the Gatekeeper. When the reality of what had happened hit her, the world again swam dizzily in front of her eyes. She collapsed onto her knees with a sob.

'No! It can't be! Where has he gone? How is this possible?'

'He said gates could only be opened in certain places,' Lautan said, wiping his eyes. 'We are fortunate he found one here.'

'Fortunate?' she cried, rounding on the old man. 'How can it be fortunate? Jann is gone!'

'But we are not. He saved us.'

'How can you be so calm?'

'I am not calm, Bakara. But there is little to be gained from bemoaning his fate.'

'Where is he? He only just came back to us! To *me*! Where did the portal take him?'

'We have no way of telling where the portal has taken him.'

The memory of her last conversation with Jann bubbled unbidden to her consciousness as she knelt in the shallow aftermath of the flood. They had been sitting around the fire on the first night of their journey, the day they left the Palace. Claire asked him about his return from the other side of the mountains.

'I know where the gates begin, and where they end. I'm not exactly sure where they go in between. But I wouldn't like to be in one when it closed.'

'Oh Baka! What awful limbo is he trapped in? Jann!'

road to duska batsirang
17th day of run'sanamasa, 966

They had only covered a few kilometres after the Gatekeeper's fall. The Fire Witch had not said a word to Lautan since agreeing to press on with their journey. They caught up with Perak, the young man's kudo, a kilometre or so down the road. The old wizard tied the animal's reins to his saddle. By some unspoken agreement they stopped at the first sign of shelter and made camp for the night.

Bakara had left the care of the animals to him and declined any food. After a while she fell into a deep sleep. Lautan pulled an almost dry blanket from the Gatekeeper's saddlebag and covered her with it before seeking a spot to settle down for the night.

When dawn broke the next day, Lautan was already awake. His fitful sleep had been disturbed by dreams of falling and loss. Friends being swept away by torrents he could not control; strangers drowning in lakes too vast for him to traverse before they slipped beneath the surface. The events of the previous day replayed constantly in his mind, especially Jann Argent's expression as the young man realised he would be pulled through the portal: a look of utter dread draining all colour from his face. He had not shared that dreadful image with the Fire Witch.

What use was he? The Water Wizard! Never had his title seemed so empty and meaningless. He could as well control the flying of the moons across the night sky as he could the rains that had fallen constantly for the last eleven days. He had counted every day. A depressing tally of failure. Without a stop to the continuing downpour there was no hope of a solution to the flooding, yet he could not even explain the rain, let alone bring it to an end. Now the pale, watery sun rose on another day of drenching and no prospect of respite.

'You're awake?'

The Witch's sleepy voice disturbed his reverie.

'Yes. I have not slept. Much.'

'I don't even remember falling asleep. Or dreaming.'

'That is good Bakara. Good that you did not dream.' He closed his mind to the replay that began again as he thought about his own dreams. 'Would you like something to eat?'

'No. Thank you. I'm not hungry.' She got to her feet, folding the blanket, looking at it with a puzzled expression. She held it to her nose, inhaling its faint scent. A tear overflowed down her cheek.

'We should make a start,' she said.

They made fair progress travelling overland. The second sweep of the Sun Hutang's course took it far to the east. The land here was firmer, allowing them to ride. Soon after midday, they intersected the river once again. Duska Batsirang now lay less than a day to the south, but they could not complete their journey before nightfall. Lautan began searching for a suitable camping spot. The familiar roar of the river spooked the animals, but the Elementals did not dismount until the road became too unstable. He regarded the fast-flowing water, his mind once more occupied with powerlessness and failure. The Fire Witch seemed lost in her own thoughts, too. No words were spoken. They continued to trudge the riverbank path, the silence broken only by the sound of the waters.

The Wizard's attention returned to the way he and the Witch had worked together the day before. There was much value in combining the Elements in the way they had. For now, he intended to conserve his strength. That final river crossing had left him empty and depleted beyond anything he had ever known. But should the opportunity arise, he would be sure to repeat the experiment. With practice, he was certain he could direct the waters into a shallower depression for the Witch to boil away with her fire. He had seen the explosive steam thus created. To what other uses could such power be bent?

Bakara, walking in front of him, turned to speak. No words came. In their place a horrified rictus creased her face as the bank of the river crumbled, collapsing from underneath her. The Witch and her kudo were pitched into the raging waters. Utan save her! She released a single bark of panic before slipping beneath the roiling waters which bore her away downstream, a hand remaining visible as she tried to grasp at one of the many pieces of flotsam sharing the river with her.

Lautan loosed Perak's reins from his saddle and swung

onto his own kudo's back, spurring the terrified beast after Bakara. The muddy path provided scant purchase but he had no time to spare the animal's feelings. Trusting to the kudo's instincts he kicked his heels into its side and rode as fast as he dared to catch up with the Fire Witch, her calls of anger and distress echoing from the deep walls of the canyon into which the river now flowed.

'Lautan! Lautan! Baka save me!' Flashes of Fire power flew from her flailing hands to splash ineffectively into the foaming river.

'Hold on Bakara!' he shouted, though it was doubtful the Witch would hear him over the river's roar. 'I am coming!'

Unable to match the speed of the current, Lautan directed his mount across a narrow peninsula of land, hoping to intercept Bakara before he lost sight of her altogether. With only his own depleted power to call on, he knew he would be unable to staunch the flow. Taking on his Water form in an attempt at rescue, such as he had achieved with the grandmother the day before, was even less likely to succeed. Those waters had been calm. These were in full flood. Perfect for rapid travel but useless for the purpose of salvation. His only hope was that the currents would wash his friend close enough to the bank for him to reach her, but as he neared the river's edge once more, even that faint hope died. With one final flare of Fire, the Witch disappeared from view as the river swept around its last curve before heading for the ocean.

'Lautaaaaaaaa…!'

Utan's beard! Had she drowned? So swiftly? The next stretch of pathway proved too perilous to persuade his kudo to take at anything more than a walking pace. Haste was required, yet he had to accept delay. It would benefit him little to drive the animal to break a leg, or to pitch him from the saddle and break his own neck. He released his white knuckled grip on the reins and left the kudo to his own instincts to find a path, and a pace, that best suited the conditions.

Rider and mount continued to follow the river's course. He called out at each new bend, but there was no sign of his fellow Elemental. With scant effort required to guide his steed, Lautan's reflections on his failures returned to haunt him. Within the space of a day, a second friend had been carried off by the very Element of which he was supposedly the master. In all his long life, Water had been the one certain thing on which he could rely. He laughed, despite his gloom, at the thought that it was his "rock". The foundation of all that he had been, was now, or ever wanted to be. From his earliest memory he had known of his affinity with Water. He had learned to control and direct it at a younger age than any Elemental before him. To have spent many decades in total control of something, and then to have that thing torn from your grasp and bring harm or even death to your friends and acquaintances and, yes, even total strangers, was hard to bear. But no matter what he tried, the rain continued to cover the land like a grey shroud at the funeral of all he held dear; like all the tears of all the mourners crying for the loss of their most precious child.

If there had only been some discernible nexus for the disturbance in the Water force, to give him something on which to focus his efforts. When the Elementals worked together to combat the evil of the Blood Clones they had a concrete, visible enemy. Created by the Blood King those terrible golems had sapped his strength, and that of each Elemental in turn. He remembered the feeling of duplication, of being in two places at once, but even then he had found the will to fight it, having a physical foe against which to pit his power. Now? The enemy, if there was one, was everywhere. In every cloud that dissolved the power of the sun every day. In every stream that gushed and foamed, eating away banks, rock and roots, and covering the land with sludge. And on every muddy path and roadway, every tree whose branches dripped and shook, every township with rivers instead of streets. Wherever he looked, his weakness stared back at him.

Behind the iron-grey clouds, the sun dropped lower. The already dark day turned towards dusk. Ahead, in the gloom, Lautan espied a flash of white on a sandbank in the middle of the river. At first he could not discern what it was. An upturned tree, perhaps? A drowned animal washed up on the bank? Or a garment torn from its owner and left to float at the water's edge? As he drew nearer, the shape moved, twisting spastically like the last flame of a dying campfire.

Bakara!

Spurring his kudo on, he rode to the riverside and dismounted. With all thought of failure forgotten, he entered the stream. At this point, so close to the coast, it had widened and slowed. Even so, he had to fight the current. Now riding atop the surface as he had done when rescuing the grandmother, he reached the Fire Witch.

'Bakara! Are you alright? Are you hurt?'

Her eyes flickered open. She moaned again.

'Lautan? Where am I?'

'Safe. Safe at last my dear Bakara. Come, let me carry you. Though you are too young to be a grandmother, I shall treat you as one for the purposes of rescue.'

He lifted her from the sandbank and fought his way back to the riverside where his kudo stood munching on a bush.

'I know not where your mount is,' Lautan said, 'or even if she has survived the maelstrom, but if you have strength to stay in the saddle, I will lead. Although night is almost upon us, we are not far from Duska Batsirang. I believe we should try to reach it tonight. A hot meal and a dry bed will soon restore your strength.'

The Fire Witch did not reply. She had fallen asleep in his arms.

court of the blood king
18th day of run'sanamasa, 966

They rode into the basilica of the Blood King's Court late on the morning of the fourth day after leaving the landing site. Sebaklan Pwalek had offered to push on, the day before, which would have meant arriving under cover of darkness, but by that time her brother had had enough travelling for one day.

'My arse is rubbed raw on this bloody animal,' he said, 'and my skin wrinkled and cold from being soaked all day long. At least give me some respite from this accursed rain. Surely one more night will make no difference? How much further is it, anyway?'

'If we continue, midnight will see us at Court,' Pwalek had replied.

For once, Kyle had to agree with her brother. Even on the warmest summer days back home they had never ridden non-stop for this long. She too was saddle sore and travel weary. She longed for a dry, warm bed and a hot meal. In the absence of those comforts, a rest beside a campfire and a bowl of reheated stew would suffice.

'I don't think I can do it,' she said. 'Let's find a camp. Tomorrow is soon enough.'

And so they had stopped at the first sign of shelter. This close to the Court, small villages and townships dotted the road. They found a proper bed after all. If it had not already been clear to Kyle that she was travelling with a man of importance, the reaction of the villagers to Pwalek's request for lodgings told her all she needed to know. She spent the night in someone else's bed. Ignoring her protests, the couple insisted she sleep in comfort while they took what rest they could on a pair of benches pushed together in their living area. As far as she knew, Douglas' experience had been similar, though of course he had not argued.

'Is this it?' her brother said as they rode through the imposing Court gates. 'I was expecting a castle! This looks more like a pile of red rocks.'

Kyle bit back a retort. Whatever she said would make no difference. He was determined to find the bad in everything, to be unimpressed by everything, and to load her with guilt for having the idea to become colonists in the first place. What he thought they could do about it now, she had no idea. Coming here was a one-way trip and she was happy to make the most of it. She had never expected perfection.

'Where's my suite?' her brother went on. 'Where's my feather bed? Where are my *servants*?'

'I don't remember anyone promising servants. Be careful, brother dear, you might end up waiting on tables yourself.'

'Pah! As if!'

'I don't think it will come to that, my lady,' Sebaklan Pwalek said, smiling broadly at her as he dismounted. 'If you will give me a moment, I will find someone to take you to your chambers. And I will introduce you to our leader.'

Pwalek handed the reins of his kudo to an ostler and hurried inside.

'Come on!' Douglas shouted over the drumming rain, 'at least let's get out of this weather!' He swung a leg over his saddle and slid gracefully off his kudo. How did he always make things look so effortless?

'What are you waiting for?' he called over his shoulder. 'Are you not wet enough yet?'

As he spoke a gust of wind drove the stinging rain into her face. She almost lost her balance and fell from the saddle, grabbing for the pommel at the last moment. Her clumsiness, a direct contrast to her brother's grace only moments before, made her cheeks flush red. Hoping any onlookers would think her colour was a result of her exertion, she dismounted and walked both animals over to the stable block where the ostler was busy unsaddling Pwalek's mount.

'Thank you,' she said to the man. 'Look after him, he has a lovely temperament and has given me an easy ride all the way here.'

'I will Miss, you can be sure of that,' the man replied. 'I treat all the animals like my own.'

Kyle hurried across the courtyard, the rain twisting and swirling around her as if deliberately trying to fly into her face. She dismissed the ridiculous idea as she stepped into the imposing entrance hall of the Court. Her brother stood inside the massive double doors, a wicked smile creasing his face.

'The rain loves you, sister,' he said. 'Are you sure you wouldn't prefer to wait outside a little longer?'

He really could be a maddening little sod at times.

'Thank you, no,' she said, refusing to give him the slightest hint that his constant jibes were finding their target. 'I'm quite happy to be under cover for now. I hope whoever looks after the rooms here has set a fire and I can get properly dry for the first time since we landed.'

A middle-aged woman dressed in a dun-coloured homespun dress approached along the hallway.

'Kyle and Douglas Muir?' she said, 'If you'll come with me I'll show you to your chambers.'

'Yes,' said Douglas, 'but it's "Douglas and Kyle Muir". As the elder I must always be addressed first.'

'Elder by five minutes,' Kyle muttered, falling into step behind her brother.

The interior of the Court was decorated with paintings, presumably of previous occupants or famous people from society. Istanian society, Kyle corrected herself, remembering the Waters woman's brief description of the local cultures. The corridor along which they walked had tall windows at regular intervals, interspersed with small cauldrons atop red stone pillars, which she assumed would be lit to provide illumination after sunset. They could have done with being lit already; the weak sunlight filtering through the leaden clouds was hardly bright enough to see by.

They followed the woman up a flight of stone steps, and after a couple more turns entered a passage where Pwalek stood waiting beside a short man in vibrant yellow tunic and leggings. A fool's cap of multicoloured material sat on the man's head. A single golden bell hung from each of its three horns.

'There you are,' said Pwalek. 'I was beginning to think the housekeeper had taken a wrong turn.'

'I wouldn't know,' replied Kyle, but her humour was lost on the Istanians.

'Douglas, Kyle,' Pwalek continued, 'may I present Jeruk Nipis, the leader of the Darmajelis of Istania.'

'You have got to be joking,' said Douglas.

court of the blood king - muirs' chambers
18th day of run'sanamasa, 966

'No joke,' replied the man in the yellow costume, 'although I maintain the appearance of the Jester when it suits me. A role that is more useful than you may think. The common people presume someone who plays the fool, is a fool, but from what I've heard, I expected better from you, young man.'

Kyle smiled, more at her brother's reaction to the gentle chastisement than the manner of its delivery. For once, Douglas was lost for words.

'If you will excuse me, Jeruk, I have matters to attend,' said Pwalek.

'Certainly, Seb, certainly,' the other replied. 'I will see you later.'

Pwalek withdrew, leaving them alone with the strange man.

'Allow me to show you your quarters,' he said, motioning to the nearest door.

They entered a large room. To Kyle's delight, a fire burned in the grate. A comfortable looking sofa sat before the hearth, with two other easy chairs on either side. She glanced around the room, taking in other items of furniture: a bureau, and a small table with two straight-backed chairs. A large window overlooked the basilica and Court gates. Outside, a pale sun reflected off the wet, red stone of the building. It brought little relief to the overall greyness of the day.

Two further doors led from the room. In front of her a smaller, single door. To her right a set of double doors stood ajar, offering a hint of a similar room beyond. Through the smaller door Kyle could see a double bed had been made up, its plain coverlet turned down ready to be occupied.

'Oh! It's delightful!', Kyle said.

'I am pleased that you are pleased,' said Nipis. 'I had the room prepared with you in mind. There is a bath through there, in the bedchamber. You may ask for hot water to be brought up whenever you like. And through here,' he continued, eyeing Douglas as he moved toward the double doors, 'you will find your chambers.'

'Gods!' said Douglas, flashing an angry look in Kyle's direction. 'Am I doomed to have you follow me around forever? Adjoining rooms now! Will I never have any privacy?'

A sudden rain squall hit Kyle's window, making her jump as the glass rattled in its frame. A bead of water found its way through the closure and ran down the inside of the pane, pooling on the sill. Douglas followed the strange man into second suite. Kyle, surprised and upset by her brother's reaction, hung back.

'There are bolts and a lock on that door,' she said. 'By all means take the key to your side, brother. It can stay locked as far as I'm concerned.'

She moved closer to the fire, her clothes beginning to steam. Through the door she could hear the two men talking. It was difficult to make out what was being said over the crackling of the fire. Reluctantly, she edged nearer to the door.

'I suppose there must be other things wrong with your room Douglas, beyond it being adjacent to mine?' she asked. 'Nothing is ever quite right for you, is it?'

His face popped around the doorframe, a strange grin giving him a manic look.

'It will do,' he said. 'It is almost the same as yours. Only larger.'

Their escort appeared to stand behind her brother.

'Please, young lady, settle yourself in,' he said. 'Order water for your bath. You will find the bell pull beside the fireplace. Take a nap. I will have some dry clothes sent up also. For now, please excuse us. I have matters to discuss with your brother.'

The last thing Kyle saw before he closed the door in her face was her brother's bizarre grin, stretching even wider. What "matters" could that man—effectively their President, no less—possibly have to discuss with her brother, of all people? They had only just arrived! And, since he obviously did, why was she being excluded? Until a few moments ago she had no inkling her brother felt that way about her. They always did everything together!

Well she would damned well grill him about it later. For now, the suggestion of a hot bath overrode any other thought. She found the bell pull and gave it a sharp tug.

Chapter 14

The buzz of conversation in the assembly area still surprised Felice Waters. Earlier Prism ships had been processed within a couple of days. Even Valiant, arriving unexpectedly, had been dealt with by the morning of the third day after she ditched in the bay. Four days had passed since the latest arrival, and Pennatanah base was still thronged with colonists. Jo Granger waved from her seat close to the back wall. Felice picked her way across the crowded room, squeezing between four-seater tables crammed with seven or eight people.

She flopped into the seat opposite Jo. 'Hi!'

Jo laughed at Felice's mock exhaustion. 'Busy!'

'Tell me. No matter how often I eat here I can't get used to this noise. It's normally so quiet you can hear the mice eating.'

'Strictly speaking, tikliks aren't mice.'

'I knew as soon as I said it I wouldn't get that past you. Bloody geneticists.'

'Although they are the closest thing to a rodent I've seen since I got here,' Jo added. 'Maybe I should do a DNA–'

'Stop right there!' Felice interrupted her. 'I'm still not halfway through my analysis. Your machine will be tied up until the end of Sanamasa earliest.'

'That's OK. The tikliks aren't going anywhere. Why is it so busy here anyway?'

'My best guess is they're not too keen on the available options. Most of them have heard about the tensions between Istania and Kertonia. They don't want to be caught up in a war. No ruler on one side; assassination of a high-ranking Palace official on the other, *and* the fact that neither side sent a welcome delegation. It all gives a poor impression of the indigenous.'

'Can't say I blame them. If I'd known more before I chose a side—even that there were "sides" at all—I would've thought twice.' Jo smiled. 'I've enjoyed being back here much more than I ever did being there.'

'Well you've been a lifesaver for my project. It would never have left the runway if you hadn't lent me the analyser.'

'My pleasure.'

Felice glanced around the room at the many small groups, each engaged in animated conversation. 'Another thing about this crowd. They're more independent than before. We used to bang on about frontier spirit and all that but in the end, when we arrived, most people were happy being led by the nose into serfdom.'

'Oi! I'm no serf!'

'No. Sorry.' Felice put a hand on Jo's arm. 'But you know what I mean. It's frightening how everyone starts off expecting to break free of their previous humdrum life and establish an exciting new one in a colony, but when they find a new community with its own set of rules—different from the familiar ones but still rules—better than ninety percent of Earthers jump at the chance. Sad really.'

'But not this lot?'

'See for yourself. I'd put money on most of these conversations being about setting up on their own. An Earther district, not tied to any other group. And certainly independent from the Reds or Blacks.'

A man at the nearest table, who had been paying more attention to their conversation than his own, turned to her.

'You're right about us,' he said. 'We were discussing exactly that. I've been wanting to ask you something.'

'Go ahead,' Felice said.

'This base. What is it used for when there are no arriving ships to deal with?'

'It's a good question. One that's been occupying my mind recently too.'

'How do you mean?'

'Before now there's always been another ship to wait for. Even when the base is quiet, we've kept a small group of people on hand, or at least nearby, to call on when the next arrival is due.'

'And we were the last.'

'Precisely. No more ships after Dauntless. So what are we for? And what are we going to do with her?'

'The Dauntless?'

'Yes. Endeavour and Intrepid were both dismantled. Some parts were used to create this base, others went into storage for tech spares. Most of it we couldn't find a use for. It's at the bottom of the bay. And Valiant is still out there too, where she fell. Seems a shame to take Dauntless apart when we've no need of those parts.'

'Captain told me she's a different breed from the earlier models. I mean, she's no good for another long trip through outer space, but her drives will keep her floating at dock for the foreseeable. Could maybe fly her round the planet for a bit. Find a new base?'

The thought of leaving the peninsula where she had spent the last ten years filled Felice with a strange mixture of dread and yearning. She had her own dichotomy with "frontier spirit." Part of her recognised how comfortable she had become with the quiet life around Pennatanah. Another long-buried part dreamt of a new adventure.

'One option, certainly. What do you think, Jo?'

'We never had chance to do a planet-wide geographical survey. We really have no idea what there is beyond these few hundred square kilometres. Maybe we could even find a place where it's not raining.'

Felice laughed. 'I'm sure that will stop. Eventually.'

'Sorry, that's a sidetrack,' the colonist continued. 'I meant, if there's no reason for this place to be a landing point any longer, could we base our new Earther colony here? It already has a lot of what we need. Except space, but we can build that. Trade with the locals. Fish, maybe?'

'The locals won't come anywhere near while Dauntless is on stand,' Felice said. 'We had a hard enough time getting the royals to visit. They hate gravnull fields and it'll be the same with the Prism effect. You'd think folk who have real magicians in their lives would be more tolerant of anything that looks like another form of magic, but they're not.'

'Didn't you say Intrepid was broken up?'

'Not until after her passengers had been processed. All of these buildings came from Endeavour. Most of Intrepid, apart from the juiciest bits of kit, is at the bottom of Pennatanah Bay.

'But to answer your question,' Felice went on, surprised to hear herself saying it, 'I can't see any reason not to base yourselves here. At least for now. In many ways it's ideal. Close to the sea, an easy ride to the forest and a couple of lakes, but still removed from Court and Palace. Maybe I overstated the trading difficulties. In the past we've sourced most of our supplies from the outlying towns and villages. It's just that we have to go there. They won't come here. But there's a comfortable certainty to it. If you fly Dauntless off to the other side of the planet, who knows what you'd find?'

pennatanah
18th day of run'sanamasa, 966

Claire rode with Patrick into Pennatanah base at the end of their fourth day since leaving the Palace. The sun, obscured by heavy cloud the whole day, was already nearing the horizon. Out across the bay its grey light turned the slow waves to beaten lead, pocked with silver flashes where raindrops hit the surface. She had never seen the site in the rain.

'It's not changed much,' she said.

Patrick lifted the edge of his hood for a better look. 'It looks older to me. Dirtier.'

He was right. The once pristine white walls of the compounds were now streaked with dirt, washed from the roofs. At street level they had been splashed with mud from passing kudai and cartwheels. It had changed in another respect too. It was busy! Even in the continuing downpour the roadways were dotted with walkers, hunched against the driving rain. The newly arrived Prism ship floated at the mooring mast in a haze of orange light, occasionally flashing a thin bolt of lightning to the base of the tower as the rain grounded surplus energy from its field corona.

'Looks like there's a few newcomers still around,' Claire said. 'Should be busy in the food hall at this time of day. Why don't we start there?'

'Fine by me.'

They turned their kudai in the direction of the large building that stood beneath the imposing bulk of the floating Prism ship. The animals snorted and tossed their heads as they neared the vessel with its pearlescent electric halo and its low hum, but the riders urged them on, speaking soft words of encouragement. Apparently the ship was less fearsome than the raging rivers they had encountered earlier. Familiar refectory sounds greeted them as they entered the hall. The noise of multiple conversations bounced from the metal walls, punctuated by the clicking of cutlery against plates, and the chink of glasses. Most of the tables were full, but a sizeable queue still waited at the servery to collect their meals.

'I don't remember it ever being this busy,' Claire said. 'Where on Earth do we start?'

'We'll just have to ask around. See if anyone has seen anything suspicious.'

'I guess. But if these rains are the fault of person or persons unknown I doubt they would even be aware of it, at least at first. I know I wasn't. All sorts of weird winds and draughts followed me around for ages. It wasn't until I walked into the main hall at the Palace that I had any clue it was me causing them.'

'I don't know what else to suggest,' Patrick replied. 'We have to start somewhere.'

They moved between the tables, greeting the occupants, explaining who they were and trying to uncover the information they were looking for without making it too obvious. It soon became clear they would cover more ground if they split up. Claire took the left of the hall while Patrick moved over to the right. She avoided a small dishevelled group of tabukki, conspicuous from the faint but unmistakable orange hue of their skin. Sitting at a table overflowing with discarded tabukka wraps was another big hint. No sensible answers to be had there.

Travelling on the Valiant at least gave her something in common with the Dauntless passengers. Everyone had seen the semi-submerged hull of the earlier ship in the bay. They were all keen to hear the tale of her unfortunate arrival. Claire repeated the story several times, and overheard Patrick doing the same. They reached the back wall of the hall together and compared notes.

'Nothing,' said Patrick.

'Same here,' said Claire. 'No one saw anyone acting strangely, or in a way that could be connected to the weather.'

'And no one heard anyone else discussing anything like that either. I don't expect that to change, but I guess we may as well get through the rest of these before we try another approach.'

Claire was about to ask what he meant when she heard a shout.

'Hello! Claire!'

Felice Waters made her way towards them across the crowded hall. 'What are you doing here? Come to check on your results?'

'Results?' echoed Claire. 'Oh! The DNA! I'd forgotten about that!' The connection between their search and Felice's project snapped together in her mind. She took

Felice's arm. 'Actually, we could use your help. Assuming you took samples from all the new arrivals?'

'Of course. That's what it was all about.'

'Excellent! Are you busy now? Could you run through the results with me?'

'I was about to have some lunch, but I can grab it to go. Meet me by the door.'

She took off towards the servery. Claire laid a hand on Patrick's arm.

'Stay in the hall,' she said. 'Finish what we started. At least you'll be out of the rain, and I'll know where to find you. I don't suppose I'll be long. I'll meet you back here.'

Claire followed Felice to her headquarters. Perhaps too grand a title for what she knew was actually a cramped office stuffed with records and files. The tiny room was even more untidy than she remembered. Piles of paperwork littered every flat surface. A capacious plastic haversack overflowing with sample bags was propped next to a large machine. Its display flashed green and it emitted an intermittent beeping noise. A wastepaper basket sat beside Felice's desk, almost buried under a precarious stack of rubbish. Discarded sheets of output and used coffee cups surrounded it, along with the remains of several "meals to go" that gave off an unpleasant sickly-sweet odour.

Felice pulled a red folder from the top drawer of her desk. 'These are the results for the Elementals I tested. You, Elaine, and Terry. I never did get a sample from Lautan, but in the end it didn't matter. You three were enough to prove my theory right. I believe there is a genetic basis for Elemental power.'

pennatanah - felice's office
18th day of run'sanamasa, 966

Claire took the results sheets and spread them out on Felice's desk. She had never seen DNA analyses before, but the similarities between them stood out even to her eyes. One or two peaks on each sheet coincided with those on the other two. Each page also showed separate peaks reaching almost to the top of the scale.

'How do these compare to, um, non-Elementals?'

Felice laughed. 'Normal people you mean?'

'Was I that obvious?'

'These spikes are all unusual. They don't appear on regular results. What's even more interesting...' she rummaged through the red folder and pulled out two more sheets. 'This one,' she said, laying the first on the desk beside the others, 'is from the girl who put out her family's fire using Water power.'

She lined up the second sheet beside the first.

'And this one is from the famous hand-in-rock guy.'

'Wow,' said Claire, 'the girl has an entirely different mix of high points than any of the other Elementals, but this guy...' She traced the graph on the last sheet with a finger. 'He has more peaks than any of the others. Five!'

'That's right. Seems logical to assume the girl's results would be a close match with Lautan. If I can ever get a sample from him it will be a simple matter to prove that theory. I can't explain the other one though. I was expecting his pattern to match Terry's. I was convinced it would be a form of Earth power that led to his accident with the rock, but—'

'I can explain it,' Claire interrupted, 'but probably best keep it to myself for now. Elaine and Petani have gone looking for this man.'

She glanced at the top of the sheet where Felice had written his name in her delicate hand. Piers Tremaine.

'It would have made their search so much easier if they'd known his name. Maybe we should've all come here first rather than splitting up.'

Claire looked at Felice. 'Something wrong?'

With one hand to her mouth, the woman was looking repeatedly over her desk. A puzzled expression creased her face. 'Hmm? No. Well, yes. What you said about Tremaine having more peaks than the others. Reminded me of something I saw a couple of days ago.'

She rifled through the paperwork on the other side of the desk, picking out two further pages.

'Here. I thought these were unusual but I was distracted at the time. I hadn't completed your samples anyway, so it wouldn't have been obvious.'

Claire took the sheets and let out a long whistle.

'Woah! Who are these?'

'Well that's a good question,' Felice replied. 'It's all a bit mysterious. Firstly, it wasn't me who processed their samples. Those results were already in the machine when I came back to the office. On top of that, the day before, we'd had an unannounced visit from the Court. Some fellow who said he was acting on behalf of the Darmajelis of Istania and was looking for two of the Dauntless passengers. He didn't know their names but from his description it was obvious he was talking about Douglas and Kyle Muir. I don't know how he'd heard about them, but he was pretty insistent.'

'Did he find them?'

'I pointed them out to him. Next day they were all gone. Him, the few men who were with him, the Muirs, and a handful of others. Seemed odd to me at the time. Especially for the brother. He hadn't been impressed with any of the options at first.'

'Can we check the board?'

'Sure.'

They hurried through the drizzle to the departure hall, where the decision board stood. When Claire and her fellow travellers had come to Berikatanya, the Black Queen had led a small delegation from Kertonia. She had described what they could expect from a place at the Palace, or the Court. Colonists posted their preferences on the board so that quotas could be filled with those who wanted what was on offer. This time round the whole process seemed to Claire to be more haphazard. The board was almost empty. Neither of the Muirs' names were on it. She asked Felice why the induction had not followed the usual pattern.

'You're right, this has been the worst of the lot really. You'd have thought we'd be better at it by now. We had no delegations this time, for obvious reasons, but it wasn't just that. A lot of them have been put off travelling by the rain. And there's been some talk of staying here and turning this into a "proper" colony.'

Patrick emerged from the dining hall.

'Thought I heard your voice,' he said. 'I think I've had a breakthrough. The last guy I spoke to. It's not one person we're looking for, it's—'

'Twins,' said Claire. 'Douglas and Kyle Muir.'

'Damn!' he said, smiling. 'How do you do that? Anyway, yes. Apparently they're a bit of an odd couple. She's OK, but he is... how did he put it? "Habitually dissatisfied." Like a grouch. But did you know they were spirited away in the middle of the night?'

Felice grinned. 'It may have seemed like that to whoever you spoke with. Some of this Dauntless lot behave like they're on a package holiday. They don't surface from their pits until lunch time!'

'We think they left early morning,' Claire explained. 'On the fifteenth. We need to get back to Court as quickly as we can. They have a three day head start over us.'

Patrick gave her a strange look.

'What's wrong? Come on, we need to get going!'

'I'm not coming with you,' he said, so quietly that Claire hardly heard.

'Not...? What do you mean, not coming with me?'

'Just that. I've spoken with several of the passengers from Dauntless. Most of them don't want to "fit in" with Berikatanyan society. They're staying here. At least until they figure out where they want to establish themselves. A separate group. A group for Earthers. I feel... I think it would be better for me to stay with them.'

He looked at Felice, avoiding Claire's gaze. She knew he was thinking about their earlier conversation. About his Juggler powers.

'With them, or away from us?'

Patrick's expression clouded to match the steel-grey skies.

'Comes to the same thing,' he said.

court of the blood king, douglas muir's chambers 18th day of run'sanamasa, 966

Douglas Muir watched the strange man in the yellow costume close the door on his sister. Good. She would hate that. Being excluded. Since they were children she had always dogged his footsteps. Clingy, like the mud in the streams and brooks they used to play in. He often thought how nice it would be to have some time alone, but it rarely happened. Now he was rid of his sister—no matter how briefly—but still not alone. He had a new companion. He had soon worked out that he would be the fool, even without the stranger's costume, if he underestimated this man. Counsellor to a dead king, leader of some kind of government committee. He was no ordinary jester.

'I hope your journey from the Earther base was not too arduous,' the man said.

'It was wet, sir,' Douglas replied, 'but otherwise comfortable enough. Your man Pwalek took care of us pretty well.'

'Please, call me Jeruk. Until recently, all referred to me as the Jester, but I believe—appearances aside—it is time to put that role behind me. As leader of Istania I must present a more sober image. It will be a start if my new acquaintances use my given name. Jeruk Nipis.'

'Fine with me, Jeruk. Can we skip to the chase?'

'Chase? Is someone pursuing you?'

'Sorry. An expression from back home. I mean, can we

get on with business? I assume you brought us here for a reason?'

'A man after my own heart. I have little love for diplomatic circumlocution. You are right, I sought you out. You, and your sister, though it is already clear to me that you are the more formidable intellect.'

Douglas' pride swelled at the man's words. He fought to control his normal reaction. This could be a test.

'Your years of counselling and advising have made you an excellent judge of character,' he said, smiling. 'What do you want from me?'

'I have it in mind that there should be Earther representation in government. Istania is host to many "colonists", and glad we are to have them. For the most part resourceful people who have contributed to our society in a number of ways. We are also aware of some unrest among the population. Concerns over our ongoing dispute with the Blacks. Others believe they are being exploited, or not given the opportunities they deserve. I should like to solve this small problem before it becomes a large one.'

'Nip it in the bud, we would say.'

'Quite so. I have heard the Gardener use the term on occasion, though it has been some time since I encountered the old Elemental. Anyway, I believe a seat for an Earther would be a powerful public demonstration of our commitment to your people.'

'But why me? You don't know me. You don't know anything about either of us.'

'I think you may already have an idea why I chose you,' Nipis said. 'But if not, then for now let us say I have my reasons. The events leading to my King's death have depleted this realm in certain respects. While it is true we still have men of courage and honour, from the ranks of the military especially, the old allegiances have fallen away. Historically the Fire Witch was loyal to Red House, but has made it clear she will not return. I never had much love for her in any case. As for the other, if the Elementals were to stick to their much-vaunted notion of "balance" then he would be here in her stead, but...'

'The other?'

'The Water Wizard. He has not been seen in these parts since the Battle of Lembaca Ana.'

Nipis seemed reluctant to say more. There was much about their conversation that Douglas did not understand. There were also undercurrents of meaning that he believed he did understand, but preferred not to give voice to. Things that had been happening to him since arriving on this wet rock of a planet. Things he did not want to talk about, even with his sister, let alone this man who offered much, apparently in return for little.

'I guess you have your reasons,' Douglas said, breaking the uneasy silence. 'I'm sure you'll explain when you're ready. Your offer is tempting. I've always thought I was destined for greatness, but I never expected it to be handed to me so soon.'

The small man smiled. An expression that, unusually for a Jester, did not suit him. It made his already enormous nose look even larger.

'Splendid,' he said. 'Well, you should rest. Perhaps a nice hot bath for you, too? There is a Darmajelis meeting the day after tomorrow. I will introduce you then, and we can formalise your position. Until then, look around. Get a feel for the place, I believe you would say. Relax. Eat. Enjoy your first few days of Court life.'

A knock sounded on the door. Without invitation, Sebaklan Pwalek entered, hurried to Nipis' side and whispered in his ear. The man stiffened, his eyes opening wide in surprise.

'Well,' he said, flashing another awkward smile in Douglas' direction, 'I think we are done here. Pwalek brings me word of something that demands my attention. If you will excuse me, I will send for you in plenty of time for our... ah... appointment.'

The two men left. Through the closed door to the adjoining room, Douglas heard sounds of his sister taking a bath. He turned the key in the lock.

*

Alone at last, Douglas moved to the window. The sun had long since set, but the courtyard shone with the light of two moons which rode high in the sky, their light attenuated by the scudding clouds. The perpetual rain ran down the glass and dripped from the lintel above. He watched the drops coalesce, turning to rivulets of ever greater size as they made their downward journey. Shame they had only one direction. What intricate patterns those drips could weave if they could retrace their steps. As the thought gelled in his mind, two thin streams of water crossed and returned, forming a watery outline resembling the cross of Saint Andrew. Douglas laughed.

'Or maybe England,' he said, moving closer to the window and fixing his attention on the raindrops. The liquid lines rotated on the outside of the pane until they were orientated like the cross of St. George.

'No,' he said, 'that fight went on too long. We left our patriotism behind in the twentieth century.'

The water pattern melted, resolving itself into the symbol of peace used by the Campaign for Nuclear Disarmament. Douglas laughed again. He looked at the rainfall, willing it to increase. His window rattled with the spatter of faster rain.

'What else can you do?' he said, imagining something unheard of. A ball of rainwater formed outside his window and shot towards the glass. Douglas ducked to his left as the golf ball-sized mass shattered the pane, showering him with fragments of glass and cold water.

'Woah!' he said. 'Excellent! I think we know why mister Jester wanted me on his side.'

Through the broken pane Douglas heard the sound of shouting. Embarrassed that someone may have witnessed his tricks, he peeped out into the silvery basilica. Pwalek stood out there, holding the reins of a large kudo which bucked and snorted at being dragged from its warm stable. The Jester struggled to mount the unhappy beast.

'Kudatuk!' he shouted. 'Bepe banyan dis jikan suk!'

Douglas did not understand what he said, but the old ostler who had taken care of their kudai earlier that day emerged from the stable block muttering under his breath.

'Never mind your complaining old man,' Nipis shouted to him. 'Hold these damned reins.'

The man moved to the other side of the kudo and grabbed hold of the bridle. He crooned to the animal, which settled a little, allowing Nipis to swing himself into the saddle. He snatched the reins from Pwalek's hands.

'I will find him, and bring him back!' he said, turning the kudo on the spot and almost knocking the old ostler to the ground. He rode swiftly through the Court gates, kicking up the wet gravel as he went.

The other men hurried for shelter, but the sight of the three of them had given Douglas an idea. Beyond the gates the moat glistened in the moonlight, pocked by raindrops. If the rain would do his bidding, as he had proved, what of a larger body of water?

He left his room, retracing his steps to the main door. Outside in the courtyard the rain continued to fall, at the increased pace he had willed. Rather than stop it altogether, which may have attracted attention from inside the building, he tried a different approach. Stepping through the doorway, he crossed the square heading for the moat. An invisible corona appeared above his head, shedding rainwater all around him. He walked as if covered by the glass case of a carriage clock, protected from the water on all sides. He should have tried this earlier. The journey from Pennatanah would have been so much more comfortable! But the questions from Pwalek and the nagging from his sister to give her the same protection would have sucked all the joy from it. Best keep it secret.

Under the washed moonlight, the moat had the appearance of liquid steel. Fed by a small brook, the ditch had a sluggish current. Douglas stopped it with a thought, watching as the water to the right of his mental barrier rose up the bank while that to the left drained away towards the outflow. From the deeper half, he forced a jet of water into the air. It rose several metres before falling back to the surface in a silvery arc. He made another, followed by a second in quick succession, intersecting the path of the first to make a three-dimensional version of the water cross on his window. Soon he had half-a-dozen sprays, leaping and cascading the width of the moat like an expensive fountain at a stately home. He laughed, exulting in this power. Maybe this world was not so bad after all.

'What are you doing?'

His sister's voice broke his concentration, sending the jets of water tumbling back into the moat.

'Practising,' he said, catching the last jet before it hit the surface and directing it full at Kyle's face. She dodged the stream at the last second.

'Argh!' she cried, her face creased with repugnance. 'You stupid prick!'

The invisible dam in the moat broke with a loud rush, cascading into the shallow side and sending a thick spout into the air. It hit Douglas before he had even noticed the dam had collapsed, drenching him from head to foot.

Chapter 15

The streets of Duska Batsirang were deserted when Jeruk Nipis rode past the outlying houses and approached the village square. The settlement lay almost due south of Court. He had done well to complete the trip so swiftly, pushing his kudo hard through the thin drizzle of the night. Fortunately the route avoided rivers or lakes, and covered mainly stony ground. With no softened earth or mud to hamper the animal they had kept up a gallop for most of the journey.

Since the strange weather began, night-time rain had been the lightest. When the malamajan was still in force the overnight rains were, when needed, torrential. The slow, persistent rain still had the same effect though. He was soaked, cold, and uncertain how to proceed. Decades had passed since his last visit to this village. With the villagers all abed, how was he to find the man he sought?

He walked his animal over to a stone trough mounted in front of the only inn, tied it to the rail, and knocked on the door. At the third attempt, a light flickered into life in an upstairs room. He knocked again.

'Alright, alright, give me chance,' came a muffled voice. Bolts slid rustily back before the door creaked open.

'What is it? What do you want at this time of night?'

'I have urgent need of a stonemason.'

'What, now? It's the middle of the night man! Are you mad? What is so urgent it couldn't wait until daylight?'

'That is my business,' Jeruk said. 'I have heard tell of a man living in these parts who excels in stone craft. Do you know who I mean, or must I wake some of the other villagers?'

The innkeeper, who had been regarding Jeruk with a puzzled expression while he spoke, opened his eyes wide.

'Simon? Is it you?'

He peered closer, holding up his candle to shine a better light.

'Simon Nehj! We haven't seen you around the village since you were nothing but a boy!'

'Yes. Yes, it is me. But I no longer use that name. I'll thank you to keep it to yourself. Now, do you know the stone worker I am speaking of or not?'

'Of course I know him. Best kept secret in the village. Piers Tremaine is the man you're looking for. He did a lot of good work at first, before he went a bit weird. Now most folk would be happy if he went away. Though some don't like the way others have taken it into their own hands. Trying to force him out. For myself I'd rather he came to the right conclusion of his own accord, if you know what I mean.'

'I know exactly what you mean. That may be something I can help with, if you'll tell me where to find him?'

'Oh, yes. Sorry. Last hut on the right, down there,' the innkeeper said, pointing. 'You can't miss it. Doesn't look like any of the others in Duska Batsirang.'

'Thank you. Sorry to have disturbed your sleep.'

'Nah. Glad to help a fellow villager. Mind how you go Simon! Tremaine's got a bit of a temper when the mood takes him.'

The door closed before Jeruk could react to the deliberate use of his old name. He started down the dark main street, leaving his kudo tied beside the trough where he seemed happy enough. After half the night at the gallop the beast needed the rest. Tremaine's cottage was obvious as soon as it came into view, just as the innkeeper had said. An unusual construction, with the chimney set in one wall instead of in the centre of the roof like all the others. A peculiar series of small wooden troughs edged the roof, catching the rain and directing it into a large barrel standing against the back wall. A light burned in the

294

window with a fierce and ruddy glow. Axe marks scarred the door in several places but it had survived the onslaught. Jeruk knocked.

'Piers Tremaine?' he called.

'Go away.'

'Please open the door. I need to speak with you.'

'Do you take me for a fool? I'm not interested in anything you have to say. Leave me alone.'

'I am not from the village. I have ridden this night from Court. I must speak with you.'

Inside the cottage, the man fell silent. Jeruk waited. Moments later a face appeared at the lighted window.

'Show me your hands.'

Jeruk held up his arms in the dim light. 'I am unarmed.'

'Very well. Wait there.'

He heard the sound of heavy timbers being set aside before the door opened with a loud protest from its hinges.

'Who are you? What do you need to speak with me about so urgently? I am not taking on any more stone work.'

'It is not regular stone work I am interested in,' Jeruk said, pushing the door wide. 'We may be able to help each other.'

'Why do I need your help?'

Jeruk fingered the axe marks. 'You need someone's help, don't you? The villagers are not exactly making you welcome in Duska Batsirang these days, from what I've heard.'

'You seem to know a lot about it for someone who turns up in the middle of the night and yet says they're not from the village.'

'I make it my business to know things. Or to have people tell me things. For example, I've been told that you are much more than a regular stonemason.'

Tremaine's face took on a guarded look in the scant candlelight. The light in the room was now much less bright than it had appeared from the outside. Trusting his instincts, Nipis pulled a soiled cloth from the low table in the centre of the room.

'This for instance.'

The cloth fell to the floor revealing a piece of stone, worked into the shape of a pyramid. To his untrained eye it looked perfectly proportioned. The rock glowed with a strange, warm light.

'What do you want?'

'I want you to come with me to Court. My name is Jeruk Nipis. I am the leader of the Darmajelis of Istania. One-time Court Jester and adviser to the late King. And I have need of... abilities... such as yours.'

'There are no "abilities such as mine," as I'm sure you know. Why else would I incite such fear and hatred among the people here?'

'Your power is rare, yes, but not unheard of. Merely forgotten. These are simple folk. What you offer them is strange. They do not like strange. Village people often dislike that which they do not understand.'

'And what about Court people?'

'Court people think what I tell them to think. I may not have power over stone, but I understand the ways of men. You could have a good life there. Your skill would be highly valued. It is enough by itself to grant you a seat in my government, but I have also reserved one or two places for those of Earth origin, so you are doubly qualified.'

'I'll think about it.'

'With respect,' Jeruk said, 'I doubt you have time for a long deliberation. The villager I spoke to earlier believes others are plotting your downfall. A sizeable group. You might even say a majority. There is no place for you here. They will throw you out. Or worse. And the threat is imminent.'

'Even so–'

'You would be wise to leave tonight. While you still can. I should add that a seat on the Darmajelis may be only the beginning for you. Many whispers reach me from even farther afield than this backwater. Powers such as yours may command equally powerful seats. Thrones, even. Come with me, Tremaine. Sit with us. Use your gifts. Or stay here and die.'

Silence fell in the cottage. Jeruk watched ripples of energy flux and wane in the strange pyramid, casting flickering shadows on the walls and ceiling.

'Ah, damn it!' Tremaine said. 'All I ever wanted was a quiet life. I never asked for this power.'

'But you have it. You cannot deny it. Use it for good. Use it for Istania.'

The Stone mage left the room, returning after a moment with a large backpack. He took the glowing pyramid and shoved it down inside the pack, which Jeruk saw was already almost full of clothes.

'You were planning to leave?'

'I didn't know what they were going to do. I wanted to be ready.'

'A sensible precaution. Come, let us be on our way. It will soon be light.'

Tremaine looked around the room. He took another sculpture from beside the fireplace, wrapped it in the dirty cloth and strapped it to the outside of his pack.

'I'm ready.'

the black palace
19th day of run'sanamasa, 966

The immense blackwood doors of the Queen's chambers resounded with heavy knocking, dragging her from a dreamless sleep with the force of a dozen kudai. Her room was dark in the absence of moonlight. It must be late if Pera-Bul and Kedu-Bul had already set.

'Who disturbs the royal rest in these Sana-forsaken depths of night?' she called.

There was no response, save for a redoubled pounding

on her doors. She pulled on a nightgown and hurried across the cold marble floor. Each new blow made the inky wood shiver, sending strange blue shadows across its face like the sparks that leapt from her fingertips on very dry, Bakamasan days. When she opened the small vision panel, the wood was hot to her touch.

'What is the meaning–' she began.

The face at the opening stunned her into silence. Beneath a shock of silver hair, its expression was twisted into a grimace between hatred and fear. The stranger stared sightlessly past her into the chamber. He pummelled again at the door with bloodied fists.

'Lendan!' she shouted, 'where are you! Where are our guards? Who is this you have allowed into our presence? Remove him at once.'

The man did not speak, but continued to hammer on the Queen's door, glaring. This was outrageous! She turned the handle, intending to confront the intruder face-to-face, but the door refused to open. It shook from the onslaught, and she could feel the latch had released, yet she could not pull it from its frame. Each time she tried another series of blue sparks traced the pattern of its grain, and a redoubled wave of heat hit her like a breath of wind from the Fire season.

'Our guards will be here directly!' the Queen bluffed. 'Be off with you, or we shall have you put to death!'

Tears started in the man's eyes, whether in response to her threat or the pain from his raw, bleeding hands, she could not tell. They welled up and rolled down his dirt-encrusted cheeks, scouring cleaner lines in the grime. As she watched, the man's weeping intensified until his face was covered with running water and the fluid gushed from his eyes like miniature waterfalls. He uttered a single, guttural sob and a jet of tears flew through the panel, hitting her in the face.

She stepped back from the door with an involuntary grunt of disgust. Before she could remonstrate again with the man, he turned away. With a shock she saw that the back of his head was not hair but another face—the face of the houseman she had engaged after the Piper's death. She clutched at her nightgown against the sudden cold of the room, noticeable now that the door had ceased emanating its waves of heat. Her fist clenched around her sheet and she sat up in bed.

duska batsirang
19th day of run'sanamasa, 966

Two days had passed since Elaine survived her fall into the raging Sun Hutang. Two days on the road under the drenching sky. Two days with no chance for proper rest, a hot meal, a dry bed, or even a break from the chafing of her saddle. Two days during which her tears for Jann mingled with the rain on her face, unremarked. The one ray of sunshine in the constant bleakness had been their discovery of her kudo Jaranyla. She stood at the side of the road as if waiting for them to catch up with her. Now slumped, exhausted, on the gentle kudo's back, Elaine rocked from side to side in time with her gait. Despite his supposed affinity with Water, Lautan fared no better. Dark circles held up his eyes. His long grey hair slicked to his head like a frozen cataract, his robe dripped rainwater into his boots.

'You really think this man is a Stone mage?' the wizard asked as they rode.

'I believe he's the most likely, of all the strange things we have seen. Knowledge of Stone and Wood has been hidden for so long, it's hard to be certain. Jann's story was quite vague.'

'The Gatekeeper only repeated what the Beragan people told him.'

'Yes, I know.' Elaine clamped her mouth shut on a more pointed retort. Her weariness and the combined irritations of saddle and rain had worn her temper to a thread. 'I meant we know almost nothing about how Stone power is manifest. It does explain one thing though.'

'And what is that, Bakara?'

'Petani and I had been experimenting with the combination of Earth and Fire power.'

'I remember. It was I who interrupted you.'

'We were on the point of giving up in any case when you arrived. We were trying to recreate the peculiar glassy rock that appeared after... well...' She felt her cheeks colouring at the memory. 'After I lost my temper. Anyhow, we failed in the attempt. But if we had a Stone mage.'

'As I understood it, the Stone mage only manipulates stone. Its history, back to its creation, its strength, malleability, endurance, all these are available to the wielder of Stone power. I do not believe the creation of the material itself would be in his gift.'

Elaine sighed. 'You may be right. If that's true, then we must hope there is a plentiful supply whenever we have need of his power.'

Lautan gestured at the mountain range to their left, almost invisible in the rain. 'Stone is much like Water,' he said, smiling. 'The supply is virtually limitless.'

Damn, the old wizard could be vexatious at times!

'Yes, obviously there are piles of rock everywhere. The question is whether a Stone mage can always work with it, or if he would need different kinds for different purposes. Such as the one I was talking about. I hoped my power, combined with the Gardener's, could create it. If we should ever need it when there is none to hand.'

'Stone is much like Water,' Lautan repeated. 'I do not ever need a different kind of water.'

Elaine held her tongue. They fell silent for the rest of their journey. It was approaching midday when they rode into Duska Batsirang, though the day's heavy cloud had completely obscured the sun.

'Where will we find this mage?' Lautan asked.

'*How the hell should I know?*' thought Elaine. 'There's an inn here,' she said.

Inside the tiny hostelry the lunch trade had not yet begun. The place was deserted, with no sign of the innkeeper. Elaine walked over to the bar, her footsteps loud on the bare, dusty boards of the floor. Behind the counter, a cellar trapdoor stood open.

'Hello?' Elaine called. 'Anyone here?'

'Hold your kudai, will you?' came a voice from below.

Sounds of barrels being moved, followed by footsteps on the ladder, did not drown out the man's continued irritation with the interruption. When he emerged, red faced, from the cellar and caught sight of Elaine's topaz-studded bangles, his demeanour changed on the instant.

'A thousand apologies, Kema'satu! Had I known it was you I would have attended immediately. Please forgive an old villager his discourtesy.'

As he spoke, the innkeeper's face turned a deeper shade of red. An artery pulsed in his neck.

Elaine ignored the man's fawning. 'We are looking for an Earther. One we believe may have settled in your village. He is known for an accident he had some years ago, with a stone.'

'Ha!' said the innkeeper, hitching his trousers over his ample waist. 'Piers Tremaine. He's a popular chap all of a sudden! You're not the first to be asking after him today. At least you didn't wake me up at dead of night. His cottage is the last one the right, down there.' He pointed in the direction of the coast. 'You can't miss it. It's the one with the strange chimney. I haven't seen anything of him today, mind. He's been keeping to himself the past few days.'

Elaine left the inn without a word, Lautan following. Unsure how far Tremaine's cottage was, they rode their kudai through the village towards the sea. True to the innkeeper's word, the dwelling clearly stood out from the others.

They dismounted outside the hut, leaving their animals to graze on the few tufts of grass growing between the buildings. When there was no response to Elaine's knocks, she pushed the door open.

'Hello? Tremaine? Piers Tremaine? Are you at home?'

'There is no one here, Bakara,' Lautan said. 'The place has an empty feel to it.'

'Yes, I know what you mean.'

The cottage felt cold inside. The hearth held no warmth. No fire had burned here recently. The air inside the place was damp, and smelt of mould. Lautan walked through into the bedroom.

'There is but a single shirt hanging in the closet,' he called. 'We are too late.'

Elaine caught sight of a ring of dust beside the fire, where something had once stood. 'Some of his belongings are missing.'

'I fear we must assume he has departed, probably in the company of whoever was looking for him.'

'I think I can guess who that is,' the Fire Witch said, her eyes flashing.

They returned to the inn. In their absence, the midday rush had started. Two villagers sat at the bar with full glasses in front of them.

The innkeeper beamed at each of them in turn. 'Welcome back, Kema'satun. Did you find him?'

'No,' Elaine replied. 'Who was it that was looking for him earlier? You never said.'

'You left before I had chance Kema'satu. It was that Simon Nehj.'

Elaine frowned. 'Not a name I'm familiar with.'

'Lived here as a youth, but we don't see much of him now he works for the King. I hardly recognised him last night in his drab travelling gear. Normally you can't miss the gaudy fucker when he's all in his yellow.'

She turned to Lautan.

'We must leave. The Jester has a half-day start over us.

302

To Court, and as fast as we can!'

court of the blood king
19th day of run'sanamasa, 966

An inexperienced rider, Piers could not control his animal at anything faster than a jog. When they reached the Court, after half a day in the saddle with only a single break to take a piss and swallow a few mouthfuls of water, he was exhausted. Nipis responded with nothing but a grunt to his requests for a break, or food. Indeed they had shared only a few words since leaving the village. Maybe it had been a mistake agreeing to come with the little man, but his powers of persuasion were formidable. In the end, what else could he have done? He had pulled up his collar, pulled down his hood, and tried to still the shivering brought on by the freezing rain. Things would be better once they arrived.

His spirits lifted when they emerged from the tree line. From this distance the famed red stone of the Court looked grey under the leaden sky. Washed with the unending rain, the squat structure resembled a jumbled pile of dead fish left too long on a riverbank. Even its unwelcoming appearance held the promise of food and warmth. They rode silently through the huge gates into a deserted basilica. His companion seemed to dismiss his surly demeanour, becoming animated as he dismounted.

'Come, Tremaine. Quickly. We must get you in out of this rain.'

Nipis grabbed his shoulder, pushing him across the courtyard. Their kudai stood steaming in the light rain, watching them go. The two men entered through the large whitewood doors into the imposing hallway, Nipis still hurrying him along.

'What's the rush?' Piers asked, shrugging off the shorter man's hand. 'It's lunchtime. Are we not eating first?'

'This way!' Nipis said, striding ahead, 'I'm soaked to the

skin. You must be too. I'll show you to your room. I can have food brought up. You will feel a lot more comfortable once you're out of those wet things.'

Piers hurried after the man, who had already turned a corner. This was his first visit to Court. Rooms and corridors opened off the main hallway in all directions. If he lost sight of the only person he knew here, he would have no idea where to go. The best course of action may be to do as he was told for now, even though following orders had never been his first choice. After a series of turns, they approached a door at the end of a long corridor. A stern-faced man with a long brown beard stood beside it, as if on guard.

'Pwalek!' the Jester declared. 'Well met. This is Piers Tremaine, the man we have been seeking. A man of very special talents.'

'Happy to make your acquaintance,' the man said in heavily accented English. He held out his hand. Piers took it.

'Likewise,' he said, with a sidelong frown at Nipis, who had already entered the room.

'Come in, come in,' he said, 'these are your quarters for the time being. I hope you will find them comfortable.'

'I had a bath prepared,' Pwalek added, 'thinking you would not be long arriving. It should still be hot.'

'Very kind, thank you,' Piers said. The thought of a hot bath sent shivers down his spine, chafing his skin against the cold, saturated cloth of his undershirt. 'You mentioned having food sent up?' he said.

The little man laughed. 'Yes, of course. See to it Pwalek. There are some things I must discuss with our guest.'

The other man withdrew without another word.

'I don't feel comfortable discussing my supposed talents with everyone,' Piers said before Nipis could speak. 'They didn't exactly make me popular in my old home.'

'Pwalek is not just anyone. Don't worry. He can keep

his mouth shut. He sits on the Darmajelis too, at my right hand. But in any case you need not hide your talents here,' he continued. 'We are desperately short of Elemental help in these troubled times. You will be welcomed, trust me.'

Piers shivered again. In his experience, those who used the phrase "trust me" were the least likely to be trustworthy.

'Even so,' he said, taking off his wet cloak, 'I still have little idea what this "talent" is good for. I don't want it broadcasting. I have a good knowledge of construction methods. That's all. Anything else I have done in the past may only be temporary. I don't understand it, even now. It may not as useful as you think.'

'Nonsense,' Nipis said. 'Please don't try to convince me your work is ordinary. You are more than just a builder.'

'I have always been a builder. That has not changed.'

'Something has changed, and you know it. Why else would you accept my offer? If you had no special powers you could have simply carried on with your life of anonymity in an Istanian backwater.'

Piers began to protest again, but Nipis held up his hand.

'Calm yourself. You can have a good life here. A seat on the ruling body, as I have said. No one need know of your abilities if that is what you wish. Pwalek will not say anything. No one even knows you are here yet. We kept the public areas of the Court clear, and guarded the corridors on the way to these chambers. Your secret is safe. Being from Earth is sufficient justification for your position. We have already appointed one Earther to the Darmajelis, so it will be nothing out of the ordinary. Relax. Take a bath. Food will be here directly. I will return later to discuss what you can expect from your work.'

'I know nothing of politics,' Piers began, but Nipis waved away his protests with a crooked smile.

'Don't worry. We will not burden you with the minutiae of Court government. You will soon fall into the way of things. Remain here for the time being,' he added. 'We regularly have other Elementals visiting Court, though I know of none here at present. Nevertheless if you desire to keep your abilities a secret it would be well for you to avoid them. Some have a habit of sniffing out power in others.'

court of the blood king
19th day of run'sanamasa, 966

Their journey back to Court was as silent as it was swift. Lautan had observed the Witch's reaction to the innkeeper's words. It went beyond mere disappointment at missing this purported Stone mage. If the man spoke truly then it was certain the Jester himself had come looking for the Earther. The layers of meaning piled up on this single event made his head spin. Trying to process them had occupied him for much of the ride between coast and Court, but even without it he would have kept his own counsel. Bakara was much changed since her fall into the river. Her temper—fiery at the best of times—now burned so close to the surface that one wrong word could result in a scorching. The Wizard already felt inadequate to deal with this awful distortion in the power of Water, without being berated by the Witch for speaking out of turn. Safer to remain mute.

That the Jester knew of Tremaine's existence was a puzzle in itself. Word of Wood and Stone had reached the Elementals scant days before, when the Gatekeeper told his tale. How had the knowledge transferred so quickly to Court? Was there yet another informer at the Black Palace, stepping into the position vacated by the dead Piper?

The Jester himself had made the journey to Duska Batsirang, rather than sending a lackey. There was the second layer to the conundrum. It revealed that he not only knew of the man's existence but also the import of his power. Should Stone fall into the hands of the Reds then the Elemental team would be further disadvantaged. This Stone mage was new to his power and not local to this world. He would not feel the same weight of responsibility to maintain balance. The Elementals treated Te'banga as an immutable rule. They would not engage in any dispute or conflict unless the opposing side was supported by equal power.

Even if the man Tremaine was aware of that aspect of Elemental Law, where was the Wood mage to stand against him? There had as yet been no manifestation of that power, as far as he knew.

Fortunately, since Lautan paid little attention to their progress, the road from the coast was straight and well-drained, affording their kudai an easy passage. Even so night had already fallen when they approached Court, the lights from its windows reflecting from their wet cloaks as they drew nearer. When they rode through the enormous gates and dismounted, Lautan's attention was drawn to a window overlooking the basilica. A wave of nausea struck him. He staggered, gripping the saddle of his beast for support.

'Are you alright old friend?' Bakara asked, hurrying to his side.

'I will be,' he replied. 'Took me unawares. Never before have I felt such power. I believe I have found the source of the rain.'

The Fire Witch's eyes widened. 'Here? Where?'

He pointed at the window. The pale face he had seen had disappeared.

'Up there. Come, we must hurry.'

They ran inside. The Fire Witch, more familiar with the interior layout of the Court than he, took the lead, taking the nearest staircase to the first floor. She navigated them unerringly to a door, indistinguishable from the others in the same corridor. From his continuing queasiness, Lautan knew she had found the right room. They entered without knocking.

A heavily-built young man with close cropped black hair, sparse beard, and pale blue eyes sat in a chair beside the roaring fireplace, his face twisted into a sardonic grin.

'I didn't hear you knock,' he said, 'but please do come in.'

Lautan strode over to stand beside the youth. Scarcely more than a boy, really. How had he come to have such power?

'You must stop this,' he said. 'I know what you're doing. I can feel it. It is wrong, and you have to stop.'

The door to Lautan's left flew open. A young woman rushed into the room. Her hair, much longer, matched the colour of the young man's, her eyes a deeper shade of blue. Almost purple.

'What's going on?' she said. 'Who are you? What are you doing in my brother's room?'

Lautan turned to her. 'You too,' he said. 'You must stop what you are doing. It is causing so much misery.'

'Doing?' she said, looking puzzled. 'What do you mean? I'm not doing anything.'

'Forgive my sister,' the boy said. 'It's not her. She doesn't even know she is capable of doing anything.'

'Douglas?' the girl said. 'What's all this about? Who are these people?'

'Well I don't know about her,' he replied, cocking a thumb at the Fire Witch, 'but this old guy—'

A familiar voice interrupted him. 'Lautan! Bakara!' The Jester strode into the room. 'So good of you to grace the Court with your presence!'

The young man's face broke into a beaming smile. He rose to his feet. 'Jeruk! You're back already!'

'Back?' the Jester said, his face taking on a ruddy hue.

'I was at my window last night when you rode out.'

'Ah. Yes. An errand. A brief excursion only.' He took the boy by the arm. 'If you will excuse us, both of you. I don't know what brings you here, but there is a matter I must discuss with Douglas.'

The Jester hurried the boy into the corridor, closing the door behind them.

'Well that's typical!' the girl exclaimed. 'He's always doing that. What is all this about anyway? Who are you people?'

'I am Lautan,' Lautan said, 'the Water Wizard of Berikatanya.'

The colour drained from the girl's face at his words.

'And I am his counterpart in Fire,' Bakara said. 'The Fire Witch. Known as Bakara, but you may call me Elaine if you wish. That is the name I used while on Earth. And your name?'

The girl looked lost. Her gaze jumped from the two of them to the door through which her brother had left, and back.

'Er... Kyle. Kyle Muir. That was my brother, Douglas. You were on Earth?'

'It's a long story,' Bakara said with a wan smile. 'I would be happy to share it with you at some other time. Right now we have more pressing matters to attend to.'

'What did my brother mean? "She doesn't even know she is capable of doing anything." What am I capable of?'

'I think you may already have some idea of that,' Lautan said. 'Have you not heard the call of the Water?'

The girl flushed again, a deeper colour. She turned away and walked to the window. Raindrops continued to wash down the panes with a muted clatter.

'I...I'm not sure,' she said. 'I thought... but... I don't know. Sometimes the rain has been... strange.'

'In what way strange?'

The girl did not reply straight away. She stood watching the rivulets on the window. At length, she faced the two Elementals.

'It dances. I mean, it doesn't always fall straight down. Sometimes it hits me in the face. I thought at first it was the wind. Until last night.'

'What happened last night to change your mind?'

'I saw Douglas. I saw him walk out in the rain, and it didn't touch him. I followed him to the moat. He was making the water do things. When I asked what he was doing he said he was practising. He made me mad. That's when I felt it. At least, I think I did. Or heard it. What you said. The call of the Water.'

Lautan listened as the girl spoke. Every word she uttered confirmed what he already knew to be true.

'You and Douglas have the power,' he said. 'We have seen others from Earth who discover an affinity with the Elements once they are here. Though none has ever been as powerful as you,' he added.

The girl's face, which had been recovering its normal hue, paled again at Lautan's words.

'I'm not powerful,' she said. 'The only affinity I've ever had with Water is a love of the sea. Swimming. I can't make it jump and dance. I can't make it rain.'

'Not yet, maybe,' Bakara said. 'But this is not something Lautan could be wrong about. With practice, you will be able to do all of those things.'

'And more,' Lautan said. 'I do not understand, even with all my years of experience, how your brother does what he is doing. But he *is* doing it, of that there is no doubt.'

'And he has to stop,' Elaine said. 'Or many more people will die. Or be lost,' she added, choking on the last word.

The girl put her hands over her ears.

'I don't believe any of this,' she said, tears starting from her eyes. 'Magic and elements and death. I don't want any of it. I just wanted a chance of a better life. I don't want power. I don't want people to die. But I don't know how to stop Douglas. I could never stop him doing whatever he wants.'

'Maybe if we work together?' Lautan suggested.

As soon as the words left his mouth, he knew it had been the wrong thing to say. The girl's teary eyes opened wide. She fixed him with a terrified look.

'No! Go away! How dare you come into our rooms and accuse us of killing people? And then demand that I help you stop my brother! He's my brother! Leave me alone!'

She ran from the room, slamming the adjoining door behind her.

court of the blood king
20th day of run'sanamasa, 966

At breakfast next day, Kyle felt conflicted. The events of the previous evening were still fresh in her mind. The strange visitors, the revelations of her supposed power, and the traditional disdain from her brother all swirled around like the cold drizzle that painted the refectory windows with a grey film. But it was Jeruk Nipis' behaviour that cut most deeply. Since their arrival the little man had soon decided Douglas was the one worth investing time and effort in. He had cut her out at every turn. With a closed door, or by whisking her brother off to "discuss matters." What were these matters they could not discuss with her? Was it so unlikely she could understand matters, contribute to matters, resolve matters? She'd had more warmth and empathy from the two—what did they call themselves?—Elementals in two minutes than the Jester had offered her in two days.

She took some small comfort, childish maybe but satisfying even so, in calling him the Jester, even if only in her own mind.

Douglas collapsed onto the bench opposite her. His small plate dropped to the table with a loud clatter. 'Quick breakfast for me this morning. Important meeting to attend.' He smiled, dipped his toasted tepsak into a runny egg, and took a bite.

'Oh?'

Putting her grudge on hold, she could not help making conversation. He was her brother. Her only link to her old life, and still the only person she really knew in her new one.

'My first Darmajelis meeting,' he said, his face flushed with excitement and self-importance. 'I get to sit with the great and the good, and discuss important matters of state.'

'If you say "important" one more time, that egg will be running down your face.'

'Ho-ho! Jealousy!'

'Quite the opposite.' Kyle forced her face match her words. 'You'll be bored to tears before the morning's done. Whereas I—'

'Oh yes? What are *you* going to be doing this morning? Something very important, I have no doubt.'

'The Elementals have invited me to... discuss matters.'

The phrase popped into her head moments before she said it. It was deliciously vague and also pointedly identical to the Jester's words. Kyle smiled, outwardly for her brother's benefit and inwardly at her sudden cleverness. His smile remained fixed on his face, a small fragment of eggy toast visible between his teeth, but his eyes turned the colour of the rain-drenched sky.

'Well, I'm sure that will be every bit as boring for you as you think my meeting will be for me.' He dropped his toast onto his plate. 'Pair of old farts deluded by their own rhetoric.' He stood, stretching. 'I suppose I'll see you later.'

Kyle watched him leave. Since her meeting with the Elementals was a total fabrication, there was no rush to finish her meal. On the other hand, she had no appetite. With a resigned sigh, she left the table. Having no real appointment to attend, and with her meagre coterie of family and acquaintances engaged on the business of government, she decided to spend the morning learning her way around the Court. It appeared confusing at first glance but on closer inspection, Kyle soon saw that the corridors were not, in fact, all the same. There was no obvious logic to their layout. The buildings had probably been extended and otherwise knocked about over the years. Slight changes in the striations that coloured the stone walls supported her theory. As time went by, her confidence grew.

Midday came and went. After walking all around the Court, Kyle's appetite had recovered. Heading back towards the refectory intending to take a light lunch, she encountered a staircase heading down. It was the first such stairway she had seen. Intrigued, she followed the curve of steps until she reached the Court catacombs. It was a cold day, but down here the air had an extra chill. No light penetrated. Only the torches set in wall sconces at regular intervals relieved the gloom.

The subterranean passages looked even more convoluted than those on the upper levels. Armed with the day's experience Kyle took careful note of anything she could use to differentiate them. Scratches on walls, a bent sconce, traces of an old nest no longer occupied by whatever creature had built it. Her attention focused on these navigational clues, Kyle almost bumped into an old man hurrying in the opposite direction, his arms full of dusty, yellowed scrolls.

'Have a care there, young lady!' he exclaimed. 'These parchments are irreplaceable!'

'Oh, I'm so sorry,' Kyle said.

'What are you doing here anyway? This is a restricted area! We don't allow just anyone to wander these cellars, you know.'

'Sorry,' she repeated, cursing herself for sounding like a scolded child, 'I'm new here. I was having a look around. Trying to get my bearings.'

'Hmph. Yes, well, stay out of here in future. I have many precious artefacts in the chambers. New or not, you will show them some respect or you will have me to deal with.'

Kyle suppressed a laugh. The wizened old man did not even stand tall enough to reach her shoulders. When hunched over his burden of tightly rolled scrolls, he was shorter still. It looked as though it was taking all his strength to carry them.

'But since you are here already,' the man continued, 'you can help me move these. If you promise to be careful.'

'Yes, of course. I should be glad to help. What are they anyway, these documents?'

'The lore and history of the whole of Berikatanya. Not just Istanian history. I have all the archives here. Kertonian too. Political, military, scientific. And Elemental. I am their Keeper.'

Kyle's ears pricked up at the mention of Elemental lore. 'Where are you taking them?'

'Many centuries ago, this Court was built over an underground lake. After all this accursed rain, the water level is rising. It threatens to overwhelm my libraries. I should be attending Darmajelis today but this cannot wait. Another day and some of the scrolls will be beyond saving. I have already relocated many of them but the lake is encroaching even on their new home. The increased moisture in the air is not helping either, though I am at a loss what to do about that. It had occurred to me to seek the aid of the Fire Witch, but with her renowned temper that could prove a dangerous move. I fear more harm than good would result.'

Down here away from the rains, Water power could offer a solution to the old man's problem. If Water could be called up, it should also be possible to dismiss it. Surely it wasn't beyond even a novice like her to drive a bit of damp out of some paper? But her power was still new. She had barely accepted its existence, let alone allowed herself to believe she could wield it. She too could cause more harm than good. Nevertheless if the scrolls contained any learning about her ability, they might provide the answer to their own plight.

'Do any of these ancient texts mention Water lore?'

The Keeper chuckled. 'Bless you child, no. The current

Water Wizard, as with all those that went before him, prefers to spend his time in liquid form. He has no time for writing.'

Kyle's imagination leapt ahead, a vision of a melting man collapsing into a bathtub spooled through her mind. She shut it down before the imaginary man could circle the plughole. Her encounter with the Water Wizard had been brief, but he had seemed pretty solid to her.

'To my knowledge,' the old man continued, 'which of course is extensive, no Water lore has ever been committed to record. It is learned by practice only, and by example from those who are already adept at its use.'

Chapter 16

The ride from coast to Court passed unremarked by Claire; her thoughts occupied by the twin enigmas of the Muirs' DNA results and Patrick's decision to remain at Pennatanah. It had come as no surprise there was a DNA connection to Elemental power. Elaine had implied as much when they first arrived on Berikatanya. She'd explained that Elementals normally married each other and gave birth to other Elementals. The baton of power was handed on through the generations. Claire was a perfect example. Air powers, inchoate on Earth, had manifested as soon as she returned to her natural home. The place where her father had been Air Mage. He never spoke of his own parents. She should ask the Queen who had been Air Mage before her father. It would not surprise her to learn it was another family member.

And now, somehow, the laws of inheritance had blessed the Muirs with a glorious bounty. One which they too had been unaware of before their arrival. Unlike Earth, on Berikatanya, eldritch power had not been squeezed out of existence by centuries of industrialisation, mechanisation, and computerisation. Maybe the twins were still oblivious to their abilities? Surely no one who knew they were the cause of so much destruction would continue flaunting their power for evil? The Elemental code forbade it, although the histories Claire had uncovered in her lengthy searches through the Keeper's scrolls were littered with examples of suhiri who used their powers to advance their own position rather than for the good of all. She knew so many power-related clichés. With great power comes great responsibility. A little knowledge is a dangerous thing. Power corrupts, and absolute power corrupts absolutely. Even those schooled in Elemental lore had sometimes turned away from good use of their magic. The Muirs had no such schooling.

Claire had been terrified by the dawning realisation that her latent power was responsible for the winds. Fortunately, by then, she was surrounded by people who could help. Now she had the chance to do the same for these twins as they learned of their abilities. But she must also be prepared to confront them if their actions were deliberate.

In their brief conversations, Patrick had only hinted at his own inner conflicts. The haunted look that came over him whenever Juggler powers were mentioned suggested they too were terrifying; even more than any of the four Elemental forces. So abhorrent that he would rather shut himself away from any conscious or accidental use of them. What kind of horrific potential would lead him to make such a choice? Patrick Glass was no coward. Neither was he arrogant or over-exuberant. Talented, yes. Thoughtful. Considerate. Gentle. Perhaps it was gentleness that steered him away from his power. Whatever it was, he would have to come to terms with it in his own time.

Her rider thus distracted, Pembwana picked a route and a pace to suit herself and the conditions. They made good time, camping in a dry spot some distance from the Sun Hutang and picking up the journey again that morning. With her animal instincts the placid kudo had found a safe crossing even with the river still in full spate. They arrived at Court soon after dusk. Entering through the enormous double doors, Claire caught sight of Elaine and Lautan on their way to the refectory.

'Wait!' she called, hurrying after them. 'I must speak with you!'

'Claire!' said the Fire Witch. 'Welcome back. We have news too.'

'I was right about there being someone on the Dauntless with Elemental power,' Claire said. 'Two people, actually.'

'Douglas and Kyle Muir,' Lautan said, his deep voice booming in the passage as if it came from an undersea grotto.

'Wha–?' Claire began. 'I mean, how–'

'They are here,' Lautan said. 'We have seen them. Briefly, to be sure, but there can be no doubt. At least one of them is responsible for these rains. Possibly both.'

'Where are they?' Claire asked. 'I must help them.'

Elaine snorted. 'Good luck with that. Especially the brother.'

Claire flashed a sceptical look at the Witch. She could not tell whether this was Elaine's customary acid tongue or an honest appraisal of the situation. In the end, did it matter?

'I see you doubt the veracity of Bakara's words,' Lautan said. 'But she has the right of it. They are both volatile, and the brother is quite extraordinarily confrontational.'

'Well, I have to try. Do you know where they are Lautan?'

'Their room is on the first floor, overlooking the basilica. But we have not seen them since yesterday.'

'I'll come and find you later,' Claire said. 'Let you know how I get on.'

'That will be a short conversation,' Elaine replied, taking Lautan's arm and steering him back in the direction of the refectory.

On the first floor landing, Claire took the corridor leading to the front of the building. She knocked on each door in turn, without response. Her need to help the twins overriding her natural propriety, she opened the silent doors and called into the rooms. All were empty. As she passed the entrance to the crypt, sounds of a heated argument reached her, echoing up the rickety old stairs.

court of the blood king
20th day of run'sanamasa, 966

'God! I can't even come down to the fucking crypt without finding you! What are you doing here?'

The man's voice, loud and brittle with anger and irritation, bounced from the stone walls of the passageway. Claire crept away from the foot of the stairs, closer to the source of the sound.

'What am I doing here? I could ask you the same question! Thought you were supposed to be at your "important" meeting?'

'We've had a brief adjournment.'

'Oh, "we" now, is it? Us very important members have been adjourned. You sound like Mr MacGowan.'

'I sound nothing like him. Keep your jealousy in check Kyle, and answer the question.'

'You can't demand answers from me, you jumped up shit. "Darmajelis" or not. You're just a Johnny-come-lately. They probably sent you down here on an errand. That's it. Errand boy. Haha!'

A deafening clap of thunder rolled down the stairwell, making Claire jump. Torrential rain clattered the narrow windows on the landing above, almost drowning out the argument. If any proof were needed that these two were responsible for the rains, the way the weather responded to their fight was enough for Claire. A chilling insight into a future she had narrowly avoided, having been taken under the Queen's wing before her abilities had fledged.

'How dare you! Will you tell me what you're doing down here or not? This is a restricted area. You could be in big trouble.'

'I know it's restricted. The Keeper told me. I've been helping him.'

'Helping him? What help could you possibly be to him? He's a Darmajelis member too you know.'

'I know.'

'We shouldn't be integrating with these people anyway.

Not until we know how things stand.'

'Is that what you're doing? Sitting with the Jester and his cronies is "not integrating" whereas me spending time helping an old man is? Give me a break.'

'Stop calling him the Jester! And where is the old duffer anyway? I've been asked to find him. He missed the first part of the meeting.'

'Errand boy!' the young woman's voice taunted.

Claire peered round the corner. The twins stood at the other end of the passage, facing each other. Flickering torchlight accentuated the lines in their faces, each creased into an angry grimace. Claire thought for one second the brother was about to hit his sister, but the moment passed. His raised hand fell to his side.

'You are an annoying bitch,' he said. 'For the last time—where is the Keeper?'

'He's down there.' She pointed down one of the many passageways that led away from where they stood. 'But he won't come. He's busy moving his scrolls. There are hundreds. He won't be done today.'

'He is summoned to the Darmajelis!' the man repeated, his face ruddy under the light from the sconces.

'He doesn't know you from a stable boy. He might come for the dwarf. You've no chance.'

'Don't call him that! I've told you, he doesn't even like to be called "the Jester" any more. He's in charge of this place now. One step down from being the King himself. Show him some respect!'

'Good grief, you talk about how I shouldn't be integrating! You're so far up the Jester's arse you're talking out of his mouth!'

The brother raised his hand again. 'Fuck you!' he shouted, 'I'm sick of you following me round like a lost puppy. Why can't you just fuck off?'

Claire stepped around the corner, out of the shadows.

'Excuse me,' she said.

court of the blood king - crypt area
20th day of run'sanamasa, 966

How *did* his sister contrive so easily to get under his skin? She always said the wrong thing; pouring scorn on any of his achievements. He had never wanted to slap her more than he did at this precise moment.

'Why can't you just fuck off?' he shouted.

'Excuse me,' came a quiet voice from the other end of the passage.

Douglas spun around, shielding his eyes from the flickering torches. A young woman with long, ash-blond hair emerged from the shadows. She took a step towards them.

'I'm sorry. I couldn't help overhearing. You shouldn't be fighting.'

'She's my sister,' Douglas replied. 'We always fight. What's it got to do with you, anyway?'

The woman smiled. 'I was like you once,' she said. 'Coming into my powers before I really knew what was happening to me. Before I had much control. My name is Claire Yamani. I was on the Valiant.'

His sister opened her mouth to speak. Douglas stepped in front of her, cutting her off physically.

'I've got plenty of control, thanks.'

'Have you? It's still raining.'

'I like rain.'

'I've seen people drowned because of this rain. Rivers overflowing. Homes washed away. Is that really what you want?'

'Why should I care about them? These primitives are nothing to me.'

The woman frowned, turned to Kyle.

'Is that right? You don't care about them?'

Douglas sidestepped to stand in front of his sister again.

'She agrees with me.'

The woman's frown lines deepened. 'Even if that were

true, it's not only "primitives" that are affected. Plenty of Earthers live in these communities. You want them dead too?'

He shrugged. The woman moved to one side, fixing Kyle with a sharp look.

'Does he always treat you this way? Ignore your feelings? Put words in your mouth? I can't believe you want people dead. You've only just arrived. You don't even know them.'

'Believe what you like, it's no skin off my nose,' Douglas said.

Kyle put a hand on his arm, pushing him gently away. 'Or mine,' she said. 'We're a team. We've always been a team.'

His anger, so hot and urgent a moment before, evaporated. Right then he loved his little sister more than he ever had.

'See?'

'But I can help you,' the Yamani woman said. 'I am the Air Mage now. An Elemental, like you. I know what you're going through. How hard it is. I can help you learn to control your power.'

He laughed. 'Oh, right. That explains a lot. Another Elemental so sure of her own power—just like the old guy we met yesterday. Well I'm doing just fine controlling my power, as you've already noticed. I didn't need him and I don't need you. And neither does she.'

'He's right,' said Kyle, 'we don't need you. We're managing fine on our own.'

'More than fine, actually,' Douglas added. 'I'm down here on Darmajelis business. So if you'll excuse us.'

He took Kyle's hand. Together they walked off along the passage toward where the Keeper was working, leaving the Air Mage alone in the gloom.

court of the blood king - piers tremaine's rooms
20th day of run'sanamasa, 966

The rain on his window made soporific sounds, yet Piers Tremaine remained wide awake. After the long journey earlier in the day, and a luxurious soak in his private bath, he had tried to catch a nap before the strange little man returned. Conspiring against his desire for sleep were the almost constant rumbling of his empty stomach, and the expectation that Jeruk Nipis would reappear at any moment. The expected food never arrived, and neither did the Jester. Piers had no idea how long he had waited since his promise to be back "shortly" but there was still no sign of him. An outdoors man by both instinct and trade, he was never happy when surrounded by walls. As the time dragged by, he became increasingly agitated. He had been instructed to remain in his chambers, but would it really be so bad if he were to explore the Court? Just a little?

Without warning, his door swung open and Nipis breezed in.

'So sorry,' he began, falling silent as he took in the scene. 'Has your meal been tidied away already?'

'It was never here to be tidied in the first place.'

The little man rubbed the hook of his nose, looking mortified. 'My apologies Tremaine, you must be starving. Did you not call for service?'

He walked over to the fireplace and yanked on a braided cord that hung beside it.

'I thought you had arranged it,' Piers said.

'I'm afraid I have been distracted by... other matters. I can only apologise again.'

'I'll live. I'm more uncomfortable with being shut away like this. It feels like I've swapped one prison for another.'

'Yes, yes, I quite understand. It must be difficult. But for now, it's important that no one knows you are here. Only for another few days. Assuming you have had time to consider my offer?'

The offer of a government position had been another

factor keeping Piers awake. Grace and favour appointments, or those with a political motivation, did not sit well with him. If a man had a role or a title, he should have earned it through honest toil, or application to learning. He had neither worked nor studied to warrant a seat on such a powerful caucus, and yet it was being handed to him on a plate.

'Well,' he said, aware that the question had been hanging in the empty air for some time, 'I...'

'I'm sure I have already explained the importance of opening the Darmajelis up to Earther representatives,' Nipis said, taking Piers' arm and leading him to the sofa beside the fire. Having been left untended, the flames had died to a ruddy glow. Wisps of reluctant smoke drifted languorously up the chimney, down which the odd spot of rain fell to hiss on the embers. Nipis tossed a couple of fresh logs into the hot ashes, throwing up a plume of sparks.

'News has reached us,' he continued, 'that the much-discussed Earther separatist movement has finally decided to establish a camp of their own. Some of your compatriots at Court are becoming restless. Talking about their future, their roles, their voice. It would be a great help to public harmony if they had a representative at the highest table.'

'I have no desire to be a politician,' Piers replied, 'and no skill in such matters either, as I'm sure I've already told you. I would be a poor advocate indeed, more likely to cause unrest than quell it. They would all wonder what I'd done to deserve such an honour. They would suspect me of corruption of some sort. I'd be worse off in the end than if you had left me behind in the village.'

'Worse off? You would likely be dead if I had left you there,' the short man said, his voice taking on a steely note. He stopped, staring at the growing blaze in front of them, seeming to consider his next words.

'There is another reason,' he said. 'I did not want to

mention it, since the intelligence is uncertain. Rumours only. And yet, it has some echoes of our traditional Elementals, so I am minded to believe it.'

'Echoes?'

'You are not schooled in such things, having been shut away in that backwater, reliant upon your own intuitions to guide you. But the Elementals, as a group, have a strong code. In particular, their principle of "balance" is of utmost importance to them. That each Element is balanced by another, and there should be equal representation in any two sides of an argument or conflict.'

'I don't understand what this has to do with me. My seat on the Darmajelis.'

'There is a balancing power to Stone,' Nipis went on. 'These two powers were long hidden from us. Knowledge of them has only resurfaced in the last few days. The corresponding power to Stone is Wood. The rumour I spoke of, is that there is a Wood mage in the Black Palace.'

He took another log from the basket beside the fire, hefting its weight and turning it over in his hands as if expecting a manifestation of this "Wood power" to emerge from it.

'So you see,' he continued, lobbing the log onto the fire, 'it is also important that our resident Stone mage sits in a position of power, to maintain the balance between Red and Black. And,' he added, getting to his feet, 'that particular seat is just the beginning. The Blood Throne remains empty. Once you come fully into your powers, who knows where they may take you?'

keeper's archives
20th day of run'sanamasa, 966

Claire let out a long sigh, and lay down her quill on the slate table. The evening had been a catalogue of frustration. Now, her last candle almost spent, she had to admit she had achieved nothing. Part of the problem lay in front of her. An ancient Air scroll almost as indecipherable as it was illegible. Age had faded the lettering to the point of invisibility, and the arcane language required every dictionary and lore reference the Keeper possessed. Each word demanded translation and interpretation in its own right as well as in the context of the document as a whole. It was exhausting.

But the main barrier to her progress was the memory of her distasteful encounter with the Muir twins. No matter how hard she tried to focus on the scroll, their conversation replayed vividly in her mind. The shock of seeing Douglas raise his hand to his sister, even if no blow had been struck. His overbearing manner, his unwarranted confidence in his burgeoning power, and Kyle's almost subservient reaction to her brother's overweening faux superiority. It jarred with every scintilla of Claire's experience as an Elemental.

When the twins left to find the Keeper, Claire had intended to abandon the crypt and seek solace in the company of Elaine and Lautan. She had taken only a few steps before the familiar smells of the catacombs and the thought of this ancient and challenging text changed her mind. It would be wasteful to pass up this chance of further study. After all, she was already here. So instead she returned to this study alcove. One the Keeper had built for her, when it became clear she would be a frequent visitor to his archives. Here she still sat, head in hands, having sought inspiration and found none.

'Miss Yamani?'

The quiet, tentative tone of a woman's voice disturbed her thoughts. Kyle Muir emerged from the shadows into the guttering candlelight. Claire bristled.

'I'm not interested in a rerun of our conversation,' she began. 'If you don't want my help, then there's nothing more to say.'

The Muir girl held up her hands, her face a mask of embarrassment and supplication.

'No, please. That's not why I'm here.'

'Really? What about your brother?'

'He's gone. Back to his meeting. A late session. The Keeper refused to attend–'

'I told you. He's busy. These archives are his life.'

'Yes, and you were right. Douglas is worried about how the J– how Jeruk Nipis will react when he returns alone.'

Claire smiled. 'Don't worry, he's still the Jester to us,' she said. 'And he is right to be worried. He might be a Jester, but he doesn't suffer fools. Anyone who works for him is not allowed to make the same mistake once. So if your brother has gone, why are you here? I thought you had both turned down my offer to help?'

Kyle blushed. 'It's not always easy for me to stand up to him,' she said, brushing away a sudden tear. 'He thinks he has already mastered this amazing power. He's always been more confident than me.'

'Overconfident, it seems to me,' Claire said.

'Yes. I've seen what's happening, what his power is doing–'

'Hard to miss. The floods have even reached down here. That's why the Keeper is so distracted.'

'Please. I know. I feel like I should apologise for him. Douglas, I mean. Sometimes it seems like I've been apologising for him my whole life. I don't know if I'm responsible for any of it. How would I know? It's all so strange. Unbelievable, really, except... it's happening. I mean, magic? I think we've landed in the middle of a fairy tale.'

Claire laughed, the bright sound echoing away down the passages. 'I know. It was like that for me too, at first.'

'See? That's why I had to come and find you,' Kyle said, taking Claire's hand. 'I want to learn. I don't really know anything about this, and I'm not the sort to pretend I do. Not like Douglas.'

She hesitated, unable to hold Claire's gaze.

'I think we could be friends. I don't know about the old

man. I was a bit awe-struck by him if I'm honest. He's been using this power for ages. But he seemed, I don't know, so aloof. So angry.'

'Are you surprised? His Element is running wild, tearing up the landscape and killing people. And you're right, he's been an Elemental for longer than anyone in living memory, and yet even he can't stop what your brother is doing.'

She pulled her hand away from Kyle's grasp. 'Don't you think that gives him the right to be angry?'

Kyle's blush deepened. Fresh tears started in her eyes. 'Yes. Yes, of course. Look, I'm sorry. I want to learn. To do things properly. Miss Yamani? Will you help me, or not?'

Claire's candle, now little more than a puddle of wax with its wick leaning to one side, smoked profusely. But the greasy, pungent brume was not the cause of the girl's tears. Was it possible she was serious about making amends for her brother's misdeeds? Lautan would take some convincing. These Muirs had cause so much destruction without any training. What damage could they inflict once they were in full command of Water lore?

On the other hand, time spent among the Elementals, learning their code as well as their craft, could give this girl the tools to climb out of the pit her brother was set on creating. Surely that had to be worth a try?

'You can call me Claire,' she said. 'And yes. I will help you.'

court of the blood king, passages
20th day of run'sanamasa, 966

One of these days Douglas Muir would not be in a foul temper, but this was not that day. It was bad enough that he had to return to this late meeting. It must be approaching midnight by now. Worse, he was coming back alone. Sent to fetch the Keeper, he had been unable to persuade the stupid old man that Darmajelis business was more important than moving a few bits of yellowed paper from one dark, smelly dungeon to another.

And his sister! Wheesht! Could she possibly be any more annoying? She had not even realised they shared this weird but wonderful power over water. And once she found out, she had been too scared to use it. If they could only work together they would be unstoppable! As usual he would have to go it alone, lead the way, and wait for her to catch up.

He stemmed the flow of anger for a moment to focus on the passages. This was his first visit to the catacombs and the dingy walkways. Unfamiliar and for the most part indistinguishable, they required concentration to navigate back to the upper level of the Court. Taking a turn that seemed familiar, he arrived at the foot of the rickety stairway with a feeling of relief. The creaking of the wooden stairs told him that someone else was on their way down. Douglas started up the flight, meeting a man at the first turn. A short, squat man, not much taller than Jeruk Nipis, he appeared to be slightly older than Douglas.

The man avoided any eye contact and stepped to one side, clearly intending to pass him without acknowledgement. With his already high confidence levels boosted by his new status, and his temper still unabated from his encounter with his sister, Douglas was in a more confrontational mood.

'What are you doing down here? You do know this is a restricted area?'

The man looked perplexed. 'Er, no. I didn't. Sorry.'

'Well? Where did you think you were going?'

'I haven't eaten since I arrived. I tried to order some food to be brought to my rooms, but it never came. Thought I'd go and look for something. I'm starving.'

'And you thought you'd find your dinner in the crypt? Don't you know where the refectory is?'

'I only came here today. I don't know where anything

is.'

'Follow me. I'll take you there. It's likely there'll be nothing left by now, but I can't leave you wandering aimlessly around the Court.'

'Thank you. At least I'll know where to go for breakfast, if I last that long.'

They mounted the staircase together in silence.

'I'm sorry for trespassing into that area,' the man said as they stepped into the main corridor. 'Down there. I'm—'

'New here. Yes, you said.'

'Are you some kind of guard, then? Only...'

'Only what?'

'Sorry, but... your accent. Sounds Scottish to me. And your clothes were not made here. I think we have something in common. Are you from Earth?'

'Well *you* must be, if you recognise a Scottish accent. I didn't see you on the Dauntless.'

'Ah! So you are an Earther! I wasn't on the Dauntless. I've been here since Intrepid. My name is Piers Tremaine.'

He held out his hand. Pathetic! Thinking they could be bosom buddies just because they came from the same rock. Douglas walked on, ignoring the gesture.

'Douglas Muir. And no, I'm not a guard. I have a much more important role here than that.'

'We *do* have something in common then. I've been offered an important role too. Perhaps we will be working together?'

Douglas barked out a laugh. 'Sorry, but I doubt that. Let's just say I have a unique position. I don't work with anyone.'

He pointed along the corridor. 'Follow this passage to the end, turn left, and the refectory is on the right a little way farther down. If you'll excuse me, I have an important meeting I must attend.'

Douglas turned on his heel and strode rapidly away. What "important role" could the wandering Earther possibly have? Nipis had made no mention of other

Earthers in the Court's employ. But the man had rooms, and an inexplicable air of confidence about him. He recognised it immediately, mainly because it was so similar to his own. But he had—what had the old wizard called it?—Elemental power. That could not be the same for this Tremaine, surely? If he had been on the planet since Intrepid and had any magical abilities, he would have been brought to Court long ago. That had been an unsettling encounter. One more thing to add to the pile of shit he'd had to deal with today.

Chapter 17

If Claire was any judge, Douglas Muir was having another bad day. Even before meeting him, she had noticed patterns in the rains. They never stopped completely, but they were lighter at night. A clue that subconscious use of Water power was the root cause. When the wielder slept, the rain moderated. Still with occasional violent squalls, most likely a side-effect of the unwitting mage's dreams. Now the identity of the perpetrator had been revealed, she could match his moods to the intensity of the storms assailing the land. During their first encounter torrential and prolonged downpours mirrored his emotional outburst, rattling windows in their frames and rendering conversations inaudible.

Today, storm clouds covered every inch of sky; black and forbidding. Heavy rain fell in sheets, with a force to bend grasses and saplings. Clearly the young man's mood was equally black. No doubt a result of the Jester's reaction to his failure, the night before, to bring the Keeper to his seat on the Darmajelis. She was happy to leave that problem to Lautan, while she concentrated on the sister, upon whose door she now knocked.

'Come in.'

As an occasional and ad-hoc visitor to Court, Claire did not have proper chambers of her own. They agreed to meet in Kyle's quarters to explore what help the more experienced Elemental could offer, and perhaps develop a plan of action for Kyle's ongoing tutelage in the arts of Water. Claire opened the door.

'Hi!' she said, before noticing the appalling decor in the room. 'Ugh!'

Kyle laughed. 'Right? I don't know how I sleep in here.'

A flower pattern print covered the walls, the only

example of wallpaper Claire had ever seen at Court. It peeled away in the corners where damp had penetrated, its surface uniformly yellow with age. The rudely drawn blooms, their colours long faded, must have been garish and unnatural when first painted. Doubtless someone on the staff believed this the most desirable suite in which to house a female guest. Kyle obviously shared Claire's opinion that it was exactly the opposite.

'It's hideous,' Claire said.

'Thank God! I thought it was just me. That maybe every room was like this. Even though Douglas's isn't. We'll have to keep our voices down, by the way. He's only next door. I don't know if he's in his room or not, but if he knew you were here he'd throw a fit.'

Claire glanced at the adjoining door.

'It's OK,' Kyle said, following her gaze. 'I took the key. I've locked it. He thinks I'm annoyed with him. Well, I am really, but...'

Her voice trailed off, leaving the room silent but for the drumming of rain on the window. The odd spot fell into the grate, throwing up small plumes of ash from the previous night's fire.

'Shall we make a start?' Claire asked.

Kyle dragged her attention back from the door. 'I suppose we should. I don't know what to expect though. I've been worrying about it all night.'

'Me too, if it's any consolation. My only experience of tutoring is with small groups. I've never done anything one-to-one. Except as a pupil, of course, when–'

'A pupil?' Kyle interrupted. 'You mean you can go to school for this stuff?'

'Yes. At least, that's what I did. It's called the Academy. I spent a few months there, taking Air classes. I assume they have Water classes too, although I must admit I never heard anyone mention them.'

'That's so weird. Is it far? This Academy?'

'Quite a way from here. It's closer to the Palace, where

I live. That's in—'

'Kertonia. Yes, I know. That Waters woman at the base told us about it. Where the Black Queen lives.'

'She's a friend of mine. The Queen I mean, not Felice. She knew my father. He was Air Mage here before me.'

'I thought you were from Earth?'

'It's a long story. It'll keep for another day. But yes, you'd probably make much better progress with a proper tutor. I can show you the basics, but—'

'What about Lautan?'

'It's almost unheard of for Elementals to teach juniors.'

'But you're...?'

'I know, but I'm different. My family are from here, but I still think and act like an Earth girl. I thought—think—we have more in common than not, so I'm happy to help. But Elementals are mostly an opinionated lot who prefer their own company.'

Kyle frowned. 'That sounds just like Douglas. I don't want to be like that.'

'Well, it's not mandatory!' Claire laughed. 'Look at me!'

'Thank God!' Kyle said again. 'I can't tell you how good it is to finally meet someone I can be friends with.' Her face clouded, her eyes reddening. 'I began to think I'd be even lonelier here than I was back home. This is supposed to be an adventure. A new start. But as usual Douglas gets all the attention and keeps me in his pocket. Brings me out when he needs to prove his family credentials. Show that he has someone he cares about.'

A tear fell onto her cheek. She dashed it away with a practised flick of her fingers.

'He can't care about much,' Claire said, 'or he wouldn't be causing such wanton destruction.'

'Exactly. It's all fake. I've only really noticed it since we landed, but looking back, he's always been this way. Only without any power, obviously. For years I've believed it was his natural charisma, but... well...'

The girl's voice, little more than a whisper to begin

with, fell silent again, leaving her with a vexed expression. After a moment she recovered herself.

'It's not, is it? He isn't strong at all. Just arrogant. I've always looked to him for answers. Or help. Always taken his nasty comments on the chin, tried not to provoke him. Finally after all this time I can see he only helps me when there's something in it for him. I don't want to be like that. Help me, Claire. Please. I want to learn how to use this power properly. Like you do.'

She swallowed. 'Like Lautan does.'

'I don't think there's much I can do here,' Claire said.

Kyle flashed her a panicked look.

'No,' she went on, 'don't worry. I didn't say "nothing". I can make a start helping you with your mental control. I can show you how to access your core.'

'Core?'

'It's what we call the part of us where the power lives. You should feel it, if you sit quietly and think about it. So we can begin with those. But you have to remember, our Elements are different. I can't teach you about Water. I don't know anything about it. You'll need a Water mage for that. There's no reason we can't ask Lautan. These are strange times. I'm sure he will do anything if it will help stop these rains. Even taking you under his wing.'

Claire paused, giving Kyle chance to process what she had said. The girl seemed more settled, now that she understood they could make a start. Claire didn't want her to focus on what the difficulties might be, but maybe it was worth risking a final hard fact.

'There is one more thing, but you might not like it.'

A frightened look passed across Kyle's face. 'What?' Her quiet voice was almost lost in the rain.

'You've already explained how domineering your brother is. You'd do better if you could take yourself away from him. At least for a little while. It's another long story, but there aren't any Elementals living here at Court now. We all moved to the Palace. Lautan and I, and Elaine—the

Fire Witch—will be returning soon. You should come with us.'

Claire watched the conflicting emotions pass across the girl's face. Hiding her feelings was something else she would need to learn if they were ever to have an advantage over Douglas Muir. He was no doubt being expertly schooled in the arts of deception by his new yellow mentor. Kyle walked to the window, watching in silence as the raindrops cascaded down the panes.

'We've only recently learned there's an inherited basis for Elemental power,' Claire pressed on. 'I've seen your results—you and Douglas. There's almost no difference between you, genetically. In fact if anything, you should have a slight edge over him.'

'That can't be right,' Kyle said, turning away from the mesmerising rain. 'Look at what he can do. I can't do that.'

'My opinion? It's just confidence. Douglas has no trouble at all being himself. Letting his power flow. You've been in his shadow so long, it's going to take time for you to believe in yourself to the same extent. We can help you with that too.' She grinned. 'You've met Elaine, right?'

Kyle laughed, releasing the tension in her face and shoulders. The point was made.

'I wanted to meet the Queen anyway,' she said, 'when we were in Pennatanah. It was Douglas' idea to come here.'

She turned back to the window, tracing the path of a raindrop with her finger. On the other side of the glass, the water dodged away, began to move back up the glass.

'I'll come with you,' Kyle said quietly. 'To the Palace.'

court of the blood king, moatside path
21st day of run'sanamasa, 966

'He must be here,' Elaine said. 'We know the Jester fetched him from Duska Batsirang. That jaundiced joker would not have made the journey if he didn't know who

Tremaine is. What he can do.'

Lautan nodded. 'Supposition, Bakara, all supposition. But grounded in fact, that is certain. I cannot disagree with you.'

They sat together on the low wall that bounded the moat, outside the ruddy walls of the Court. Out here, conversations could be had without risk of being overheard. Much of the Southern Blood Plain which they overlooked was now submerged. In the distance the edge of Ketakaya forest was dimly visible as a dark mark behind the drab curtain of rain.

'And yet we have not seen him. Doubtless the Jester is keeping him safe somewhere, for reasons of his own. His schemes are legendary. He will have something in mind for Tremaine, of that we can be sure.'

'Damn him!' Elaine said, small tongues of flame licking from her fingertips, only to be quenched by the persistent rain. 'And damn this rain!' she cried, brandishing her extinguished hand at her companion. 'It even douses my temper!'

'It is good you can mock yourself, Bakara,' Lautan said, his voice as deep and liquid as the drowned plain beside which they sat. 'If we lose our sense of humour, then we have lost all.'

'There is little to laugh at, to be sure. Jann gone, our purported Stone mage in the hands of the Reds. I myself am incapable of mastering Stone—or at least the making of it—and my Fire is useless against this constant downpour.'

Lautan laid a hand on her arm. 'Not useless Bakara! Do not say so! We have worked together to great effect, though we have yet to find a perfect solution. The fault is more mine than yours.' He held out his hands, catching the cold drops as they fell. 'This is, after all, my Element. I believed my mastery of it complete. Such conceit. I have been taught a lesson by a pup young enough to be my grandchild!'

'He's teaching us all a lesson, old friend. Me as much as anyone. What are we doing here? I cannot see any benefit in remaining in this sorry place a moment more.'

'Here you are! What are you doing out here in the pouring rain?'

Claire approached from the Court gates, holding a cloak over her head.

'Ah, Sakti. Well met. We were wondering when you would be done with your studies,' Lautan said. 'We thought it wise to speak outside, since we can no longer be certain of anyone's loyalties.

'Present company excepted, of course,' he added, inclining his head in Claire's direction.

'And I had just about decided we should return to the Palace,' Elaine said. 'We didn't mention it yesterday, but we were too late to find Piers Tremaine. By the time we reached Duska Batsirang he had already gone. We haven't seen our errant Stone mage, but Lautan and I believe the Jester has brought him here.'

'Well, I was late too,' Claire said, looking for a dry spot on which to sit and deciding against it. 'You found the Muir twins before I did. But I think I've repaired the damage a little.'

'How so?' asked Elaine, levering herself off the wall.

'Your return to the Palace is well timed. Kyle Muir wants to come with us. Learn what she can about how to be an Elemental. We were hoping you might help her, Lautan?'

Lautan too rose to his feet, a rare smile creasing his lips. 'Indeed I would, Sakti. Mayhap there is something I can do to restore balance to the Elements after all. My own, in particular. It would be my honour to school the young lady in the art of Water.'

'Where is she?' Elaine asked.

'I told her to wait inside,' Claire replied. 'No point both of us getting wet.'

Lautan fixed Claire with a stern stare, while his eyes

held on to his smile. 'Your diplomacy does you credit, Sakti,' he said. 'You did not wish to embarrass me with the presence of one who tests my abilities, nor the young lady by possibly subjecting her to my wrath. It was well done. Have no fear. It is clear her brother is my bane. She has no part of this barajan.'

Claire squinted at Lautan from beneath rain-bejewelled brows. 'Barajan? I don't believe I've heard that term before.'

Lautan smiled. 'Neither has anyone else my dear Sakti, for I have only this moment coined the word.'

'Clever,' Elaine laughed. 'New rains. Now we have a name for our nemesis.'

'We have a name for his destructive works Bakara. We already knew the name of Douglas Muir.'

'Come then,' she said, striding back towards the gate. 'Let's go. The sooner we leave this place, the sooner we will arrive back home.'

'Give me a moment to retrieve my notes on the scroll I've been working on,' Claire said, hurrying ahead.

crypt
21st day of run'sanamasa, 966

'I hoped I'd find you here.'

The man's voice, leaping out of the gloom behind her, startled Claire. She spun around to see who had been doing the hoping, almost knocking her small pile of parchments off the table. A squat man in his mid-twenties stood half in shadow beside the entrance to her alcove. His red-brown hair shone in the light of the torch she had rested in a sconce. The flickering flames glinted from amber flecks in his dark blue eyes, which appeared almost black in the shade of the crypt.

'You're in luck,' Claire replied, 'I came back for these notes. I've not seen you at Court before. Why were you looking for me?'

He hesitated, unable to meet her gaze. He covered his mouth with one hand.

'I... it's embarrassing.'

Claire held out her hand.

'I'm Claire Yamani,' she said. 'Air Mage of Berikatanya. I'm often here studying, but right now, I have to go.'

'Please, wait. I know who you are. That's the embarrassing part. I overheard your conversation with the Muir girl yesterday.'

'You were here yesterday too? How long have you been stalking me?'

'I wasn't. I mean, I haven't been. I was trying to find my way around Court. I haven't been here long. Don't know where anything is. But my chambers are adjacent to the Muirs. I heard Kyle leave her room last night and thought she might be going for food. Like I said I don't know where anything is, so I followed her. Only she wasn't heading to the kitchens, she was coming here.'

'You still haven't told me your name.'

'Sorry. I'm Piers Tremaine.'

His words sent an electric shock through Claire. 'The Stone mage?' she asked, the words out before she could stop herself.

Tremaine took a step forward, his eyes wide. 'How...? No one knows about that except the man who brought me here.'

'Sorry to shatter your illusion of secrecy, but we've been looking for you as long as he has.'

'We?'

'Myself and the other Elementals. Those who—'

'Yes, I know what Elementals are. I've been on this planet for more than nine years.'

'Right. You were on the Intrepid. But we only learned of Stone power a few days ago. Didn't take us long to join the dots with the famous story—'

'Of me getting my hand stuck in a rock. God, will I ever be rid of that?'

'Right, well, we set off to find you. We figured you must be confused, or frightened, or in need of some guidance. Or all three. But the Jester beat us to it.'

'Calls himself Jeruk Nipis now.'

'He'll always be the Jester to us.'

'You said the same to Kyle last night.'

'You heard that? What else did you hear?'

'I heard you offer to help her. I heard the kindness in your voice. You have such an easy way about you. Not demanding. Not persuading. Not cajoling. You just told it like it is, and then left it to her to decide what she wanted to do. That's so different from the way I've been treated. It's why I came looking for you.'

'You need my help too?'

'I need someone's help. Maybe not with the power, but someone who knows what's going on and can explain it to me. I'm so scared of doing the wrong thing.'

'That depends on your perspective. Right and wrong. It's not always clear cut.'

'True, but if you're only ever seeing one side, it's hard to make the call. Which is right. If there is a right.'

'So you don't need help with Stone power? That's good. None of us really know anything about it. We couldn't help you if we wanted to.'

'But you know it exists.'

'A friend of mine—Jann Argent—was told about it while he was away. Travelling. It combines two of the Elements we *are* familiar with. Earth and Fire.'

'I suppose you know those Elementals too.'

'Of course. The Fire Witch is here right now actually. We're getting ready to return to the Palace. None of us live here at Court any more. The Gardener is away fighting the floods. We need help too, as it happens. Maybe we can both do each other a favour? Especially if you're adept with Stone.'

'Well I don't get my hands stuck in rocks anymore, let's put it that way,' Tremaine laughed.

'That's a start,' said Claire, laughing with him, 'but it will take more than that to beat Douglas Muir.'

'I met him last night too.'

'And?'

'He's a prick.'

Claire laughed again, a loud barking laugh that echoed along the dark passageway like a pistol shot.

'Say what you really mean.'

Tremaine smiled. 'Full of his own importance. Confident of his power, even though he can only have been using it for a few days. So I'd say you were spot on when you told Kyle you think her brother is overconfident. I'm not that sure of myself and I've been experimenting with Stone power for years.'

'What have you done with it?'

'Little things. More of a craft than a power, I guess you'd say, if you saw them. I used it occasionally in my building. When the villagers weren't looking. I've not done anything big with it.'

He shrugged, his face colouring slightly under the torchlight.

'Nothing on the scale of these rains, I'd have to admit. Maybe Muir is right to be so confident.'

'But Stone is a second-level Element,' Claire said. 'Don't sell yourself short. However powerful Douglas Muir is, he is only controlling Water.'

'Only.'

She smiled again. She was beginning to like this young man's self-deprecating sense of humour. 'Yeah, OK. You got me. Water can be pretty devastating. At least the way he uses it. But I'd bet on Stone being stronger. Want to come with me to the Palace, and find out?'

'I want to work with you,' he said, 'you and the other Elementals. But for now, I think I can be more use here.'

'How come?'

'The Jester intends to enrol me onto his Darmajelis in a few days. Muir will be there. He doesn't know I'll be attending too. If I can stay here a while longer, maybe I can suss out their plans.'

'Be careful. From what I've heard, he has a wicked temper.'

'Which one?'

'Both of them, really. If they realise what you're doing, you'll be a marked man.'

'I've had a lot of practice keeping secrets. Don't worry. I'll find out what I can and join you at the Palace once I'm sure I can get a good head start.'

court of the blood king
21st day of run'sanamasa, 966

For once, he had to admit, it had been a good day. OK there was his weird encounter with that chubby little Earther guy the night before. And his return to the meeting chamber had been... uncomfortable. Having to concede his failure to persuade the Keeper to join them. But since then, things had been going pretty well for Douglas Muir.

He strode across the courtyard towards his room, throwing a weak dome of power over himself to shield against the gentle drizzle falling from the black night sky. He did it without thinking now. As natural as breathing, and almost as effortless. Passing into the building between two blazing torches, he let his power wane.

He stopped for a moment, watching the rain. He still could not work out how it continued with no conscious effort on his part. The truth was, though he would never admit it to anyone—even his sister—he could not stop it. Easy enough to increase it. He could call up a torrential downpour in an instant, and had become adept at commanding standing water to do his bidding. But once he ceased trying, the rains would reduce to this persistent slow drizzle. Still, it was a small thing. Nothing to spoil his good day. He had not even had an argument with Kyle so far. He hadn't seen her since he dragged her away from the Yamani woman the night before, but he doubted even she could get a rise out of him today.

He knocked on her door, entering without waiting to be invited.

'I know it's late—' he began, the words dying on his lips. A chambermaid was stripping Kyle's bed. In the corner of the room, her wardrobe hung open, empty.

'What are you doing?' he demanded, grabbing the maid's arm and spinning her round. 'Where is my sister?'

The girl shrunk from his grasp. 'I beg your pardon sir, I was told to change the bed. Last I saw of young Miss Muir she was headed for the stable block.'

Douglas hurried from the room, his good mood evaporated. Breaking into a run across the courtyard he flung back the stable door.

'Hello? Where are you man? Come out!'

The startled face of the old stable hand peered around a thick wooden pillar at the other end of the stables.

'I'm here sir. What can I do for you?'

'Where is my sister? I was told she came here earlier. Did you see her?'

'Indeed I did master Muir. I saddled her kudo myself. You need have no worries on that score. My saddles never loosen.'

'When was this?'

The ostler stroked his chin, considering the question. Surely it could not be hard for this puddle brain to remember what happened earlier the same day?

'Well it would be after lunch, sir. Quite a long time after, I believe. But before dinner sir, near as I could say.'

'Alone? You let her go alone?'

'Mercy's sake young master! No! She had the two Elemental ladies with her—Air and Fire. She'll be perfectly safe with travelling companions of such renown.'

'Ach!' Douglas cried. 'Fetch my mount! *Now* man!'

He grabbed his saddle from the rack while the old man

hobbled to lead Pembainang from his berth, where the animal had doubtless expected to spend a quiet night. Douglas' anger at being abandoned by his sister—in favour of those meddling Elementals of all people—left no room for a scintilla of sympathy for the animal's well-being. He threw on the saddle, cinched it, and dragged the kudo through the stable doors.

Outside in the courtyard the rain had intensified. A direct consequence of his mood, no doubt, but even the freezing deluge on his face did not quell the rage that boiled inside him. Pembainang bucked and snorted at the change in temperature and the stinging raindrops. Douglas threw a shield over them both and swung into his saddle. Behind him, the old ostler stood in the doorway, shielding his eyes from the slanting downpour.

'Be careful how you go, sir!' he shouted over the drumming of the rain on the stable roof. 'Roads'll be slippery in this. His hooves, sir! Mind his hooves!'

Douglas kicked the kudo into a gallop, steering him between the Court gates. He had not covered more than a few metres before he had to rein the animal in, or risk breaking its legs. He stopped, staring along the dark path through the intense downpour. The surface of the roadway was already submerged by run-off, treacherous and uncertain. His mount quivered with cold and fright. Where was he going, anyway? He could not be certain where the Elementals had taken his sister. The Black Palace seemed their most likely destination, but that was a guess. They could be headed anywhere. In these conditions the Palace was more than a dozen days away. What was he thinking? No provisions, no wet weather clothing, and his anger making the roads next to impassable.

'Ach!' he shouted again, raising his fist at the rainclouds, invisible in the dark above his head. He slumped in his saddle, momentarily losing his mental focus and allowing his shield to drop. Pembainang gave another violent shiver under him. It was no use. Kyle was gone.

345

For once, his little sister had made her own decision. He dropped from the saddle and dragged the spooked animal back into the basilica.

'Take him,' Douglas yelled, throwing the reins to the ostler, who still sheltered beside the stable door. The old man flashed him a grateful smile that faded quickly under Douglas' glare. He caught the traces and led the kudo into the stables with a few gentle words. Douglas remained alone in the courtyard, allowing the full force of the rain to reach him. He stood stock still under the torrential, stinging drops, his fists clenched until his knuckles shone white.

Chapter 18

The appearance of Besakaya Forest, looming into view through the slate-grey curtain of rain, shocked Elaine into a paroxysm of regret. The sudden loss of Jann Argent hit her hard, leaving her with no thoughts to spare for Petani. He had been defending his beloved gardens and vegetable plots against the deluge since they parted company days earlier. She seemed fated always to be separated from at least one of her companions. First Jann—Oh! Jann!—and now as she journeyed closer to the Gardener, so she left Lautan behind. The ancient Elemental had elected to remain at Court so Tremaine would not feel isolated.

Lautan had met their party that morning in the basilica as they prepared to leave. 'I understand your concern, Bakara, but the increased intensity of these rains speak to a greater level of power from Douglas Muir. If my senses do not deceive me, we have little time left before he is capable of overwhelming us. I believe it unwise to leave our young Stone mage alone in this nest of vipers. He has but newly joined our company. To abandon him now would be unseemly and unfair, but may also leave him defenceless against the Jester's machinations. And I have yet one more reason to remain,' he added, glancing around the courtyard. 'The longer I am here, the more likely I am to gain some insight into how the Muir boy is achieving this trick with our weather. There has to be a way to stop him before he comes fully into his power.'

His words had worried her. If this was what Muir could achieve when not in complete control, it would take more than Lautan alone to stop him. In the end she had accepted that the Water Wizard was not to be persuaded. They had parted, agreeing to meet at the Palace as soon as he could get away.

After a full day's gruelling ride they passed the westward boundary of the Besakaya. Elaine reined her kudo Jaranyla to a halt and spun her around to face the others.

'We should break our journey here,' she said, 'see how Petani is faring.'

Claire and Kyle had been riding side by side deep in conversation. They joined her under the forest canopy.

'I'd rather press on,' Claire said. 'We need to take Kyle to the Palace as soon as we can. I must speak with the Queen about her training. If Lautan is right, she'll need a crash course if she is to have any chance of helping us with what's to come. He's already said he'll help once he rejoins us.'

'Who is Petani?' Kyle asked.

'A friend,' Elaine said. 'The fourth Elemental—Earth is his Element.'

'And his passion,' Claire added. 'You should see his gardens. He could grow flowers in a desert.'

'I'd like to see that,' Kyle said. 'Would it take long to reach him?'

'We will have to stop soon anyway,' Elaine said. 'We're losing the light…'

She had a bad feeling about her Elemental partner. From a slow start their friendship had blossomed, helped by their shared efforts to create stone. The old man was grounded in his power in a way Elaine had never quite matched. It was more than the difference between their Elements. She admired his passion for all things Earth-bound; was awed by his ability with growing things. And she had abandoned him when he needed help the most. A day added to their journey would make little impact on them, but could be of immense help to the Gardener.

'…so we may as well overnight at the Project. It's only a slight diversion and we'll be more comfortable there than camped at the side of the trail.'

Claire raised no further objection. Elaine directed her

mount along the forest path towards the Project, the others falling in behind. They reached the camp as night fell. Under the light of torches set around the campsite, all looked serene and orderly. Only at the limit of the lit area could they discern hints of the devastation the floods had caused. Dark outlines of fallen trees severed by the ghostly white fingers of exposed roots.

Petani trudged towards them from the main camp fire, his face deeply lined, his shoulders hunched.

'Well met, Bakara!' he called, 'and Claire! Good to see you both again! Who is this?'

They introduced Kyle, avoiding any reference to her latent power or her connection with the cause of the destruction.

'How goes it, old friend?' Elaine asked, once they were all seated around the fire pit with steaming bowls of Nembaka's famous stew cradled in their laps. 'Have you salvaged anything?'

The old man stared into the fire before replying. When he raised his eyes to look at her, they brimmed with tears.

'No,' he said, choking on the word. 'You can see for yourself tomorrow. There is almost nothing left. Most of the crops are underwater. And the gardens...'

He stopped, unable to speak. Elaine moved to his side, putting an arm around his shoulder.

'I have been trying to create channels,' he said, after recovering himself a little, 'to divert the water, you know? But every day the deluge continues. My earth works break down. Washed away by the constant floods. The levels rise higher than the day before. Only yesterday we lost the dunela and bolabisaman. The duntang have been submerged for four or five days. If we can't drain them soon they will rot in the ground.

'The problem here is the same one I had at the Landing. Too much water, not enough rock. If I could make rock channels, they would persist, but the soil here is deep. There is no bedrock. I mean, there is, but it's down deep. Too deep for my Earth sense to reach. I have nothing but clay, sand, and soil to work with. And gravel too of course, which helped with drainage until this deluge came upon us. None of those materials are enough to withstand the water's power.'

Under Elaine's arm, Petani shook with emotion. He was beyond exhausted already, but she knew he would never stop trying to save his plantation.

'I'll help,' she said. 'I will stay here with you. Together we can solve this conundrum.'

'We cannot stay,' Claire said, aghast. 'I'm so sorry, Petani. I know how much this means to you. But we have to take Kyle to the Queen. She...'

Claire's voice tailed off. She looked at Elaine, obviously hesitant to reveal too much of Kyle's story. It would do no good to give the old Elemental something else to worry about.

'You go,' Elaine said. 'Get some rest tonight and start out again tomorrow. I will stay here and help Petani.'

Claire began to object, but Elaine silenced her with a look before turning her attention back to the old man.

'I have had some success working with Lautan,' she said. 'He conceived the idea of diverting water into pools, which I could boil away with Fire. It was exhausting work, but effective.'

Petani looked horrified. 'You cannot boil the water here! It lays over plants and crops alike. They might yet survive if we can only drain the area, but not if they've been cooked!'

Elaine bit down on her temper. Her friend was tired and stressed.

'I wasn't suggesting we boil it where it is,' she said gently. 'I said Lautan and I diverted it. He could do that with his power. Here, we will need to channel it.'

'I already told you–'

'I know. Your channels don't last long. But they won't have to. Just long enough to take the water somewhere I can use my Fire.'

'Did you say clay?' asked Kyle.

'What's that, young lady?'

'Just now, when you said there isn't enough rock here. I thought you said there was clay.'

'A little, yes. In patches.'

'Can't you make your channels with pottery then? All our drains back on Earth were made of pot. If you have clay...' She glanced nervously at Elaine. 'And Fire...'

A thrill of renewed hope shivered through Elaine at Kyle's words. She flashed a grateful smile at the girl.

'It's definitely worth a try!' she said, turning to Petani. 'Let's talk more about it in the morning. We're all tired, and maybe not thinking clearly. Things will look different after a good night's sleep.'

Petani looked unconvinced but did not argue any further. After a while, people started to drift off to their ahmeks and huts.

The following day, Claire and Kyle rode out as soon as they had breakfasted. Elaine and Petani picked their way between flooded areas of the Project, trying to identify both a spot suitable for a small lake, and a source of clay. There was little to be found, but they fashioned what they gathered into simple half-pipes which Elaine fired. With the help of the Project team, Petani set about creating drainage ditches, lining them at intervals with short lengths of pipe.

'You know this won't work?' he said, once the water had started to flow.

Elaine kept quiet, waiting for the lake to fill to a point where it would boil without damaging any precious vegetable matter.

At first, it looked as if the Gardener was wrong. The water boiled away, Elaine expending enough Fire power to keep the depth stable as more flowed in. Crops began to peep out from the flooded areas. But before long Petani gave a cry of frustration.

'See? There they go.'

As they watched, the sides of his ditches collapsed between the half-pipe sections and the flow of water ceased. Elaine let her power drop, turning her back on the steaming lake and staring at the semi-flooded ground. Damn it! The soil here was so soft. They needed something stronger.

'We will have to try again with stone,' she said. 'Maybe we will have more success making it with a mixture of gravel, sand and clay? At the Palace we could not bring enough raw material into the Fire. Here, it lies everywhere, right at the surface. Surely it will not shrink from my Fire? All you need to do is hold it while it cooks. We can't give in yet.'

road to the black palace
22nd day of run'sanamasa, 966

Kyle Muir waited until the ramshackle campsite had disappeared from view behind the trees before speaking.

'You wanted to stay, didn't you?'

She studied Claire's face as the Air Mage considered her question. The Air Mage! Her mentor! This whole journey flipped between nightmare and dream in the turn of a moment. Even the hard, steady rain could not dampen her mood this morning.

'I would've preferred to stick together,' Claire replied at length. 'We're stronger that way. Makes it easier to deal with any problems the rain drops into our path. Especially with Elaine. Bakara as the locals call her. She's the most powerful Elemental. Or maybe it's just her temper.'

The two women laughed.

'Why do you all have two names?' Kyle had puzzled about this for some time but only now plucked up the courage to ask. Claire was the most approachable of all the Elementals.

'Two names? Oh, I see what you mean. Well, we don't.

Not all of us. Lautan has always been Lautan. He remained here when the other Elementals fell to Earth through the first portal. They took Earther names during the time they were there. A few years for some but decades for others.'

'How come?'

'I don't really know how, or why, but the portal wasn't like a static doorway. Maybe a water analogy would work for you.'

Kyle laughed again. 'Try me.'

'I sometimes think of it like a hosepipe. Water enters at only one place—the tap—but it comes out wherever the hose is pointing. So if you're watering a garden, all the water ends up in the same garden, that would be Earth in this case, but it's sprayed on various parts. So anyone travelling through the portal ended up in separated in time.'

'I don't get it.'

'Sorry, it's not a very good analogy. A hose just points at physical places, but the Earth end of the portal moved through different points in time too. Elaine only spent four years there. But Petani, who you've just met, was a young man when he fell to Earth. He was there for more than thirty years.'

'Wow! What does it feel like? Falling through a portal, I mean?'

'I don't know. It was my parents who were caught by the vortex. My father was Air Mage at the time. My mother didn't have any powers. At least, none that I know of. They never talked about it. When I came here I had no idea who they had been.'

'Did they come back with you?'

Claire fell silent. They rode on for some distance before she replied, her eyes red with emotion.

'My father was killed before we left. Muggers. My mother came with me, but she died in a cryopod accident during the trip.'

Kyle stopped her kudo in its tracks.

'God, I'm so sorry. I know how you must feel. I'm an orphan too. Our parents died in a car crash soon after we moved to the States. That's one reason I've always been so close to Douglas. He treats me like shit, but he's the only family I have left. We're twins, but he calls me his younger sister because I was born a few minutes later than him.'

They rode on, reaching the edge of the forest by midday and stopping long enough to water the kudai and eat a small meal. When they emerged from the partial shelter of the trees into the full force of the storm, it had worsened. A vertical shroud of water fell, the rain bouncing back off the stony surface of the road. For a while the riders struggled to control their frightened mounts.

'That must have been hard, coming to a new planet all alone,' Kyle said, once the animals had settled into a nervous walk.

'I was never really alone. Something must have drawn us all together. All us displaced Berikatanyans, or their offspring. We were all on the same ship. Elaine, Terry— Petani I mean—Jann, and Patrick.'

'I don't know them.'

'Jann Argent was lost on the road to Duska Batsirang. Elaine wouldn't tell me much about what happened. The floods swept him away. Patrick was born on Earth too, like me. His father was the original Pattern Juggler. Patrick inherited his powers. You probably won't meet him either. When we travelled to Pennatanah to look for you, he decided to stay.'

Kyle started to ask a question, but Claire held up her hand. 'Don't ask me about Juggler powers. No one knows. Not the Elementals, not the Keeper. Not even Patrick. At least, he didn't. He went exploring and found his father's house, but he clammed up even tighter than Elaine when I tried to ask him about it.'

Kyle heard a roaring sound in the distance. As they rode, it grew louder until it almost drowned out their conversation. Cresting a small rise in the road, the source of the noise was revealed: the Sun Hutang, now in full flood. Racing past the crumbled remains of a bridge, the raging river carried large tree trunks and other debris washed from the banks.

'Wait!' Claire cried. 'Don't ride too close to the edge.'

They stared at the torrents of muddy water for a moment.

'How are we going to cross?' asked Kyle.

'When we came this way originally, Lautan stemmed the waters with his powers while we all shuffled across behind him.'

Kyle shivered. 'I can't do that!'

Claire continued to stare at the river. A wry smile creased her face. 'Sorry, no. I wasn't suggesting it. I doubt even Lautan could stop this now. The current is way stronger than it was. We'll have to ride upstream for a bit. It flows down from Tubelak'Dun. If we make our way into the foothills we will find a crossing place.'

'Did you have many friends, back on Earth?' Claire asked after they had been picking their way uphill beside the river for a while.

'Not really. Why do you ask?'

'I've been thinking how unusual you two are. You're very close. Most Elementals are loners. Jann told me about a conversation he'd had with Elaine soon after we landed. Elemental powers are transferred genetically, but they— we, I mean—don't easily to form relationships. Not that kind anyway. When they do get together, they normally have only one child. I never heard of twins before. Or even regular brothers or sisters.'

'What does it mean?'

Claire shrugged. 'Maybe nothing. But I saw your gene patterns. You have a stack of Elemental genes. Much more than any of us.'

'Did you make friends here? At the... what did you call it? The Academy?'

Claire laughed, loud and long.

'What's so funny?'

'The idea of having friends in that place! My few months there were even lonelier than my solitary years on Valiant. Half of them resented me for being the Air Mage, even though when I started I couldn't blow out a candle with my powers. The other half were scared of me. Not exactly a good environment for forming friendships.'

'Why were you alone on your Prism ship? Was that something to do with your Mum's cryopod accident?'

Claire recounted the tale of her trip on the Valiant while they rode. They found a suitable crossing place, and kept to the higher ground where the rains had not saturated the pathways. She picked up the story again when they stopped at the base of Tubelak'Dun, searching out what little shelter they could from the rains, which had continued unabated all day.

'Five years!' Kyle said, aghast, once Claire's saga came to an end with the Captain of the Valiant finding her on the bridge. 'I would've gone mad, alone all that time. Isn't Valiant the ship that crashed in the bay?'

'Yes. That's yet another story. One that will have to keep until tomorrow. I'm bushed.'

'So many stories! I can hardly wait 'til tomorrow!'

The rest of their journey passed in similar fashion: more rain, more storytelling. Claire recounted the rescue of the passengers from the downed Valiant, her arrival at the Palace, the shocking revelation that her father had been Air Mage, and her months at the Academy. Kyle returned the favour with the few stories she could think of. Her life, so far at least, had been a lot less colourful and eventful than her mentor's. Maybe that was all about to change. Around mid-afternoon on the fourth day of their journey, the Black Palace came into view on the other side of the Sun Besaraya valley.

'Oh! It's so pretty!' Kyle cried. 'It looks like a fairy castle!'

The Black Queen's pennant flew from the high central tower. Matching smaller flags decorated each of the other towers.

'Except in black,' she added after a pause.

Under the continuing downpour, the Palace looked as though it was fashioned from black glass.

'The Queen's engineers have been busy,' Claire said, pointing into the valley. 'When we left, that bridge was out too.'

Below them, the Sun Besaraya flowed every bit as fast and deep as the Sun Hutang. Fortunately for the travellers, a new bridge had been constructed. It spanned the width of the river and a dozen metres further onto each bank. Now, it should withstand even the worst flooding.

'Come on,' said Claire. 'If we hurry, we can be there before dark.'

court of the blood king & surrounding villages
22nd day of run'sanamasa, 966

By mid-afternoon on the day after his Elemental companions had left, Lautan had to admit he was spent. Without Bakara's help, his efforts to stem the floods around the Court had been nothing short of futile. Should he have travelled with them after all? The Stone mage Tremaine appeared to be faring well on his own. Lautan had sought the young man out late the previous evening to inform him of their plan.

'Is there aught you require of me?' Lautan had asked.

'It's good to have you on my side, but I can't think of anything right now. I've not been to that promised government meeting yet, so it's hard to say. All this waiting around is very frustrating!'

'We cannot leave until you have gleaned as much information as you can from the Jester's caucus, but we should have a plan for our departure.'

'I'll know more once I find out who the other attendees

are. I may be able to grill them outside of the meetings too.'

The young man attempted to explain how the application of heat to the discussions would help. He met with limited success. They concluded that the longer they remained, the more likely it was that Tremaine's position would be uncovered. The young man had then referred to himself as a "mole", but that had confused Lautan even further. At length they agreed to meet regularly but infrequently, to reduce their chances of discovery to a minimum. If matters progressed as expected they planned to leave Court no later than the end of Run'Sanamasa.

Discussions with the Stone mage thus curtailed, and with his other companions absent from the Court, Lautan had a great deal of time on his hands. Time he knew he should fill with something other than wallowing in the depths of frustration at his inability to counteract Douglas Muir's outlandish power.

His presence annoyed the young mage. It would likely engender greater extremes of weather. So he kept away from the corridors of power as far as possible, staying at the Keeper's pleasure in the old archivist's spare room. There was much for him to do, though as yet he had enjoyed little success. The moat level around the Court continued to rise. Lautan began to wonder how high it must reach before the Jester himself would instruct the Muir boy to desist.

In the few small villages surrounding the Court, he won some minor battles. Redirecting young, newly-formed streams created by breaches in local river banks; holding flood waters aside while whole families found a place of safety; rescuing livestock stranded in the midst of swollen rivers. But the limitations of his powers, and how much their earlier successes had relied on Bakara's assistance, became more obvious with each passing day. It weighed on his mind like sacks of grain loaded onto a kudo's back. Each more painful than the last until the poor animal collapsed under its yoke. He was not yet at the point of collapse, but it could only be a matter of time. Rarely had he expended his power with greater frequency or duration. The galling truth was that rarely had he done so with less effect. After countless decades of experience, monumental successes, and acclamation as the Water Wizard of Berikatanya, he was now disenfranchised by a young man. Barely more than a boy! Newly arrived without training, without knowledge, without acclaim, but with a seemingly limitless supply of raw power.

What chewed at his confidence and his self-belief was that he simply did not understand how Douglas Muir was doing it. The malamajan, widely seen as the pinnacle of Elemental success, had stood for centuries. Created by the greatest Water Wizard of all time, sustained through the combined efforts of Water mages ever since, it should have been immutable. Rain in sufficient quantity for the season, where it was needed, for as long as it was needed, at a time to cause least inconvenience to the populace. Even the Earthers with their glowing blue technologies and their interstellar space ships, could not control weather to that extent. It was—had been—a marvel. Lautan stood in the shadow of the Court of the Blood King, drenched by the heavy downpour that plastered his grey locks to his face and his robes to his body, and admitted that the ancient masterpiece lay in ruins. He was unable to conceive how it could ever be rebuilt.

pennatanah
23rd day of run'sanamasa, 966

The delicious irony was not lost on Felice Waters. In her cramped office, she stood beside her printer holding the latest genetic test output. From her experience with the mountain of results that preceded it, she could interpret the pattern with a glance. It showed low-level Earth power was latent in the subject. The irony arose from the identity of that subject: Jo Granger. The woman who provided the gene sequencer in the first place, and taught Felice how to use it. The woman who, since the start of her pet project, Felice had become very close to.

It was a worry.

The current batch of colonists were an odd bunch. The majority of them far less willing than their predecessors to fit in with Berikatanyan culture and living arrangements. Most remained at the base, still trying to decide where, and how, they would live. Felice had contributed to several of those discussions in recent days. Dauntless was the last scheduled Prism ship, the fourth of four. There was nothing now to keep her here, manning her post. Even in the long gap before Valiant's doomed arrival, she always knew another ship would come. That was no longer true. What was she to do? She had no skills as an artisan. Her experience was all security related. Her expertise, organisational. She was a good motivator, team builder. A people person. Just the sort of person a new colony of Earthers could use. She had not yet admitted it to herself, but she had already decided to join them.

And now this. A woman she had begun to think of as a girlfriend—potential girlfriend at least—had powers. Might have powers. Did it make a difference? Others in the same group had similar results. None of them had manifested yet. Maybe they never would. Felice hated prejudice of any kind. To discriminate against fellow colonists or—worse— lovers, would grind her gears. It was not her.

She stood, finally owning her instinctive decision. Someone knocked.

'It's open.'

Jo Granger stuck her head around the door. 'There's a rider,' she said. 'From Istania.'

Felice grabbed a coat from its peg and stepped out into the rain. Heavier today than usual, and colder. The rider came at speed, their kudo's hooves sliding dangerously on the treacherous roadway. Felice could not make out who it was at first. It rode like a man, but the rider's features, obscured by a hooded cloak, were further blurred by the slanting rain. As he rode nearer to the base, she recognised a colonist from her own ship, Endeavour. He had left for Court almost ten years before. She gave her mental catalogue time to retrieve his name. Every colonist had passed through her hands at some time. She remembered them all. Sure enough, as he passed the first of Pennatanah's squat buildings, his name popped into her mind: Kuan-Yin Ning. Some kind of engineer back on Earth, if her recollection was correct. He reined the kudo to a slippery stop in front of the two women and dismounted, unfastening a small travelling pack from the saddle.

'Hi,' he said, pulling off his hood. 'Do you have room for one more here? Things not so good around the Court right now.'

'Welcome back Ning,' Felice said, taking his kudo's reins. 'Come inside, you look like you could use a hot meal.'

She tied the animal outside the canteen building and ushered Ning through the doors. In the middle of the afternoon the main hall was almost deserted. A few late lunchers sat in one corner, eking out their last coffee for want of something better to do. The usual small group of tabukki occupied the opposite corner, each of them staring vacantly at Felice without recognition.

'You can change into some dry things through there. I'll see if I can fill a plate for you from what's left.'

The messenger was soon seated in front of a plateful of what looked like an explosion in an ethnic fusion kitchen. Once he had made sufficient inroads into the still-steaming pile to take the edge off his hunger, he sat back, smiling.

'Thanks! Hadn't eaten since yesterday. I rode all night.'

'What's the hurry?' Jo asked. 'Surely it can't be that bad at Court? We would have heard before now.'

'Someone has to be first with the news. Just hope you

don't shoot the messenger.'

He took another mouthful. The two women waited for him to continue.

'Rains are worse than ever,' he began. Felice hoped he would not take too long to reveal something they didn't know. 'Lautan is at Court, trying to help. Poor guy seems almost powerless. Word on the street is the rains are connected with the new arrivals. Too much of a coincidence that they started just before the last ship docked. We had a few of them come to Court. Not as many as usual. But then things started to get weird.'

'In what way?' Felice asked.

'It wasn't one thing,' Ning replied. 'The Jester called more frequent Darmajelis meetings. Orders came flying out faster than we could handle them. Then there were the Elementals. After seasons with only the Air Mage paying us the occasional visit, suddenly all of them were there. All except the Gardener that is. And these newbies. Three of them—a brother and sister, and another guy—were treated to some of the best rooms in the guest wing. No one knew why. Then the brother turned up at one of the meetings. Earther representative, someone said. Supposed to make us all feel included. Well, let me tell, you this guy—Douglas Muir—is not the kind to include anyone. Arrogant young pup, strutting around the Court barking orders at anyone who comes within a couple of metres.'

'Muir is on the Darmajelis?' Felice said. 'That was quick!'

'I'm guessing his sister wasn't best pleased either,' Ning continued. 'They had an enormous bust up and next thing we know, she's gone. The Air Mage and the Witch went too.'

'They all left together?'

'No one will say, but it's a fair guess. Muir has been in a foul mood ever since. Mind you, we all have. This damn rain doesn't help. We've been expecting it to tail off but it seems to be getting worse! In the end I decided to bail.

Before the Court goes under water. We've heard the rumours about an Earther colony. Figured I'd throw my lot in with them.'

'The more the merrier,' Jo said.

'Yes, I'd pretty much come to the same conclusion before you arrived,' Felice agreed.

Jo Granger jumped to her feet. 'Really?' She beamed a thousand-watt smile and threw her arms around Felice. 'That's the best news I've had since I got here!'

Felice returned the unexpected embrace. 'Pennatanah won't be submerged any time soon,' she said to Ning once she emerged from her clinch. 'We're too high here, and the ground is too rocky. If we're ever overwhelmed the only things left above the surface will be the Duns.'

She stood, intending to leave the young man to finish the rest of his meal in peace. Her conversation with Claire Yamani came back to her.

'Do you know anything about drive systems?'

the black palace - throne room
23rd day of run'sanamasa, 966

Their kudai's hooves clattered over the long wooden bridge, the echoes underneath swept away by the fast-moving river. In the gathering gloom the granite walls and turrets of the Black Palace towered over her, dark and terrible. From the other side of the Sun Besaraya, it had been impossible to see how massive the Palace was. Normally fascinated by water, whether standing, flowing, or rippling in waves against a shore, Kyle now ignored it. Her full attention was riveted to the imposing black structure which they swiftly approached.

When Claire spoke of it, and of the Black Queen, it was always in warm tones. She painted a picture of a happy, friendly place where the Elementals gathered in safety and worked with common purpose for the greater good. That image jarred with this cold, stark edifice. The incessant rain drove icy blades into her head and shoulders. Her white hands were almost frozen to the reins. There seemed nothing warm or friendly about this place.

They rode through the gates as the last grey shadow of the rain-washed sun disappeared behind the mountains. In the Palace basilica, torches had already been lit, smoking and sputtering with each fat drop of rain that hit them. A young stable boy hurried out to take their animals.

'Welcome home Sakti,' he said, his expression shining with unabashed awe. 'Miss,' he added, not recognising Kyle.

They ran inside, shaking their cloaks in the vast hall.

The interior of the Palace was as cold and bleak as the outside. Black slate floors met black marble walls, punctuated at intervals by tall blackwood doors. Thick columns of polished obsidian supported the high vaulted ceilings, their blackness relieved occasionally by golden sconces in which flaming torches blazed, and intricate filigree details. A tall houseman in black-and-gold livery approached them from a doorway to their left.

'Sakti,' he said, bowing low. 'The Queen is in her chambers. She expressed a desire to see you on your return, no matter how late. The kitchen staff delivered her meal not long since. I'm sure she would be most gratified if you were to join her. Both of you,' he added, with a nod in Kyle's direction.

Without a further word, the man spun on his heel and returned in the direction he had come from. Claire took Kyle's arm.

'Come on. May as well get it over with.'

Kyle felt sick. She hesitated. Claire pulled at her arm.

'I was joking, silly!' she laughed. 'You will love the Queen. And she will love you. She adores having Elementals at the Palace.'

Claire led her through a bewildering labyrinth of corridors and staircases, each one as black as the last, each with its torches blazing, each with a different set of huge paintings or impressive sculptures decorating the hall. She pointed out a portrait of a distinguished-looking man as they walked.

'That's my father, in his Air Mage robes.'

The raiments depicted in the painting were well named. They drifted around the man's form like gossamer, suffused with a faint blue colour rendered almost iridescent by the artist. After what seemed an age they reached a set of double doors, larger than any they had seen so far. Claire knocked.

'Munlak!' called a subdued voice from the other side.

They entered. The Queen sat on a wide window seat, surrounded by richly embroidered cushions, a half-empty plate beside her on a small blackwood table. Her demeanour could not have shouted "regal" at Kyle any louder if a thousand courtiers had stood behind her with trumpets blaring and banners waving.

'Claire!' the Queen said, standing and gliding across the room towards them. 'Welcome home! And who is this you have brought to visit?'

'Thank you, your Majesty,' Claire replied. 'This is Kyle Muir, recently arrived from Earth on the Dauntless. The last of the ships we expected.'

'Ah yes,' the Queen said.

She proffered a hand. Unsure of the protocol when meeting royalty, Kyle shook it. A small frown bisected the Queen's brow momentarily. 'Have you eaten? Please do have something. They always bring too much.'

A table set against one wall bulged with food. Kyle's stomach ached at the sight. They had not eaten since setting off that morning. She hesitated, wanting to grab as much as she could fit on a plate. There must surely be some rule about the Queen going first? Or Claire maybe, as the senior Elemental? Come to that, the Queen didn't even know Kyle was an Elemental. She was glad Claire had not yet mentioned the rains. The last thing she wanted was to get off on the wrong foot with one of the most powerful people on the planet.

'Most gracious, your Majesty,' Claire said. 'We have not eaten since this morning.'

'Then go ahead,' the Queen said with an open handed gesture towards the spread. 'I have already eaten more than enough! Take whatever you wish.'

Claire nodded at Kyle, who needed no more encouragement. She set to, filling the largest plate she could find.

'Has the housekeeper sorted out rooms for Kyle?' asked the Queen, 'or is this just a flying visit?'

'Actually, we need your advice ma'am,' Claire said. 'Kyle has shown some aptitude with Water, so I wondered if you could arrange a place for her at the Academy, as you did for me?'

'I'm sure that would be possible Claire dear,' the Queen replied, 'but if Water is her Element it wouldn't do any good to attend the Academy.'

Kyle stopped dead in the process of piling up her plate, a bread-crumbed skewer of barawa fish in her hand. She opened her mouth to ask the obvious question, but bit down on the fish instead, belatedly remembering a fragment of royal protocol. Someone who has only moments before been introduced to a Queen does not bark questions at the first opportunity. Fortunately, the Air Mage appeared to be equally astonished by the Queen's words.

'How so?' Claire asked.

'There are no mages or scholars of Water at the Academy,' the Queen said, retaking her seat in the window. A continuous cascade of rainwater ran down the panes, the storm having settled to its overnight drizzle. 'Water mages are few in number, widely spread, and tend to keep to themselves. You must have noticed that no one ever talks of a Water guild. They hardly ever meet with each other. Historically all Water adepts have been self-taught.'

'Then perhaps the Keeper—' Claire began.

The Queen cut her off. 'Nothing to be gained there either, I'm afraid.' She turned to Kyle. 'Water lore has, as far as anyone can determine, never been committed to record.'

'He told me the same,' Kyle said, feeling her face redden. 'The Keeper I mean.'

The Queen glanced over at Kyle, sending a bolt of electric fear through her and quelling her appetite. 'You said the girl had shown promise,' she said. 'Does Lautan know of this? And where is the old boy anyway? Did he return with you?'

'No, your Majesty. The Water Wizard remains at Court, for reasons I should discuss with you. As for his appraisal of Kyle, they have met. He has agreed to tutor her, once the opportunity arises.'

The Queen's eyebrows rose, disappearing beneath her glossy black fringe. 'Indeed? Has he? Then what use would an Academy seat be? There is no better teacher in all of Kertonia. You are honoured, my dear. I hope you realise?'

Kyle curtsied involuntarily, cursing herself for the unwonted gesture. 'I do, your Majesty. I am in awe of his long experience and easy manner. I would strive to emulate him. He is a very kind and generous man.'

'He is the Water Wizard of Berikatanya!' the Queen declared, before softening her features and smiling at Kyle. 'And yes, I too have found him kind. A very astute observation.' She turned to Claire. 'In Lautan's absence, perhaps you could take the young lady under your wing?'

'I have already offered, ma'am. We will work together until the Wizard's return. She is proving an adept student and has already almost mastered the basics.'

'What is Lautan doing that we must discuss?'

Claire looked at Kyle. It was clear she did not want to talk with Kyle present, but she still had half a plate of food. She looked at the spread. It was all delicious. Better than anything she had eaten since waking up on Dauntless.

She glanced back at Claire, embarrassed to find her friend smiling at her.

'What?' she said.

'Fill your plate again,' Claire said, 'and take it to my rooms. We'll arrange proper accommodation for you tomorrow. You can stay with me tonight.'

'Yes, that would be best,' the Queen agreed. 'It will give the chambermaids time to air a bed properly for you. It doesn't take long for bedclothes to become stale and damp in this awful weather! I shall arrange a room close to Claire's, since you will be working together. Take as much food as you wish.'

'Thank you, your Majesty,' Kyle said. 'It's all amazing.' She hesitated. 'But I don't know where Claire's rooms are.'

The Queen pulled on a bell cord. Within moments another man in black livery, with slightly less gold than the other man, appeared at the door.

'Please show Miss Muir to Sakti Udara's chambers,' the Queen instructed, 'and bring hot water and fresh towels for her bath.'

The liveried man waited while Kyle filled her plate. The Queen returned to her seat at the window. An uneasy silence fell over the room. As the Queen's heavy double doors closed behind her with a soft click, Kyle heard the Queen break that silence.

'Now then, what's all this about Lautan?'

Chapter 19

The Queen's question hung in the air as the door closed on Kyle Muir.

Claire had spent days trying to work out how to approach this subject. Now the moment had arrived, she still didn't know which was best. Slide in sideways? Start from the beginning and hope the Queen would pick up enough hints to realise what Claire was about to reveal? Or present the bare facts and follow up with reasons later. The Queen stared silently, expectantly, at her, a half-smile fixed quizzically on her lips. Claire's courage had deserted her.

'These are strange times,' the Queen said, apparently as keen to fill the silence as Claire was to maintain it. 'The empty Blood Throne should give us an advantage over the Reds, and yet we are frustrated at every turn. First the problems at the Landing, and lately these accursed rains. I have had such feelings of disquiet these past few days. One might even call it dread. This news of Lautan—does he have tidings of a solution for the rains? Or at least their cause?'

'It is all connected, your Majesty,' said Claire, taking her cue. 'You remember Jann Argent returned recently?'

'Yes of course. When you all took off so suddenly, he travelled with you. I remarked on it at the time, surely you recall?'

'I do. And I must apologise again. But as we said at the time, our various journeys were of the utmost urgency.'

'And you said you would explain in due course. Is that what this is all about? Your deferred explanation?'

'In part your Majesty, yes.'

'Please, Claire. I have told you many times. When we are alone you must call me Ru'ita.'

369

Lamplight caught the splashes of grey hair at the Queen's temples. They were much wider and longer now since Claire had noticed them last, and joined by smaller streaks all through the monarch's glossy black locks.

'Forgive me. Even after all this time it still feels strange to have a Queen for a friend. I will try to remember.'

She took a small plate and filled it with a few choice morsels from the Queen's table. Seating herself in the window at the opposite end from the Queen, she began.

'The Gatekeeper's quest was successful. When he returned, he brought news from the other side of Temmok'Dun.'

Claire gave the Queen an abridged version of Jann's long tale while picking at the food on her plate. She refilled it twice while the story unfolded, prompted by occasional questions. When she came to the part about Wood and Stone, she hesitated again.

'The revelations of the northern people, the Beragan, struck a chord with me Ru'ita. One of my earliest memories on this planet that I've never been able to repeat, or explain.'

'I'm not sure I understand, my dear.'

'That makes two of us.'

She recounted the brief and inexplicable surge of power at the Forest Clearance project, when she laid a hand on the trunk of a rare tree at the edge of the clearing.

'What made it even stranger, was how it echoed the dream I had on board Valiant. We aren't supposed to dream in cryosleep. I guess I must already have been returning to consciousness when my cryopod began to fail. It was so real. So vivid. And the rush of power from the Wood—I've never felt anything like it. I passed it off as an early manifestation of my Air power. But when Jann told us of Wood and Stone, the connections snapped together in my mind like pieces of a jigsaw puzzle.

'What is it Ru'ita? Are you alright?'

The Queen, her skin always as pale as moonlight, had

turned an even whiter shade. She trembled as she sat by the window.

'Are you cold? Let me fetch you a wrap.'

'No. Not cold. I mentioned my feelings of dread, but now... your talk of dreams... of wood. It... Oh, Claire! I have had such nightmares of late. My sleep has been disturbed for many days. Since the time of the rains. I put it down to that. To the worry about the floods and how the rising waters were affecting our people. But these visions contain more than torrents of water and rivers in full flood. I am in them, somehow grown taller, bolts of lightning striking me from all directions. Or, perhaps, coming from me. I can feel the electric power surging through me, frightening in its intensity. The dreams have often been so terrible as to wake me in the middle of the night. And in them all, in my hand, a shaft of dark wood. Hot to my touch, so hot I can hardly hold on to it. Yet in my dream I know I must not let it go.'

The Queen fell silent. A single fat tear rolled down her cheek, mirrored by a massive raindrop on the window behind her.

'What does it mean?' she said, dashing away the tear with the back of her hand. 'What does it all mean?'

Claire's moment had arrived. She must not shrink from it. 'Ru'ita, you have often told me that my father was your most trusted advisor. In such a role, there must have been times when he had to tell you things that were difficult to hear. You've also said how grateful you are that I have stepped into his place. Brought Air back to the Palace, and taken over where my father left off.

'Well, now it's my turn to tell you something hard. Something frightening. Almost unbelievable. The Bera'n explained to Jann how Wood and Stone were sent South along with all the other first-level Elements. The Elders did not trust the Binagan—the wild people—to use these powers. They were each given artefacts to suppress their use. A kind of antidote. The powers are not normally antagonistic, but when brought into close enough proximity they can cancel each other out.

'So the Stone Mage—the Banshirin in the tongue of the Bera'n—was given a wooden staff. The Elders referred to it as the mace. The first Banshirin treated the mace as if it was an ancient artefact of power—a badge of office—thus ensuring it would be revered by his descendants and remain close to them at all times. If not actually in their hands, then beside their bed, or somewhere in their living quarters.

'And the Wood Mage, the Kayshirin—'

Claire stopped. The Queen was staring at her wrists. The obsidian bands that never left her, day or night, glinted in the lamplight, each of their polished black surfaces reflecting the monarch's ghostly white face. With shaking hands, she reached up to take the circlet from her head. Made of the same dark stone, set with an ebony diamond in its centre, the crown too was worn constantly. Claire could not remember ever seeing the Queen without it.

'The Wood Mage,' she continued, her voice quavering, 'was given artefacts of Stone to quell her power.'

The Queen lifted her gaze to meet Claire's. She held out the dark diadem. Her eyes, red-rimmed and bloodshot, brimmed with tears.

Claire swallowed past a sudden lump in her throat. She laid a hand on the Queen's arm. 'Yes,' she said. 'It is quite common for our powers to be revealed in dreams.'

The Queen's hands fell into her lap. 'It's impossible,' she said, her gaze flicking between Claire and the crown. 'I'm the Queen. I cannot be a Wood mage. I've never... felt any power. Never... I don't even know what Wood magic can do.'

'No one does,' Claire said. 'But whatever it is may well give us an edge in the coming battle. If you can learn to wield it in time.'

'Battle?'

'Lautan has discovered the cause of these rains.'

Claire returned her plate to the still-bulging table. She completed the saga of their journeys to find the new Elementals, Water and Stone, and the events at Court.

'So Lautan is unable to prevent this?' the Queen asked as her tale concluded.

'For now, no. He will not give up the attempt. For the present he has stayed at Court to help Piers Tremaine. I will do what I can to train the sister, Kyle. She is entirely innocent of any Elemental wrongdoing. But when Douglas Muir comes fully into his power, I believe it will take all of us to overcome him. It is not only a matter for Water. Air and Earth and Fire must play their parts, too. As must Stone, and... Wood.'

The Queen looked aghast. 'I have no idea where to start with such power.'

Claire smiled. 'I can help, if you will allow me?'

The gratitude that shone from the Queen's face at her words made tears start in Claire's eyes.

'Would you?' the monarch asked, her voice taking on an uncharacteristic shy note. 'I am certainly unable to do it alone, especially if our need is urgent.'

Claire took the Queen's hands in her own. 'Take off the bands. Leave the Palace—all this black stone must also suppress your powers. I'll come with you to the woods. I expect your power will be easier to wield there and I can guide your first steps with it. But most important, take heed of what your innermost thoughts tell you. Seek out that staff you have dreamt of. See what happens.'

The Queen returned her smile weakly.

'I will try,' she said, 'though it will seem strange to be without my trinkets. I have always thought of them as badges of office.'

'If we have understood the message the Gatekeeper brought back,' Claire said, running a finger around one of the Queen's bangles, 'you should think of them as shackles.'

the black palace
24th day of run'sanamasa, 966

The sound of voices drew Elaine onto her balcony. She collected a cloak from a chair beside the window. The early morning rain, no more than a heavy mist, suggested the Muir boy must still be asleep. Stepping out, she was reminded how much she loved this room. Claire had recommended it. Partly for its proximity to her own chambers, but also for its view over one of the Palace's four atria. The quadrangle had been set with shade-loving plants, chosen by Petani. Their white flowers required little sunlight. They provided some relief from the uniformly black walls. Only the noonday sun was high enough to illuminate the flagged courtyard. The area had not seen sun since the damned rains began.

Below, in the atrium, Claire coached the Muir girl. She was attempting her first power pulse. Claire's early experience of this invocation was a favourite campfire story. One that Elaine never tired of hearing. Having had her share of bullies over the years, both here and during her brief time on Earth, she loved any tale of them being put in their place, embarrassed, or otherwise defeated. Claire's was one of the best. Apparently the power pulse was not restricted to Air. It also formed part of the armoury of a Water mage. Claire must have chosen it as a teaching method because her own experience was equally valid with Air or Water. Her pupil had clearly mastered the art of accessing her core with surprising speed if Claire thought she was ready to move on to the next lesson.

As Elaine watched, Claire explained the principles to the girl before demonstrating with an Air pulse. The blast of energy crossed the courtyard in an instant. It cut a visible path through the heavy mist and rebounded off a window in the opposite wall with a spray of tiny droplets. After a word of encouragement from the Air Mage, Kyle tried the trick for herself.

Nothing happened.

Claire murmured further words of support. Muffled by the mist and distorted by echoes from the Palace walls, they were inaudible from where Elaine stood. Kyle tried again, still with no success.

Elaine pursed her lips. If Kyle Muir had been her pupil, she would have lost her temper long before, and abandoned the lesson. Claire's patience and perseverance were impressive. Elaine only ever had one way of explaining anything. If the hapless soul under her tutelage could not grasp the concept from that, they would be on their own. Luckily for the Guild, Fire was covered at the Academy. In ordinary circumstances she would never think of offering her services as a teacher. And yet it seemed obvious an injection of temper and aggression would serve the girl better than the Air Mage's calm and measured approach.

On the other side of the atrium, the Queen appeared on her own balcony. As befitted the monarch, her suite stretched the entire width of the building. Its veranda was deeper and more ornate than any other. The royal crest, set in the middle of the outer wall, dripped a steady stream of rainwater onto the flagstones below. Elaine caught the Queen's eye. The two women nodded at each other wordlessly.

This Queen was a strange one. Elaine's relationship with the Blood King had been antagonistic at best. It often spilled over into full-blown arguments, with ripe insults thrown in each direction. They had stopped short of physical violence, but they were both hot-blooded individuals. Each with their own—often different—sense of right and wrong. They came close to blows many times. In a strange way, Elaine missed the old man.

But the Queen? She was the polar opposite. Claire often commented on her warmth and dry sense of humour. Something Elaine had never experienced. Early days, maybe. The Fire Witch had not yet spent a full season at the Palace. Yet despite the Air Mage's assertion of the Queen's good points, Elaine could not see it. To her, the woman was always cold and aloof. Cold! A word that did not sit well with Fire! Give the monarch her due though: she had welcomed the opposing Elements of Earth and Fire into her domain without question. She treated them all as equals, alongside her long-standing allies Air and Water.

A cry of triumph barrelled around the walls of the atrium. The target of Kyle's pulse, a small statue fashioned from polished blackwood brought from Claire's chambers for the purpose, arced into the air. It bounced off the flagged floor of the courtyard and came to rest a metre or so from the trough. When the echoes died away, Elaine heard Claire explaining that in time, Kyle would learn to bisect the statue with a narrower and more powerful water jet. A more difficult test which combined elements of control, focus and aim to hit the wooden figure with enough force to cut it in half without knocking it away.

Ironic, that a lesson in Water taking place several metres below her balcony had taught her something too. Careful explanation, discussion, and even diplomacy could resolve a situation more effectively than brute force strength. Even for the most powerful of combatants. The revelation resounded through her mind even louder than the echoes of the women's voices in the cold, dark atrium.

the black palace - refectory
24th day of run'sanamasa, 966

What a brilliant morning! Not literally—Kyle hadn't seen the sun since arriving on planet. But even under the iron-grey skies and depressing drizzle her brother had initiated, nothing could dampen her spirits today! She had created a power pulse of Water! A real spell! No, not spell. What was it Claire called it?

'What's that word you use instead of spell?'

They were in the Air Mage's chambers, changing into

dry clothes.

'Jamtera. It's from old Istanian. Even the Keeper isn't sure where the word originated.'

'I guess I should start to learn some of the language.'

'You'll be fine around the Palace. All the natives have been exposed to English for ten years. They consider it a badge of honour to speak fluently. It's almost as cultivated as it was to use French in England in the fourteenth century. But when you're travelling away from here, it's good to have enough words to get by. Like being in a foreign country back on Earth. The locals appreciate you making an effort with their language.'

'You've not been here that long, and you're pretty good.'

Claire blushed. 'Thanks. Kertonian lessons were on my curriculum at the Academy. To be honest, it isn't that hard to learn. Only a few rules. Simple vocabulary. You'll soon pick it up.'

The refectory buzzed with conversation as they entered. They had missed the lunch rush, but the inclement weather meant many were reluctant to leave the comfort, warmth, and dryness of the long bench seats. Several lingered over a last cup of hot katuh. The two women filled their plates and joined the Fire Witch.

'You did amazingly well this morning,' she said as they took their seats.

Kyle flashed her a quizzical glance.

'I didn't see you in the courtyard.'

The Witch smiled. 'I had eyes in the sky. I was watching from my balcony. As was the Queen,' she added. 'I think you impressed her too.'

Kyle felt hot. 'Thanks. I surprised myself. It's all down to Claire really. I would never have come this far, this fast, without her help.'

'Elaine's right, you did well for a first attempt. Don't get cocky though. There's a long way to go before you're as good as your brother, and I'm sure he's not standing still either.'

'If I ever can be as good as him,' Kyle said. The weight of expectation settling around her shoulders was almost palpable.

'I've seen your test results, remember. I *know* you can be as good as him. Different maybe—your genetic fingerprints do vary—but definitely as strong.'

'That makes sense. Obviously we're not identical twins.'

'A lot of it is confidence anyway,' the Fire Witch said. 'If you have the natural ability, which you clearly do, the only thing standing in your way is you. Perhaps I can help with that?'

Kyle was about to protest that she was doing perfectly well under her friend's guidance when Claire leant across the table and laid a hand on the Witch's arm.

'Are you serious? You'd be doing me a huge favour. The Queen has asked me to... spend some time with her today. If you could take over tutor duties—just for the rest of the day—that would be great!'

'Come on then, eat up!' Elaine said. 'We've a full afternoon's practice ahead. No time to waste! Sounds like the first thing I have to add to the curriculum is "getting out of your own way"!'

Claire stacked her plates and cutlery. 'I'm sure I'll be back later today. For now, I'll leave you to enjoy the rest of your lunch together. Maybe we can all share a glass of wine this evening?'

Kyle nodded, her mouth full. The invitation gave her a warm glow. She still could not get used to the idea that Elementals wanted to help her. But even away from the problems her brother was causing, they actively wanted to spend time with her. There had not been even the slightest hint that they blamed her for Douglas' actions.

'It's like I've emerged from a shadow,' she said.

'Sorry?' said Elaine.

'Oh. Train of thought. I meant my progress since

leaving the Court. It's almost as if Douglas was casting a shadow over me, drowning out my power with his own.'

'I don't know of any Elemental way he could do that. Like I said, it's more likely a psychological thing. You're in awe of him. Thinking he's always better than you.'

Kyle knew she was right. She had never even admitted it to herself. It was doubly hard to admit to someone else. But the Elementals had already helped her so much.

'It's still hard to accept. He's my brother. I don't think he did it deliberately. It's just how it's always been. He jumps into things full pelt. Takes life by the throat and gets on with it. Water magic is just the latest thing to take his fancy.'

Elaine's face clouded over.

'Don't get me wrong,' Kyle said, mortified this dynamic woman would think her disrespectful, 'I know it's the most powerful, most dangerous thing he's ever done. I meant, well, he won't see it like that. To him, it's a toy. I don't believe he's given a thought to the effects of what he's doing on other people. He just wants to test the boundaries. See how far he can take it. What's the biggest thing he can do with this new power? He's like a junkie, searching for the next high, and the next high, always wanting it to be bigger and better than the last.'

'That's what makes him so dangerous,' Elaine said. 'With the kind of power your genes have given you, none of us know what the limits are.'

Kyle shivered. 'I don't think I can stop him on my own. Not in time. I'm going to need help. Everyone's help.'

'We know. We're all here. Well, Lautan will be here soon, and Petani will come when we need him. You'll see. Together, there's nothing we can't fix.'

She rose to her feet. 'Come on then, let's get to it.'

Out in the courtyard the morning drizzle had developed into a downpour.

'Change of plan,' Elaine said. 'We'll get soaked out here

trying to practice what you were doing yesterday with Claire. Why don't you see if you can shield us from this rain first?'

'How?' Kyle asked, but the answer came to her almost before the question had left her lips. She stared up, raindrops splattering on her face and in her eyes. She could feel the rain on her skin, of course, but for the first time she felt it with her mind too. If she concentrated, she could see every individual drop. Predict their path, and the instant at which they would hit the ground, or the trough, or Elaine's cloak. Not only predict it. Control it. Stop it.

'Try–' Elaine began, but Kyle held up her hand, both to signal her need for quiet and to express her power. She reached out, physically with her hand and mentally with her new-found ability. The confidence swelled in her with each passing moment. The rain slowed. Encouraged by that small beginning, Kyle intensified her efforts. The rain in the courtyard stopped. High above them, beyond the level of the Palace roof, it continued to fall. Reaching the building, it careened off to the side, diverted from its natural course by Kyle's exertion of will.

'Yes!' cried the Fire Witch. 'Yes! Well done Kyle!'

the black palace & surroundings
24th day of run'sanamasa, 966

She felt naked.

It was ridiculous. She was dressed exactly as before, with the sole, tiny exceptions of two stone bangles around her wrists and a stone diadem on her head. Yet these three outwardly insignificant changes were filled with import and, yes, more than a little dread.

For as long as she could remember, the obsidian tiara had adorned her brow whenever she was awake. It had been passed down through her family since before written records were kept. Her grandmother had called it Mahok Ginkadaya, though the Keeper had not found any reference to the name. The bangles too stayed with her permanently. She slept in them, bathed in them, ate in them. She could not recall a time when she had been without them. Perhaps the artefacts' provenance and history all lent weight to her Air Mage's words. If not for her implicit trust in Claire, and the few clues in support of her strange story, she would have found the whole thing quite literally incredible.

And her dreams, of course. Nightmares of increasing intensity which had plagued her sleep since the Gatekeeper set out on his quest. As if her subconscious mind had foreknowledge of the revelations he would bring back. It cried out to her to accept the heritage of which he spoke, after the decades of denial. How her hands had trembled as she slipped the bangles off her wrists in the privacy of her quarters that night! Could it really have been yesterday? Yes, only a single night had passed. A night for once devoid of visions. Yet still she had slept fitfully, waking at intervals as her hands crept beneath her pillow. Her sleep-dulled mind had puzzled at the strange sensation before drowsily recalling that she no longer wore the bangles.

Now, she determined to complete the second step Claire had suggested. Without her baubles, she experienced strange sensations all through her body. Reluctant—no, if she was honest, embarrassed—to discuss the feelings with anyone, she sat alone in her chambers. The tingling, hot flushes, and bone-deep aching waxed and waned. Concentrating, she found could bring on a perception of wood, or quell it. Her living quarters contained several items fashioned from it. A fruit bowl, table and chairs, and the imposing kaytam doors. Blackwood, as the Earthers called it. Each different variety had its own appearance, beyond the colouration and grain pattern visible to the casual observer. It was as if she saw them in another dimension, though she was at a loss to explain the subtle differences for anything except the doors. They almost shouted at her. Ironically, the kaytam suggested a protective force, greater than the simple physical blocking of an entrance. With the application of Wood power— once she had learned how—she knew the doorway would become impassable to anyone to whom she denied access.

A knock came as she focused on the door, making her jump.

'Come.'

Claire entered.

'Are you ready, Ru'ita?'

A shiver ran down her spine. 'No, but I've never let that stop me.'

The thought of leaving the stone cocoon of the Palace, and discovering what might ensue once she took herself beyond its influence, filled her with trepidation. Her hands began to shake anew. On their way out, they passed the Palace refectory, where Claire's young protégé was taking a late lunch in the company of the Fire Witch. The two were deep in conversation.

'Shouldn't you–?' she began.

'Elaine is looking after Kyle for the rest of the day. You are my priority right now.'

The rain, heavier than in recent days, sounded loud against the hood of her cloak. Drawing the heavy material more closely around her, the Queen stepped onto the path beside the Palace moat. They headed for the nearby wood, hoping that Claire was right and the proximity to its many trees would have the desired effect. What was that, exactly? The desired effect? What would be the effect, and did she really desire it? Less than a day had passed since she learned of her supposed potential. Not nearly long enough to come to terms with the knowledge. But she was Queen! Over the years she had grown used to meeting challenges head on, rather than letting them stew. She had no patience with endless meetings, counselling sessions, and debates. Better just to get on with it. If it proved more than she could handle, so be it. Nothing had ever had that effect on her, but if anything could, it was probably the discovery and use of a second-level Elemental power.

For Sana's sake! Even the Elementals themselves had only learned of second-level powers mere days before! Some of them had been using their power for a lifetime. Even lovely Claire, every millimetre her father's daughter, who had only known of her inheritance since Tanamasa, had that much more experience than her. There was a parallel there though, which both informed and bolstered the Queen's approach. The girl who walked beside her had been through so much. Plucked from her life unimaginable distances away, catapulted through the void on one of the Earthers' fabulous spaceships, and left alone on that ship for five years having discovered her mother's corpse. Thrown into Palace life on her arrival, with the revelation of being part of the Air dynasty added to the mix for extra flavour. Remarkable, really, what she had achieved, all with good grace and humour. Surely a Queen of Kertonia could do no worse? She was about to find out.

The pair walked through the outermost, sparsely growing set of trees and entered the heart of the forest. Claire had been silent for most of their walk, which the Queen appreciated. Now they had reached their first destination, she turned to speak.

'At least we have some shelter here from the rain!'

The canopy was thick, even at the edge of the treeline. What little rain was not stopped, condensed into fat droplets that fell at intervals from the broad leaves, making a splattery, woody music of their own. The Queen had never taken an interest in botany. She did not recognise the many varieties of tree the forest was home to or know their names. But with her burgeoning Wood sense, she could differentiate them easily. Whatever perception had been unlocked seemed to work below the level of her traditional senses. At least, that was the only way she could think about it. The trees did not sing to her. They did not glow. They did not smell any different. And yet on some subliminal level, they were doing all of those things.

Kaytam, Ponektu, and Kayati all revealed themselves to her in subtle ways that, before now, she had not noticed.

'I can almost hear them,' she said, smiling.

Claire clapped her hands. 'Excellent!' she cried. 'Exactly what I hoped for! The quiet here will help too. Help you still your mind. Try it now, while I'm here. Don't think of anything in particular. Just open yourself to the feelings that the forest conjures. Once you begin, you will soon hear a louder song. Your own song, from your core. But that will come later.'

At first, the sensations were those of her familiar senses. The fresh smells of wet fern, wood, and bracken. The occasional shriek of a bird or scurrying of a small animal, set against the constant backdrop of the whispering rain. As her mind became accustomed to these and ignored them, she began to discern a different impression. Not a sound, exactly, nor yet a smell. A strange combination of every sense and one to which she could not put a name. In her excitement she reached for it mentally. It receded.

'Be still,' Claire murmured. 'It will come.'

The Queen smiled, feeling the colour rise in her cheeks. 'Thank you. It's hard not to compel it.'

They meandered along the many paths through the forest, often retracing their steps or finding a chosen route had returned them to the starting point. Some tracks were wide and floored with leaf litter and chips of bark left by foraging animals. Others, narrow and overgrown, were imperceptible until they were almost upon them. Each revealed new delights. Flowers and ferns, protected from the worst of the rains by the forest canopy, flourished in their many forms, colours, and varieties of fronds. Small creatures darted out in front of them. Frightened by the unexpected presence, they plunged back from where they came, chittering a warning to their fellows. After much wandering, the Queen began to notice a change in her thoughts.

'I think...'

'Yes,' said Claire. 'I thought so.'

The Air Mage stood back, as if allowing the forest a clearer path to the Queen. 'Let go any expectations or preconceptions,' she said. 'You are used to being in control. Set that aside. At least for now. Open your mind fully to the power of the woods.'

Within moments, the whole forest became suffused with a deep blue colour.

'Oh! Look at that!' said the Queen, with a sharp intake of breath.

'What?'

'The colour! It's so beautiful!'

'I don't see anything. Nothing has changed. This must be part of your power. You're doing really well. Remember not to reach for it—let it come to you.'

The blue had begun as a diffuse fog covering the whole of the visible woodland. Now, it coalesced around a single pathway to the Queen's right.

'Over there! We need to go that way.'

'*You* need to go that way,' Claire said. 'I have a feeling you should do this next part on your own.'

She began to panic at the thought of being abandoned by the only friend who really understood Elemental power. The forest blue dimmed. But she was the Queen! And on the evidence of today, she was also a Wood mage! Maybe she did not need help after all? She fought down the feelings of dread.

'Perhaps you're right Claire. I will go on alone. You've helped so much. I shall find you on my return, let you know what happens.'

Without waiting for the Air Mage to comment further, the Queen made her way along the path still lit by the pulsating blue light. It continued for some distance before she came to what at first appeared to be a clearing. Emerging from the dense undergrowth, she saw that it was not, after all, a natural opening in the wood. An area the size of the Palace basilica had been blasted from the forest by the many bolts of lightning. A frightening side-effect of the Muir boy's constant rainfall. Trees lay felled across the gap. Others had collapsed onto their neighbours, precariously balanced at the mercy of the wind or further lightning strikes.

To her left, a Durmak tree had been hit, causing a shaft of wood to split from a main branch and fall to the ground. Of all the trunks, branches, and twigs around her, this one "sung" the loudest. Its smooth surface, shorn of its bark, was limned by more crepuscular blue light. Perhaps two metres in length and about as thick at its base as a man's arm, the shaft tapered slightly towards one end. The other end betrayed the violence with which it had been wrested from its parent tree.

She reached for it, intending to carry it back to the Palace and investigate why it called to her so strongly and plainly. As she hefted the branch in her right hand a cry of surprise and pain escaped her lips. She dropped the wood and stepped back. Although betraying no outward sign of fire, it was as hot to her hand as a cauldron of boiling water.

the black palace
24th day of run'sanamasa, 966

It was late. The two moons Pera-Bul and Kedu-Bul had risen long before, their silver discs ghostly behind heavy cloud. Kyle was wet, cold, and exhausted.

After her initial success diverting the rain from the atrium, Elaine had suggested leaving the Palace. Flooding of the surrounding area was becoming a severe problem for the local villages. The Fire Witch thought they could combine practice with a chance to offer help to the Queen's subjects. They had spent the day together, Kyle listening carefully to Elaine's barked explanations of how to increase her power, and then attempting to put that new knowledge to use.

'You need to let your anger out Kyle!' the Witch had said. 'It will help with your power.'

'Claire told me I needed to stay in control. Keep my emotions to one side.'

A momentary cloud of irritation passed across the Witch's face, mirroring the scudding thunderheads above. Kyle was sure she would throw a fit of temper, but the older woman took a deep breath.

'That's true when you need fine control,' she said. 'But for raw energy, your anger can help. How do you think your brother is doing all this? Do you think he's calm? On an even keel? Or is he mad at something? Or even, everything?'

All told, it had been a day of mixed success, but the occasional failure had only spurred her on to greater efforts. She had taken the Witch's advice and let slip her frustrations. A little. With that, she had increased her range and protected ever larger areas from rainfall, as well as diverting some of the smaller floods, to the great relief of a handful of villagers. More significant flooding had defeated her, but as usual Elaine had been there with a terse word of encouragement.

'Even Lautan would struggle with this,' she said. 'Don't beat yourself up, you've done some good work today.'

'Hi you two! How's it going?'

Claire approached from the direction of the Timakaya forest.

'Thank Baka!' the Witch cried.

Claire laughed. 'That good?'

'Oh don't get me wrong, your girl's been amazing. But I'm spent. She's all yours.'

Without another word or a backward glance, the Fire Witch was gone. Kyle didn't think she'd been amazing. Now her favourite Elemental had returned, there was one "amazing" event from the previous day that she wanted to explore further. Completely by accident, the pair had discovered the effects of combining their Elements. For a brief moment, while trying to sustain Kyle's efforts, Claire's own Elemental power had spilled out, adding its force to Kyle's own. The result had been instantaneous and unexpected. Adding a surge of Air to Kyle's control of Water shredded the floodwaters into a fine spray that exploded into the atmosphere, spreading over an enormous area of ground. Claire's mercurial mind had instantly grasped the significance of the event.

'Wow! So it's not only Elaine and Lautan who can work together,' she had said. 'She can boil off his diverted water, but we can spread it out so it takes longer to accumulate at dangerous levels. And,' she went on, 'once we stop these accursed rains, think of the possibilities for irrigation! Petani will be so excited!'

Kyle's thoughts had been taking another direction during the course of the day.

'Now you're back, can we try something?' she asked. 'Yesterday we combined our powers, but with your power acting on mine. What would happen the other way round?'

Claire's eyes widened. 'I have no idea,' she replied. 'Why don't we try it?'

So they did.

The effect was entirely different. Adding Water power to an existing jamtera of Air created a dense fog. The impenetrable grey blanket hung in the air before the slanting rain dispersed it.

'This would be great in battle!' Kyle said. 'Imagine how disorientated the enemy forces would be if they were surrounded by this!'

Claire grinned. 'You're already starting to think like an Elemental!' she said.

With little physical or mental strength remaining, Kyle had decided they should call it a day. They sat beside a roaring fire in Claire's chambers holding aching hands around oversized mugs of panklat.

'This is way better than the hot chocolate at home,'

Kyle said.

'I know!' Claire laughed. 'I have to limit myself to one a day or I wouldn't fit my clothes!'

A comfortable silence fell between them. Kyle's thoughts turned back to the events of the day. She had surprised herself with her progress. Despite her fatigue, she felt ready to make an attempt to quell her brother's power. During her lessons, she had sensed how Douglas was creating the rain. Unsure of her strength compared to his, she at least now had an idea how to counter it. Claire would never agree to it though. She had already expressed a concern that Kyle was over-reaching.

'I think I'll finish this in my room, if you don't mind?' she said, trying to keep her voice calm. 'I'd like time to process everything that happened today, and think about where I'd like to take my lessons tomorrow.'

Claire looked surprised, but in a good way.

'That's a great idea,' she said. 'I always thought that was one of the few downsides of learning at the Academy. The pressure was on all the time. Very little downtime for students. I often wished I could have a timeout to do exactly what you said. See you for breakfast?'

'Sure.'

Kyle headed for her chambers, staying only long enough to set down her mug. The boost of energy from the panklat had reinforced her determination to make the attempt tonight. The memory of Water power was still fresh, and her resolve had yet to weaken. She hurried through the Palace corridors, deserted now most courtiers and staff had retired for the night. The main doors were already closed and bolted. She slid back one enormous iron bolt and cracked the door. Outside in the basilica the rain fell steadily. Douglas must still be awake: the strength of the downpour had not lessened to the fine drizzle that always accompanied his sleep. Kyle grabbed a cloak from one of the pegs in the hallway and stepped out into the night.

Under the heavy drops of the barajan, she stood quietly, summoning her power. She felt the now-familiar ache begin deep in her mind as she accessed her core. Reaching out with the power, she searched for her brother's influence, found it, and began to push back. Slowly at first, but with increasing intensity, she conjured the dak-jamtera to counteract his malign efforts. To her profound amazement, her attempt began to work.

For a few seconds.

Douglas Muir's counterattack began immediately and with frightening ferocity. Transmitted by the Elemental force they both shared, intensified by their common genes, heritage, and experience, Kyle could almost feel his anger through the Water. The rain above the Palace turned from shower to monsoon as quickly as opening a tap. Stinging heavy raindrops, falling so swiftly they still held the chill of the high atmosphere, raked her cheeks. She did not notice them. Her mind was held in thrall by her brother's riposte. Her body became rigid, her arms flung out spastically, the fingers of her hands spread into claws. She gave a single bone-crunching shiver before dropping to the ground in a dead faint.

The last thing she saw as her consciousness ebbed was the Queen's pennant. Rent from the flagpole by the lashing rain, the ragged cloth flew down like a crippled black bird, landing in a crumpled heap beside her on the courtyard stones.

Chapter 20

She stood alone and naked under a torrent of rain more powerful than anything she had ever known. The icy downpour had torn the clothes from her frozen body. It beat relentlessly against her flesh, threatening to strip that from her bones too. The rain fell so fast she could not feel the separate drops. Instead she was tortured by constant pain, as if she had stepped in front of a harvester and been caught in its myriad whirling blades.

It was dark, but she knew her friends all lay dead, out there in the blackness. Left alone to face the mad wizard Muir, she tried to summon her Fire, but the biting rain against her head made thought all but impossible. Only instinct remained. There was no shelter, no respite from the deluge. From somewhere, she heard a drum. No, many drums. Hundreds of separate drumbeats, repeating an arcane, irregular rhythm she could not follow. Was it a call to arms? Had the Queen finally decided to mobilise against Douglas Muir? How could she march her forces through *this*? No kudo could be persuaded outdoors under this liquid assault. The war was lost before it even began. An inexorable feeling of utter hopelessness washed over Elaine. She began to cry. For the loss of her friends, her failure as an Elemental, and her inability to prevent mad Muir from submerging the entire country underwater. Sobs wracked her numb body. She fell to her knees on the carpet.

Carpet?

Elaine opened her eyes. The frenetic drumbeats of her dream resolved into rain, hammering against the windows. One of the smaller panes had shattered from the force of the storm, allowing a chill wind to blow in. She had fallen, naked, to the floor. Crouched on the rug beside her bed, her awful nightmare receded. She stood, ignoring the pain in her knees, grabbed a nightgown, and crossed to the window to see if she could plug the hole.

Outside in the basilica, a figure lay on the ground. Dimly illuminated by torchlight shining through the Palace windows, the body sprawled at an unnatural angle on the flagstones, unmoving. Raindrops bounced up all around it, spattering. Saturated strands of long black hair stretched toward the nearest gutter, dragged by fast-flowing rivulets. Kyle!

She pulled on a cloak and ran from the room, hammering on the Air Mage's door as she passed.

'Claire! It's Kyle! She's in the yard!'

Without waiting for a response she ran on, out into the storm. She splashed across the courtyard, the stone flags gritty beneath her bare feet. Her cloak flapped open. The cold rain slashed her flesh, echoing her dream. Surely Kyle was not dead? She lifted the young Water mage's head.

'Kyle! Kyle! Can you hear me?'

Claire ran from the building to join her. Kyle murmured something inaudible, but her eyes remained closed.

'We have to move her inside,' Elaine said, shouting to be heard over the roar of the storm against the granite walls and polished flagstones. She reached for Kyle's shoulders while Claire took her feet. The girl's clothing was covered in fine grit splashed from the basilica floor. As the two Elementals lifted her, an explosion detonated, shaking the ground as if an earthquake had struck. The Air Mage dropped one leg.

'What the—?'

To Claire's left, a large block of granite, part of the castellated North turret, rolled to a stop, leaning heavily on the Palace wall. Above, silhouetted against the ghostly shadow of the moons behind the heavy clouds, the gap it had left was starkly visible.

'Hurry!' Elaine said, 'there may be more to come. The

rain must be eroding the mortar.'

They carried Kyle's unconscious body inside.

'Fetch a towel, and something to cover her with. We have to warm her up.'

She held out her hands, palms facing upwards. After a moment's concentration, red flames appeared in each hand, flickering higher and hotter with each passing second. Heat suffused the hallway. Kyle's clothing began to steam. Claire returned carrying a blanket. She screamed, staring at the doorway.

'What is it?' Elaine asked, jumping to her feet. Her Fire died away. Jann Argent stood there, his pale face and dark-rimmed eyes betraying his exhaustion. He stepped over the threshold and collapsed onto the slate floor.

'Dear Baka!' Elaine shouted, rushing to his side. 'I thought you were dead! Where have you been?'

'Got a bit lost,' he said, before his eyes rolled up and he passed out.

'What in Baka's name is going on?' Elaine demanded, her frustration boiling over. 'Fetch help, Claire. A guard. Someone to help carry them. We can't manage both of them between us.'

The Air Mage ran off to summon one of the guards. Elaine retrieved the blanket and lay it over Jann Argent, summoning her Fire once more to warm his chilled flesh. She brushed a strand of wet hair away from his face.

'I thought you were dead,' she repeated.

*

The two invalids were attended by the Palace physician. Many Earthers had a romantic notion of life in a medieval society. When it came to injuries and affliction, the reality was not so attractive. Fortunately the Gatekeeper and the young Water Mage were not injured. Their only illness— exhaustion and exposure—was nothing that could not be cured by warmth, rest, and hot food. Claire agreed Kyle should spend the night in her chambers where the Air Mage could keep an eye on her. Jann Argent lay in Elaine's bed, the covers pulled up to his chin, while she kept vigil over his sleep.

What an eventful night! The officer on duty, Pena-gliman Lendan, had been agitated when no one could find the Queen. Someone in authority had to supervise the care of the sick, and decide what to do about the damage. More than two months had passed since the Piper's death and the Palace hierarchy still had not found a replacement. The man had been at the heart of everything to do with the running of the place. His absence was as obvious as the hole in the North tower. Certainly the Pena-gliman was not equal to the task.

'If this rain doesn't stop soon,' he said, 'the Black Palace will come crashing to the ground.'

'A bit of it already has,' Elaine replied laconically. 'It missed us by metres!'

'I must make sure everyone is kept inside, until I can find a stonemason to repair the damage. Can you at least slow the rain? One of you Elementals? It is even more intense now than yesterday. There are leaks everywhere and my guards report there are several other blocks on the parapets which have been loosened.'

Annoyed by his disrespectful tone she had sent him off to find a mason. Jann had called to her from the bath, where he was soaking away the aches in his bones.

'You could do it. I've seen your gentle side. Don't pretend it doesn't exist. Your Fire doesn't have to be flames of anger. You showed me that in the hall.'

'I thought you were unconscious.'

'I was drifting in and out, but I felt your power. It buoyed me up like a warm Bakamasa day. Or the glow from a homely hearth.'

Elaine had never been described as "homely." Rather than being annoyed, she was touched by Jann's comment. She left him to dry off, returning to her bedchamber to stare out at the rain. It continued to fall in heavy torrents. He had been semi-conscious! Did he hear the pain in her voice? And her relief that his fall through the gate had not been fatal? She shook her head at the embarrassment. The lessons had been coming thick and fast for her of late. First Claire, showing her what could be achieved with patience and dedication. And now the Gatekeeper urging her to let loose her gentle nature. She hated the idea of making herself vulnerable. Gentleness led to hurt. In the privacy of her rooms, with the soft sounds of bathing reaching her from the next room, maybe it was worth a try. Distracted by the thought of Jann Argent emerging naked from her bath, she had brought up her power. Surrounded the Palace with a suffusive warmth strong enough to repel the rains. She couldn't maintain it for long, but it would at least give the building a chance to dry out. May even prevent further damage.

A short while later Jann stirred, turning onto his back beside her. The heat Elaine generated had warmed the entire Palace. She had held her power up for longer than expected, but the mental effort was beginning to tell. Her eyelids had been drooping for some time. She had to keep shaking herself awake, or walking around the room to dispel the torpor. She was supposed to be keeping watch! For the sixth time, Jann threw off the blankets, exposing his naked torso. His hairless chest and chiselled abs set a different kind of fire burning in Elaine's stomach. A fire she had long thought permanently quenched. She got up to leave the room; put some distance between herself and temptation. Jann's eyes flew open. He grabbed for her hand before she moved out of reach. There was fire in his eyes too.

'Don't go,' he said.

outside the black palace
24th day of run'sanamasa, 966

In the clearing the rain had intensified, falling now with angry purpose. A deluge of leaves joined it, ripped from their twigs and branches and cast to the forest floor by the vertical river of rain. The durmak shaft lay where it had fallen, wet and glistening under the moonlit cloud cover. The Queen was forced to take refuge once more beneath the canopy. The raindrops fell like myriad tiny knives, stabbing at her head and face, shoulders and hands.

Perhaps she had been too quick to bid farewell to her young friend and Air Mage. While she roamed the forest, night had fallen. Racing clouds thickened over the moons, bringing a period of darker gloom to the glade in which the strange blue light of the shaft continued to glow. In this new dimness the light of other trees too shone out once again, all in different shades of blue. Faint echoes of her earlier first sight of Wood power. Surely the shaft could not still be hot? Had it even been hot at all, or was it only her reaction to touching a length of her Element, in its place of origin? She remembered Claire's story of her venture from the clearing in Besakaya forest. How the inexplicable surge of power had taken her by surprise. Maybe that was it? If she had not dismissed the girl she could have asked her. She was accustomed to hearing counsel before making any decision. This new world of Elemental power had sapped her confidence, but she was still Queen.

Braving the blades of rain, she stepped out into the clearing once more to retrieve the wood. Tentatively, she plucked it from its resting place, steeling her mind in the expectation of another burn. None came. The wood was cold to her touch. Cold and wet. In the failing light, she examined it more closely. The lightning bolt had stripped it of its bark, revealing the smoothness beneath. A knuckle about a third of its length from the narrow end provided a perfect handhold, as if naturally fashioned for the purpose. Better than anything the Palace artisans could craft. The heel of the shaft, where it had been torn from its parent tree, still showed signs of the force of that removal. Ragged splinters of riven wood hung from it. The surface at that point was anything but smooth. It looked as though it had been chewed by a kuclar. Perhaps there was something her craftsmen could do after all? Shave off the shards and make the branch look more like a staff.

She started back for the Palace, conscious of the lateness of the night and the silliness of being out here in the worst storm so far. But wait. Why worry whether or not her artisans could do anything with her new staff? She was, allegedly, a Wood mage. Was there not something she could do herself? She should be capable of feats to surpass even the most highly trained woodsmith, limited as they were to using hand tools and brute strength.

It would require a different approach to the way she had slammed her doors earlier that day. This was delicate work. A real challenge of control and careful expression of power, for one in the early days of her apprenticeship. Still, who would know? If she failed, she could still hand the matter over to someone adept with the more traditional methods.

The Queen found a fallen tree on which to perch while she concentrated on the task. Back under the heavy canopy, the forest lay almost entirely in darkness. Only the eerie blue glow from the shaft provided any illumination. It reflected from her white skin, giving it a supernatural appearance. She laughed at the thought. This was all beyond her understanding. It seemed appropriate she should also look otherworldly.

Focusing her mind on the shattered end of the shaft, she reached out to the wood, and simultaneously in to that mysterious core of power she had so recently discovered. With a soft cry of delight, she felt the power begin to flow. Slowly at first, but with increasing intensity. Would it be too strong? Unsure how to control it, she abandoned higher thinking and let her instincts take over. Before her eyes, the splintered end of the shaft began to close. The fibres of wood knitted themselves back together until only a smooth stump remained. Not just any stump. The broad end of the shaft had fashioned itself into a perfect heel for the staff. As the last sliver of wood moved into place, the blue light of the staff flashed once and went out. The Queen sat on the log, in total darkness, listening to fat water drops hitting the leaf litter all around her.

court of the blood king - darmajelis chamber
25th day of run'sanamasa, 966

Douglas Muir was already in a foul mood before he even arrived at the chamber. How dare she? How dare *they*? His anger alone would have been enough to raise the storm outside to the level of a monsoon, but it was a targeted rage. In the vicinity of the Blood Court, the increased rainfall was noticeable. For the Palace, he was actively making it unbearable. That would teach those jumped up "Elementals" not to unlock his sister's potential and use it against him! While she had been here, with him, she knew her rightful place. As she had always done. By his side, but in his shadow. He was now, and had always been older, wiser, and stronger. And more deserving of the fruits of whatever endeavour he engaged in. Kyle was welcome to the leavings; his was the glory.

And now these lesser Elementals had whisked her away from his influence, filled her mind with bizarre ideas no doubt. At least one of them—he had a good idea who—had been coaching her in the use of their shared power. He had felt it! Like a ripple in the Water, expanding in concentric circles through the strange currents of force even he did not yet fully understand. Bad enough that she was learning. May even come to equal him in time, though the prospect seemed unlikely. But when she turned her burgeoning Water power in his direction, attempted to counter his works and quench the rains, that brought the red mist down in his mind. The blind rage had momentarily prevented him from accessing the source of his power. Feelings of panic had risen up. That he would lose this new-found special ability. Return to the mediocrity that had tormented him all his life. It soon passed. He regained his focus and struck back, with instinctive force. Whatever had happened all those kilometres away at the Black Palace, Kyle's influence disappeared from the ether. A small part of him hoped he had not hurt her too badly. He silenced it with a shake of his head. He was late for the Darmajelis meeting. He had more important matters to think about.

The chamber was already full when he entered. Fuller than usual, actually. Douglas glanced around the room to see which seat was newly occupied. He found it as the Jester took to his feet. The annoying Earther he had met and challenged in the crypt five days before.

'Douglas!' the Jester said, beaming. 'Finally, we are all assembled. Let us make a start.'

Douglas claimed his seat, his eyes never leaving the new Earther's face. Surely this could not be the "important role" the man had talked of? The Jester had made no mention of him before now.

'Before we get to the main business, I have one special item to add to the order paper,' the Jester continued. 'I should like to formally introduce our latest member to the assembly this morning. Gentlemen, this is Piers Tremaine. I've asked him to represent the Earther community in our meetings and work to improve our relationship with the colonists, whether they have only just arrived...'

The annoying little man nodded in Douglas' direction as he said this, pausing for effect before continuing.

'...or been here for several years, as in Piers' case. Perhaps I can ask you to give the group a brief background of yourself and your time on Berikatanya, Piers?'

'Thank you, Jeruk,' Tremaine said, getting to his feet. Douglas watched a smug smile play over the man's fat lips. He was clearly an idiot. 'And thank you all for giving me such a welcome. I hope to fulfil the duties of Earther representative to everyone's satisfaction, but if my efforts ever fall short please do tell me. I can only improve with your feedback.'

Was he doing it deliberately? Emphasising his role? Douglas was the Earther representative! Why did they need another? The upstart continued with his recap. He mentioned his arrival on the Intrepid—a fact he seemed inordinately proud of—and how he had spent his time doing stone work for a minor village. That was about it. Oh, and made some sculptures. No doubt very pretty. Nothing to warrant a seat here. His biggest achievement so far appeared to be making the right diplomatic noises. Anyone could fawn and scrape. Douglas had real power. Tremaine was coming to the end of his little speech. Maybe now they could get on with some real work.

'...and so I was surprised to hear a knock on my door at that time of night, but even more so when I opened it to find Jeruk standing there, offering me a place on his Darmajelis.'

So that's where he had been going that night! Douglas jumped to his feet.

'Sorry, am I missing something?'

'Please observe the rules of debate, Douglas,' the Jester said. 'Piers has not finished his address.' He was smiling, but Douglas could see the dangerous look in his eyes. Damn the man.

'Rules be damned. I don't need to listen to any more of his story. Why is he here at all, that's what I'd like to know? You already have an Earther here—me! We don't need another!'

'What we need or don't need is a matter for me,' the Jester replied. 'Be careful where you take this Douglas. If you are implying there is room for only one representative from the Batu'n–'

'You'll choose him over me? Is that what you're saying?'

A sharp blast of rain hit the chamber windows, rattling them in their frames. A momentary look of fear flashed into the Jester's eyes. The unguarded moment was quickly extinguished as the Jester regained his composure, but it was enough for Douglas.

'Because he is so much more important than me, isn't he? So dynamic. Is that why you went to bring him here in person, when you sent your minion to fetch me?'

Sebaklan Pwalek, seated at the Jester's right hand, started to object. Nipis silenced him with a gesture.

'Enough!' the Jester said, raising his voice. 'How, when and by whom you were both brought here is immaterial. The "why" is the important thing. You are not the only one here with Elemental powers young man.'

The revelation sent a thrill of unease roiling into the pit of his stomach.

'Powers? Him? He's a mason for God's sake!'

'I work with stone, yes,' Tremaine agreed, staring unflinchingly at Douglas. 'Not always in the traditional way.'

His irritating smug smile reappeared on the man's face. So his sculptures were made with some kind of stone power? Big deal.

Douglas barked out a disdainful laugh. 'Is that it? His magic makes pretty knick-knacks? Mine could drown the world! But if that's the way you want it Jeruk, then fine! You need me more than I need an interminable series of boring meetings and jibber-jabber.'

He jabbed a finger in the Jester's direction as he spoke. A second torrent of rain lashed the chamber windows, making the entire meeting jump.

'I am the real Water Wizard! Your Lautan is no match for me, and I'll prove it!'

Douglas turned, sending his chair crashing to the floor, and strode from the chamber.

court of the blood king - douglas' chambers
25th day of run'sanamasa, 966

Douglas burst into his chambers, slamming the door into its frame behind him. The air had a damp chill. His fire had not been lit—the chambermaid expecting him to be occupied at his meeting until later—his bed had not been made, and his table was empty of food. Only the lashing of the rain on his windows disturbed the silence in the room.

'Ach!' he screamed, sweeping a vase off the table to shatter against the wall. 'Damn them! Damn them all!'

He had called himself the Water Wizard before storming out of the chamber, but until that moment he had not believed it. Now, with his temper flaring, his mind opened not only to the possibility of that truth, but to higher powers previously dammed behind a wall of his own uncertainty. This Elemental magic was slippery. His first attempts to take control of what he had already been doing unconsciously had been easy. Too easy, it seemed. At some level he admitted something he would never have spoken of openly. He had been arrogant. The ease with which he had grasped and wielded this power allowed him to assume there was nothing more to it. He had been powerful indeed, in those first days. Beyond anything he could have imagined. But there *was* more to it.

If his anger had unlocked the sluice gates of the dam holding his higher powers in check, what would open them? More of the same? That would not be difficult. His sense of betrayal was absolute. He would never return to that pathetic rabble. Did not even want to be in the company of the supercilious troll who thought himself entitled to rule simply because he had spent years whispering in the Blood King's ear. Well, the King was dead, and the throne vacant. Open to anyone who could defeat other challengers, according to the rules of succession. Only there were no other challengers. Or at least, not until now.

Even with the power he had used so far, no one could stand against him. The withered old man who everyone graced with the title Water Wizard had not attempted to raise a single thought against Douglas. Lautan's attempts to quell his power in more circumspect ways had all been futile. He had defeated his sister, new to her own power, in moments. And now he had access to even more potential, assuming he could discern the trick of it. Was it rage? Or something more subtle? He had been angry before. His temper only delivered more violent rains. Something else had occurred today in the Darmajelis chamber. Something different.

Of course! Stupid! He had already thought how much stronger he was than Lautan, without making the connection. It was not his anger that opened a path to higher power, but self-belief. Even something as simple and insignificant as conferring the title Water Wizard on himself had been enough to start the Water flowing. He walked to the window, shards of broken pottery crunching under his boots. Behind him, the door opened. It was the chambermaid.

'Sir? Can I–?'

'Not now!'

The girl closed the door again hurriedly. Douglas gazed out at the lowering sky, shedding its burden of rain as it had done for days. He need only trust himself. It was a feedback loop. He understood the concept from high school. A small amount of confidence would deliver a result, increasing the confidence and in turn increasing the result. What was it that dullard careers master had said? Fake it 'til you make it. Was it possible he could believe— or pretend to believe—long enough to start the process? He searched for a water metaphor. Yes. Calling himself Water Wizard had started a drip. What he needed was a torrent.

He stared at the sky. Let his mind wander. Thought of the possibilities of unlimited power. The clouds darkened.

Slowly at first, but with gathering speed, the thunderheads multiplied and blackened until the sun was all but obliterated behind a bruised blanket. The rain, already heavy, turned rapidly to a uniform deluge, as if the Blood Court had been built under a cataract. In the basilica below, courtiers and servants ran for cover, their faces filled with pain and fear. Was that it? Was that all he could muster? No. He was the Water Wizard. This was only rain. Bodies of water too were his to command. He turned his attention to the moat. Watched it rise and boil until it crested the drawbridge, spilling over into the courtyard, flooding the stable block, and running through the main doors like a racing river in full torrent.

Chapter 21

The Black Queen awoke slowly, her sleep-befuddled mind confused by the strange feel of her bed linen, the abnormal absence of background Palace hubbub in her room, and the confection of strange smells reaching her nose. Had the lack of her treasured obsidian bangles disturbed her sleep again? No, this was different. Her bed had a soft, springy quality she had never noticed before.

A large, cold, extremely wet drop of rainwater fell on her cheek.

She opened her eyes. She had not slept in the Palace at all. The crepuscular forest still surrounded her, the bed nothing but soft moss and fallen leaves. Despite its beggarly construction, and the chill of the gloomy wood in which it lay, this "bed" had provided the best night's sleep she could remember. Her new-found durmak staff lay under her hand, its wood dark, the blue light which had limned its smooth form the night before now extinguished. The reason for this escaped her. Was it an innate property of the wood? Would it only be visible in darkness? Or did the wood remain quiescent because she was no longer calling on its power? Best not to question it. Let things play out in their natural course. When the time was right, she would understand. For now, she was content to be. And more than content that her sleep had been free of disturbing dreams and terrifying nightmares.

She brushed the leaf litter from her clothes and gave the staff a closer examination. With the benefit of the muted daylight filtering through the forest canopy, she could discern more detail. Having dried out overnight, the wood felt warm to her touch. Was it unnaturally warm? An echo of that flash of heat the shaft of wood had given her the previous day? Or was it only her imagination? A faint grain pattern criss-crossed its smooth surface in a series of swirling lines almost like an ancient, long-forgotten script. Holding the staff brought her Wood sense to life once again, the surrounding trees each beginning a muted song of their own. She calmed her mind and let the feelings develop, exploring them and analysing them. Trying to direct their growth to test the limits of her control.

It was clear that the power of this higher Element, in common with the more familiar Elements, could be used for good or evil. Right there, in the depths of the forest surrounded by what she was quickly learning to call *her* Element, she promised herself to only ever use it for good. That ethos informed all her actions as Queen. There was no reason to change it now, with the discovery of a higher power. Her father taught her that greater power merely conferred greater responsibility. Even so, her philosophical side would not constrain her use of Wood power in an attack, if it should prove necessary during their current troubles.

So far she had not uncovered a combative aspect to this magic. The staff sang its strange woody song to her and told the tale of its natural lambent energy, strong with healing and renewal. Her dear Piper had taught her much about music. What she sensed was not really a song as such, but the wood's story did have different levels. The healing part was its melody, and elements of counterpoint and rhythm were there too. The ability to lift and carry suggested itself, and its affinity with growing things conferred the potential for augmentation and revitalisation.

With these exciting new pathways, thoughts, and capabilities thrumming in her mind, she turned back toward the Palace, intending to seek her Air Mage's counsel regarding Elemental development. She shuddered. How strange! She had spent her whole life in that Palace, calling it home and never questioning it. Now, open to the possibilities of Wood power, returning indoors felt like entering a tomb.

Staff in hand, she arrived at the forest edge once more. The stony path alongside the moat showed new signs of wear from the constant rain. Facing another drenching on the short walk to the Palace gates, the Queen stamped the heel of the staff against the roadway in frustration. A shockwave of Wood power shot through her, competing with the physical jarring sensation from the staff. The sky darkened, turning black within seconds. Enormous rainclouds, leaden and forbidding, rolled across the grey sky, blotting out what little sunlight had broken through. The new clouds added their load to the already heavy rain. It fell now in curtains, cold and sharp on her skin.

A coincidence surely? Even so, all thought of exploring her power further evaporated. The Queen pulled her cloak tightly around her and hurried towards the Palace, hunched against the icy deluge. Before her eyes the river level rose until it breached the bank and flooded the path on which she stood. Within seconds she was wading against the current, the force of water threatening to wash her legs out from under her and carry her off downstream.

the black palace
25th day of run'sanamasa, 966

The great gates of the Black Palace stood closed and barred when the Queen fought her way back to stand before them. She rapped on the smooth dark surface with her staff.

'Ho there! Open these gates. Your Queen requires admittance!'

With embarrassed haste and grovelling apologies the guardsmen complied. They had been busy sandbagging the threshold, trying to stem the wash from the path outside. As the Queen entered, a sluggish wave of muddy water followed her before the guards could close and rebag the gap.

Inside the Palace the huge hallway thronged with

townsfolk, forced to seek refuge. Many of their homes had been swept away, others flooded to the rooftops. The Queen moved among them, listening to their stories, offering a word of encouragement, dry clothes, and hot food. Elaine, Claire, and Kyle came over to join her in the centre of the courtyard. She shrugged off their gaggle of questions and concerns regarding her overnight absence from the Palace. There were more pressing matters to attend to.

'Is there nothing you can do, young lady?' she asked, addressing Kyle directly.

The unseasoned mage had a sickly pallor, which darkened at her words. She flicked a lock of black hair off her face, avoiding the Queen's gaze.

'I have tried your Majesty,' she replied, her voice almost drowned by the noise of the crowd. 'Once. But Douglas sensed what I was doing in an instant.' She glanced up and down the hallway. 'This all started as a result. He has a wicked temper.'

'This, and Kyle in a dead faint,' added Claire, 'from which she is not yet fully recovered.'

'There must be more to it than that,' Elaine said. 'It was bad enough last night when we found Kyle passed out in the courtyard, but today's deluge is ten times worse. Someone else has pissed him off even more than you did Kyle.'

The Queen inclined her head toward the young Water mage. 'My apologies Kyle, I should not have been so hasty with my words. I know how it feels to be new to your powers. I myself had a bad scare out there on the road. The river almost washed me away. We are lucky so many of the townsfolk made it safely here, but surely some will still be trapped out there, or worse?

'Perhaps,' she continued, 'if you will allow it, I can help with your fatigue?'

She tightened her grip on the staff, raised it, and closed her eyes. To the others' obvious surprise, a faint electric blue light began to glimmer around the edges of the wood. Within moments, Kyle's pallor diminished. The beginnings of a rosy glow blossomed in her cheeks. The tension left her shoulders and she relaxed, smiling.

'Wow! I feel like I slept for a week and woke up on a bed of eiderdown.'

'Well, I don't know what eiderdown is,' said the Queen, 'but I'm pleased you are feeling better.'

Kyle bowed. 'Thank you, your Majesty.'

'That was most impressive your Majesty,' Elaine said. 'I could use some myself, though I caught a little benefit from the backwash.'

'As did I,' said Claire. 'Whatever you have been up to since yesterday, ma'am, you have made remarkable progress!'

The Queen regarded her staff. 'This has helped. It is almost like having the forest by my side, and drawing on its healing powers. I hope it will be of some help to you all in the coming battle.'

Kyle blanched once again. 'I know I have to confront Douglas. I won't pretend the prospect doesn't scare me witless. I may need a constant supply of your curative balm ma'am, to get me through it.'

'We must all work together,' the Queen said, thumping her staff on the slate floor. 'It will take nothing less than our combined efforts, I am sure, to defeat this scourge. And on that subject,' she added, 'where are Lautan and Petani?'

court of the blood king
25th day of run'sanamasa, 966

It had been a long day, amusing and interesting in parts, but mainly tedious in the extreme. Government business was not for him. The meeting had dragged on until the early part of the evening. Apart from the single highlight of Douglas Muir's childish outburst, it had been a series of interminable debates on the minutiae of government. The increasing side-effects of the boy's rains; the mobilisation of more forces to something called "the Valley"; and so on and so on until Piers had felt his eyelids drooping. The monotonous drone of Tepak Alempin's voice reached him from the distant end of a long, echoing tunnel.

When the chance presented itself, he made his escape, bolted down a hurried meal, and retired to his chambers. He disliked going to bed right after dinner. In future he would be sure to leave those dreadful meetings in time to eat, whether business was concluded or not. He had barely crawled into bed when someone hammered on his door.

'Tremaine? Tremaine! Open up!'

The Jester's voice was unmistakable. What the hell did he want now? Had he not had his pound of flesh from Piers today already? He crossed the room and opened the door.

'What can I do for you Jeruk?' he asked, in the most diplomatic tones he could muster.

'We need your help. Urgently. Come on, man! Get dressed. You can't go outside in your nightclothes!'

'Outside?'

'Come on!'

Piers threw on a jerkin and a pair of breeches, grabbed a cloak from the back of his door and joined the Jester in the hallway.

'What's all this about? What kind of help do you need from me?'

'Stone help,' said the Jester. A deep frown creased his forehead and made his already prominent nose stand out even more. 'You'll see. Come on!'

The little man hurried off towards the main hall. Piers followed. There was nothing to be gained by further questions until the nature of the problem became clearer.

'It's Muir's damned rains,' the Jester said as they reached the bottom of the staircase. 'They're flooding the

Court!'

He pointed. A superfluous gesture; under the flickering light of many torches Piers could see the entire hallway lay underwater. As he watched, the flood rose to lap over the riser of the third stair.

'Do something!' the Jester cried. 'Before we all drown!'

'What did you have in mind?' Piers asked, trying not to laugh. There was a delicious irony in all this. It had after all been the Jester's idea to bring the Muirs here in the first place.

'Damn it man! You're a Stone Mage aren't you? This is all coming from the moat. Raise a barrier, or something. Quickly!'

Piers sighed. He had not paid much attention to the Court's architecture on his arrival. He had no idea how the moat was constructed or even where it was exactly. He could have used Lautan's help, but the Water Wizard had taken great pains to ensure the Jester remained unaware of his presence.

'I'll have to go outside. I can't do anything from here. Fetch the Keeper.'

'The Keeper? What use will that old goat be? He's not adept with stone too, is he?'

'Just fetch him,' Piers said, entering the water. 'I may need his ministrations when I'm done.'

The Jester started to argue but fell silent under Piers' stern gaze. He ascended the stairs while Piers waded towards the door. Outside the rain continued to fall, as always. Fiercer now: he could almost feel Muir's anger in every drop. Perhaps it had not been such a good idea to annoy the hot-headed young man after all. It seemed Piers could not stay out of trouble for long in this world.

When his foot hit the moat border, the water was up to his chest. The icy chill had already seeped into his flesh, sending shivers through him. Best get this done. Hypothermia could not be far behind, and his concentration would fail long before that, making his power inaccessible. He reached out with his mind, feeling the outline of the stones. He could sense their size and weight, and the type of rock they had been cut from. He was familiar with it. Much the same stone as he had often used for his sculptures. He could use a similar approach here.

Under his influence the stones began to swell and stretch. Careful not to thin them to the point of breaking under the weight of water, he raised a strong but narrow barrier. There was little material to work with. He could not bring the foundations of the wall into the mix without undermining the structure altogether. If it collapsed back into the depths they would be lost beyond redemption.

Slowly, the wall of stone rose to breach the rain-dappled surface of the flood. How much higher dare he raise it? The rains continued. They would likely worsen until Muir was stopped. Perhaps he could do something about that on his return to the main building. For now, he would have to make his best guess. Piers stopped the wall perhaps fifteen centimetres above the water level. At the rate it was rising that should give them time enough to deal with Muir.

The water drained from his improvised flood defence as Piers made his way back to the gate. He too felt drained. The blackness of the night flooded into his mind, dimming his sight and turning sounds to strange remote echoes. Using his power in earnest was a completely different thing from using it to craft—what had Muir called them?—knick-knacks. He had gone beyond himself. As he strode out of the shallows onto the stony path, he staggered and fell to his knees. He shivered uncontrollably. The gate in front of him dissolved behind encroaching darkness. Dimly, as if from the bottom of a fathomless pit, he heard the Keeper's voice calling to him.

'Piers! Piers! Are you alright? Let's get you inside.'

court of the blood king
25th day of run'sanamasa, 966

'Lautan! Wake up!'

The Keeper's hissed imperatives filtered through his sleepy mind. He rubbed his eyes. 'Wha...? What's this? What do you want?'

'You must come,' the Keeper replied. 'Piers needs our help.'

He snapped awake at the words, the fog of sleep dissipating instantly. He levered himself out of the tiny cot. His breath clouded the chill air of old man's quarters.

'What is it? What has befallen him?'

'Easier to see for yourself. I have had him taken to his chambers, and persuaded the Jester to leave him in my care. He thinks I am down here searching for a remedy.'

The two men hurried through the catacombs, climbing the cobwebbed wooden stairs that would bring them up closest to Tremaine's suite. At the sight of the young man's pallid face, Lautan gasped.

'What is wrong with him?' he repeated. 'What has happened?'

The Keeper gave the Water Wizard a brief recap of the night's events.

'I believe his Elemental exertions have exhausted him,' the Keeper concluded. 'I have no remedy or medical aid for that here.'

'I too am unaware of any treatment,' Lautan said, feeling his spirits fall at yet another dilemma he was powerless to prevent. 'Beyond rest, warmth, and sustenance.'

'I think the time has come to remove him from the malign influences here,' the Keeper said. 'His feud with Douglas Muir is only fuelling our troubles, and the Jester will continue to demand more from him until there is nothing left.'

Piers' eyes fluttered open. He reached out a hand for Lautan.

'Claire,' he whispered. 'Said... I would follow.'

His head fell back onto the pillow once more.

Lautan's gaze flicked between Tremaine and the Keeper. 'That is good. They will be expecting us at the Palace.'

Whatever counter-attack could be mounted against Muir would be more successful with all the Elementals working in concert. They must brave the open road once more.

'You have the right of it,' Lautan said. 'I must convey him to the Palace. We have done all we can here. Whatever intelligence he has gathered will have to suffice. We cannot risk staying any longer. Though how he will undertake the journey I do not know.'

'I am sure this is exhaustion only,' the Keeper repeated. 'He will recover with rest if he avoids using his power for a time. As long as you can keep him warm and make sure he has enough water.'

'Finally, something that is within my power,' Lautan said with a wry smile. 'But how will he ride? He cannot sit in a saddle as he is!'

'Follow me. The head ostler is a close friend. He will have a solution.'

Lautan hefted Tremaine's unconscious body over his shoulder and followed the Keeper back down the deserted staircase. The old man took the lead, plucking a torch from its sconce. He ducked onto another stairway, its opening hidden behind racks of parchment. Sweeping away ancient cobwebs with the burning brand, he chose their direction at each junction without hesitation.

'These passages were built by the old King. Mind your head here, they are very low in places. Their existence has long been forgotten by anyone who does not spend their days poring over the archives.'

Lautan's back ached from the effort of carrying Tremaine, and bending double to avoid cracking the young stone mage's head against the uneven roof. At one point they had to carry him between them, crouching under an overhang of rock. Moments later the passage began to climb. Lautan was astonished when they exited the obscure tunnel into the back of the stable block.

'Kepka Tuala!' called the Keeper. 'Are you here?'

'What's this?' said a sleepy voice from a hay-filled cot set against the wall. 'Pelaran? What are you doing here at this time of night?'

'We need your help old friend,' the Keeper said. 'These good people must leave Court tonight, on your fastest kudo. And your most reliable,' he added. 'As you can see, the Stone mage is unwell. He cannot ride unaided.'

'I have just the thing,' the ostler said, all trace of drowsiness gone in the face of his friend's need. 'It will take me a few moments to fit it to Jiwambu. She is the most placid of my animals here, but also the most able. Your friend will be safe on her back.'

Lautan set Tremaine in a hay stall. The stone mage did not stir. Dark circles surrounded his eyes. His pallor had worsened; dark veins clearly visible through his skin. Lautan removed a wisp of cobweb from his face, and sat beside him to share the warmth of his body.

The ostler was as good as his word. The assortment of leather straps, buckles, and harnesses he produced looked complicated, but he assured Lautan its use was straightforward.

'Slip his legs through here,' he said, executing the instructions as he uttered them, 'and strap this part to the saddle.'

Between them, the three men lifted Tremaine into the saddle. The animal stood perfectly still, as if understanding what was required of her. The ostler fastened the strap he had indicated to an attachment point on the pommel, and pulled it taught. He had already fitted the contraption's specially adapted jerkin to Tremaine's legs. Its upper half wrapped around his chest and could be fastened to the reins to prevent the rider slipping sideways.

'There,' said the ostler, stepping back and casting an experienced eye over the entire rig. 'You can set a good pace with him belted in like that. You understand how to get him off, and back on again when necessary?'

'I do, thank you Kepka Tuala', said Lautan. 'You have been most kind.'

'You must leave,' said the Keeper. 'The Jester may return to Tremaine's room at any moment. If he discovers him gone, he will alert the guards.'

Lautan clasped the Keeper's withered hand. 'Then this is farewell. We will do our best to counter Muir's magic. Anything you can do to help from here would be most welcome.'

'I will attempt to bring the Jester to his senses,' the Keeper assured him, 'though any move against young Muir will likely only inflame the situation.'

Lautan nodded. There was no more to be said. He swung himself onto his own kudo, took Jiwambu's traces in his other hand, and rode out into the torrential rains.

Chapter 22

Dawn broke the next day with a sickly grey cast. At her window, Kyle Muir looked out on the drowned landscape with a hollow feeling in the pit of her stomach. In the face of the Elementals' best efforts, water levels continued to rise under the unremitting rainfall. Working with Elaine in a kind of journeyman's equivalent to the double act the Fire Witch had with Lautan, they had attempted to "divert and boil" the floodwaters until darkness fell, with no noticeable effect. Douglas must have been awake late, his anger still driving the extreme rains almost until midnight. Had it not been for the Queen's healing energies, the floods would have been even worse. When the deluge finally abated to a heavy drizzle, the ground floor of the Black Palace was underwater. Food supplies had been moved out of harm's way, courtiers and servants alike offering space in their rooms, doubling up with beds and finding spare bedding for couches and armchairs, in an effort to house several hundred refugee villagers. The stream of bedraggled humanity had continued to flow into the Palace well after dark, almost as fast as the water itself.

Douglas would soon be awake again and the heavier rains would resume. Another day and the Palace would be submerged altogether. Gathering her resolve, Kyle dressed and knocked on Claire's door. Her knock was answered immediately.

'You're up too,' the Air Mage smiled as the door opened.

'I have to try again,' Kyle said. 'Have you seen it out there? We can't afford to wait any longer.'

'You're not strong enough! It's barely more than a day since your first attempt. That almost killed you.'

'I know, but we won't solve this problem by acting on

417

the effect of my brother's magic. I have to stop it at the source. I have to stop *him*.'

'How?'

Kyle sat heavily on the edge of Claire's rumpled bed. 'I don't know. Not exactly. But I feel like I have more control over the power now. Working with you and Elaine yesterday, well, it kind of rubbed off on me, you know? Made me stronger, somehow.' She shrugged. 'I can't explain it. But I know I have to try. And it has to be today.'

Her friend did not reply at first. She looked at Kyle with a mixture of concern and pride, before walking over to her window and gazing out at the devastation they had failed to prevent the day before.

'We will need the Queen,' Claire said, still staring at the drowned landscape.

Relieved that Claire seemed now to be on-side with the idea, Kyle joined her at the window. 'Yes,' she said. 'I definitely can't do it without her help.'

'I wish there was something I could do too.'

'You've already done loads,' Kyle replied. 'Will the Queen be up?'

'Maybe not, but she won't mind being woken for this.'

Kyle waited while Claire dressed in a tunic and breeches, an outfit that in its simplicity declared this was a working day. The two Elementals hurried to the Queen's quarters. They found the monarch, too, had risen early.

'Good morning, Claire,' the Queen said, dismissing the royal guard with a wave of her hand, 'and Kyle. This must be important for you to call before I have even taken a bite of breakfast.'

Kyle's spirits fell. 'Oh, your Majesty, I am so sorry. I would never—'

The words died on Kyle's lips as she noticed the Queen was smiling, a wicked glint in her eye.

'It's never too early to receive my Elementals, dear, but I cannot resist a little joke. What can I do for you?'

Claire explained Kyle's intentions, and her need of the

Queen's healing Wood powers. Without a moment's hesitation the Queen took up her staff from where it rested beside her bed.

'I am ready,' she announced. 'When do you mean to start?'

'Now is as good a time as any ma'am,' Kyle said. 'I had hoped to begin before Douglas wakes. I believe,' she added, glancing out at the continuing drizzle, 'we are still in time.'

'Very well,' said the Queen. 'Where would you like to undertake this task?'

Kyle thought for a moment. She would have preferred to be away from the Palace, but since the floodwaters surrounding them were several metres deep, that was impossible.

'Somewhere outside,' she said, 'where I can better sense the effect I am having. Your balcony, perhaps your Majesty, if you wouldn't mind?'

'Of course,' said the Queen. 'I will remain inside. I would prefer not to be drenched again if it can be avoided. I can send you my help just as well from in here. Whenever you are ready, my dear.'

Even though Claire was a friend and the Queen a staunch ally, Kyle still felt the pressure of their stares as they waited for her to make a move. This was it. Possibly her last, best chance to stop her brother. It still felt wrong—no, not wrong. Strange—opposing him, but she knew she was on the right side. Whatever past injustices or recent slights had taken root in his imagination and driven him to bring down this blight on his new world, nothing could justify the devastation he had caused in such a short time. Suppressing a yammering cry of fear that welled up inside her, Kyle stepped out onto the Queen's balcony.

Below, the atrium where she had so recently made her first faltering attempts with Water stood empty. The echoes of the earliest few fat raindrops of the day carried up to her from the flagged floor. Douglas was waking. She had no time to lose. Focusing her attention to the core of her power, Kyle reached out. She sensed her brother's influence with frightening clarity. After the days spent working with her Elemental friends, she felt she understood his strength. It was pervasive, covering every part of the land, but she could feel it becoming stronger as her thoughts turned toward the Court. If the best she could do was to constrain his effect there, then at least Kertonia would be free. She wanted to do more. The Istanian people were every bit as vulnerable to his power as the Queen's subjects. Every bit as deserving of saving and restitution. But she could only do what she could do.

Slowly at first but with increasing confidence, Kyle raised up her own Elemental strength, felt it flowing through her like a torrent of ice-blue water. Putting all thought of failure from her mind, she sent out her power across the land.

everywhere
26th day of run'sanamasa, 966

Kyle Muir's Water influence surged out over the drowned fields and villages from where she stood in the Black Palace. Concentric circles of power spread like ripples on a gigantic pond, invisible to normal eyes. Above the black granite edifice, the rain stopped instantly. Unlike her earliest faltering attempt to make a shield for her practice atrium, this was a permanent cessation. It affected the Palace itself, the grounds, moat, river, and three local hamlets. For the first time in almost a month, no rain fell. Charcoal clouds rolled back, revealing a crystal clear sky set with the burning jewel of the Berikatanyan sun, spreading its warmth and light unimpeded as it had not done since the Muirs' arrival. As it rose, gaining in strength, the ground began to steam.

Farther away the overnight drizzle, which would ordinarily have turned to rain under the control of

Douglas' waking mind, instead became a dense mist, rolling and boiling once the sun's warmth began to heat the air. Without constant replenishment from the unnatural rains, floodwaters abated. Treetops appeared, followed by shrubs and the roofs of the tallest houses. Before long lower-lying ground emerged, adding its steam to that from the higher places. The landscape resembled a post-apocalyptic wasteland covered in an unearthly fog, sidling away from the light of the sun like the grey memory of an ancient vampire.

On the road from the Blood Court, Lautan rode his kudo out through the edge of the rain and into the morning sun. Behind him, strapped to the saddle on Jiwambu, Piers Tremaine remained unconscious, though a hint of a smile played over his lips as the sunlight struck his face. Lautan reined the animals to a halt and looked back. The curtain of rain receded rapidly in the direction from which they had come, as if drawn by an invisible hand. His Water sense told him this was Kyle's doing yet, as with her brother, he could not discern how she was doing it. No matter how, the fact of it gave him renewed hope. He spun his kudo toward the Palace and kicked the animal into a fast gallop over the drying roadway. Snickering at the sight of the sun, Jiwambu matched his pace effortlessly.

At the Forest Clearance Project, Petani stepped from his ahmek into a rain-free morning. He gazed at the sky, wondering at this change in fortune. Ignoring Umtanesh's invitation to break his fast, he set to work rebuilding his seed beds and plantations, whistling as he toiled.

Across the whole of Kertonia, and a large swathe of Istania, local people emerged from whatever shelter they had found, giving praise to whichever of the four Gods they worshipped. Some had been trapped for days in the upper storeys of their dwelling places, worried about how they and their animals would survive. Others had abandoned their homes altogether, finding sanctuary in caves or byres built on higher ground. Sharing a space with a few saptak, though not something they would have done from choice, was infinitely preferable to being stuck indoors with no food or potable water, or drowning in the flash floods that had beleaguered the land since the start of the rains. Now, slowly, they picked up the threads of their lives once more.

At the Blood Court, the rains still fell. Not as strong as they had been at the height of Douglas Muir's ire the previous day, but still heavy enough to maintain the level of flooding around the red stone building. Lying in his bed, the self-styled Water Wizard tried to free his mind from the dreams which had infested his sleep during the night. Even fully awake, his room felt out of kilter. Something was not quite right and he could not put his finger on it. If he had to define it, he would have called it mental indigestion. He threw back the covers and walked over to the window. The view over the Court's basilica and beyond toward the dark forest of Alaakaya resolved his conundrum.

With the speed of long practice, Muir sent up his Water sense. Moments later, he froze, a sneer of disgust creasing his face. The feeling of another's influence in the Element was unmistakable.

'Bitch,' he said under his breath.

court of the blood king
26th day of run'sanamasa, 966

No doubt about it, that snot-faced little bitch of a sister had finally learned how to manipulate the rain. She had spent her entire life trailing after him like a sad puppy even though she was only a few minutes younger, coming back for more no matter how many times he tricked, kicked, or picked on her. Now she was trying to stop him.

The lesser of them in terms of ability, obviously, and relatively new to it compared with him, her attempts were clumsy and weak. Even so, her efforts at countermanding his power meant his rains would never be as strong as they had been. So what? He had been bored with rain for the past few days anyway. He only kept at it because it was causing grief for the treacherous gnome he had thought was his friend. He would happily have drowned the little fool. Ha! Fool by costume and fool by nature. How the hell did he think he could run a country? Even a flea-bitten little backwater like Istania. The idiot had come knocking the night before, demanding Douglas open his door, stop the rains, help with the floods.

'Why are you doing this?' the buffoon shouted through the wood, as if it was not obvious to anyone with a half-functioning brain. 'I offered you everything, and this is how you repay me? Floods, drownings, and mayhem? Stop it at once! Stop it now, or I will have my guards break down this door and drag you to the tower.'

'Go away,' Douglas had replied. 'Do you think you have yet seen the full extent of my power? Any more threats from you and I will bring down a torrent on your head so deep you will think the present rains are a summer shower. Leave me alone!'

As expected, that had been enough to give the idiot pause. He crawled away and had not been back since. For now, Douglas could keep his door locked. The leavings of last night's meal still littered his table. As usual there was enough to last him three or four days. After that, if he was still here, he would have to think again.

He should never have let Kyle persuade him to come. With her clever word paintings of a new life in a rural idyll, supported by an armful of glossy brochures, it had been an easy sell. The covers sported happy, good-looking frontiersmen and women. A marketeer's mix of ethnicities, energetically cutting down trees, building homes and raising families. It had been Kyle's first original idea in living memory, coming here. Maybe that had thrown him. That, and her infective enthusiasm. Yes, that was exactly it.

It had infected him, like a virus attacking when he was at his lowest ebb. They did not have much, back on Earth. Few friends—OK, one friend—and poor job prospects after finishing their respective college courses. The future looked bleak. Their successful applications for the Dauntless seemed like a lifeline. With hindsight, it looked more like a rope to hang themselves with.

Still, he had his power. An unexpected bonus. Now he had learned to use it, and his fun with the rains had come to an end, what else was it good for? Something greater than anything he had done so far. Something that would make that deformed joker sit up and pay attention. Pay him some respect. The answer came to him like a splash of cold mountain spring water in the face. The sea!

So far he had wielded his power only on rain, rivers, and lakes. Fresh water? Pah! That was for girls. Let his sister work her pathetic magic on it. He would prove himself a master of seawater. With its untold depths and almost limitless volume, nothing was beyond him. He laughed at the Jester's panic when scarcely more than a metre of water flooded his draughty castle. Let's see how he reacts when a few million litres of ocean come rolling over his head!

Douglas sent out his Water sense. He had not seen the ocean since leaving the coast soon after they arrived. Though his sense of direction had never been the best, it did not take him long to find it. Find it, and summon it.

road to the black palace
26th day of run'sanamasa, 966

The Black Palace appeared in the distance as Lautan crested a nearby hill and reined his kudo to a halt. It glinted in the low morning sunlight, the land around it still blanketed with mist rising from the heated wet earth. There had never been a more welcome sight. He was pleased to see the bridge over the Sun Besaraya had been repaired since he set off for Duska Batsirang from the Queen's sanctuary eleven days before. Kyle's efforts at suppressing the rains were most successful this close to home, but the rivers were still dangerously full. After half a day's riding from Court, he did not have the strength to stem the flow of an engorged river to make a crossing.

Behind him, Jiwambu had taken advantage of the pause in their journey to crop some grass at the side of the path. His companion, strapped to the placid kudo's back, had remained unconsciousness the entire journey. Lautan had set the fastest pace he deemed safe, trusting to the instincts of their mounts to slow down if they needed to. They had not stopped, save for two occasions when he had tried to force some water into the Stone mage, to no avail. The young man must by now be badly dehydrated. Putting his worry aside, the Water Wizard set off once again. Their journey was almost done. He prayed to Utan that the Palace medics would be able to help Tremaine.

The kudai flew down the incline towards the bridge. Lautan felt Kyle's influence all around him, suffusing the atmosphere with suppressive Water power, holding back the clouds. Confusingly, he could not detect any opposing Elemental force. If the Muir boy still wielded his power to maintain the unnatural rains, it would have been obvious. After these many days of failing to counter it, Lautan had become sensitised enough to recognise the unique flavour of Muir's power. Now, it was gone. Even if Kyle let her influence drop, there would be no further rain. It was a puzzle.

They crossed the bridge. The river, though fast-flowing and muddy, and still carrying detritus washed from upstream, was no longer foaming and roiling. The risk of a breach of its banks had receded. All along the riverbank on both sides, pools and puddles had formed as the floodwaters drained back into the Besaraya. Though it would take many days for the land to return to normal, progress had already been rapid.

On the final stretch, with the Palace gates visible through the mist, Lautan sat bolt upright in his saddle, gripping the reins until his knuckles showed white. A new Water influence washed over his mind, bringing with it a thrill of fear and dread. Though the kudai were already at a gallop, he spurred them on with a shout and an urgent kick to the flanks. The danger had not passed. He had been a fool to believe it. Muir had turned his attention to a new toy. One that could spell disaster for the whole of Berikatanya.

the black palace
26th day of run'sanamasa, 966

Claire Yamani stood in the basilica of the Black Palace currying her kudo Pembwana, the morning sun already warm on her back. Such a normal thing for her to do, yet it felt rare. Today was the first day since the beginning of the month that the rain had stopped. Her heart swelled with pride at the thought it was her young apprentice who had brought this about, early this very morning. Was apprentice the right word? They worked with different Elements but Kyle Muir still looked on Claire as her mentor. Pupil, then? Not that it mattered. They were more friends now than pupil and master. Mistress. Whatever. There was nothing like combing out the knots in your kudo's coat to make the mind wander!

Claire moved around to Pembwana's other flank as another kudo barrelled into the basilica. It was Lautan! And he had a second rider in tow. Disturbed by the commotion the Palace ostler emerged from the stables. A deep frown creased his face as he strode over to remonstrate with the Water Wizard.

'What's this?' he said, taking hold of reins. 'Get down off this poor animal at once, man! Can't you see she's almost dead with fatigue?'

The kudo did indeed look spent. Flecks of white foam

covered her coat and raucous panting wracked her entire body. Her legs shivered as she stood there. Lautan dismounted.

'My apologies Kepka Lemda. My need was imperative. Please take the best care of her. She has brought me here in the nick of time.'

He turned to Claire. 'Sakti, it is good to see you again. Tremaine needs urgent medical attention, and once that is done we must meet directly. It may seem as though the danger is past, but in truth the worst is yet to come.'

The old Wizard's words sent a thrill of fear through Claire. She suppressed it. The Elementals had faced peril before. Whatever came their way now they would face it again, and be every bit as successful as they had been in the past.

'I will fetch the Queen,' she said, ignoring the puzzled expression that flitted across Lautan's face.

The Queen took no persuading, on hearing her assistance was required. When they returned, Lautan had unstrapped Piers from his saddle.

'It took three to hoist him into this saddle,' the old Elemental said, 'but I think two of us could get him down, if you will assist me Sakti?'

'Of course,' Claire replied, stepping to the other side of Tremaine's mount.

They lifted him with surprising ease. He weighed almost nothing.

'What happened?' Claire asked.

'He exhausted himself raising the moat wall around the Blood Court to hold off the floods,' Lautan replied. 'While standing chest-deep in the icy waters. I believe it was the largest stone work he had ever attempted, and in such conditions! It was a notable effort.'

'Set him here, in the shade,' the Queen said. 'Claire, would you fetch some water from the stables?'

She gripped her staff more firmly and closed her eyes. When Claire returned with a small bowl of water, a fine blue light had appeared from the staff, tracing the lines of its grain pattern and pulsating with lambent energy. Lautan's face was a picture of astonishment.

'What is this?' he whispered. 'The Queen? With a staff of power?'

Claire filled him in briefly with events at the Palace in his absence.

'Utan's beard!' he said once she had concluded her tale. 'The Stone Mage and the Wood Mage together for the first time! And just *in* time,' he added. 'What we face now will take all our combined efforts to overcome.'

Piers Tremaine opened his eyes, looking fearfully from face to face. 'Mmph,' he said, as his gaze fell on the water bowl in Claire's hand.

She knelt beside him and held the bowl to his lips while he took a few gulps.

'Not too much at once my dear,' the Queen said, placing a hand on Claire's wrist. 'Let him breathe.'

'I'm alright,' Piers said. 'I mean, I feel better. Much better now. Hungry though.'

Lautan chuckled. 'I'm not surprised. It is almost a full day since you ate anything. Let us take you inside. We have important matters to discuss. Where are Bakara and the others?'

'Patrick has not changed his mind,' Claire replied. 'He has stayed at Pennatanah. We've had no word from Petani. He must still be labouring in the Forest. But Bakara and Kyle Muir are here. I will fetch them. And Jann.'

'The Gatekeeper is returned?' Lautan asked, his eyes wide. 'That is welcome news indeed. We will certainly have need of him. Go, Sakti. Bring them. Let us meet in the refectory, where Tremaine can take sustenance.'

'The refectory is too public,' the Queen said, tapping her staff on the flagstones. 'I don't suppose the news you bring is good, Lautan?'

The Elemental shook his head silently.

'In which case we should discuss it in private. Take

Tremaine to my chambers. I will have food brought up, and I shall stop by the Witch's rooms on my way. Claire, if you will find your young protege and Jann Argent?'

'I will your Majesty. I know where they will be.'

'Splendid. Let us make haste then. It sounds like there is not a moment to be lost.'

the black palace
26th day of run'sanamasa, 966

Lautan remained standing as the others filed into the Black Queen's chambers. He had sat Tremaine in a comfortable chair by the fireplace. When Sakti Udara entered, she filled a plate for him and pulled over a straight-backed chair to sit beside him and help with his food and drink. The girl was a wonderful role model and an excellent Elemental. She had grown immeasurably since he first met her, in both power and maturity. It was clear the Muir girl thought highly of her too. Her face positively glowed with adoration whenever she looked in Sakti's direction. She smiled and bowed slightly at Lautan before taking the window seat and gazing out at the sunlit morning. The restored brightness of the day was a result of the girl's powers, he reminded himself. He should take a moment to congratulate her personally once this brief conference was ended.

Bakara had arrived with the Queen, eschewing any victuals and taking one end of the longest, plushest sofa in the room. She made no comment. The Fire Witch's patience was thin at the best of times but she was making a good effort to keep it in check. Ordinarily she would have demanded he explain himself upon seeing him. Perhaps the presence of the Queen was having a dampening effect on her acerbity.

The Gatekeeper was the last to join them. Sakti offered no explanation when she had arrived alone, neither did he mention it. Bakara patted the cushion beside her and he took the seat without comment.

'Well, Lautan,' the Queen said, 'what news?'

'Two things, Majesty,' he replied, after a moment's gathering of his thoughts. 'Firstly, Kyle's success with her Water powers reached as far as Besakaya. A most impressive accomplishment, young lady. Rarely has such power been wielded by one so young, and so new to the Element. I am sure in time you will exceed even your brother's mastery of Water.'

Kyle blushed deep red to the roots of her long black hair. She smiled, and inclined her head politely in his direction, but said nothing. Diplomacy as well as power. Clever girl.

'This was a great success, yes,' Lautan continued, 'and it has had a beneficial side-effect which I shall return to later. But it has also led directly to my second subject: the deadly peril that now confronts us. Faced with his sister's confrontation, the Muir boy has abandoned his efforts with the rain. Though Kyle's influence did not reach Court, I sense the rains have stopped there too, since he is no longer creating them.'

'What is he doing, then?' the Gatekeeper asked, his clouded expression every bit as dark as the thunderheads that had blotted the skies until this morning.

'He has turned his attention to the ocean,' Lautan said, the words renewing his own trepidation as he uttered them. 'He is raising a tsunami.'

Kyle's face turned white even as she nodded. It was clear she too had felt the change in her brother's power, though possible she could not explain or interpret it. Claire and the Queen let out a horrified gasp in unison. Piers Tremaine leaned forward, his knuckles white on the arm of his chair.

'What can we do?' he asked, his voice faint but steady. 'What can *I* do?'

'You can get well!' Sakti replied, placing a hand on his arm and urging him to sit back.

'It sounds like there's no time for that!' Piers replied. He looked straight into Lautan's eyes. 'Am I right?'

'Yes,' he replied. 'Even now Douglas Muir is raising the tides, though he is still at Court. We still have time to beat him to the coast.'

'The coast?' the Queen said. 'If he can raise a wave from where he is, can you not stop him from here?'

Lautan felt his eyes pricking with embarrassment, thoughts of his previous failures welling up behind them. 'He is powerful, Majesty, as you have seen, but he is not yet as skilled with salt water as I. It is my preferred medium. As you know, I even live there when I can. With Kyle's help, it is possible I could attenuate the effect he is causing.'

'Well, then–' the Queen began.

'But,' Lautan continued, 'it is unlikely he will stay where he is. Once he divines how close the ocean is—and it surely will not take him long—he will go there. The effect of his power in such close proximity to such a vast volume of his Element will multiply the effect manyfold. We must go. And we must leave now,' he added. 'If we can arrive before him, we stand a chance of stopping him.'

'Where, exactly?' asked the Queen.

'Utperi'Tuk is the closest point of the coast to the Blood Court,' Elaine said. 'Where I went to summon you Lautan, before the battle of the Clone Rout.'

'That is correct, Bakara,' he said. 'Utperi'Tuk is our destination.'

'It is more than a day's ride,' the Queen said. 'Can we be there in time?'

'We, Majesty?' Lautan replied, before he had stopped to think what he was saying. 'Will you be gracing us with your presence?'

'No Lautan, I will not be gracing you,' she said, standing, placing the heel of her staff on the floor in front of her and drawing herself up to her full height. 'I will be helping you. I am the Kayshirin. The Wood mage. I am one of you, and I shall do my part. Though I am not entirely certain what that part will be. You did not answer my question,' she went on. 'How will we reach the coast in time to stop Muir?'

'Travelling there from here would normally involve a break in the journey overnight. But since haste is imperative, we must eschew comfort and ride hard. It is no more than half a day at a fast gallop. If we leave now, with fresh kudai and no stop, we can be there by midnight.'

'Piers isn't well enough for such a journey,' Claire said, moving to stand beside the Queen.

Tremaine began to protest, but the Queen held up her hand.

'Then there at least is the first answer to what my part will be,' she said. 'With the healing power of my staff I will ensure all of us arrive fresh and ready for whatever the night may bring. I have not been on a midnight adventure since I was a girl. When do we leave?'

The machinery of the Palace swung into action at the Queen's command. Provisions were readied and packed into saddle bags. The stable team selected their six strongest, fittest, and swiftest kudai, and saddled them for speed. Lautan expected the Queen to complain that her own kudo Pembrang was not among them, but like a true leader—and a true Elemental, he had to add—she said nothing. A good general did not question the decisions of their team.

Claire and Kyle joined Lautan in the basilica while the stablemen were saddling their animals.

'What was the side-effect?' Kyle asked him.

'Forgive me, young lady. What?'

'When we were in the Queen's chambers you were talking about my success against Douglas. You said it had a beneficial side-effect and you'd tell us about it later, but you never did.'

'Ah yes.' Lautan thought for a moment. 'Imagine a water channel,' he said, 'full of water, flowing freely. And then something happens to connect a larger channel to the side. It could be a pipe, that has a larger bore pipe spliced onto it. Or a river, where the bank collapses and opens up a larger channel. Most of the water would divert into that larger channel, leaving the smaller to run dry. Or almost dry,' he added after a pause. 'That was me. The smaller channel.'

'And Douglas was the larger.'

'Exactly. Once I realised what was happening, I could do something about it. I have been managing water flows in one way or another, my whole life.'

Shortly after mid-morning all the preparations were complete. Under the cool, bright, Sanamasan sun, the team of six mounted up.

'Lead on, your Majesty,' Lautan said.

The Queen stared at him, a half-smile on her face, the late morning sun striking blue highlights in her long black hair that at first he took for flashes of Wood power.

'You must stop thinking of me as your Queen, Lautan,' she said. 'I am an Elemental now, and we have more need of haste and power than we do of airs and graces. Since we are going into battle at your behest, against an adversary skilled in your Element, *you* lead on.'

Without further comment, Lautan turned his kudo and led the troupe out through the Palace gates.

Chapter 23

Kyle could not believe the change in the Queen. They had been riding all afternoon and evening without a break. If she had expected anyone to call time on the ride, it would have been her. Dressed all in black leather and riding an unfamiliar kudo, even though this one was just as deep a shade of black as the Queen's favourite mount Pembrang, she looked every bit the warrior Queen. Warrior Elemental, she corrected herself. But there was more to it than simply turning her back on pomp and comfort. She had thrown herself into the role with unmistakable fervour. Almost as if she had been preparing for it all her life, while only pretending to be Queen.

From what she'd learned in conversation with Claire, perhaps that was the truth after all. The Queen was a Wood mage, cocooned in a Palace of stone, who had now metamorphosed into a powerful and terrifying butterfly.

Under the light of the twin moons, Kyle could see the outline of a large forest squatting at the foot of the mountains to their left. When they reached a fork in the road, the Fire Witch reined her kudo to a halt.

'What is it, Bakara?' Lautan asked, turning his own steed around to stop next to her. 'We must press on. We are more than halfway there.'

The Witch pointed to the left-hand fork. 'This is the road to Besakaya,' she said, slightly out of breath. 'Petani is close by. I should go for him. It will not take long. We will have need of his power at the coast.'

The other riders gathered around them, their mounts' laboured breath steaming in the silvery moonlight. Lautan did not hesitate.

'It is a wise suggestion Bakara,' he said. 'Go ahead. We will continue to Utperi'Tuk. Join us there when you can.'

434

He spun his kudo round again and rode off without another word, the others falling in behind him on the moonlit path. Glancing behind her, Kyle saw that the Fire Witch and her mount had already disappeared against the blackness of the great forest.

The last of the journey passed in silence, their pace too fast for conversation. An experienced rider, Kyle held her reins loosely against the pommel of her saddle. She could feel the strength and confidence in the animal, and did not want to give it distracting signals. She had little fear of falling, trusting her mount, but the road was dark, heavily potholed after the rains, and the animal was tiring rapidly. She did not truly relax until they arrived at the coast. As they approached the cliff tops, the ocean came into view, heaving and rolling like a bathful of quicksilver in the moonlight. Lautan slowed the troupe to a trot before stopping at a crossroads where the path split into three.

'The first path leads to a ledge on the face of the cliff,' he said. 'Its location is ideal, but it is too narrow for us all to work in harmony. I believe we would be better placed atop the cliff itself. There at least, if we are not successful, we may have time to take shelter from the wave.'

There was no dissent. As far as Kyle knew only the Fire Witch, of their present company, had visited this place before. They were content to follow Lautan's lead. At the end of the path, it gave way to tussocks of grass and sedge, and bare rock. Dismounting from her kudo, Kyle walked to the cliff edge. They had ridden to the south side of a small asymmetric bay. On the opposite side another cliff top, smaller in length but slightly taller than the one on which they stood, reflected the sound of booming waves from the cove below. A large section of its seaward edge had broken away and fallen into the water. It caught the incoming swell, sending up powerful plumes of foam which broke against the bluff, painting it dull silver under the waning moonlight. Kyle looked out at the rolling ocean. A gasp of horror came unbidden from her throat.

'Oh, my God,' she said. 'Is that...?'

In the distance, close to the contour of the horizon, stars winked out in a straight line running parallel to the coast. Illuminated by the low moons as they slipped slowly toward setting, a wall of water rose from the surface. She could not tell how tall it was already, but it was growing taller by the moment.

'Yes,' said Lautan, 'that is the wave. We do not have much time. Kyle, I will need your assistance. The swell has its own momentum that we cannot countermand, but the volume is another matter. We may still be able to attenuate it.

'Gatekeeper! If there is aught you can do to divert any of the wave, that would be most helpful.'

'I will search for a gate,' Argent replied, scowling, 'though it is unlikely I shall find one.'

'Ru'ita,' Lautan continued, turning his attention to the Queen. Kyle was impressed. He had taken her at her word and was no longer addressing her as "your Majesty." This was only the second time Kyle had heard the Queen's given name.

The Queen approached, having led her kudo to a fresh patch of grass.

'How may I be of help Lautan?' she asked.

'You are essential to us,' Lautan replied. 'This will require sustained effort at the highest level by Kyle and myself.' He turned to Kyle. 'It will be the hardest thing you have yet attempted young lady,' he said. 'I can say that with some authority, as it will also be the hardest thing I have yet attempted. Ru'ita, we will need a constant supply of healing energy. Whatever you can do to buoy us up will be most welcome.'

'I shall do my utmost,' the Queen replied.

A blue light sprang from her staff, outlining the shape of the wood. Wisps of cerulean smoke emerged to curl and writhe in the night air.

'There is a task for our Stone mage, also,' Lautan went

on. 'Though I am loathe to ask, since it will require a gargantuan effort.'

'You want a wall,' Tremaine replied.

'You are ahead of me, I see,' Lautan smiled.

'It's obvious,' Tremaine said with a tortured expression. 'If you can't stop the wave then it will overwhelm the land. You need a wall as a backstop.'

'Are you up to the task, Stone mage?' asked Lautan.

'Let's just say you're not the only one taking on something that's the hardest thing they've ever tried.'

Tremaine was grinning, but Kyle could see the dread in his eyes. He must still be weak from his ordeal at the Blood Court. Half a day's hard riding had not helped. As the twin moons rode their orbits toward the top of the opposite cliff, he turned and walked after Jann Argent to the precipice. Lautan took her hand. Together they turned to face the oncoming tsunami.

court of the blood king
27th day of run'sanamasa, 966

He exulted.

Wielding power over fresh water had been fun. Compared to sea water though, well, there *was* no comparison. His days of footling around with rain now felt like the first staggering steps of a child learning to walk. Immersing his mind in the almost limitless depths of the ocean was like returning home after a lifetime in the desert.

Douglas Muir stood at his open window, oblivious to anything that went on around him at Court. Below, a constant stream of peasants had been returning to their homes now that the floodwaters were receding. Had he noticed them he would have laughed at the futility of their journeys. Though they did not know it, they would soon be washed back here on a tide of salt water. There had been no further hammering at his door. The threat of even fiercer rains had been enough to keep the yellow dwarf away. Had he overheard the Jester's plans to oust him from his chambers, and from the Court, this too would have been a source of immense amusement. Pretty soon there would be no Court left for him to be ousted from.

None of these mundane matters breached his concentration. Instead, he stretched his Water senses out over the land, coast, and shallows, to the deepest part of the ocean. Bin-segar, they called it. The Wild Sea. The land-locked Istanians had never ventured onto its rolling surface save to catch a few fish in the shallowest waters. Their boats, inasmuch as they deserved the title, were nothing more sophisticated than hollowed out tree trunks. They had never travelled to other lands. Did not even know if there were other lands to travel to. He despised their lack of adventure, of sea-going lore, and of vision. He had spent most of his life living beside the ocean. An accomplished sailor, swimmer, and fisherman, his love of water had clearly foreshadowed his latent Water power. But whatever magic there had ever been on Earth was long spent; only the more prosaic water-based activities had been available to him.

Here though, on his new home planet, the world was quite literally his oyster, though his mental examination of the seas had not yet revealed the presence of anything like an oyster. He flexed his power, revelling in the feel of the brine to his Water sense. Experimenting with its movement and mass, currents and depths, volume and density. He could not have given numbers to these things. Could not even have described them to anyone, except possibly his sister and the old fool she had fetched up with. He had no need of words. Right now he was more interested in deeds. It had taken fully half the time he had spent standing at that window, but at last, after much coaxing and great expenditure of energy, the ocean had started moving to his bidding. Wild Sea? Ha! These fools had no idea how wild it was about to become!

He was tired, but only in the way muscles became tired

after a period of intense exercise. Tired with an associated sense of gratification. Of accomplishment. And he had accomplished. Far out at sea, his wave had begun. Imperceptibly at first, at least above the surface, but with gathering pace and momentum, it grew. Night had long since fallen but Douglas had no need of light either. He had no notion of time. His Water sense brought him all the information he needed. More than he needed. It had begun telling him of another influence. No, two other influences. Damn them! His fucking sister and that meddling old man! They were trying to stop him. Again! Worse, they were succeeding. His wave had not slowed, but it was diminishing.

Douglas came to his senses, as if waking from a dream. His room swam into focus. His skin chilled from the open window, his clothes damp with his own sweat. His legs ached. The power he could bring to bear on the sea was attenuated by distance. If he was to have any chance of achieving his ultimate aim, especially in the face of resistance from his two Elemental adversaries, he must travel to the coast. Grabbing a cloak from his nightstand and unbolting his door, he hurried out into the darkened corridor.

In retrospect he was surprised to find no guard posted there. That idiot Jester could not have poured water from a boot if the instructions were printed on the heel. Douglas ran down the main staircase, across the basilica, and into the stable block. All was in darkness.

'Hello! Hello there! I need a hor– a kudo!' he shouted.

Disturbed by his loud entrance, the animals in the stable shuffled, knocking into each other and snickering with annoyance.

'Where you be going at this time of night?' came a sleepy voice from the back of the building. The head ostler emerged from his pathetic crib, carrying a lantern in one hand and picking straw out of his hair with the other. 'Jester said you wasn't to be allowed a mount anyways. Be off with you. Disturbing the peace after midnight. I had my way you'd be hanged.'

'Yes and if I had my way, you'd be drowned,' Douglas replied, 'and I think you know which one of us is more likely to get their way, hmm?'

'Where you going I asked? None of these here like long night journeys.'

'To the coast. The nearest part to here. Whatever it's called.'

'Utperi'Tuk be the nearest. What you want to do there? Nothing but rocks and foam. Awful place.'

'That's my business. I don't have time to argue about it. Are you going to saddle me a kudo or not?'

'That's a long ride,' said the man, ignoring Douglas' question, 'even at a gallop. Won't be there before dawn. Utperi'Tuk? In the dark? With one of my kudai? I don't think so. Go ahead and drown me. Young fool.'

Douglas raised his hand. The ostler flinched, the light from his lantern dipping and swooping across the walls, floor, and a large table bearing several saddles. His gaze fell on the table. A simple affair constructed from broad planks and rough-hewn tree trunks. He walked over to it and lifted off one of the saddles, stroked a hand across the table's smooth surface.

'Never mind an animal,' he said, upending the table, 'I'll take one of these.'

'Oi! What you doing? Have a care there!' the ostler cried.

The contents of the table spilled onto the floor, saddles rolling in the dust. The old man scrabbled to retrieve them one-handed, his lantern swinging dangerously close to the bales of straw piled against one wall.

'Oi!' he shouted again. 'That's my table!'

Douglas kicked at the table top from behind. Three strong blows were enough to dislodge a plank. He righted the table again and pulled the timber free with both hands.

'Thank you!' he said. 'This will do nicely!'

He ran out into the night, the stableman following him to stand at the door shouting curses. Reaching the moat, Douglas jumped in without hesitation. He held the board beneath him, closed his eyes, and accessed the core of his power. The waters swelled under him, churning and foaming. Concentrating his power to create a familiar pattern, Douglas brought up a series of small waves on the surface of the moat. He paddled a few strokes, and jumped onto the plank. Holding a rolling tide of water under the wood large enough to carry him forward, he set off in the direction of the coast, surfing a wave for the first time since leaving Earth.

utperi'tuk
27th day of run'sanamasa, 966

Kyle allowed herself a moment of self-congratulation. She stood beside Lautan. The Water Wizard's energies thrummed in her mind even as she augmented them with her own. She could feel their effect on the gathering wave. Douglas would be incandescent with fury once he discovered what they were doing. That, too, gave her added incentive. Finally, after a lifetime of believing herself inferior to her not-that-much-older brother, she too had emerged from her cocoon. Like the Black Queen blossoming into a true Wood mage, Kyle had come of age. Comfortable with her power, certain it would continue to grow and develop, she now stood not only physically beside the Water Wizard, but also metaphorically. They were a team.

A successful team, too. Sure, they could not stop the wave entirely. Kyle's Water sense told her that. If they continued as they were, by the time her brother's wave reached the shore it would be only a metre or so larger than a regular breaker. They might be soaked, but they would be in no danger. Maybe they could turn up the volume just a little? She turned to the Queen, intending to ask for more healing energies.

From the corner of her eye, she caught sight of something on the opposite cliff. A spray of water jetted out from the rock, arcing down to the ocean below. Something else tumbled with it. Hard to be sure at this distance, in the dark, but it looked like a large plank of wood! What the hell? Now there was movement on the cliff top. Her Water sense beat her eyes to the figure's identity. Douglas was here!

'Lautan!' she cried, momentarily losing focus on her Water.

'I see him!' the old Wizard replied. 'Do not be distracted Kyle! His presence here gives him vastly more control over the ocean. We must redouble our efforts.'

Douglas stood at the extreme edge of the rock, his arms held wide as if embracing the ocean. Faintly, above the noise of the regular waves crashing against the cliff, Kyle heard his voice. It was impossible to hear the words but her Water sense told her he was invoking his strongest power.

'I must concentrate on him,' Lautan shouted. 'If I focus, I believe I can prevent him from compelling the tsunami to grow. But it is already vast. You must continue trying to diminish it, Kyle, without my help.'

Kyle quailed in the depths of her mind. She clamped down on her fear, willing it to be silent. She could do this. Even alone, without the power and experience of her Water partner, she was up to it. And yet, she was tiring. Already the first tiny hints of a limit to her magic began to distract her.

'We will need all of your power, your– Ru'ita,' she said. 'However much you can give us.'

The Queen gave an almost imperceptible nod. She raised her staff above her head, holding it in both hands, and closed her eyes once again. Bolts of clear blue flame shot from the staff like forked lightning. The energy hit Kyle and Lautan, suffusing them with its eerie light. She felt renewed. Invincible. She too raised her Water power to levels previously undreamt of, sending it out over the wave tops toward the approaching tsunami. Beside her, she could feel Lautan's constraining influences working on Douglas. The old man was matching her brother, almost blending with him like a confluence of two great rivers.

Another bolt of energy, this time red and gold, flew over her head. It struck the ground beside Douglas, knocking him off his feet.

'Well come, Bakara!' Lautan shouted, not taking his eyes off the opposite cliff for an instant. 'Not a moment too soon!'

Kyle hardly dared to look, yet the sight was irresistible. The Fire Witch sat upon her kudo, her arms aloft. The amber bangles around her wrists glowed like rings of lava. Fire shot once more from her hands, arcing across the space between the two cliffs in Douglas' direction. He had recovered his balance. Moments before the second fire bolts struck, two massive gouts of water appeared from nowhere and landed on the flames, quenching them completely.

Douglas shouted something, his words lost in the gap. A third mass of water materialised above the Witch's head. It fell over her with a loud splash. Her kudo reared in terror, pitching her from the saddle before it took off at a gallop, away from the cliff top.

'Ugh!' Elaine said, spitting water from her mouth. 'This is war!'

As she got to her feet, a cry came from behind them. 'Petani!'

It was Tremaine. He came running to join the group.

'Am I glad to see you. I cannot work with the stone here. The cliffs are ancient and crumbling. The rock is so old it is more like earth than stone. I believe it may be more susceptible to your powers than mine.'

The Earth Elemental and the Fire Witch shared a glance.

'Perhaps...?' he said.

'Do you think?' she replied.

'What are you talking about?' Tremaine said.

'Petani and I have tried to make stone before,' Elaine said. 'We were not successful. But perhaps this material will be more responsive to our influences. If he can supply it, then I can fire it. Once it is molten it will at least be closer to stone than it is now. You may then manipulate it. In any case the attempt is likely to be more productive than exchanging Elemental insults with Muir over there. Let us leave him to the Water wielders.'

She walked over to the cliff edge, Petani and Tremaine following. Kyle heard the Fire Witch gasp.

'Look!' she said. 'The sea is pulling back from the cliff. Like an enormous tide rolling out.'

'There is raw material to work with now,' Petani said. 'The waters have revealed it. Better work with that than the cliff itself, and risk undermining our position here.'

'That is good news,' Lautan said, 'but there is also bad. If the seas are receding it means the tsunami is almost here. We do not have much time.'

utperi'tuk
27th day of run'sanamasa, 966

Kyle shuddered at Lautan's words. They were running out of time! Already feeling the limit of her power, she had to redouble her efforts to reduce the height of the wave while Lautan held Douglas back from making it any taller. Visible now at the limits of the bay, the tsunami blanked out a huge swathe of sky. It rose above the horizon like a dark, rippling blanket. On the opposite cliff, Douglas continued to shout his exultation as his creation swept towards the coast. There was panic in Petani's voice as she heard him debating their approach to the problem of the wall.

'We must try a different method Bakara,' he said. 'The

last time we attempted this I could not compel the earth to come to the fire. Give me a moment to summon and hold it before you let loose your flame.

'How much will you need?' he asked, turning to Tremaine.

The Stone mage regarded the ocean, his face a mask of fear and doubt.

'The wave is strong,' he said. 'If I have any chance of deflecting it the wall must be fashioned in a double parabola. I must construct an arc across the bay from north to south to funnel the waters into a smaller space. That itself will slow the wave down, but it will not be enough. The wall must have a curved face perpendicular to the arc.'

He cupped his hand in the air to show the others what he meant.

'From top to bottom. As the wave breaks against the wall it will be turned back on itself, creating a massive eddy that will interfere with the rest of the wave behind it.'

'How much earth?' Petani repeated.

'I have never attempted anything of this magnitude,' Tremaine replied. 'Just give me whatever you can summon. I cannot have too much.'

The old Earth Elemental faced the sea. He looked down at the exposed shingle of the beach. Kyle saw his body tense as he brought up his power. She took a few steps closer to the cliff edge, knowing she had to keep focused on the wave but unable to resist the temptation of watching the others' efforts.

Below, in the shadows of the cliff, the sand, small rocks and pebbles of the naked sea bed were moving. Assembling themselves into a tall pile of earth stretching as far as she could see. The speed with which the pile grew amazed her but she remained silent, not wanting to disturb Petani's concentration.

'When–?' asked the Fire Witch.

'Now,' Petani grunted, closing his eyes.

Kyle assumed he was preparing to hold the earth in the path of Bakara's Fire power. She expected to see bolts of flame shoot from the older woman's hands, as they had done when she attacked Douglas, but there was no visible sign of Fire from the Witch. Instead, after the briefest of pauses, the rock pile below them began to glow. Within moments it had started to melt, and flow together. Between them, Petani and Bakara created a river of magma right there on the beach.

'Whenever you're ready Tremaine,' the Witch shouted.

Now it was the Stone mage's turn to apply his eldritch power to the molten rock. Kyle had seen examples of his craft before. Compared to what he was now attempting, they were as motes of gravel beside a mountain. Her new-found Elemental sense baulked at the immensity of the task. The magma began to move, rising up above the beach and stretching out around the bay. In the blue light of the Queen's Wood power, Tremaine's face looked ghostly pale. After a few seconds he staggered, reaching out to steady himself against an outcrop of rock.

'Ahh!' he exclaimed. 'I cannot hold the wall for long while it is molten. The stone begins to fall as I raise the next section.'

'Finally, something I can do!' Claire said. 'I will need your help Kyle! Remember how we used our Elements in combination?'

Out in the bay, the tsunami reared out of the water like a leviathan. There was no time for her to affect it any further, but she could help with the wall. She glanced at Lautan for confirmation. Sensing her hesitation, he nodded, once. It was enough.

'What shall we do?' she asked.

'We must raise a spray behind where Piers is lifting the wall. If we can douse the magma the rock will set in place. He won't need to waste energy holding it up.'

Kyle grasped the concept instantly. Turning her attention to the shallow water in front of the approaching wave, she pulled it closer to the coast. The Air Mage summoned a powerful gust of wind that whipped up Kyle's waves into a heavy spray. Between them, they directed the flying droplets at the wall. Gouts of steam rose hissing into the night air as the rock hardened beneath its impact.

They continued to work in concert for a few moments, but progress began to slow. The molten magma ran down the beach in the direction of the cliff where Douglas stood, but it was not rising up fast enough. Tremaine fell to his knees.

'Ru'ita!' Claire called. 'He needs your help.'

The Queen had been feeding a constant stream of blue light to the two Water Wizards. At Claire's words, a third line of healing energy flew from her upraised staff, striking Tremaine in the middle of his back. He regained his feet and began working on the wall again. Kyle could see the Queen herself was tiring. The three bolts of healing were thinner than the two which had helped her and Lautan. Now that she was not working on the wave...

'Leave me, Ru'ita!' Kyle said. 'Concentrate on Tremaine.'

Lautan waved a hand in compliance. Their streams of blue attenuated and died, latent wisps of power curling away to evaporate into the night. With the Queen's energy focused entirely on the Stone mage, the wall of lava rose up and stretched away across the bay, taking Kyle and Claire by surprise. They hurried to match the pace of the sea wall with their spray. The curving parabola of rock hit the far cliff, its surface rising up above the edge, cutting off Douglas' view of the wave just as it began to break over the furthest point of the bay.

'I can no longer hold him!' Lautan cried. 'He is too strong, and I am almost spent!'

Sure enough as the edges of the tsunami broke, the central part, still some hundreds of metres out in the bay, surged to terrifying new heights. The sound of her brother's manic laughter echoed across the space between the cliffs.

Around both sides of the bay, the tsunami struck the ends of Tremaine's wall.

'Bakara!' Lautan yelled, his voice hoarse with his exertions. 'We may have one last chance! If you are done with the wall, come to me. We need steam!'

The Fire Witch hurried over to stand by Lautan's side. They exchange brief words, inaudible from where Kyle stood, but then Lautan raised his voice.

'Stand away from me Bakara, while we make the attempt,' he said. 'I am deeply connected with the Muir boy. I fear what may happen.'

His face an ashen grey from his exertions, Lautan faced Douglas across the void. At the extreme limits of his strength, he raised his arms. From the Fire Witch's wrists, two incandescent jets of white fire spewed out, hotter than anything Kyle had yet seen. The tongues of flame writhed around each other, creating a spinning cone of fire right in front of Lautan. With a roar, Lautan thrust both arms towards the fiery funnel, clasping his hands together to form a wedge, his fingers pointing straight at her brother. Powerful streams of clear water shot from his finger tips, joining together into a single concentrated jet that flew through the fire, to be flashed into superheated steam.

The bolt of steam crossed the void in an instant, striking Douglas in the middle of his chest. He screamed, the bolt stripping his clothing and flaying his flesh from his torso before he could blink. As the scorching steam emerged from his back, her brother collapsed, falling from the promontory into the wave he had created to be dashed by it, already dead, into Tremaine's wall.

Lautan let out an agonised howl of pain. Unable to believe what she was seeing, Kyle watched, horrified, as the old Wizard swelled and bloated before bursting into a fine spray of gold-flecked liquid that spewed over her. She grabbed Claire, their anguished cries echoing as one into the night. Seconds later, the tsunami struck the wall in front of them with a deafening roar. Tons of water, its momentum undiminished by the death of the one who had created it, crashed against the still-warm stone, flying up in a silvery curtain before falling back against the tide. Huge gouts of spray overflew the structure, drenching the Elementals and threatening to drag them from their feet. Tremaine clung on to the rock, Petani crouched and hugged the Earth, summoning the last vestiges of his power to immobilise himself against the ground.

Kyle screamed again as a final surge of seawater spewed over the wall directly towards where she, Claire, and Elaine stood. There was no time to avoid it, but in any case she was rooted to the spot with terror. Her Water power utterly spent, her connection with Lautan lost, she knew it was over. They had saved the land, but they could not save themselves. And at the last, she had been too weak to save the others. Though dead, her brother's mocking voice still echoed in her mind. She fell to her knees with a guttural sob.

'Nyaaa!'

A hoarse cry of gargantuan effort came from her left. His face twisted in a grimace of determination and horror, Jann Argent stood with his eyes squeezed shut. His fingers curled at unnatural angles, his elbows dug into his sides. Moments before the water struck the Elementals, Kyle glimpsed starlight. A gate opened up in front of her, swallowing the surge before snapping shut with a hollow pop. The Gatekeeper collapsed face down against the grass in a dead faint.

Kyle stared dumbfounded out into the roiling ocean while the waters receded. Within the space of a few moments she had lost the brother she had wasted a lifetime trying to impress, and the new-found mentor she had only known for a few days. She remained on her knees on the wet rock, wracked with uncontrollable sobs, her powers useless to prevent the tears that flowed.

court of the blood king
27th day of run'sanamasa, 966

Fingers of late evening sun struck the dancing motes of dust in the air of the chamber. Jeruk Nipis did not notice them. He sat at the head of the long table, his head in his hands. His closest friend and advisor angrily laid out the extent of their failure for the assembled group. Jeruk had called this gathering as an "extraordinary" meeting. An excuse, only, to ensure that those members who were not aligned with the Puppeteers—principally the Keeper and Jurip—could be excluded.

'It's a fucking disaster,' Pwalek said. 'I don't think we could have fucked it up as bad as this if we'd planned it.'

'Is it really as bad as all that?' the fat, bearded arsehole Grissan said. 'We're all still here, aren't we?'

'More by luck than judgment,' Pwalek replied, rounding on the man. 'The Darmajelis was supposed to show how Istania could be ruled without a monarch. How we could bring the people together—Earthers too—and live harmoniously and productively without bowing and scraping to Royals or Princips. Well, that turned out well didn't it?

'Our pathetic attempts at controlling those Earthers resulted in one death and one defection, and the almost total destruction of the entire land. Not just Istania, but Kertonia too! Outside this Court, the populace is on the verge of outright rebellion. They think us incompetent at best, and thoroughly corrupt at worst. They're demanding a King. Again! A bloody King!'

'I wish them luck in their search for one,' Jeruk said with a sneer. 'And somewhere for him to sit.'

In the Throne Room beyond the chamber door, what remained of the Blood Throne sat in a puddled heap of distorted red rock. Piers Tremaine's last definitive refusal of the most powerful seat in the land—the complete destruction of that seat and a guarantee that no one would ever occupy it again.

'This is no time for jest!' Pwalek exclaimed. 'Far from removing the upper tiers of our government, all we've done is guarantee they will continue. We're further from our goals now than when we started! Like I said: a fucking disaster. Oh yes!' he went on, hardly pausing for breath, 'and in case you've forgotten, all the surviving mages and Elementals—including Wood and Stone—are now aligned with the Black Queen under the Kertonian banner. We only just learned of the existence of those last two and already we have thrown away any chance of ever influencing them or their use. If not for the Queen's passive nature, we'd have been overrun already.

'So we've lost control of the government, of the people, and of the Elementals. Is there anything left? No. Nothing is under our aegis any more. Anything could happen.'

Pwalek leant on the table, staring down at Jeruk. He could smell the foul odour of the man's breath as he finished his rant.

'It wasn't that long ago,' Pwalek said, 'when we were still hiding ourselves away in that dank basement cellar, that you told us there had to be a way to rid ourselves of "these insects." You were going to find it. That sounds like an empty promise to me now Jeruk. If we were ever in control of anything we certainly are not now. I for one cannot see how we ever will be.'

Jeruk sat in silence for a few moments, mustering his thoughts. There was no denying the truth of his friend's words, even though he bristled at the way Pwalek had delivered them. He took his head out of his hands and straightened his new tunic. Leaving his Jester persona behind, he had had this one made in the colours of Red House: a deep, rich crimson, stitched with golden thread.

'There have been victories and setbacks since I uttered those words, it is true,' he said. 'We are rid of one of the largest insects though. The one that lived right here at Court and provided some of our worst headaches. We have seen off pretenders to the throne, and secured more reliable informants in the Palace of the Blacks. And one of those we thought of as an ally, who in the end proved false, has been taken care of for us. Albeit by some who now give us another, different problem.

'But we are no longer hiding below ground. We are ruling. That must count for something. It is a step along the road, only, to be sure. But as our dear Keeper is so fond of remarking, the journey of a thousand days begins with a single step. We have made that beginning, Seb. We must take courage from it. Have we yet found the way to fulfil my promise? No. But you judge me too harshly when you call it an empty one. Our work is not done, but it is most definitely begun.'

the black palace
29th day of run'sanamasa, 966

A slight breeze blew through Kyle Muir's bedroom. Slight, but cold. She pulled the covers up to her chin and turned over to cuddle her pillow. With only two days remaining before they entered the last month of Sanamasa even her thick, soft coverlet was not up to the task of keeping her warm. When her stubborn denial failed to soothe her aching limbs, she sat up in bed, the last foggy traces of sleep falling away as she tried to remember why the window was open in the first place.

Ah yes. The sound of the soft malamajan rains—restored now that her brother's malign influence was defeated—had disturbed her sleep. She had wanted to see it. To experience the feeling of the gentle rain on her face and understand, with her deepest Elemental cognition, the rightness of it. Still half asleep she had reached out with her Water sense and grasped without conscious thought how it was done. The feeling of utter contentment that comprehension brought had carried her back to sleep in moments.

It felt good to be back at the Palace. It felt like home. Their return journey had been fraught. Even summoning the energy to leave Utperi'Tuk required all their courage and resolve. Still mourning the loss of Lautan someone, she could not remember who, had suggested they should make a start back. They gathered their few belongings, tracked down their kudai to whatever shelter they had found from the explosions of Elemental power that had filled the night, and headed back inland. Conversation had been stilted. Many of their party did not want to talk at all. They cradled their mental exhaustion and psychological wounds close to themselves. Unwilling to share. Kyle had ridden beside Claire, her closest friend and mentor, and they had exchanged a few words.

'Why did he die?' Claire asked.

'It was... like a back blow. Because of his connection,' Kyle replied.

'Connection?'

'He had to almost meld himself with Douglas. To reduce my brother's ability to raise the waters. Like tuning into his wavelength of power. When Lautan was connected so closely, there was always a risk he would be unable to stop a backlash once Douglas died.'

'He knew it would happen, didn't he?'

Kyle had ridden on for some distance before she trusted herself to answer.

'Yes. At least he knew it *could* happen. Was most likely to happen. He warned the Witch to move away. He must have been worried she would be caught in it too. She provided half of the power that killed Douglas.'

'But she wasn't connected. Not in the same way.'

'No. He sacrificed himself so we would be safe.'

Her voice had broken then, and the two Elementals rode on in silence. They made slow progress. On the journey to Utperi'Tuk the imminent danger had spurred them to cover the whole distance at a gallop. In the aftermath, there was no urgency, nor indeed any energy left in them or their mounts to travel at more than a walking pace. As the sun rose and set on the day of the tsunami, they realised they would have to make camp. The provisions they had carried with them since leaving the Palace the day before were untouched, so they stopped and broke their fast in an uneasy silence.

Kyle expected to at least grab some rest before continuing the journey, but in the end none of the group could sleep. Claire's gentle sobbing, a few metres away from her, was enough to keep Kyle awake. Every so often someone would make a comment, or get up to poke the fire. Animal sounds seemed somehow louder and more terrifying. At one point Piers, alone of all of them, had dropped off but woke with a shout wrenched from whatever nightmare his slumber had served up. That was enough for the Queen.

'This is ridiculous,' she said, getting to her feet and folding her groundsheet. 'We may as well press on. At least there will be comfortable beds and hot food once we reach the Palace.'

So once more they had ridden through the night, arriving at the Palace gates shortly after daybreak. The Palace staff had wanted to make a fuss but the Queen gave them short shrift. She ordered the refectory cleared so the seven of them could eat in peace. After, they had all retired to their own chambers, with their own thoughts. Kyle slept the day through, waking only that once to watch the malamajan. She was still aching, but not as bone-deep tired as she had been on their return. It was a wonder she had made it into bed.

The sound of low voices drifted up to her window. It was Claire, and the Queen, walking beside the river. Kyle dressed and joined them.

'Lovely day for a walk,' she said as she approached.

'I do hope you are well rested,' said the Queen.

'Yes, thank you,' Kyle replied, unsure whether to address her as "your majesty" again now, or whether she still considered herself more Mage than majesty. She still held her staff, though its light was not in evidence. For now, it remained only a piece of wood.

'I hope you are too, both of you.'

'Getting there,' Claire said. 'We were discussing the ceremony.'

'Ceremony?' Kyle said.

'We must organise a feast. To honour Lautan's memory,' the Queen said, her face an unreadable mask.

It was clear she felt Lautan's loss as keenly as any of them. Of all the Elementals, she had known him longest.

'Now that your brother is defeated, and poor Lautan has gone, we must also introduce his replacement. Our new Water Wizard. The occasion cannot be allowed to pass without some pomp. We shall have a double ceremony. Sadness and happiness. I think the other Elementals will appreciate my efforts in giving the event that balance.'

Having spent all of her time on Berikatanya so far in the company of Douglas or Lautan, Kyle had never met any of the other Water mages. Did not even know how many there were. She had no idea who they were talking about.

'Like a party, you mean?' she said. 'Great! I can't wait to meet him. I hope he'll be as good a teacher as Lautan was.'

The Queen laughed, her peals of mirth matching the tinkling sound of the river.

'Kyle, dear, it's you. You are the Water Wizard of Berikatanya now.'

...oooOooo...

Glossary

Abbaleh
Small, web-building creature similar to a spider

Ahmek
Large, portable dwellings similar to tents. Ahmeks are made from heavy material that doesn't lend itself to being carried by individuals or even small groups, so their use is restricted to the military, or semi-permanent camps like the Forest Clearance Project

Air Mage
The Elemental who controls Air

Alaakaya
Forest behind the Court ("Medium wood")

Albert Yamani
Claire's father. Previous Air Mage of Berikatanya

Alempin
A Tepak of the Blood Watch who has a seat on the Darmajelis

Baka
The god of the Fire Element

Bakamasa
"Fire season"—the Berikatanyan equivalent of Summer

Bakara
Elemental name for the Fire Witch

Banshiru (banshirin)
Stone magic (or one who wields it)

Barajan
The term Lautan coins for the "new rains" that begin during this volume

Barawa fish
A blue fish, considered a delicacy

Batarian
The language of the people who live north of Temmok'Dun

Batugan
Of, or pertaining to, the Batu'n

Batu'n
Berikatanyan term for Earth people (both languages)

Bepermak
Food suitable for consuming when travelling. The contents vary, but are tightly wrapped in edible leaves (similar to dolmades) for both preservation and portability

Beragan
The name for the people who live north of Temmok'Dun ("civilised people")

Berjengo
An Elder of the Beragan, with a particular interest in, and knowledge of, their history

Berikatanya
Local name for the colonised planet, home to the Elementals & Princips

Besakaya
Berikatanyan forest, part of which is undergoing the Forest Clearance Project ("Great wood")

Binagan
The Beragan word for the people living south of the mountains. Translates as "wild people"

Bin-segar
Wild Sea

Black Queen
Unofficial title of the ruler of Kertonia

Blood Watch
The honour guard of the Blood King

Bogdan Dmitriev
The captain of the Dauntless

Bolabisaman
Berikatanyan vegetable. Closest equivalent to an onion

Borok Duset
Eastern Mountain ("Devil's Boil")

Bubayem
Dark purple Berikatanyan fruit grown in the southern regions

Bumerang
A Berikatanyan fruit, red in colour and similar to an apple

Buwangah
Cloud fruit wine

Car'Alam
Berikatanyan term for the Ceremony that led to the opening of the vortex

Cary Cabrera
A member of Felice Waters' team at the Pennatanah landing base

Celapi
Berikatanyan musical instrument similar to a guitar

Claire Yamani
Daughter of Albert and Nyna Yamani who makes the journey to Perse aboard the Valiant

Clone rout
Alternative name for the Battle of Lembaca Ana

Court
Home of the King of Istania

Dak-jamtera
See jamtera

Dauntless
Prism ship—intended to be the last ship to make the journey to Perse—completes its journey at the time of this story

Darmajelis
The governing body of Istania, led by Jeruk Nipis, constituted in the absence of a monarch following the death of the Blood King

David Garcia
Team leader of the forest clearance project

Dingas
Berikatanyan animal prized for its tender meat

Dipeka Kekusaman
An Elder of the Beragan, she is sensitive to the presence of Elemental power

Douglas Muir
A passenger on the Dauntless, which completes its journey during this volume. Brother to Kyle

Dumwheat
An experimental cereal crop created by crossing wheat brought from Earth with the local Berikatanyan grain used to make tepsak

Dunela
Berikatanyan vegetable

Duntang
Berikatanyan equivalent of a potato

Duska Batsirang
The village where Piers Tremaine lives and works (Duska is the term for an inland village)

Duske Pelapan
The village to which Patrick Glass travels in search of the lore of his father (Duske is the term for a coastal village)

Duske Raj'Pupu
The village where Sepuke Maliktakta lives

Eladok
A bird of prey native to the Temmok'Duk mountains. Its beak is laced with highly poisonous saliva

Elaine Chandler
Fire poi artiste with Miles Miller's Marvellous Manifestations travelling circus who later makes the journey to Perse aboard the Valiant

Elemental
A supreme mage who can control a single Element. Leader of the corresponding Guild

Endeavour
Prism ship—the first to make the journey to Perse

Endurance
Prism ship—intended to be the third to make the journey to Perse, but destroyed by a failure of its Prism drive

Eradewan
The governing body of Kertonia, led by the Black Queen

Etrumus Kepalawan
A villager from Duske Raj'Pupu who leads the rebellion against Sepuke Maliktakta

Felice Waters
Senior officer at the Earther planetary immigration station at Pennatanah Bay

Fire Witch
The Elemental who controls Fire

Ghantu
Berikatanyan bird that lives in woodlands. Known for its screeching call

Gravnull
A technology that nullifies gravity, allowing vessels equipped with it to hover. Used in planetary flight, not for space travel

Guild
An assembly of Mages

Haande
A suhir of the Earth Element who works with Petani at the Valley harbour project

Hampanay
Derogatory term for a non-native who displays ability with Elemental powers

Harimeladan
The Keeper of the Queen's Purse and member of the Eradewan

Hodak
A rank in the Queen's forces

Intrepid
Prism ship—the second to make the journey to Perse

Istania
Local name for the Blood King's realm

Istri
Wife of Penka

Jambala
Berikatanyan fruit, often juiced to make a refreshing drink

Jamtera (and dak-jamtera)
An expression of Elemental power. Equivalent to a "spell" in traditional magic. Dak-jamtera is the corresponding defence or counter-spell.

Jann Argent
A colonist who journeys to Perse aboard the Valiant. Later revealed to be the Gatekeeper

Jaranyla
The name of Elaine's kudo—chestnut mare ("Horse of the Flame")

Jarapera
The name of Patrick Glass's kudo ("Horse of the Artisan")

Jeruk Nipis
Full name of the Yellow Jester, who installs himself as head of the Darmajelis

Jester
Principal advisor to the Blood King

Jo Granger
Plant geneticist who helps Felice Waters with her DNA analysis project

Jojo grass
Tall Berikatanyan grass often dried and fed to animals

Juggler
See Pattern Juggler

Jurip
Head of the Kertonian military, occasional attendee at the Eradewan

Kamesa
Beragan word for town

Katuh
A hot beverage

Kayshiru (kayshirin)
Wood magic (or one who wields it)

Kaytam
Black wood native to Berikatanya

Kedewada
The Beragan maturity ritual

Kedu-Bul
Smaller of the two moons of Berikatanya

Keeper of the Keys
Custodian of the Court keys, archives, and ceremonial costumes

Kema'katan
The "power pulse" air spell

Kemasara
a generic honorific title conferred out of respect (in Istania). Literally "eminence"

Kema'satu
An honorific title conferred on Elementals out of respect (in Kertonia), literally translated as "force of nature"

Kepka Lemda
An ostler at the Black Palace

Kepka Tuala
Head ostler at the Blood Court and friend of the Keeper of Keys

Kepta
Honorific title for a village leader. Equivalent to a mayor

Kepul Seri
A fire mage. Leader of the Fire Guild until the Fire Witch resumes the guild leadership role

Kertonia
Local name for the Black Queen's realm

Ketakaya
Forest between Pennatanah and the King's Court ("Small wood")

Ketiga Batu
Berikatanyan term for Earth (both languages)

Keti Caraga
Beragan word for the people relocated south of Temmok'Dun ("the warring tribes")

Kilpemigang
Keeper of the Coin at the Blood Court, has a seat on the Darmajelis

Kinchu
Small Berikatanyan herbivore similar to a rabbit

Klikeran
Decorative material made from the shells of marine creatures found in shallow coastal waters and used for all manner of trinkets in Berikatanyan culture, notably for fret markers on celapi

Krupang
Beragan word for crutch

Kuan-Yin Ning
Earther who returns to Pennatanah seeking sanctuary from the political turmoil and flooding at the Blood Court

Kuclar
Big cat, native to Berikatanya, that lives in forested areas

Kudo (pl: kudai)
Berikatanyan word for horse (in both Istanian and Kertonian)

Kyle Muir
A passenger on the Dauntless, which completes its journey during this volume. Sister to Douglas

Lautan
Elemental name for the Water Wizard

Lem Tantaran
Valley Plain

Lembaca Ana
Berikatanyan name for the Valley of the Cataclysm. Location of the original Car'Alam ceremony which opened the vortex.

Lendan
A Pena-gliman in the Queen's forces who accompanies her to the Valley for an inspection of the harbour works

Luki
Beragan word for tree bark

Lum-segar
The ocean at the mouth of the Valley ("Mud Sea")

Luum
Beragan word for moss

Mahok Ginkadaya
Historical name for the obsidian tiara worn by the Black Queen. Although its derivation has been lost to history, the name comes from an ancient tongue and means "the crown that cools the power"

Malamajan
The rain that falls on Berikatanya once the sun has fully set ("Night rain"). Instigated centuries ago as a result of a powerful Water spell

Martuk
A stonemason of Duska Batsirang who attempts to take over one of Piers Tremaine's building projects

Mizar
One of the major rivers of Berikatanya. It rises in the foothills of Tubelak'Dun and flows through the forest of Besakaya before reaching the western coast.

Mungo Pearman
The full name of the Purple Piper

Nembaka
One of the Berikatanyan natives working on the forest clearance project

Nerka jugu
Berikatanyan expletive (literally "hell's teeth")

Nyirumi
A suhir of the Earth Element who works with Petani at the Valley harbour project

Olek Grissan
One of the more verbose Puppeteers

Palace
Home of the Queen of Kertonia

Panklat
A creamy sweet hot beverage flavoured with local spices

Parapekotik
Court musicians' town

Patrick Glass
Graphic designer who later makes the journey to Perse aboard the Valiant and befriends Jann Argent. Later revealed to be the Pattern Juggler

Pattana
One of the Berikatanyan natives working on the forest clearance project, now retired

Pattern Juggler
Controller of Elemental forces during the Car'Alam ceremony. Capable of directing forces to achieve particular aims, but not of generating those forces in the first place

Pembrang
The name of Black Queen's kudo—black stallion ("Black Rider")

Pembwana
The name of Claire's kudo—black mare ("Bearer of the Wind")

Pena-gliman
A rank in the Queen's honour guard

Pena-lipan
A rank in the Blood King's forces (equivalent to pena-gliman above)

Penjal Mpah
The senior Elder of the Beragan people

Penka
An elder from the village of Duske Pelapan who comes to the Black Palace in search of Patrick Glass

Pennamatalaya
A young woman of the Beragan people who finds Jann Argent's unconscious body during her kedewada, rescues him, and subsequently nurses him back to health

Pennatanah
Earther Landing point (Land of the newcomer)

Pennatanah Bay
Landing site for the colony program

Per Tantaran
The battle plain on the border of Kertonia and Istania

Pera-Bul
Larger of the two moons of Berikatanya

Perak
The name of Jann Argent's kudo—silver stallion

Permajelis
The ill-fated "peace council" which the Black Queen attempts to set up in the wake of the Battle of Lembaca Ana

Perse
The colony planet first targeted by humanity

Petani
Elemental name for the controller of Earth power

Piers Tremaine
An Earther stonemason who arrived on the Intrepid and took up residence in Duska Batsirang

Pilgrim
Character who inhabited the Valley of the Cataclysm

Piper / Purple Piper
Principal advisor to the Black Queen

Pondok Pemmunak
Villager of Duska Batsirang who commissions Piers
Tremaine to build a house

Ponektu
A species of Berikatanyan tree

Princips
Generic term for senior courtiers / landowners / Blood
King & Black Queen

Prism drive
See Wormwood star drive

Prism ship
Colony ships powered by the Wormwood "Prism" drive

Pun'Akarnya
The new mountain created as a result of the final battle in
Book 1 of this trilogy

Puppeteers
A shady group of dissidents led by Jeruk Nipis who plot
and scheme to overthrow the monarchy in favour of a
more egalitarian form of government

Ra-mek
A larger and more opulent version of an ahmek for the
exclusive use of royalty

Racun
a poison secreted by the glands of several Berikatanyan
animals

Rampiri
Ancient term for combining Elemental powers to create more powerful effects

Rebusang
The meat stew eaten at the forest clearance project

Blood King
Unofficial title of the ruler of Istania

Rektan Malikputran
Best friend, and right-hand man, of Sepuke Maliktakta

Remalan
Months

Rohantu
The blood clones. Literally "soul phantom"

Sakti Udara
Elemental name for Air Mage

Sana
The god of the Air Element

Sanamasa
"Air season"—the Berikatanyan equivalent of Winter

Sangella
Claire's maidservant

Saptak skin
The cleaned, dried, and stitched skin of a Berikatanyan ruminant, used to carry water

Seba-tepak
A rank in the Blood King's forces

Sebaklan Pwalek
Long-time confident of Jeruk Nipis and a fellow
conspirator/Puppeteer

Sepuke Maliktakta
Distant cousin of the Blood King and leader of the village
of Duske Raj'Pupu

Sickmoss
A variety of Berikatanyan moss that induces violent and
immediate nausea on contact

Suhir Haande
See Haande

Suhir Nyirumi
See Nyirumi

Suhiri
The Berikatanyans name for mages who are not
Elementals

Su'matra
Berikatanyan name for the people

Sun Besaraya
The river that runs from Temmok'Dun to the coast at
Lembaca Ana ("big river")

Sun Hitaraya
The river that has its origins on Borok Duset and joins
with the Besaraya southwest of the Black Palace ("black
river")

Sun Hutang
The river that winds from Tubelak'Dun, through the
Forest Clearance Project to the coast south of Duska
Batsirang ("forest river")

Sun Lum
The river that runs from Borok Duset to the southernmost coast ("mud river")

Sun Penk
The river that runs from the centre of Tubelak'Dun to join the Sun Besaraya northeast of Lembaca Ana ("short river")

Sunyok
A Berikatanyan eating tool

Tabukka
A Berikatanyan narcotic leaf

Tabukki
Those who are addicted to tabukka

Tana
The god of the Earth Element

Tanamasa
"Earth season"—the Berikatanyan equivalent of Autumn

Tanaratana
Berikatanyan native who replaces Pattana on the team working with Petani at the harbour project

Te'banga
The agreement between Elementals whereby they divide their loyalties and efforts evenly between the ruling houses

Telebi Ana
The bay at the harbour project site

Tema'gana
Istanian equivalent of Kema'satu

Temmok'Dun
Northern Mountains ("Wall of the World")

Tenfir Abarad
The town north of Temmok'Dun where Jann Argent
recuperates after his journey

Tepak
A rank in the King's honour guard. Equivalent to an army
captain.

Tepsak
A Berikatanyan bread

Terry Spate
Horticulturalist and gardener who makes the journey to
Perse aboard the Valiant and befriends Claire Yamani.
Later revealed to be the Earth Elemental

Tiklik
A Berikatanyan rodent, similar to a mouse

Timakaya
The forest close to the Black Palace, where the Queen
finds her staff ("Eastern wood")

Trapweed
A rapidly growing form of plant life, similar to bindweed
but much stronger and faster growing. It reacts to any
movement by wrapping itself around the unwary intruder.

Tuakara
Fire Witch at the time the Te'banga was first agreed.
Distant ancestor of the current Fire Witch

Tubelak'Dun
Western Mountains ("Spine of the World")

Umtanesh
One of the Berikatanyan natives working on the forest
clearance project

Uta Tantaran
The Northern Plain—land between the Black Palace and the foothills of Temmok'Dun

Utamasa
"Water season"—the Berikatanyan equivalent of Spring

Utan
The god of the Water Element

Utperi'Tuk
Coastal region close to the Red Court ("Sea Nymph's Cove")

Valiant
Prism ship—the third to make the journey to Perse

Valley of the Cataclysm
see Lembaca Ana

Water Wizard
The Elemental who controls Water

Wormwood star drive
Propulsion system for the colony ships which reaches near-light speed. Known colloquially as the "Prism" drive since it focuses energy through a series of extremely dense prisms.